Light in the Darkness

PAINTING THE MISTS, BOOK 3

PATRICK G. LAPLANTE

Published by:
Patrick G. Laplante

Third edition, 2020
ISBN: 978-1-989578-08-7

Dedication

To those who have lost hope.
May you find the light that guides your way.

Author's Note

Thank you, everyone, for your continued readership. As usual, it is a pleasure to continue writing for you all. Your compliments inspire me, and your feedback is much appreciated.

This time, I'll make it a short note. As you read this book I want you to consider how state of mind can affect the choices people make. For example, say a small child decides to run away from home. He is fed up with his parents who love him dearly and have only his best interest in mind. From an outsider's perspective, the child is irrational. In truth, the child is emotional, a flesh and blood human like the rest of us that makes mistakes.

This book, as the title suggests, is about finding light in the darkness. It is about finding hope amidst suffering. It is about overcoming depression, anxiety, and fear. And finally, it is about responsibility and belonging.

Prologue

The darkness was suffocating. A man was floating alone in an endless ocean, and he had been there for God knew how long. Countless years had passed since his last human interaction. In fact, he no longer remembered his name. He simply… existed.

The only variance to the man's existence was an occasional wave or gentle murmur. Yet try as he might, he could never reach those voices, and he could never break free from the water that contained him. He used to fear the darkness, the unknown, but now it had become a part of him. He was one with the darkness, and one with the water surrounding him.

One day, he became aware of another existence. It, too, was trapped in the darkness. He couldn't see anything, so he assumed it was a serpent. After all, he could think of no other creatures that were so long and thin. Normally, such a beast would strangle him alive and swallow him. Yet he felt kinship with it, a connection of sorts. They were companions in the darkness, inseparable friends. Even the cruelest devil would never kill the only other creature in existence, lest madness take him and drive him to ruin.

Humans couldn't live alone. That was what made the darkness so unbearable for the man. He faintly remembered the last breath he had taken, in the outside. His water-filled lungs longed for fresh air. With air, he could speak. The more he thought of it, the more he wished he could befriend that coiling snake.

Time passed by, day by day. Each moment was torture for the man, but he endured until the day that he finally saw it— the light. At first it was only a single sliver, a ray of light shining upon his gloomy surroundings.

Light. I had forgotten what it looked like. After all these years, I can't bear to look at it and can only keep my eyes closed in fear. And yet he could *feel* the light on his skin. He needed it.

He forced himself to swim toward that sliver, which pulsated and grew with each passing moment. He swam with arms that had weakened with time. The strength of a grown man eluded him, and he felt as weak as an infant. But he didn't give up. No man who had ever seen the light could return to the darkness. As the man struggled, he felt the coiling snake tighten up around him, holding him back.

Come with me, he thought. *The light is so much better than this emptiness. Hold on to me, and I'll take you out to see the world in all its glory.*

The coiling snake seemed to hesitate before finally loosening up and letting him swim once more. It didn't let go, however. It simply clung to the man and waited for him to lead the way out.

After what seemed like an eternity, he finally felt himself making progress toward the ever-widening rift. Now it seemed to attract him. The rift was there just for him, waiting for him to crawl through to a better world. He exerted all his strength to finally pull himself against the opening, only to find out that it was too small for him.

I will not *let this stop me. I* will *pull through this rift that I've waited for all these years.* Since he couldn't pull himself through, he would simply squeeze through. And he would bring that snake along with him. He first pushed his hand through the rift, and he felt nothing but cold beyond it. But if there was light, he could stand a little cold. Anything was better than the darkness. So he shoved his arm in deeper until he finally had his elbow through.

That was when he felt the "others." He felt the hands of giants guiding him. He heard the soft murmurs that he'd heard all this time.

Have they been calling to me? Have they been trying to find me? He wasn't sure, but even if they were enemies, he'd still charge through that portal and out into the sunlit world.

The giant hands latched on to his arm, gently guiding him out. He cooperated with them, forcing his head through the tiny crack. *Even if my skull shatters, I'll force my way through!* He felt immense pain as his head began squeezing through the portal. Surprisingly, it didn't resist him; instead, it began expanding, accommodating him. It pulsed as it seemed to try to pull him through. Both the portal and the man were working in tandem, matching their rhythm to pull him through to the other side.

With great effort, he finally pushed his head through the opening. His mind shook as a massive headache overwhelmed his every sense. The pain was soon relieved as he and the snake were pulled through the portal into a mysterious, cold world.

Despite the cold, and despite his closed eyes, he felt that he was in the right place. This was the world of light, the world where he belonged.

He clutched the snake and shivered as a large cloth dropped down on him, drying off the water that had drenched him in the darkness. The water was finally gone, so he opened his mouth and breathed in with all his strength. That first breath was painful, and he let out a shrill roar as he swiftly exhaled.

Right, I've forgotten how to breathe. Time has atrophied my lungs, so I need to take things step by step. He instantly recovered and began taking in fast, shallow breaths. Each one spread warmth throughout his body to his weak limbs.

"Let me give you a hand," he heard a loud booming voice say. He didn't have the strength to resist as a giant hand patted him down and helped him wipe himself off. "Finally, he's here after all this time."

"He's beautiful," the quivering voice of a woman said. He felt two large hands firmly grip him in the towel, and the giant lady took him to her chest. For the first time in what seemed like an eternity, he felt warmth. Perhaps getting treated like an infant wasn't so bad.

"What should we call him?" the man's voice asked.

"Let's call him Cha Ming," she replied weakly.

It was raining outside. While Diyu was hardly a humid place, its proximity to the Yellow River ensured a dense miasma of soul vapor constantly rising to the clouds above. It accumulated day by day, eventually materializing as a soul monsoon. The plant life in Diyu welcomed this refreshing downpour, which revitalized many soul life-forms and brought color to their ethereal limbs.

Every soul monsoon brought about the birth of many spiritual life-forms all over the city. Countless creatures used the energy to break through to the next level. Yama would have done the same if he hadn't reached the limits of this realm. As much as he yearned to leave, he was bound by duty to serve for all eternity. The universe depended on his unrelenting efforts and impeccable work ethic, which was why he found himself outside his office tower in such wretched rain in the first place.

Yama was elegantly dressed and carried a magnificently crafted umbrella. Not only was its handle carved from jade, but the various runes on the both the handle and the fabric made sure that not a single speck of rain could land on his carefully crafted suit. It was a Hades Limited Edition suit from a few aeons ago. Collecting suits and drinking tea were two of his few hobbies. Fishing was the other.

He hailed a taxi that just happened to pass by the building, only to have it splash a puddle of soul water off the street and directly onto Yama's umbrella shield. He smoldered in rage but held himself back, lest he destroy the entire city block. That would be a public-relations nightmare, and their department was already working triple overtime.

A few moments later, another taxi stopped and ushered him inside. It sped off at ten times the speed of light toward the center of the massive city. Yama didn't often go downtown. Everyone kept telling him that it was the best location for an office, but he'd never seen the appeal. There was nothing to *do* downtown, and it was easy enough to host a half dozen coffee shops and a few premium restaurants inside the office building. Besides, the commute downtown during rush hour was atrocious.

For now, however, the car plowed ahead at full speed, dodging thousands of cars to save precious minutes. Driving a taxi like a stolen vehicle was a time-honored tradition throughout the universe. Yama didn't mind, of course. If he'd wanted a reasonable driver, he would have hired a rideshare driver. That sort of company was all the rage in Diyu nowadays. He couldn't be bothered trying out the service, however. He questioned whether they had the proper insurance and training.

Traffic soon slowed to a crawl, and the skyscrapers of Diyu's downtown core shone brightly in their magnificence. This was the *true* city that never slept. Each high-rise building was over ten li tall, and some even pushed a hundred. Thankfully, slowing to a crawl was a relative term. In gridlock here, cars still managed to travel at half the speed of light.

I hope I won't be late.

Yama took out his communicator when he felt a vibration affect his true soul. It was a soul message from Usama, the man he was meeting.

Where are you? it read.

He deftly typed in a few words in reply. *Be there soon. Traffic is backed up, but I should be there in about thirty minutes.*

Time flowed differently in Diyu. Thirty Diyu minutes was akin to several years in some mortal realms, but only a passing second in others. Even Yama wasn't sure why this happened, but he knew that the brightest minds in the Underworld were studying the subject with utmost vigor.

Soon, the taxi broke through the gridlock and dropped

Yama off in front of a posh-looking establishment. Usama stood there waiting for him, wearing a familiar red Hades suit. Also limited edition, if he wasn't mistaken. The shorter, bearded man handed him a cigar as they walked past two large bouncers and made their way into a large banquet hall. They passed by several thousand tables before finally arriving at a small one reasonably close to the stage, where speeches would be given.

Another short man with curly hair stood up to greet him and shook his hand. "Usama's said so much about you. It's great to finally meet the legend in person. My name is Judah, at your service," the man said jovially. Yama nodded, and they sat down, enjoying complimentary spirit wine as they waited for the event to begin.

"Good wine," Yama commented. "Desolate Steps vintage, forty-sixth great kalpa[1], if I'm not mistaken?" he said while savoring its full body. Such exquisite wines not only calmed the mind but soothed the soul. This bottle was extremely expensive, capable of funding a thousand of his employees for ten Underworld years.

"I never thought you'd be such a wine connoisseur," Judah said.

"Well, it comes with age, I suppose. You have no idea how many hobbies I've gotten to try since the beginning of time." Yama sighed self-deprecatingly. He wasn't sure why, but he instantly had a good impression of the man. He had a pleasant demeanor, obviously the type of man people flocked to. In Yama's experience, this type of person would easily become the

---

[1] An ancient Buddhist time unit representing about 1.28 trillion Earth years. It is related to the birth, stability, destruction, and subsequent emptiness of the universe until it is finally reborn.

core of his group of friends. He was slightly envious. Despite having lived for aeons, Yama's friends didn't number more than a few dozen.

"Judah, Usama said that you know a way to help alleviate my staffing problems," Yama said, cutting to the chase. "I must admit, Usama has done a great job filtering through the billions of potential contractors, and I've already reached out to several who are clearly deserving of full-time, permanent employment. But I'm curious—beyond temporary workers, what help could you possibly provide?"

The short, curly-haired man nodded understandingly. "I understand. Being lord of the Underworld and all, you certainly have a very high-level perspective. However, I think that is *exactly* the problem."

Before he could continue, the clear sound of a bell rang out, and tens of thousands of servants flocked out to the various tables. The bustle continued for a few minutes before they finally disappeared, leaving only the finest dishes for the guests to enjoy. Broiled Star Anemone, Poisoned Dragon's Liver, and all sorts of exotic delicacies were included in what Yama could only assume was an extremely expensive meal.

Despite priding himself on his Spartan lifestyle, Yama filled his plate with gusto. The first few bites he ate were heavenly, so much so that he almost cried. The others at the table looked on with shock as the man single-handedly polished off a quarter of the dishes on the table. They didn't dare complain, of course. The man could technically reincarnate them, mere spirits, with a single thought.

After finally sating his demonic food lust, he looked around and realized his impropriety. He put away his cutlery and cleared his throat before speaking. "My friend, what exactly do you mean that my perspective is too high level? After all, I'm extremely familiar with the inner workings of my company, and anything my employees can do, I can do better."

"Right," Judah admitted. "You're so capable that you often do not realize the problems of lesser souls. But that isn't what I meant. Your status is so lofty that you've ignored the governance of the Underworld, letting the free market decide what's best and only interfering in extreme cases."

"That's right," Yama said proudly. "The free-market system is well known throughout the universe as the best way to allocate scarce resources with alternative uses[2]. Literally billions of kingdoms and countries of the past seventy-two great kalpas have failed due to inappropriate government intervention, and a smart man learns from the mistakes of others."

"Rightly so, Your Highness, rightly so," Judah praised. "Of course, there are exceptions, as you know. Things like primary roadways are best done by the government, as are a few other select activities like law enforcement and the military. But have you ever thought of the *structure* of government? More importantly, have you thought of the way taxes are structured, specifically?"

"What do taxes have to do with anything? It's common sense that everyone should pay into the system. However, successful people have benefited more from the system and should be taxed at higher rates." The lord of the Underworld had given much thought to this in the past.

"In principle, you're correct," Judah acquiesced. "Heaven shares the same opinion. As does the demon world. But

---

[2] Reference: Basic Economics, 5th Ed. by Thomas Sowell. It's a good read, and I highly recommend it.

did you know that Hell[3] and the Immortal Realm have recently introduced tax reform which has greatly affected the Underworld?"

Yama frowned when he heard this. After all, he didn't meddle much in foreign affairs, and the Underworld had always been a strictly neutral party. He hadn't even interfered in the Twenty-Seven Universe Wars that had devastated the entire cosmos. In some, the devils attacked Heaven, and in others, the angels attacked Hell. Sometimes, the demons decided that they were the rightful rulers of the universe and staged a large-scale rebellion. Throughout all these genocides and righteous crusades, the Underworld had kept its neutrality.

How dare they hurt Diyu.

Seeing the man's agitation, Judah acted quickly to defuse the situation. "It's not as bad as I made it out to be. You see, your current taxation system consists of a five-percent flat tax and a progressive tax that can reach as high as fifty percent. Meanwhile, you've also eliminated corporate taxes, which is a good move with respect to attracting businesses and having your economy prosper. Meanwhile, you also have a hefty consumption tax of ten percent, and it's impossible to avoid ever since you digitized currency several aeons ago.

"What Hell and the Immortal Realm have done is to cap the progressive tax at twenty percent. And because of this, their economy has thrived."

The lord of the Underworld pondered in silence before giving the short, blue-eyed man the okay to continue. "You see, this has enabled them to retain top talents in Hell and the

---

[3] In Chinese mythology, Hell and the Underworld are not the same thing. The Underworld is simply a place that judges people and handles reincarnation. Hell, on the other hand, is the lowest realm one can be reincarnated to, reserved for sinners and devils.

Immortal Realm. In addition, many souls have flocked away from Diyu to take advantage of the favorable tax treatment. If that wasn't enough, these are all your most capable people. They're leaving, and only the unambitious and the unskilled are left behind."

"How do you propose we counter this?" Yama asked in a worried voice.

"I ask that, in your capacity as lord of the Underworld, you support me for mayor in the upcoming election. My platform is very simple: cut spending and cap the progressive tax at ten percent. We'll then increase the consumption tax to twenty percent to make up for lost revenue. The people in Diyu will be discouraged to consume and waste resources, but they'll be able to save beyond their wildest dreams.

"Ambitious souls would flock from everywhere, knowing that after slaving away for a few millennia, they'll be able to retire peacefully in the Blessed Isles in Heaven, among other various exotic locations. With the Diyu advantage, skilled workers will flock to the Underworld. Then, attracting talented individuals will become much more manageable."

The lord of the Underworld nodded seriously, but he wasn't born yesterday. Politicians liked to meddle in all sorts of things, and he was sure that this man was no exception. "What other pieces of the platform should I know about?" he said shrewdly.

"Oh, nothing major. I want to remove the following pieces of art in the city. They're atrocious, and whoever made them should be ashamed of themselves." Judah passed him a list of the supposed "art" objects that City Hall had approved as a part of mandatory art spending. Fortunately, Yama agreed. They were *terrible*, and the person who'd approved them needed to be fired.

"Anything else?" the ancient man asked.

"Yes, I want to regulate the movie industry. And the book industry. Nothing too major—I just want to ban the use of time travel as a literary tool. Same with dream worlds," Judah replied between bites.

"What's wrong with those? It's not like it affects children's morals, and it doesn't really affect anyone negatively..." Yama replied hesitantly. Truth be told, he had a friend in show business that did these things quite often. He was a terrible writer but an excellent friend.

"Let me ask you something," Judah pressed on. "Have you *ever*, in the countless *aeons* you've lived in this universe, seen good usage of time travel or dream worlds in movies? I mean, when used seriously. When used ironically as a literary trope, it doesn't really matter."

"You do have a point," he admitted begrudgingly. The only good ones he'd seen were parodies of the genre. "Fine. It's a deal."

Chapter 1: Washed Up

Cha Ming woke to the sounds of chirping birds and crowing roosters. He heard children playing and dogs barking just outside his window. He opened his eyes to see a single ray of sunlight illuminating the otherwise dark room.

Where am I? he thought. He tried to get out of the small bed, only to realize that he was utterly incapable of moving.

Why can't I move? he thought in a panic. The feeling of being completely helpless was overwhelming. While the first part of his life was one filled with sadness, this past year had been full of freedom and adventure. In that world, the helpless were often preyed on by powerful cultivators.

The panic lessened when he realized that he was lying in a warm bed in a wooden house, not a cell. Despite being unable to move his limbs, he didn't discover any restraining devices.

Perhaps I can use qi to invigorate my body and get out of bed, he thought. He then tried to circulate his cultivation base. This simple act felt like thousands of tiny daggers cutting through his entire body. His screams quickly attracted footsteps to his bedroom door, which was opened without ceremony. He immediately hoped for some answer, but as soon as the person entered, Cha Ming fainted.

Consciousness returned to Cha Ming some time later.

"Don't try to move," an authoritative voice said, "and don't circulate your qi." Cha Ming opened his eyes to see a middle-aged man with short-cropped black hair. The few streaks of silver and his wrinkled features was a testament to the many hardships he'd suffered in his lifetime.

Cha Ming caught a faint whiff of medicinal herbs coming from the man. However, the man wasn't wearing a traditional cultivation robe, nor was he wearing a spirit-doctor uniform.

Is he just a common man who practices medicine? Cha Ming wondered. To his knowledge, medical doctors who didn't cultivate were rarer than a phoenix feather or a qilin's horn. After all, even the most novice apothecaries could prepare medicines that were much more effective than a mortal doctor.

Before Cha Ming could say anything, the man handed him a bowl of what appeared to be medicinal tea. The pungent liquid was light green, and it smelled so foul that he wondered whether the man had poisoned it.

"Relax," the doctor said. "It's just a simple medicinal liquid that eases irritation in the throat and soothes the symptoms of dehydration. You've been unconscious for a full month, after all."

A month. Cha Ming took the bowl and drank it instinctively. He only realized what he'd done when he felt a burning sensation as the liquid wandered down his throat and into his stomach. It felt like hot needles had pierced his entire esophagus. Just as he began to curse the man silently, he noticed that the burning was becoming a cooling sensation. More importantly, his parched throat felt moist and painless. "Good medicine!" he said.

"It's just a simple concoction," the man said self-deprecatingly. "You can find much better medicine at an apothecary's if you can afford it. Unfortunately, not everyone in this world can afford the best medicine. Or practice it."

"Eh? The paralysis is gone?" Cha Ming lifted his arms and wiggled his legs. He sighed in relief at the knowledge that he wasn't paralyzed from the neck down. Such a fate would have been worse than death.

"Yes, I stopped administering the paralytic after you woke up last time," the man replied. "I don't often treat cultivators, so I wasn't sure how you would react when you woke up in a strange place. A mere mortal like myself could be killed in the blink of an eye.

"It didn't occur to me, however, that you would try to circulate your qi right away. I'll need to make a note that a qi-restraining concoction is recommended when treating such patients. I trust that you've noticed circulating your qi is *extremely* counterproductive for someone in your state. Please don't try it again in the future, as I can't afford to treat you in perpetuity."

Cha Ming was puzzled. "In the future? You mean for the next short while, correct? How much longer must I wait before my qi pathways and meridians heal?"

The man's pitying look spoke volumes. "I'm afraid that, to my knowledge, it's impossible for you to heal your qi pathways," the man said slowly. "Your qi pathways are a complete mess, and even the finest doctor wouldn't be able to fix them. Fortunately, your dantian—and as such, your cultivation—is intact. Regrettably, you have no way to deliver the qi in your dantian to the rest of your body. While you might be able to soak up a bit of qi while cultivating, your efficiency wouldn't even be a tenth of the usual. Besides, accumulating qi without being able to spend it is a pointless endeavor."

Cha Ming wasn't sure how to react. The cultivation world was one where the strong flourished and the weak were trampled on. He had begun a whole new life full of possibilities. Had this new road finally come to an end?

"I understand that this is difficult to accept," the man continued. "I also know you likely won't give up so easily. Please wait a few days and get used to your body's condition before attempting to cultivate, that's all I ask.

"You must practice some sort of body-refining technique, or it would have been impossible for you to heal to such an extent in only a month. You washed up on the shore near the village. Some kids found you, and a few adults in the village carried you to my office. You had fifty-seventy fractures, thirteen torn ligaments, and you were covered in cuts and bruises from head to toe. Many of your muscles were torn, and your internal organs were a mess."

Seeing the doctor's hesitant expression, Cha Ming closed his eyes. "Please continue. I can take it."

"Your organs are failing," the doctor said in a grave voice. "While I may not be very good at treating injuries, I pride myself on my diagnosing skills. While inspecting your body, I noticed that most of your organs have suffered severe burns. The damage to your qi pathways has made it difficult for them to recover. The only reason you're still alive is because of your unreasonably sturdy body. I'm not sure how long you'll be able to last. Days... weeks... months..."

Cha Ming understood what wasn't spoken. Years were not an option. "Can I have some time alone, please?"

The older man nodded before walking toward the door. "Come find me if you need anything," he said. "Lunch is at noon."

As soon as the door closed, Cha Ming began weeping. Not only had he lost his ability to cultivate, but he could die at any moment. Both he and Huxian were doomed. While he wasn't sure where the baby fox was, he was certainly alive. Cha Ming lay in his bed, dejected. Myriad memories, thoughts, and dreams passed through his head, and he unknowingly fell asleep.

A six-year-old boy with brown hair and hazel eyes opened the door to a small wooden shack. The door creaked as it opened.

I'd better find some grease before the hinges rust over, the young boy thought. He was carrying a pouch of rice, cabbage, and some tofu. It was all he could afford to buy for the time being.

As he entered the shack, he heard the usual snoring sounds coming from the single bedroom in the house. It wasn't his, of course. His father slept in the bedroom while he slept on a thin mat in the living room. The boy sighed and got to work. He started a cooking fire and took water from a bucket and mixed it in with rice in a pot.

He then chopped up the cabbage and the onions. By the time he finished, the blazing fire had died down somewhat, and it was now at the ideal temperature to cook. He hung the small pot up above the fire and installed a cooking plate above it. He placed a large wok above the cooking plate and began putting in the few ingredients he had available.

He poured in oil, and then dropped in the onions and cabbage. These were best added first, as they required much time to get tender. Frying them lightly helped. He added in a small amount of soy sauce to the dish, as well as cooking wine, before adding in the tofu and letting it simmer. After a half hour, he placed the dish and the rice in two large bowls on the table and placed two smaller bowls with chopsticks on placemats. He also set two small cups near the bowls and poured boiling water in each of the cups. They were too poor to afford tea.

The boy then mustered up his courage and slowly opened the door to his father's room. The smell of liquor assaulted his nostrils, but he crinkled his nose and continued crawling through the litter-covered room. Tattered robes, used undergarments, and a multitude of empty bottles made it difficult to maneuver to the small mat in a corner of the room. His father lay there sleeping. He reeked of wine, the only thing he found solace with in their wretched world. His left hand clutched the stump that remained of his right arm. His father was a cripple.

"Father, dinner is ready," the boy said. He waited a few moments before repeating himself, but to no avail, so he walked up to the larger man and began shaking him. The man only grunted and turned over. He sighed and prepared himself mentally before crawling over his large body and doing the only thing that would surely wake him up—he touched the man's stump.

As expected, the man swept out with his right arm. He was prepared, crossing his arms in front of his chest and dissipating much of the blow. Despite this precaution, however, he was still knocked onto the floor. Fortunately, he'd taken note of every bottle in the room and managed to position his limbs so that bottles didn't shatter as he tumbled.

He looked toward his father, who had woken up from his daze. "Is that you, Cha Ming?" the man said. His face was tinged with regret and shame at what he'd just done.

"Dinner is ready," the boy said. The man nodded, waving him off. Cha Ming returned to the kitchen and began cleaning dishes. He heard the sounds of splashing water and the clinking of bottles as his father fished around for an acceptable set of clothes.

He hadn't always been this way. Before Cha Ming was three, he hadn't touched a drop of wine, making sure to carefully feed the growing boy three times a day. However, everything changed after Cha Ming's first birthday. He got fired because his disability caused him to drop an important order he was carrying. It was the last place in town that was willing to employ him. Ever since then, he'd been drinking. Whenever Cha Ming asked where he got the money, he just mumbled something about a military pension.

Still, it was his father, and he would take care of him. They ate dinner together but didn't say much. He knew how much Cha Ming did. After their short meal, he took out a few silver coins from inside his room and placed it on the dinner table. Money for groceries for the next week. Cha Ming swept them up as he cleaned the table and washed the dishes. The crash of bottles from the bedroom let Cha Ming know that his father had resumed drinking.

That night, like the many nights before, he brought out his mat to the living room along with two thin blankets. Despite the loud snoring coming from the adjacent bedroom, the exhaustion of his days of work overcame him, and he finally fell asleep.

It was dusk when Cha Ming woke up again. He looked around and saw a set of simple clothes and sandals. He also noticed his bag of holding had been placed on the table beside him. It was damaged, ripped in three separate places. Using his soul force, he opened the bag with great difficulty. A quick account made him realize that he was both grievously wounded *and* broke.

All that remained in the bag were three golden crystals from the gold formation eye, a few Barrier Breaker pills, three Foundation Establishment pills, and the black-and-white orb Elder Ling had left for him. Every bit of crystalized elemental essence and every spirit stone, and every last drop of ink had been used by the Monkey King when he made the formation. Cha Ming had also used all his talismans in the final battle in Fairweather.

He sighed, then willed the Clear Sky Brush to appear. Unsurprisingly, the elemental characters on the brush were dull. He peered inside the Clear Sky World and discovered that none of the liquified elemental essence remained. Not that it mattered—painting talismans and his Seventy-Two Earthly Transformations Technique required qi as a guide. Without qi, he had lost his profession.

He looked at his ruined bag of holding regretfully. It was a very useful item, and he wasn't sure where to store his items.

Wait a minute, he thought, *can the Clear Sky World hold these items just like it did the liquified elemental essence?*

He used one of the gold crystals to test out his theory. To his surprise, it disappeared when he willed it to, storing it safely in the Clear Sky World. He sighed in relief and collected the remaining items. He also made a note to buy a new bag so he could camouflage his Clear Sky Brush's storage capability.

A short while later, Cha Ming walked into a narrow wooden

hallway. It was a short hallway that led to four rooms. Six pieces of art decorated the walls. They were beautifully framed, even if the contents were not particularly impressive. The paintings had clearly been made by children. Despite the lack of skill displayed, Cha Ming felt a little warmer when he looked at them.

He continued down the hallway into a living room, which doubled as a dining room. Wonderful smells emanated from the kitchen, and he could hear clanging pans and sizzling food. He was about to go in and greet the doctor when that same middle-aged man walked out into the dining room from the opposite direction. He was accompanied by a little girl. She seemed a little pale, and Cha Ming confirmed that she was sick when she let out a light cough.

A few sharp sounds came from the kitchen, and a middle-aged woman walked out. The little girl darted out and hugged her.

"How is she?" the woman asked the doctor.

He shook his head and smiled. "No need to worry, my dear, she just has an infection in her lungs. Feed her one of these pills every day for the next two weeks, and she'll get better." He handed her a bottle of pills before continuing. "Make sure to feed her lots of soup and tea. Avoid cold drinks. She should also get at least twelve hours of sleep every day."

The woman seemed relieved. "I made supper while you were treating her. I'll bring it out shortly."

The doctor nodded in appreciation. After an incense time, the mother, her daughter, the doctor, and Cha Ming were all seated at the table.

"This young lady is called Jin Xia, and this is her daughter

Wang[4] Yi," the doctor explained. "Jin Xia's husband is Wang Cai, a carpenter in the village." He thought for a bit before shaking his head in embarrassment. "My apologies, you just woke up today. My name is Li Yin. What's your name, young man?"

"My name is Du Cha Ming. Many thanks for saving my life," he said, smiling. The young girl was hiding behind her mother's sleeve shyly while the rest ate. Cha Ming guessed she was around six or seven years old.

"I'm sorry, she's a little shy," Jin Xia said. "Please forgive her." The little girl continued to shyly observe him as he ate from several vegetable dishes and ignored the meat dishes. The doctor and the mother saw this but said nothing.

"Little Yi was one of the kids who found you," Li Yin said between mouthfuls of food. "She and three of her friends were playing by the shore when they found you washed up. They tried to carry you to my office but had to stop after a dozen feet. That's when they gave up and ran to me for help."

Thinking of the river, Cha Ming's thoughts wandered. He thought of the dark waters, and he thought of his friends. He thought of Wang Jun and the promise he could no longer fulfill. The man had given up ten years of his life for nothing. Finally, he thought of Huxian. If there was a way to cancel their contract of brotherhood, he would do it. Now, he could only implicate his friend. After all, they both shared a life, and if one died, the other would as well. That, and it was very unlikely

---

[4] Chinese names are usually presented with the family name first, and the given name second. In this case, Wang is the family name and Yi is the given name. In China, it is common for a woman to have a different surname than her child because the family name is passed from the father. The wife's family name is rarely ever changed, as it is considered dishonorable to her own family.

that he would survive his next shared tribulation with Huxian.

The rest of their dinner passed in awkward silence, and the mother and her child left soon after. Cha Ming recovered his faculties shortly after they left. He saw that Li Yin was busy looking through a book, so he picked up the dishes and took them over to the kitchen. Fortunately, a pot of boiling water had been prepared in advance. He used a brush and soap to scrub away at the pots, pans, and bowls before setting them out to dry. Then, seeing as the older man was busy, he went back to bed and rested.

The next morning, he woke up at dawn. He looked around and confirmed that it hadn't been a dream. He was injured, and his future was ruined. Still, he felt hungry, so he walked out of his room and saw that Li Yin had yet to awaken. Since the man was taking care of him, he prepared a breakfast consisting of rice porridge and some vegetables he saw lying around. He also found some pickles and prepared them as well. Li Yin arrived just in time to see him setting the table.

"Thank you, my boy," the older man said before sitting down. They ate breakfast in silence. Once breakfast was over, Li Yin retrieved a teapot and served a cup to each of them. Cha Ming drank in silence, but his despondency was very apparent.

Li Yin hesitated before speaking. "You looked happy when you were cooking breakfast and cleaning the dishes. People need to keep busy, or their inner demons will keep gnawing away at them. This is a hard time in your life, but you can't let yourself get lost in thought."

Cha Ming didn't respond, so the man left him to his brooding.

Chapter 2: Crystal Falls

The air was chilly in the small village where Cha Ming had washed up. It was noticeably colder than Green Leaf City or Fairweather City, indicating that he had teleported far north. When he had asked Li Yin where the village was located, he simply replied that it was a secret. All he could let Cha Ming know was that the town was called Crystal Falls. It was named after the gigantic waterfall beside the village, which shrouded it in mist and humidified the air. It sparkled in the sun, often manifesting rainbows when the light passed through.

The village was in an isolated valley, and strangers were rarely permitted inside, while very few who left could ever come back. This was a strange policy for any village, as isolationism would make trade and exchange of knowledge extremely difficult. Still, he didn't bother pressing the issue. After all, he didn't have long to live. Besides, the people were very friendly. Children ran around and played, and everyone walked with smiles on their faces.

Cha Ming asked a stranger for directions, and they kindly

directed him to an indoor shop in their small merchant district. No one answered when he knocked on the door, so he let himself in. The soft sound of ringing bells served as both a gentle warning and a greeting, a promise that someone would be there soon.

The jewelry store was unlike any he had ever seen. Typically, goods would be on display behind glass cases to prevent theft. The people in this town clearly trusted each other, as pieces of jewelry were left out in the open for anyone to touch. While there was jade and silver, he noticed a distinct lack of gold and other precious stones. What he did find, however, was a multitude of bright, clear stones fashioned into jewelry and ornaments.

There were earrings fashioned from long crystals the size of his fingers. There were statuettes carved from that same clear stone. He also saw several timepieces and necklaces, but strangely very few rings. The ones he did see were fashioned with plain silver and completely unadorned with decorative stones.

"Can I help you?" said a wizened old man who walked up to the counter. He seemed to have just woken from a nap, given his disheveled appearance. As Cha Ming walked over to the counter, the man placed a pair of spectacles on his wrinkled face. Cha Ming took out three gold crystals the size of a fist and gently placed them on the counter.

The man gave him an excited grin before picking up one of the crystals. He observed it keenly with a large magnifying lens, then he used a metal instrument and easily dented the crystal's soft surface and nodded in appreciation. "You're looking the sell these?" he asked Cha Ming, who nodded in response.

The man thought for a while before taking out a notepad

and scribbling on it unintelligibly. Then he frowned. "You're not very familiar. Are you new around here?" he asked.

"I'm afraid I washed up on shore a month ago," Cha Ming said wryly. "My name is Cha Ming, and I've been staying at Doctor Li Yin's residence for the past month."

"Right, right," the man replied while nodding. "Little Chin told me about that. It's nice to see you've made a good recovery. My name is Xu Peng." He continued scribbling on his piece of paper before making an offer.

"You're in luck, young lad," the man finally said. "We don't get a lot of gold around here, so anything I fashion with them will sell like hotcakes. The last time I got my hands on any gold was five years ago. For Li Yin's sake, I'll give you a good price. Five stones and twenty shards apiece." Cha Ming looked puzzled when he saw the fifteen stones a quarter the size of a fist, followed by sixty shards as big as the tip of his pinky. They weren't clear or lustrous like the stones on display, but they were obviously made from the same material. Moreover, the material looked familiar.

"Spirit stones?" Cha Ming gasped in shock. This was the first time he'd seen spirit stones so strangely cut. There was a continent-wide standard on cut and quality, so the irregular shape surprised him. He could also feel a gentle warmth emanating from the stones. If he hadn't been injured, he would have tried absorbing the qi trapped in it to test the quality. Simply by judging by the intensity of their aura, these stones were not low-grade stones. Rather, they appeared to be mid-grade spirit stones. He had never seen high-grade stones before, so he couldn't discount the possibility.

"I'm not sure what they're called," the man said. "We've used these as currency for over two hundred years without any issue." He didn't seem to want to talk more on the subject. Cha Ming was happy to exchange the gold crystals for something with actual value, so he quickly agreed to the exchange.

If I'm not mistaken, three shards are equal to a mid-sized spirit stone, Cha Ming thought, then quickly turned glum once more. It was a very ironic situation; the town had excess spirit stones, but he had no ability to use them.

A quarter hour later, he walked down the street and went into another shop. There were no outdoor stalls in this town, at least not yet. The winter cold had not yet subsided, and any perishable goods would freeze out in the open. He wandered through the small store with a basket in hand and picked up some onions, some cabbage, and some tofu—the ingredients for a dish he had made far too often in the past.

A pleasant young lady met him at the till, where she tallied up the total cost of his order. "That will be five specks," she said.

"Specks?" Cha Ming asked, confused.

The woman frowned slightly before a look of enlightenment flashed in her eyes. "Ah! You're the new guy in town who's staying at Li Yin's!" she said, her face flushed with excitement. "How is the world outside? Have you been on any adventures? Are you single?"

A veritable barrage of questions assaulted Cha Ming, who stood there not knowing how to respond. Thankfully, a middle-aged lady sensed his plight.

"Go to the back, little girl," the woman said. "It's not good to scare away customers." She shooed her off before continuing with the transaction. "I've heard that you're new in town. I don't suppose you have any money on you?" she asked.

Cha Ming looked at her helplessly and placed a pile of shards in front of her.

"Oh? So you *do* have money." The woman snatched up one of the shards and took out forty-five diamond-like crystals and placed them back in front of Cha Ming. "There are fifty specks to a shard, and fifty shards to a stone."

"Thank you very much for the explanation. I feel relieved now," Cha Ming said. Not only could he now purchase food, but it seemed that the goldsmith had also been very generous with him. He packed up the food and headed toward the entrance.

Just as he was about to exit, the middle-aged lady yelled out. "Make sure to take care of Li Yin while you get better. He's good at treating people, but he never watches out for his own health!"

Cha Ming turned around and nodded before heading back toward the doctor's residence.

Cha Ming and the doctor sat in silence as they ate. Li Yin had a dull look, though Cha Ming didn't feel slighted. He had seen that same expression when the doctor ate the day prior, and in his humble opinion, he was a better cook than he was. Not that he would ever say such a thing. What concerned him more was whether he would appreciate the lighter fare.

"I see that you don't eat meat," the man said suddenly.

Cha Ming nodded.

"Why?" he continued.

"Because I don't want to hurt animals, and I'm perfectly capable of surviving otherwise," Cha Ming replied.

"You've done this all your life?" the man asked. Seeing Cha

Ming nod, he continued eating. "I'll be sure to add a note in my dietary research. If you don't mind, I'll have you fill in a questionnaire later so that I can tabulate data on your eating habits, history, when you started cultivating, etc."

The man's comments brought a rarely seen light to Cha Ming's eyes. "What other research do you conduct aside from dietary research?"

"All sorts of research: anatomical, diseases and their prevention and cures, infection, psychology, herbology, surgery, and anything else that can help mankind flourish."

"Surgery? You perform surgery as well?" Cha Ming asked.

The doctor nodded. "Yes, surgery is very important for medicine for the masses. Specifically, severe trauma might require an amputation, and severe bone fractures have trouble healing without surgery. I sometimes do some operations on internal tissue damage, but these are very tricky, and the risk of infection is very high."

Cha Ming marveled at the man's dedication. Spirit doctors made the need for invasive surgery irrelevant. Moreover, invasive surgeries were extremely risky. Even back on Earth, surgeries had only been successful for the past two centuries. Infection had killed over ninety percent of amputation patients, something which was only alleviated with proper sterilization and cauterization.

"Do you wash your hands and wash the patient before performing surgery?" Cha Ming asked.

"Before and after each one," Li Yin replied. "In the course of my research, I've discovered that agents of disease propagate through filth on human hands and bodies. I educate every patient I treat on this aspect. My data indicates that constant hand washing has greatly reduced the incidence of disease in town. Fortunately, it's only a small town of 10,000 people. A larger data set would be unmanageable by me alone."

"Do you sterilize the metal instruments you use and the string you stitch with?" Cha Ming pressed.

The doctor thought for a bit. "Yes, it makes no sense that only human touch would transfer…" he muttered. "But how to clean effectively. I could use soap, but is this treatment harsh enough? If I use boiling water, perhaps…" Without saying goodbye, he returned to his office and shut the door.

Such dedication and open-mindedness, Cha Ming thought. The doctors on Earth, in their arrogance, refused to accept the possibility that doctors could spread disease. In fact, when hospitals began to deliver babies, the death toll greatly increased since doctors refused to wash their hands even after surgeries and autopsies. The first man who brought up this concept was shunned by the entire medical community just for implying that doctors should wash their hands between patients.

A warm feeling suffused Cha Ming as he realized that these simple words he said might bring relief to countless mortals in the future. It was like a small speck of light in the darkness that was his current life.

Even if I can't fight, and I won't live for very long, maybe I can put some of my limited knowledge to good use in this small village, he thought. *At least it's better than doing nothing for the last few weeks or months in my life.*

Unbeknownst to Cha Ming, the concept of surviving for only days had been pushed to the back of his mind.

After the doctor's abrupt departure, Cha Ming cleaned the dishes and went back to his room. It was time to attempt circulating his qi a second time. This time, he didn't circulate it at maximum capacity. Instead, he sat in meditation and guided his soul force to his dantian, where he could observe the situation. His dantian was intact, just as the doctor said. It was covered in multiple seals that traveled to and from each organ in a loop.

As he looked through the qi pathways leading outside of his dantian, his expression turned grim. Aside from the first half inch leading from his dantian, the remaining ones were a mess. They were covered in cuts and lesions, and sometimes entire sections were missing. And regardless of whether the qi pathways were whole or damaged, they were all covered in black burns, which limited their flexibility and caused them to be full of tiny holes.

When he arrived at his organs, his expression became ugly. His kidney, bladder, lungs, and large intestine were the most damaged. That explained why he was only able to take short breaths and was feeling increasingly lethargic. Conversely, his heart, small intestine, spleen, stomach, liver, and gallbladder were functioning at only a little over half capacity. These functioning organs were the yin and yang organs that he had refined via Seventy-Two Transformations. They were mostly whole and only slight burnt.

The more damaged organs were a different matter. They were charred black, and in some cases, up to thirty percent of the organ had turned to brittle coal. He felt his kidney barely keeping up, the consequences of its inactivity very clear to Cha Ming. Over time, his blood would become full of impurities, and he would eventually be poisoned to death.

Closer to his extremities, his meridians and qi pathways had suffered less severe damage. However, they were still burned beyond recognition. Using them to deliver qi to his extremities for techniques would be impossible. These pathways were extremely important for cultivation speed. Even if he did manage to cultivate, he would be limited to around ten percent of his original capacity.

Still, he had to try. He gritted his teeth and attempted to circulate the tiniest amount of qi possible. A searing pain shot all over his body, but it was still bearable. He continued this way for a quarter hour before increasing the flow of qi slightly. Pain ravaged his body for what seemed like an eternity. He saw several of his brittle meridians burst, causing qi to assault his muscles, which spasmed in response. Cracks appeared on several of his organs. Finally, an immense amount of pain in his lungs caused him to cough up blood.

Following his futile attempt, Cha Ming collapsed in bed. The pain was tolerable, but the dejection he felt was not. Was there truly no hope?

He woke up the next morning to the sound of crowing roosters.

"You look pale," Li Yin remarked as they ate breakfast. "Did you try circulating your qi again?" he asked.

Cha Ming nodded, ashamed of his disregard for the doctor's instructions.

"It's difficult to let go of what you've lost," Li Yin said. "Try not to coop yourself up in here. It's bad for your mental health. It will do you some good to walk around a little. Personally, I enjoy going near the woods and watching the kids play."

Cha Ming accepted the advice in silence.

Seeing his dour mood, Li Yin fetched a kettle of boiling

water and poured tea for two. It wasn't the best tea, nor was it the best tea set. However, it did remind Cha Ming that things weren't so bad. There had been a point in his life where he'd had no teapot and no tea to brew.

"Now that you've finally evaluated your body's condition, I have a few other recommendations for you," Li Yin said between sips. "First, don't run. While your mind can take it, your heart cannot. Second, don't drink. Your liver is damaged, and you will poison yourself to death. Third, don't eat too much salt, because your kidneys are now functioning below their necessary capacity. Finally, talk to people."

The last comment surprised Cha Ming. He looked up at the doctor, who smiled before continuing. "People are social creatures. Without interacting with anyone, they will lose all hope. It is better to live in the company of a devil than to live alone for all eternity."

With these words, the doctor put his dish down and closed himself up in his office once more.

Cha Ming went out for a walk later that afternoon and followed Li Yin's advice. As he walked, he saw a man through a window. He was sitting at a bar and drinking away his sorrows. Unfortunately, Cha Ming already knew what this would do to a man. He had sworn never to drink, and he wasn't about to start such a terrible habit now.

He continued walking until he reached the edge of the woods, where he saw a group of six children playing. They were playing a game called *Swords*, something he was very familiar with. Each child would take a long branch, and they would attack each other just like they would with swords. Cuts and bruises were inevitable.

The exchange between these children made him smile. Kids

were a loveable bunch—quick to anger but quick to please. The sight made him mourn his lack of a childhood. Yet he didn't look away. Before long, he realized that there was a smile on his previously bitter face.

Good doctor, he thought. He watched them for an hour. Only in his dreams could he have such a childhood.

Chapter 3: Bloody Mary

Clip. Clop. Clip. Clop.

The sounds of hooves and turning chariot wheels broke the peaceful silence in the forest. It wasn't an absolute silence. Rather, gentle chirping, cawing, and slithering sounds could be heard if one was attentive, as could the rustling leaves and blowing wind. A convoy was traveling through these woods on a soft clay road. It consisted of three wagons and six guards on horseback. Each wagon had one driver and two cloaked figures riding at the front. The front wagon was led by a man with long silver hair, who was also the leader of the convoy.

"So you see, Miss Lan, that is how I established my empire," the man said. "It was *difficult*, of course, but thirty years of hard work have enabled me to retire in luxury and leave the family with my eldest."

"Fascinating," she said dispassionately. She wished she didn't need to talk to the old man, but unfortunately, it was part of the job description. Not every mercenary mission was a harrowing adventure. Most were like this one—uneventful.

It was the intimidation of having a mercenary in the first place that brought the profession value. Their ability to defend the convoy if things went south was a form of insurance.

Where's a good fight when you need one? she thought.

She heard a twanging bow, and an arrow lodged itself directly between the lead driver's legs, pinning his clothes to the carriage.

Ask for the Devil, and he shall appear.

The convoy didn't react as expected to the sudden act of aggression.

"Ah, I was wondering when you would come," the convoy leader said, unperturbed.

The nearby bushes rustled, and six young men holding bows with nocked arrows walked onto the clay road.

"You know the drill, old man," one of them said. "Just put fifty spirit stones in a bag and toss it over. We don't want to hurt anyone, but everyone who crosses the bridge must pay the toll."

The older man nodded. He took out a small sack, which had evidently been prepared for this event, and tossed it over. "Off you go, boys. Go enjoy yourselves."

The young men walked off cheerfully. After they had gone a fair distance, the older man urged the horses forward. Then, everyone in the caravan heard a bloodcurdling scream.

"Have mercy!" a young man shouted when he saw his brother's arm fly off.

Gong Lan walked toward him. She had pulled back the hood of her cloak, and a spray of blood drenched her face. The young man paled as he tried to escape.

The other four reacted quickly and shot Gong Lan with an arrow apiece. She quickly dodged two of them and cut the other two in midair with her sabers. She then charged forward like a bloody whirlwind and rapidly decapitated two of them. The others dropped their bows and attempted to run. In response, she unleashed two beams of bloody blade qi that felled them from behind. There was no remorse or anxiety on her face after killing the six men, only excitement.

"Why did you have to kill them like that?" an angry voice said. It was the old man, the caravan leader. He was livid, which Gong Lan found terribly ironic given that he'd just been robbed.

She frowned before replying. "I've been charged with protecting your convoy. They robbed you, so I retrieved your possessions," she explained before tossing a bloody bag of spirit stones to the older man.

His eyes narrowed. "You're here to follow my *orders*. I did not *ask* you to act, and the situation was under control. These thugs have been here for years, but they've never charged an exorbitant amount. All their gang does is occasionally enforce a toll so they can drink and have fun. I've seen *much* worse in my days. Besides, they've always kept the area clean of *actual* brigands. Not only have you brutally killed some petty thieves, but now they're going to come at us for revenge. You've killed us all!"

Gong Lan was about to retort, but she suddenly heard the sounds of several swift footsteps. In the distance, she saw a few dozen angry cultivators charging with weapons and howling at the top of their lungs.

"Avenge our brothers!" they yelled.

Finally, Gong Lan thought. *A good fight.* She ignored the merchant and licked one of her blades before leaping into the fray.

Not one of the brigands lived to tell the tale.

Gong Lan sat in front of an oak desk, sulking. The ticking sounds of an exquisitely crafted timepiece exacerbated her boredom. She didn't want to be trapped in this little room, but her brother had insisted. From the other side of the thin wall, she heard one party shouting and arguing and another party firmly trying to calm him. She heard "psycho" and "devil" mentioned more than a few times by the angry party.

After a half hour, the conversation ended. The calm voice agreed to a full refund and a guarantee that she would never be assigned to the angry client again. The other side snorted loudly before storming out of the building.

The door creaked softly as her brother opened it shortly after. Her face flushed red with shame as she reflected on the trouble she had just caused him. While she wanted to fight for a living, she didn't want to ruin her brother's company in the process.

Maybe I should find a different way to adventure and make money, she thought.

Her brother didn't walk to his desk as expected. Instead, he dragged a small wooden chair over and sat down in front of her. "Little sister," he said, "what's come over you?"

She didn't reply and kept her eyes downcast. They'd had this conversation many times before.

"Look at me when I'm talking," he said softly.

Her eyes darted up and looked at him. He had a calm and assuring demeanor. He didn't look angry, only concerned.

"Do you remember that I said to come look for me if things become overwhelming?" he asked.

She nodded in response but did not reply.

"If there's something bothering you, you need to tell me," he continued. This is the fifth customer you've frightened away since you came back from Fairweather. I've heard people describe you as psycho, crazy, insane, bloodthirsty... anything you can think of. They all say the same thing—that you're out of your mind and you need to be locked up.

"Be honest with me, Lan Er. Are you in control, or have you lost it? This is serious." Her brother was usually kind and comforting. Now, he was stern and rebuking.

This is why I don't want to say anything, she thought. *I know you'll be disappointed and yell at me when I finally screw up. Just like Dad used to.*

The former Blood King realized that he'd raised his voice and took the time to calm down. "Gong Lan," he said, "even I'm not immune to fits of rage. Didn't I tell you? Back in my youth, I lost control and ended up killing several of my friends. I can *never* forgive myself for that. I *need* you to tell me when you can't handle things anymore. I know where to get help. Just trust me, okay?"

He didn't wait for her answer before getting up and leaving the room. Gong Lan continued staring bleakly at the floor.

"You went crazy after a decade of slaughter," she mumbled. "Compared to you, I'm just a weak failure." She sat there moping for a half hour before finally getting up and going to the only place that could help her forget her shortcomings: the tavern.

Somewhere in Green Leaf City, three mercenaries walked into a bar. The loud crash resulting from their collision alerted all the patrons, who shook their heads in disdain. The three mercenaries cursed loudly as they walked around the building to find the entrance. The instant the trio entered, they were greeted with glares and silence.

"Nope. Not this one. I must have the wrong bar," said the leader of the group, who broke into a cold sweat from the concentrated killing intent directed their way. "Come along with me now, boys. We're going to the *other* bar now."

One of his drunken companions began speaking in protest, but the leader hurriedly shushed him and escorted the trio outside. Once they'd left, the bar patrons returned to their conversations.

"Have you heard about the Blood Queen's latest exploits?" a man asked his companions. They were seated at a small, elevated table. The four of them nursed large mugs of ale. They weren't particularly inebriated. The night was young, and only those with serious drinking problems were already out for the count.

"What did she do *this* time?" another man asked.

"Well," the original man replied, "she killed six young boys near Meadowlark Bridge. You know, the ones who hardly cause trouble. Her employer was pissed. If that wasn't enough, the remaining thirty-four in the gang attacked in anger. She slaughtered *them* all without any hesitation."

"But those men weren't proper thugs," the third one said. "Heck, I don't think they've killed or raped anyone. The worst thing they ever did was beat a few men to a pulp. Plus, it's not like their toll is that high. I've been on that route a few dozen times and they only asked for fifty spirit stones each time. That's ridiculously cheap."

"Right," the original continued. "Otherwise, why would I have mentioned it? The Blood Queen always kills at the drop of a pin. If it wasn't for her brother, she'd be damn-near unemployable. Over the last month, she's killed a hundred and forty people. None of them were honest folks, to be sure, but only two or three of them deserved death."

The man sighed. "She should just go back to doing what she's good at: the arena battles. Then she'd only be killing two or three people every few days instead of massacring a small thieves' village like she did last week. The pay's got to be better in the arena as well. Plus, I really miss—"

The man suddenly stopped speaking as a young woman dressed in red leather walked in. She walked through the crowd and sat at the bar. Her twin sabers gave off an ominous vibe, abruptly cutting off all conversation people were having about her. This was, coincidentally, eighty percent of the conversations being held at the time.

"One Bloody Mary," she said. The bartender was used to this order, so he fixed one up right away. Of course, he made it just the way she liked it. He mixed in various herbs, giving it a rich metallic flavor. He didn't pause after making the first one, which she downed instantly. It was only after giving her the fourth consecutive one that her face became flushed, and she finally slowed down.

The mercenaries who had just been discussing her finally

built up the courage to talk in whispers again.

"I wonder if she'll start another fight tonight?" the second mercenary said. "Does anyone want to bet? Twenty spirit stones says she will."

The first mercenary rubbed his brow. "You know it's just charity if I take that bet. Give me twenty-to-one odds and you're on."

The second man begrudgingly accepted. He'd be crazy not to take free money.

The third mercenary sighed and got up from his chair. "Looks like it's my turn again. I'll go get Sergeant Feng. Be back in a jiffy."

The other two men nodded. The first week, the bar hadn't had a clue about how to stop the Blood Queen every time a fight broke out. Then one day, Sergeant Feng came out and drank with her. She started a fight, as usual, but the results weren't nearly as devastating.

Ever since then, they'd come up with a schedule where different regulars would go fetch Sergeant Feng as soon as she came in. His drinks were on the house, courtesy of the incredibly nervous bar owner.

Still, he couldn't complain. Her usual rabble-rousing had done wonders for attracting clientele. The trick was to get her to start a fight to keep the customers happy, while somehow minimizing damage.

Sergeant Feng fit the bill just right.

"I heard about your latest 'exploits,'" Feng Ming said as he hunched over the oak bar. He held a glass of baiju[5], which he drank hot. It was the way noblemen drank, and while Feng Ming didn't exactly strike others as nobility, some things just couldn't be hidden. It was in his bones.

Gong Lan was nursing her ninth Bloody Mary of the night. Unlike most nights, she wasn't energetic and rowdy. Rather, she was lethargic. She laid on the bar, cradling her head with her left arm. "You're not here to judge me, too, are you?" she said, looking like she could break into tears at any moment.

"You can drop the act," he said. "I know you don't care what they think. But I think you *do* care what some people think. What did your brother say this time?" He'd just finished his baiju, so he hollered for another one.

"I don't know what it is," Feng Ming said after taking a sip of his new drink, "but I could never get around to liking cocktails or beer. It's like my stomach can't tolerate anything more than the more concentrated liquor. I have no idea how you can tolerate so many of those god-awful concoctions." He pointed to the Bloody Mary in her hands. Having had a sip before, he knew full well how that blood-flavored drink tasted. Even describing it as an acquired taste would be a bit of a stretch.

Gong Lan sighed. "I'm always disappointing him. I always cause trouble for him, but I can't help it. Not everyone can be as strong as him, you know. I just feel like, compared to him, I'll never achieve anything in my life." With that thought, she chugged the rest of her Bloody Mary and ordered another one.

Feng Ming looked at her flushed face with amusement. "All

---

[5] Baiju is a distilled Chinese alcoholic beverage, either made from sorghum or rice. Its alcohol content is usually thirty percent or more.

right, that's what you *think* he thinks. But what did he actually say this time?" He chugged the remainder of his baiju and ordered yet another. It seemed like since his trip to Fairweather, his resistance to alcohol had shot through the roof. He vaguely remembered someone speaking about a special constitution and resistance to poisons.

Gong Lan sighed once more. "He talked about how he'd gone crazy before and killed a bunch of his friends. Then he had to get help." She then looked at Feng Ming intently. "He asked if I needed help, but it's only been a couple months. He took the same path for a decade before it was too much for him. If that's not calling me out as weak, what is?" Her voice was now tinged in anger.

"Calm down, calm down," Feng Ming said. "I think he truly cares about you. Besides, not every martial art suits everyone. You used to be so kind to everyone. I'm worried about you, Gong Lan. Your brother cares about you deeply, and so do I."

"Oh?" she said with a coy smile. "So you care about this pretty lady, do you? How about you take up my offer this time? We'll walk on upstairs, and I'll give you a night you can never forget." She bit her lips when she said this, and a surge of warmth spread down to Feng Ming's lower abdomen.

"Do we really need to go through this every time?" he said while rolling his eyes. She got off the bar stool and stood up beside him, putting her arm on his chest and looking up into his eyes. Her coquettish actions almost caused him to lose control.

"Why don't you just accept? Just this once. It's so boring here, and I could use a little… *excitement.*" Her choice of words caused him to shudder uncontrollably.

"I think I'll pass again," he said. "You'll be the first to

know if I change my mind." He called for another drink, and the bartender came by with yet another steaming hot cup. He didn't bat an eye when he saw Gong Lan's behavior. He'd seen it too many times before.

There were two main reasons why Feng Ming had always refused her advances. The first one being that her brother was a monster, and he'd rather fight five devils than the Blood King. The second and more important reason, was that he had a feeling that their definitions of "fun" and "excitement" might be vastly different. She was much stronger than him—how could he possibly resist if she decided to kick things up a notch? No, it was best to stay friends with someone like her.

Gong Lan pouted in disappointment as she got back to her drink. Feng Ming noticed a flurry of spirit stones exchanging hands after she got back to her seat. She had clearly become the most popular betting attraction in the city. It didn't help that Feng Ming still carried his past reputation as a popinjay. His current military exploits were a state secret, and bragging about them was prohibited.

"You should really take your brother up on his offer," he said seriously. "He has experience in these matters. Just give it a try. There's no way he'd ever do anything to hurt you."

She sighed at these words and lay back down on the bar. Her face was extremely flushed, and her eyes fluttered as she fell asleep.

Well, its about time I take her home, he thought.

He quickly settled Gong Lan's tab with the bartender and threw her over his shoulder. Now the only tricky part was how to handle her antics when she suddenly "woke up" when he laid her down in her bed. She'd undoubtedly try to pull him in, as she always did.

The bar was quiet as Feng Ming carried Gong Lan out of the bar. The door closed, and hundreds of voices shouted out at the same time. A few people cheered loudly, while the majority groaned.

"Your free ride ends here!" the first mercenary said to his colleague.

The second begrudgingly put his twenty spirit stones on the table, while the first was elated. After so many losses, he'd finally won something.

Across the bar, several such exchanges took place. Some shouted "retribution!" Others shouted "I win, finally!"

Everyone then looked at the barkeep, who was on his knees, thanking the heavens for their mercy.

Chapter 4:
The Bar Maid and the Lord

A young lady was serving drinks to customers in a bar. She wore a mauve hairclip to complement the mauve dress she wore. This was the best way to make tips, she'd discovered. Unfortunately, it came with many undesirable side effects.

She heard whistling and catcalling as she walked past a table of rowdy men. They were all residents of Stonefell, a remote outpost near the spirit woods. Naturally, there was only so much to do in a town of 1,000 people, so most mercenaries flocked to the only bar in town.

Hong Xin had fled as far as she could before she finally ran out of food and money. She'd sold her horse to stay the night, not knowing what do next. Fortunately, the owner of the bar happened to be looking for a tavern wench. She was hired straightaway.

Serving as bar maid had not seemed like a bad idea. As far as she knew, one only had to serve food and drinks, make pleasant conversation, and look pretty. Yet she had gravely underestimated the gall of drunken men. Every night, she returned to her room in tears, covered in slap marks and overwhelmed with all the unsavory attention she'd gotten that night. That wasn't counting the bruises that she obtained every time one of her customers grabbed her wrists or fondled her.

Why did I have to run away? she thought. *Should I call it quits and go back home?*

A sharp slap to her buttocks ended her train of thought and caused her to drop a tray full of drinks as she fell backward. She got up carefully to avoid cutting herself on the broken glass, but to the pleasure of the various men in the establishment, her clothes were soaked. She could only blush in shame as her now transparent clothes stuck to her body, accentuating her generous curves and ample bosom.

She ran to a small closet and retrieved a broom, mop, and pail. She tried to hide her embarrassment as she cleaned the mess up in her revealing attire. Once she finished, she headed over to the owner, who ogled her while crossing his arms in displeasure.

"That's getting deducted from your pay," he said. She nodded silently, not daring to make eye contact.

"Can I go dry myself off now?" she asked. Her face flushed red with shame.

"No, I don't think so," he replied. His face was covered in a lascivious grin. "You're still on the clock, and your break isn't for another forty-five minutes. Just bear with it for now."

She gritted her teeth but continued her work. It would have been rather simple to dry herself off using her fire qi. She wasn't *completely* useless, having reached the fifth stage of qi condensation a short while ago. At least, that's what she kept repeating to herself. She knew that she'd been far outstripped by her friends at school. Still, there was no use wishing in life.

That had gotten her nowhere, and she knew better now than to rely on the sympathy of others.

The last time she'd dried herself off like that in front of customers, she was reprimanded and fined for "scaring" the clientele. Another time, she'd ducked into a room before drying herself off. She was only away for five minutes, but she was fined for taking a break before her allotted time. Her boss's behavior was getting increasingly unreasonable, but there was nothing she could do. She was poor and miserable, trapped in this small town in the middle of nowhere.

So she continued serving the customers their drinks in her wet attire. The orders were far more frequent than usual, and they likely had bought extra drinks to stare at her lecherously as she served them. Despite the large number of orders, she was careful to avoid the various feet that tried to trip her or the occasional spill on the uneven wooden floor.

Another slap to her soaked bottom came out of nowhere, causing her to yelp in surprise. Her eyes were red, and she was on the verge of tears, but she held them back. She didn't spill her drinks this time. At this point, butt slapping was the least of her worries. When a customer got drunk enough, she'd sometimes be grabbed from behind and fondled in all sorts of inappropriate ways. At most, these customers only got a slap on the wrist.

This world is so unfair, she moaned inwardly.

Later that night, the customers had gone. Her dress was dried, and she sat at a small wooden table, eating her meal for the night. The sound of clinking coins made her eyes dart up to the owner, who held them in his meaty fist.

"That's five silvers for the night, and three silvers from tips from our generous patrons," he said while smiling. She knew it was a lie, of course. She'd noticed how many silvers had been placed on the table after customers departed. However, she knew arguing wouldn't do her any good.

"Unfortunately, you broke some expensive mugs and spilled some drinks," he continued. "Not only that, several clients complained, and I had to refund them their money. I'll take away six silver, so that leaves you with two. No complaints, right?"

She looked to the side and avoided eye contact. She was used to it.

The man then walked up behind her and placed his large hands on her tense shoulders. He dug his thumbs into her muscles as if he were giving her a massage, but she found his actions revolting and not relaxing in the slightest.

"Xin Er," he said, "I know a much better way for you to make money. You could make ten silver an hour, and I wouldn't even care if you took long breaks between… *sessions*. If you're scared because you're inexperienced, you don't need to worry. I'll train you free of cost."

She shuddered when she heard these words and felt his breath beside her ear. Her heart palpitated, and her whole body tightened as she forced herself away from him.

"Fine, have it your way." Her boss walked off unhappily.

She looked longingly at the two silver coins on the table, which she took to the bartender when she finished her meal. He handed her the usual and shot her a sympathetic look. Although he was a healthy young man, he was the only one in the establishment who didn't look at her in a perverse manner.

"It'll only get worse," he said, sighing.

She knew what he was implying. However, as an employee, he couldn't tell her to quit directly. She thanked him and took the two flasks of wine up to her room. That night, like every night, she drank herself to sleep.

Huxian lifted his small head up when a pack of wolves brought him yet another beast carcass. Like most times, it was a small one. However, beggars couldn't be choosers. He munched in satisfaction as the wolf pack looked at him, salivating.

"When are you guys going to catch something bigger?" he asked coldly. He'd perused his inherited memories intensely these past few weeks, and his predecessors agreed on one thing: Spirit beasts and demon beasts respected power. Being nice with them never got you anywhere. He used beast language when he spoke now, something that all spirit beasts understood innately.

The wolves shuddered in fear before their pack leader gulped and spoke up. "Lord, there is nothing bigger to hunt within the limits of our territory. We don't dare hunt outside it, for fear of attracting retribution from the other lords."

The wolves cowered. These words had to be said, but the consequences of uttering them could be disastrous. They could only hope that this young lord kept his temper under control.

Huxian grunted when he heard this. "What's the weakest lord's strength? Where can I find him?" he said while stretching out his limbs.

The wolves shuddered when they heard the cracking of his bones. In front of Huxian, they couldn't help but prostrate themselves in fear and awe. It was a complete suppression that stemmed from their very blood.

"Lord, I'll explain to you right away," the leader said excitedly. "The weakest nearby lord is a demon ferret. He is a first-level demon beast that controls a territory twice the size of our current territory. Regrettably, this means that us canines have been reduced to beggars in that same territory. Instead of being their natural predators, we've been reduced to second-class existences there."

This didn't surprise Huxian. This was what every spirit beast did when they took over a new territory. They elevated the status of their subservient beasts, enslaved the rest, and monopolized the resources. Every legendary herb or mushroom growing in the territory would be reserved for their use alone. This way, the strong thrived and the weak faded.

Huxian's presence increased as he began to walk out of the shadows. This was the first time he was revealing his full form to the wolf pack. Now that his wounds were ninety percent healed, he could afford to head out. The wolves gasped and whined when they saw his two dazzling tails. He had kept them hidden, so they'd assumed that he was an ordinary demon fox.

But he didn't show his true appearance to others quite yet. Instead, he camouflaged himself as a normal two-tailed demon fox. He walked forward proudly, and his orange and white fur was a sharp contrast to the motley gray colors of the wolf pack. The wolves cowered as he released his aura, an aura five times more powerful than he had let on before.

"Great Lord!" one wolf gasped. "With a two-tailed demon fox leading our territory, there's no way that those stupid ferrets can continue monopolizing this area."

Huxian ignored their comments and walked out of the cave, and the pack of wolves followed him proudly. He was now six feet long and carried the aura of a conqueror.

The forest seemed to come to life as he walked through it. Various spirit beasts came out of hiding and prostrated themselves before him. He didn't deign to look at them but continued walking. These spirit beasts didn't feel slighted in the least; they might have died of fright if he'd paid attention to such lowly servants.

Soon, their group arrived at the border. The demarcation of land was clear as day, as both sides had urinated to indicate their respective territories.

"Come out and meet your maker, you stupid ferret!" Huxian growled. The forest before him became a flurry of activity, as dozens of spirit ferrets charged out and looked toward him with murderous glares. They didn't dare charge, however. This was clearly the lord of another territory, and only their own lord would stand a chance against him.

"You dare!" a squeaky voice sounded out from behind the woods. Soon, a large ferret appeared. It stood four feet tall on its hind legs, and its massive teeth were over six inches long. The wolves near Huxian paled when they saw those glistening teeth but didn't dare cower and stood firmly behind their lord. This was their chance for success, their chance for revolution!

"Here's how this is going to work," Huxian growled. "Immediately hand three quarters of your territory to your father[6] and scram!"

His intimidating aura surged, and the dozens of ferrets cowered behind their leader, who was slightly affected by the bloodline suppression. They cast fearful glances at his two

---

[6] An insulting form of self-address in Chinese culture. Addressing yourself as someone's father has obvious implications and also indicates that you expect the other person to respect you like they would their own father.

wagging tails, an unusual sight in these woods.

"Come now, give me some face[7]," the demon ferret said. "I can tell that this esteemed sir is a powerful demon beast that deserves a much larger territory than he currently has. How about I give you *half* of my territory, and we call it quits?"

The lesser ferrets whispered amongst themselves in surprise. This kind of compromise would only happen when one lord felt disadvantaged against the other.

"I've changed my mind," Huxian replied. "You can scram the hell out of your territory with the rest of your weasels, and I'm taking the whole thing!"

The demon ferret's face contorted in rage. "You're going too far," he snarled. "How could this lord[8] be left without a territory? You can clearly snatch some territory from the other lords. If you keep pushing, I'll fight you, and we'll be mutually wounded. How will you hold on to your territory then?"

"You overestimate yourself," Huxian replied in a grave voice. "Very well. If you want to fight, let's fight!"

The demon ferret's eyes narrowed as he ordered his minions to fall back. The dozens of wolves that had followed to witness this battle retreated as well. The surrounding circle became a holy dueling arena where their leaders would decide the fate of their respective species. Squeals, squeaks, growls, and howls filled the air, and the tension was palpable.

The demon ferret was the first to make his move. Ferrets were creatures of the forest, with tenacious vitality. They were

---

[7] Chinese culture often refers to giving face. When you give in to someone when you shouldn't, you are giving them face and respect. When you withhold respect that is owed, you are not giving face, or slapping them in the face. This ties in with the concept of family and personal "honor."

[8] An arrogant way to describe oneself. "This King" and "This Emperor" or "This Sovereign" can also be used in this manner.

naturally attuned to earth and wood. Their skin was thick, their bones were hard, and their regenerative capabilities were nothing to shake a stick at. The demon ferret's squeaky howls pierced the air, and energy from the earth glowed as it seeped into his skin like a raging river.

Huxian saw this happening but didn't stop it. He was here to show his dominance and expand his territory. He wanted to grind that ferret's face into the ground and bite through its skinny neck when it was at its strongest. As he waited, the earth transformed into a yellow armor on the surface of the demon ferret's fur. Its sharp claws and fangs had increased in length by fifty percent, and the ferret had grown to twice its original size. It now looked like an enormous badger lord, a king of the weasel family.

Despite his increased stature, the armored demon ferret didn't slow down in the slightest. It darted out toward Huxian, using extreme speed to take a quick swipe at the fox's neck. A look of glee appeared on its face when its claw made contact. However, it was replaced with disappointment when it realized that it had just struck an afterimage. Huxian had swiftly moved out of the way and placed himself behind the ferret. He still didn't attack; he simply yawned.

"Are you sure you want to do this?" Huxian asked provocatively. "Your father could beat you even without racial abilities. Why don't you bite off your left leg, kowtow three times, and scram? At least this way I won't be forced to kill you."

This further enraged the demon ferret, who immediately burned his blood essence while charging toward Huxian. His speed increased by fifty percent, and he slashed out with both his claws and his impressive fangs. However, he was suddenly stopped by an overbearing pressure.

"Burning your blood essence isn't very sportsmanlike." Huxian growled. He was now surrounded by an aura of pure white light, and his two tails fluttered in the wind.

The aura ate away at the ferret's armor, causing it to break down piece by piece. When the armor disappeared, his fur began burning soon after.

"Mercy, my lord. I'll be your servant!" the demon ferret shouted. It wasn't that the demon ferret didn't want to move— rather, he couldn't. The suppression ate away his demonic qi and pierced his defenses.

Huxian ignored his pleading. He revealed his fangs and approached the demon ferret at a steady pace. Saliva dripped from his mouth; after all, demon-beast flesh cores were nutritious supplements.

The demon ferret cowered as he approached him, not daring to say another word. It was then that Huxian heard a loud voice.

"Stop," the voice said. "As per the rules of this mountain, the demon ferret's territory is yours. However, you may *not* kill another lord in my territory in ordinary circumstances. Do I make myself clear?"

Huxian frowned as he pondered. The voice was coming from the peak of the mountain, and the aura that accompanied it was far more powerful than he was. Clearly another demon beast had taken residence on the mountain, one that was much stronger than him.

Things being as they were, Huxian grunted and dispelled his Aura of Purification. The demon ferret gasped and kowtowed three times in succession. The spirit ferrets accompanied him and kowtowed three times as well.

"Take your brood and get the hell out of Lord Two Tails's territory," Huxian said. He was in an extremely bad mood. Just as the ferrets were about to take off, he yelled, "Wait!" The ferrets turned around. "Leave six corpses of peak ninth-level ferrets. The rest of you may leave."

The demon ferret looked at his brethren with an expression of anguish, but his claws slashed out and killed six of his closest brothers. In the wild, anything could be done for survival.

Huxian looked up to the peak of the mountain, and the lack of response confirmed that this was allowed. "Take these corpses back to my cave," he growled. The spirit wolves were happy to comply. From now on, wolves and foxes would rule over this expanded territory.

As the wolves reveled, the spirit deer and other larger animals mourned. The ferrets had never bothered them, preferring to feast on spirit fowl and other small critters. Wolves and foxes would have no such appetites.

That night, Huxian ate the six spirit ferret corpses, bones and all. He let out of sigh of relief as his wounds fully healed and his power edged a little closer to the early stages of the Purification Realm. Demonic qi surged throughout his body, strengthening his bones, flesh, and blood. His core also grew a tiny bit.

As Huxian strengthened himself, he thought about the mysterious entity at the peak of the mountain.

It's a good thing I kept all my aces up my sleeve, he thought. *Who knows if I'll have to fight that guy in the future.*

Chapter 5: Fracture

Sweat dripped down Cha Ming's chest as he trembled in pain. He was completely focused on his latest idea: healing his meridians with the Creation Qi Manipulation Technique. He gritted his teeth as he extracted a wisp of white qi from his dantian and directed it to a creation seal that led to the outside. Slowly but surely, it wandered through the opening and to the undamaged inch or so of the qi pathway.

It was difficult to force the qi through the charred black tunnel. To his surprise, the charred surface quickly became coated with a new layer of qi-pathway material. However, the pathway was much smaller than before. It could be rebuilt, but the technique could not remove any damaged materials.

Still, something was better than nothing. The qi continued traveling down the pathway, depleting itself as it created. In some cases, entire holes were patched. In others, the pathway was entirely missing, so the technique was able to create a brand-new pathway. However, his joy was short-lived. He soon arrived at a location where the channel was ragged and torn beyond recognition. It was also filled with charred debris.

As the qi swept across these remnants, a thick coating appeared on the surface of each piece. Cha Ming grimaced when he realized that the pathway he had worked so hard to repair was completely blocked off.

This was the straw that broke the camel's back. His technique clearly mentioned that the human body could at most accommodate six sets of meridians. Therefore, he couldn't create a new pathway.

Depressed and dejected, he laid in his bed, staring at the ceiling. Before long, he drifted into a deep sleep.

Cha Ming panted heavily as he struggled against a large ball of wool. It was shearing season, and this sheep was still covered in its thick wool coat. It had fallen into a shallow ditch and couldn't get out unassisted. As a helper to a local farmer, it was Cha Ming's duty to rescue any sheep that were lost or in precarious situations.

Sweat ran down his brow as he inched his way forward, pushing his stubborn charge up the steep slope little by little. Finally, a half hour later, Cha Ming laid down on the pasture grass. His shirt was drenched in sweat, and all his muscles burned intensely. The sheep he had rescued, seeing Cha Ming completely covered in a salty liquid, proceeded to lick his arms and bare chest.

This isn't the first time, nor will it be the last, he thought. After catching his breath, he continued to guard the sheep as they grazed. They were close to the woods, and it would only be too easy for wolves or foxes to prey on the unsuspecting herd. That was why he always brought a long wooden staff with him wherever he went. Fortunately, these predators feared humans instinctively. As such, he could easily fight them off with a few wide swings.

Time flowed by quickly, and the clouds were tinged in red as dusk settled. It was time to bring the sheep back to their resting place, so Cha Ming patiently herded them away from the woods. As he walked past them, he noticed an unusual silence.

Must be wolves again, he thought. The smaller animals in the forest always shied away from their natural predators. Just like he expected, four silhouettes darted out from the woods toward one of the weaker sheep in the flock. Cha Ming grasped his staff firmly and sprinted toward them, hollering. He wasn't trying to kill them, only scare them. It was much too difficult for a lone boy to accomplish.

As he approached, the wolves growled at him and didn't move back. This was unusual behavior but understandable given their mangy appearances. They were skin and bones, and desperation flickered in their fierce eyes. Unfortunately, desperate wolves were the trickiest. Cha Ming swung his long staff and hit a wolf's head, and it whined but still stood firm.

He heard a sharp bleating noise as one of the younger sheep was bitten in the neck. He watched on helplessly as they dragged its corpse off. The two wolves facing him slowly backed away, their fangs bared. Cha Ming could only sigh and continue herding the agitated sheep back to their resting place.

He traveled back to the village after sunset. It was dark out, but a few people hung lanterns up to illuminate the communal street. He carried two large pails of water from the well with great difficulty. As he made his way toward their small shack, he noticed a few silhouettes. Frowning, he continued toward the house. He was greeted by the older farmer who employed him, the village mayor, and a friendly neighbor. They didn't appear very happy.

"Cha Ming, we have something important to tell you," the mayor said gravely. Seeing Cha Ming's confused expression, he sighed and continued. "It's not easy to say this, but it needs to be done. Your father passed away this morning."

Cha Ming dropped both pails in shock. His strength left him, and his legs buckled. His eyes were red and tearing up. "What happened?" he asked in a quavering voice.

The mayor sighed once more. "Fisherman Zhu found him downstream from the bridge, floating in the river. It was clear that he'd fallen to his death. We weren't sure if it was accidental or not, but then we found a note in your home. I'm afraid your father ended his own life."

Hearing this, Cha Ming sobbed uncontrollably.

Why did you have to do this? he thought. I was working so hard to support us both. It would have been no problem for us to survive. Since there is such a thing as filial piety, don't you owe it to me, your son, to continue living?

As such thoughts ran through his mind, the three adults waited for him to recover. Eventually, Cha Ming stood up and wiped away his tears.

"Can I see my father's body?" he asked.

The mayor nodded. "I'll take you there very soon. Come look at the letter before we go." His voice was soothing and reassuring. He had no doubt gone through this process many times before.

Cha Ming followed them in and saw a note on the kitchen

table, along with a pouch. Tears streamed down his face as he read the note.

Dearest Cha Ming,

I'm sorry I was never a good father.

Life has been difficult for me, but it's no excuse. My memories cause me great misery, and I can't help but drown my sorrows in liquor every day. These days, I've been thinking about what to do. I have little money left, and you won't be able to support us both adequately. Besides, I'm tired and lonely. It's time I move on and meet your mother.

Here is the rest of my life savings. It's not much, but it can get you somewhere far away if you so choose. Your mother and I were both cultivators. Unfortunately, we were both crippled in the war. It was those injuries that caused her death shortly after you were born, but she never regretted having you. And neither have I.

I tested your aptitude long ago, and it wouldn't be a problem for you to attend a publicly funded cultivation school. Alternatively, you can stay here and enjoy a peaceful life, away from war and its atrocities. The cultivation world is a brutal place, full of schemes and greed. I'm sure you can handle it. You are much stronger than I was at your age.

This meager amount of money should get you to the nearest city. Or it should be enough to buy a farm. It's up to you. Whatever you choose, I wish you a happy life. Once again, I'm sorry, but I miss her so much. I hope you can understand.

With love,

Du Xie Ming

Cha Ming was inconsolable over the next few weeks. He buried his father next to his mother and mourned for three days and nights at their graves. Then, he continued herding sheep for another two weeks. After getting paid for his services, he resigned and began planning his journey to Green Leaf City. The dangers of the cultivation world might be plenty, but he couldn't bear to stay in his small town, despite the kindness of its residents.

He had chosen to become a cultivator. It was the very first real choice he'd made in this life.

Cha Ming woke the next morning and prepared breakfast for himself and Li Yin. It was a daily habit for him, one of the few useful things he could do to help the generous doctor. It gratified him to see that, at the very least, he could take care of the man who saw dozens of mortal patients every day. He didn't ask for any payment, but the villagers helped where they could. Every day, they received various baskets of food, bandages, and herbs.

"Have you thought about what you're going to do?" Li Yin asked as they ate.

Cha Ming laughed helplessly. "What *can* I do? I'm a cripple, and I don't have long to live. If I didn't have someone who depended on me, I'd consider throwing myself off a bridge."

He kept his eyes down, ashamed of what he'd just said. Just admitting that he would consider suicide seemed to push him into a deep pool of cold water, a darkness he couldn't escape from.

"I was like you once," Li Yin said softly, seeing Cha Ming's discouraged expression. "My father was a spirit doctor. One of the best in his clan. He tested me when I was young, you see, and I was evaluated as a third-grade talent with full innate soul force and dual water and wood affinity. It was like a dream come true.

"My father was equally excited. Not every spirit doctor has the good fortune to teach his profession to his child. As a result, I was fed countless medicines in my youth. My father made me study anatomy and spirit-doctor theory. Because I was young, I didn't train my qi or body. Instead, my father made me perform several drills to increase my soul force. He was so excited…"

Li Yin looked up and stared into Cha Ming's eyes. "And then I tried cultivating. I successfully formed a qi cyclone on my first try. What great fortune! But I was happy too soon." He paused and sighed.

"The instant I attempted to circulate the newly condensed qi, my meridians were overwhelmed. They shattered and were torn to bits. Fortunately, the remainder of my body didn't suffer much damage. Yet I was destined to be a cripple for the rest of my life.

"Later, my father discovered that I had a rare innate disorder that caused the walls of my meridians to be weak and brittle. I noticed as he explained this that his countenance had turned cold. He stopped speaking to me soon after. I lost all status in the clan, and all I could do was maintain a feeble existence. Only my mother still showed affection to me, but her expression of disappointment was unbearable.

"Angry and disheartened, I ran away from the clan. No one stopped me, of course. It was still my dream to become a doctor. If I couldn't become a spirit doctor, then I would become a mortal doctor!

"I pestered countless academies for admittance, but reality

has always been the harshest teacher. I was laughed out of many establishments, and they always informed me mockingly that those who couldn't cultivate couldn't practice medicine. Eventually, my funds ran dry, so I became a clerical assistant for a lowly apothecary.

"I continued studying, as I was determined that it was possible to heal the sick without qi or spirit medicine. Soon I saved up enough silver to open a practice in a small shack in the slums of the city. I treated many commoners who were sick and injured using common herbs, acupuncture, and joint-manipulation techniques. I used the results of these early treatments to modify what I had learned from my early education, and after twenty years, I created a book containing all the knowledge I'd gleaned.

"I was convinced that the spirit doctors would be pleased. After all, my medicine was very effective, but I was only practicing on commoners. Not only would this not infringe on their lucrative market, it would relieve them from the pain of having to deal with the world's common people."

He sighed. "I was naïve. They said that I was dirtying the name of doctor. Spirit doctors hold themselves to a high standard—how could they allow someone like me, who did not meet these standards, to practice? Therefore, they burned my book and banned me from practicing medicine. If I were caught practicing, they would imprison me, all in the name of preventing harm to innocents. The very same innocents they refused to treat themselves.

"I could only run away and practice in seclusion. As a cripple, I may not be able to do as much as a cultivator. But that *doesn't* make my life worthless. There's always something that can be done. Even if you have a week left in your life, you can still use that strong body to build a house. You can still find *something* you can help the world with."

Finishing his cup of tea, Li Yin stood up from his chair and went to treat his next patient.

Weeks flew by. The sun was shining brightly as farmers tended to their fields and sheepherders tended their flocks. Cha Ming saw children playing in the fine summer weather as he walked. They did the usual things that young children did: running through the woods, jumping off tall things, and beating each other with sticks. These children had yet to learn caution and considered themselves invincible.

Cha Ming was carrying a large stack of wood for Li Yin when he saw their naïve horseplay. He was carrying a 200-jin bundle, much more than most men could carry. His current limit was about one quarter of his former strength. Any more and he would begin to feel pain.

I guess it isn't so bad to live out the rest of my days like this, he thought.

He performed many menial chores every day, helping villagers. With each day that passed, Cha Ming continued coughing up blood and feeling more and more lethargic. It would only be a matter of time before he kicked the bucket. He hadn't tried recreating his qi pathways since the last incident. He did, however, continue cultivating passively for eight hours every night. It was something he could do instead of sleeping, and the process comforted him.

After arriving at the doctor's house, he stacked the wood underneath a thick canvas awning that protected it from the rain. These mundane tasks were therapeutic. There was much need for such help in the village, so he hustled to pick up his next batch of wood. This one was for Grandma Li.

He walked back to the forest and hefted a large axe that had been specially crafted for him. A few vicious chops were all it took for him to fell a tree that was two feet thick in diameter. He cut it into smaller pieces, then split and bundled the freshly cut wood. The entire process took less than an hour, which was much faster than what a mere mortal could accomplish.

As he carried the bundle back, he observed the young children and their horseplay. This time, they were playing on the rooftops.

Maybe I should tell them to stop, he thought.

Suddenly, he heard a cracking sound followed by a scream. He quickly dropped his bundle of wood and ran over to the other side of the house, where he saw a boy bawling in pain. His leg was deformed due to the fall and clearly broken.

"There now," Cha Ming said in a soothing voice. "I'll take you to see the doctor. He'll fix you up, don't you worry." The boy tried his best to put on a brave face but ultimately couldn't stop himself from crying. As Cha Ming picked up the young boy, he saw a few kids walking up to him with guilty looks plastered on their faces.

"And that's why you don't play around on rooftops, kids," he said. "Learn your lesson before you break your leg like little Bing here."

After the quick scolding, he walked toward Li Yin's house at a brisk pace. Fortunately, only the boy's shin bone was broken. This sort of break wasn't life threatening.

A short while later, Cha Ming was sitting on a chair looking at the boy while the doctor made his assessment. He saw him touch several spots on the boy's leg and ask about pain. He knew from Li Yin's explanations that he was verifying circulation.

The doctor's scientific mind amazed Cha Ming. He had dropped several hints over the past two months, superficial information that he had gleaned over his lifetime on Earth about the circulatory system, immunity, and the like. Li Yin quickly took inspiration from the slightest hints and implemented them within a few days of study. In fact, he had devised all sorts of potential experiments he could use to verify each theory.

"Cha Ming, I'll need your help for this," Li Yin said.

Cha Ming nodded. It was the reason he'd stuck around for so long. At first he wanted to continue fetching firewood, but Li Yin said he needed a pair of strong arms.

"All right, little man, just sit still and be brave. Can you do that for me?" the doctor asked. "This will hurt a little, but not much. You can take a little bit of pain, right?"

The boy nodded and put on a brave face. "All right, Cha Ming, I need you to force these two bones apart and realign them as I guide. Are you ready?"

Cha Ming nodded, and at the doctor's signal, he used a fraction of his strength to adjust as the doctor indicated. The boy screamed and struggled, but fortunately, Li Yin had anticipated this and kept him still. He continued to guide Cha Ming with one hand until the bone was finally set in place. He then created a splint with wood and cloth.

"Remember, this will swell a lot and hurt a lot, but you must *not* remove this splint until I tell you to. Is that clear?"

The boy nodded miserably.

"Now that that problem is fixed, how did you break your finger?" the doctor asked.

"This?" the boy asked, perplexed. He held up a finger, which was quite red in the middle. The finger was clearly crooked and aching. "This happened last week. We were playing sword fighting with sticks, and I got hit on the finger. It hurt pretty bad, but it's getting better."

"I see," Li Yin said. "You've broken your finger, and it's already started healing. If it continues healing, that finger will cause you problems for the rest of your life. You should let me fix it."

The boy hesitated, but he ultimately nodded in acquiescence. He had seen the doctor many times before and trusted him unconditionally.

"That's a brave boy," Li Yin continued. "Now, I'm sorry to say that this is going to hurt as well, though not as much as the other bone because it's smaller. You're brave enough to handle that, aren't you?"

The boy winced but didn't protest.

"Cha Ming, when a bone is broken, it sometimes comes together at a strange angle and heals together. Unfortunately, when you heal this way, it will lead to deformities in the bones. His finger won't function properly, and it will hamper his progress in life. I need you to break his finger again, at this point here." He pointed to the finger.

Cha Ming frowned, but at the doctor's orders, he snapped the boy's finger like a chicken bone.

Chapter 6: Hope

The boy howled in pain but quickly calmed down. Cha Ming worked with the doctor to set the bone in the right position, and Li Yin made another splint for the finger to heal properly.

In the end, they took the boy back to his mother, who was waiting in the dining area. She had prepared a lunch for them in her restlessness, so they ate together before the mother and child finally left. Cha Ming returned to carrying wood, but the vivid scenes he'd experienced kept playing through his mind as he worked.

Do I need to destroy my qi pathways before rebuilding them again? he thought. *Do I need to clear the rubble before building new supports for the collapsed tunnel?* He recalled how missing sections of qi pathways had been quickly replaced by brand-new material. However, even lightly burned walls would lead to new meridians, which were much thinner than before.

He had a theory, but *how* he could accomplish it was a different matter. Unfortunately, his qi channels could not be destroyed by regular means. He could break them down forcefully by circulating his qi, but it was far too painful, and the debris left behind wouldn't be removed. Besides, he couldn't circulate his qi for more than three seconds before passing out.

Then, a crazy idea popped into his head. *What if I try using my destruction qi to clear away the rubble? I could first coat my meridians in creation qi to shield them, and slowly work my way forward. I would destroy a little bit, then create more as soon as it's destroyed.*

His mind continued to race for the remainder of the day. He worked quickly to finish all his duties before returning to his room. He shivered with excitement at the prospect of recovery.

Cha Ming rested his mind for an hour before projecting his spiritual force inward. He focused on his dantian and the several severed and damaged qi pathways. This time, he paid extremely close attention to the seals on his dantian, which enabled qi to flow to and from his qi pathways.

There were many pathways leading from his dantian to his kidney, so he chose a badly damaged one he had not experimented with yet as a starting point. Taking a deep breath, he gently gathered a wisp of the dark, destructive qi that inhabited the star between his qi lakes. It cycled continuously between the elements in a destructive fashion—wood destroyed earth, earth imbibed water, water doused fire, fire melted steel, and steel cut wood. It struggled fiercely as he pulled it out from its natural resting place.

Fortunately, the calamity lightning had done more than just injure Cha Ming. The baptism of lightning had greatly strengthened his soul, and he was now at half-step foundation establishment. Therefore, he used brute force to stabilize the struggling qi, which upon sensing the presence of absolute power, became gentle as a kitten.

The first step is establishing a qi seal. Everything he was trying was purely experimental. The Creation Qi Manipulation Technique was not designed to handle destruction qi, after all. Therefore, Cha Ming had to make many of his own inferences. The first inference was how to create a qi seal with destructive qi. Judging from the form of all other qi seals in his dantian, he decided that it should take the shape of a black star.

The qi seal for wood, for example, was created using the character for wood. It was the same for all the elements, but the creation qi seal was not a character. It simply existed as a white circle, as though any attempt to represent it as a character would be considered blasphemy.

He first grabbed a wisp of creation qi and gathered it on the circular seal, acting as a buffer between his dantian and his destruction qi. He was performing a dangerous experiment, and any slight mishap could pierce his dantian, leading to the complete ruination of his cultivation. At that point, recovery would be truly impossible.

Seeing that his buffer was established, he carefully guided the black wisp to the white circle and used it to draw a black line on the circle. He sighed in relief when he saw that his dantian was not pierced by the qi's destructive power. Following the first stroke, he quickly drew four more. To his surprise, the instant he completed the star, it flashed briefly before glowing with eight colors. There were five colors representing the five elements, a white circle, and a black star. The eighth color was ash gray, and he wasn't sure what this signified. However, he was quite pleased to see that the experimental qi seal had been completed successfully.

The second step, destruction before creation. Cha Ming

gritted his teeth as he slowly urged the small wisp of black qi through the newly established qi seal. The instant it touched the badly mangled qi pathway, extreme pain made Cha Ming convulse slightly. Compared to creating qi pathways, destroying them was unimaginably more painful. Fortunately, his soul was formidable. This allowed his mental state to bear the extreme pain and force the black wisp a little further down.

Cha Ming felt like countless razor blades were ravaging his insides as he continued to direct the wisp of destructive qi toward his kidney. Still, he pressed on. This was the last straw he could grasp, and if he was successful, he might be able to save his life. With luck, he could restore his ability to cultivate.

Worst case, I drop dead, he thought. *It's better to die trying than to give up hope.*

This single thought guided him through the process like a light in the darkness. He continued inching farther and farther until he reached his kidney. When he arrived at the kidney, he didn't stop. Instead, he used the black wisp to destroy the surface where a ruined qi seal lay. He wiped this qi seal out of existence, then carefully traced a black star where the seal had previously been. After the last stroke was completed, he finally ran out of destruction qi.

Fortunately, I managed to finish clearing a single pathway, he thought before retracting what remained of his inky black qi. After it returned to his qi pool, he directed the misty white qi to the same qi seal. It passed through effortlessly, and as he directed it, he witnessed the creation of the most beautiful qi pathway he had ever seen. It was flawless, a much better product than his original creation. Better yet, he felt that this new qi pathway was far more flexible and durable this the ones he had been born with.

Compared to the pain he'd suffered while clearing the rubble, the pain of creating a new pathway was like scratching an itch. In a way, the pain felt *comfortable*. It took him less than a tenth of the time to completely empty out his creation qi and form a complete qi pathway. As soon as he formed the circular seal, the same eight-colored mutation as before led to the creation of a hybrid qi seal.

He breathed a sigh of relief as soon as the deed was done. After retracting the white qi, he was about to begin cultivating to recover his qi when a thought struck him: Could he use this hybrid qi seal with *all* the elements? His dantian was brimming full with five different qi lakes. He didn't hesitate to grab a wisp of green wood qi and force it through the hybrid qi seal. As expected, it passed through without a hitch.

As it passed through, he noticed the qi pathway strengthen, and the dematerialized flesh beside where the destruction qi had passed began to heal over. It continued until finally pouring into his badly damaged kidney. He gasped in shock as the damaged organ sprang to life. While he couldn't heal the charred remains of the organ, its function had increased significantly.

Once the wood qi was completely exhausted, he switched to water qi. The instant the water qi poured in, he felt the fluids in the organ regenerate. It began functioning at a much higher capacity. Next, as he poured metal qi in, he felt the blood in his organ increase. Then, earth qi stabilized its structure, and finally, fire qi catalyzed the whole process. Although he wasn't sure exactly how well it was functioning, his rapidly decreasing lethargy was a good indication.

He sighed in relief when the process was completed. As he withdrew his consciousness from his body, he realized that it was already late in the evening. He felt a stabbing pain in his bladder as the urge to relieve himself struck without warning. He hobbled over to a small bucket in his room and sighed in relief as he filled it with hot urine. The process brought him great pain.

Am I passing a kidney stone or something? he thought. *And what's that smell?*

It took him a quarter hour to painfully finish the process before he retrieved a small lamp. He lit it, only to discover that the bucket was filled with a blackish red fluid. He swirled it around slightly, hearing a noise akin to sand in the bottom.

He wrinkled his nose and stuffed the bucket in a corner of the room. He planned to show it to the doctor in the morning.

Finally, after wandering back to his bed, exhaustion hit him like a sack of bricks. Sleep took him instantly.

Cha Ming woke up the next morning to the wonderful smell of breakfast food. His stomach grumbled intensely, so he immediately obeyed it and sprang out of bed. After washing his face, he proceeded to the dining room, where he saw a large breakfast laid out on the table. He heard the doctor in his office, patiently discussing medical matters with his patient.

Not wanting to disturb him, he walked over to the table and ravenously ate whatever was in front of him. He hadn't felt so hungry in a long time. Even spending a month unconscious hadn't made him so famished.

Li Yin walked in just as he was finishing his meal. "You

finally decided to come out of your room after three days, I see."
The man grunted. Seeing the look of confusion on Cha Ming's
face, he continued. "I checked up on you several times over the
last few days. For three days, you were sitting in a meditative
posture, and I didn't want to disturb you. This morning, I saw
that you were sleeping, so I made you breakfast. Given that
you can't cultivate, I'm surprised you could stay in a meditative
state for so long."

Embarrassed, Cha Ming explained his recent experience
with the clever doctor, who listened attentively. After their
discussion, Cha Ming also fetched the bucket of foul urine he'd
excreted when he woke up from his session.

"Fascinating!" Li Yin exclaimed. "It appears to me that,
since you've managed to restore some level of qi flow to your
kidney, it has cleared the debris that had been accumulating
over time and was slowly poisoning you. If what you say is true,
then the immediate threat to your life from kidney failure has
disappeared. I'm happy for you. Truly." The older man's eyes
sparkled for a moment, but an expression of loneliness quickly
replaced his previous excitement. This too vanished swiftly and
was quickly replaced with his usual calm demeanor. Then, a
bell rang from his office.

"Take your time today and rest, my boy," Li Yin said before
heading toward his office. "I need to go see another patient."

It took Cha Ming three more days to recover his qi, and ten
shards had been ground to dust in the process. The damage

to his meridians and qi pathways made it very difficult to absorb ambient qi, so the concentrated essence in mid-grade spirit stones was ideal for his recovery. He considered himself extremely fortunate to have washed up in a place where spirit stones were so abundant.

He soon realized that the process of healing his qi pathways would take far longer than he originally estimated. The process could even take two years, depending on the circumstances. Further, at least half of this time would be spent resting and recuperating.

These three days, he had done a considerable amount of thinking. He was currently useless in battle, and his injuries could only be aggravated if he was exposed to any violence or dangerous situations. This meant that, ideally, he should stay within the village the whole time. These thoughts continued to linger when he successfully cleared and rebuilt another two pathways. With each qi pathway he unblocked, he felt one step closer to gaining his life back.

It was now summer, and the scorching heat had forced many people back indoors for shelter. Cha Ming was no exception. His bedroom was rather small, so after purchasing the supplies he required, he sat at a small desk in the living room and began practicing his calligraphy.

He wrote whatever came to mind as his paintbrush flowed. There was no qi involved, but he kept his spiritual force active at all times, striving for perfection with every brush stroke. As he wrote, he thought of his kind teacher, Elder Ling, who had kindly taught him without asking for anything in return. So many coincidences had shaped his life in the past year. In addition, he'd had many instances of luck, such as finding the Clear Sky Brush, his cultivation technique, meeting Huxian, and meeting the man in the brush. Yet he had suffered no true hardships.

Now it was his turn to suffer. And this penance would last many years. Here he was, lost and friendless. He could only carry on and make the best of the situation.

"That's very good penmanship you have there," a voice said from behind him.

Cha Ming turned around and saw Li Yin, who nodded appreciatively. "You write quite fast as well."

Cha Ming sighed and continued writing. "I learned calligraphy when I became a talisman artist. Although I can't currently use qi, I can still continue practicing this skill. Besides, it focuses my mind and soothes the soul."

"Quite right," Li Yin said. "I have a job for you if you're interested."

"Oh?" Cha Ming asked. "Whatever it is that you need me to do, I'll be happy to oblige." This was the first time the doctor had ever asked him to do anything directly. He owed the man his life, so he would never hesitate to help him with something.

"Come with me," he said. "I'll show you something."

Cha Ming followed Li Yin into his office. There, he noticed a messy desk and a few bookshelves. The doctor walked past these and proceeded to a large wooden closet. He opened the lock on the handle and opened it, revealing a dozen large bound books. There were also over a hundred scrolls that lay bundled in a pile.

"I must confess, I haven't been the best at taking notes all these years," the doctor said. "I have so much research, and so many patients, but very little time."

He then walked up to one of the large bound books and opened it for Cha Ming to see. Every word written within it was hastily scrawled in what could only be described as "doctor's script." In other words, the contents were nearly illegible.

"These are my life's work," Li Yin continued. "They contain all my accumulated knowledge on medicine, and every book contains general groupings in each subject. For example, this book is about the human skeletal system. There's another book on organs, and another one on qi pathways, meridians, and acupuncture. There is also a large book on disease.

"What I'd like you to do is read through these, condense and amalgamate the content, and write it legibly so that new doctors can easily learn the content. Can you do it?"

Cha Ming gulped but eventually nodded. It was a very tedious task, but at this point he had a very substantial amount of downtime. Further, if he started with the book on meridians and qi pathways, then followed up with the book on organs, he would stand a much better chance in succeeding in his experimental recovery process.

"I'll start tonight," Cha Ming said, grabbing the large book on qi pathways. He didn't dare idle for a single moment. His life and his future were at stake.

Chapter 7: Arrest

G ong Lan shivered as she woke. It was dark, and a musty smell assaulted her nostrils when she breathed. It was cold and damp where she lay, rough even. Definitely not a bed. Moving her legs, she heard the rattling of chains being dragged across a hard surface. Stone, if she wasn't mistaken. Her eyelashes fluttered as she finally looked around what appeared to be a dark cell.

She winced in pain as she sat up on her stone bed. Her ankles were bloodied and covered in sharp lines, a cruel reminder that at some point, she'd tried to force her way out of the iron fetters.

How did I get here? Why am I in a cell?

Blurry memories surfaced as she searched for the answer. She recalled a pickpocket taking an elder man's pouch. There was a chase. A group of hoodlums who were harassing a young woman. She remembered flashes of steel and a spray of blood.

And then... nothing. She couldn't remember anything after that.

Despite the blood on her ankles, her usual despondency over the past months remained. After much trial and error, she'd discovered that it was other people's blood that she craved. She had thrown herself into many dangerous missions but had also botched many peaceful ones. After many months, her brother couldn't take it anymore and refused to give her further assignments. She couldn't blame him, of course. Her lust for blood was rapidly eroding his loyal client base. However, he had yet to realize the consequences of his actions.

At first, there were only a few extra brawls in the tavern she frequented. After a few weeks of collateral damage, she was banned from every tavern and bar in the city. As such, she was forced to drink alone. No one wanted to be around her when she was inebriated. After her only outlet was snatched away, her temper became increasingly volatile. Only Feng Ming and her brother could stand to visit her. Even then, they only came by once a week. After all, they were both busy men with full-time jobs.

Now she'd hit rock bottom. She had killed a few hooligans for pickpocketing. The punishment clearly didn't suit the crime, something she only realized in retrospect.

What do I do now? Do I wait here and rot in prison?

Her train of thought was derailed when she heard footsteps in the hallway. Keys jingled as the lock to her door clicked open.

"Visitor for prisoner Gong Lan," a dull voice intoned.

She couldn't see who it was, as the torchlight from the hallway was the first light she had seen since waking. A familiar-looking figure walked in, and the door closed behind him.

"You're a really impressive prisoner," the man said. "You've just gotten here and you're already in solitary confinement. Your reputation precedes you, Blood Queen."

Some blood queen, she thought. She was clothed in rags; her signature red leather armor had been stripped off by God knew who. Her treasured sabers were missing as well. *Maybe that's for the best.*

"You look dashing as always, Feng Ming," she said. "Have you come to grant me my last wish before they execute me?"

Feng Ming chuckled wryly. "That depends on the request. What would you have me do?"

"Me," she replied. Sadly, he had fought off all her attempts to date.

He chuckled again. "I'm afraid I can't help you there. Not only would your brother kill me, but those chains and the stone bed would make things very uncomfortable."

"You mean exciting?" she replied.

"And that is the third reason, the reason I've always turned you down in the first place," he said. "I think our definitions of excitement are very different. Anyway, I don't think they'll execute you. They'll likely keep you detained for many years. Your brother's too damn powerful, after all, so the city lord has no choice but to accommodate him. However, accommodation and capitulation are two completely different things."

In other words, he could reduce the punishment, but the punishment had to be severe enough to appease the masses. Anything less than her current punishment would greatly weaken the city lord's authority. Sparing her life was already giving her brother a lot of face.

"You need to take care of yourself," Feng Ming said. "I'm going on a mission in a couple days. It'll be a long one. Take this time away from killing to reflect on why it was that you got into this mess in the first place. What were you fighting for? I refuse to believe that the kind-hearted Gong Lan I first met would strive for power only to mindlessly slaughter innocents."

They sat in silence for a while, after which Feng Ming walked over to the steel door and knocked. He glanced at her once more before walking out.

I walked down this path to protect my friends. I tried my hardest not to be a failure, but now I've become the biggest of burdens. Father was right—I'll never amount to anything.

Thinking of her friends and family didn't help. It only made the thick walls and steel door that much more alienating. She felt so lonely suddenly, yet all she could do was suffer in silence.

A week passed. It was difficult to tell time in the dark cell, so instead she counted the meals she ate. Despite everything she'd heard about people getting themselves thrown in jail to get three square meals a day, the truth was disappointing. Every evening, the jailor would bring by a small chunk of meat, a pitcher of water, and a loaf of bread. To many people, this chunk of meat would be a godsend. However, that single meal was barely enough to sustain her. She wasn't used to starving like this, but she supposed she didn't deserve better.

Gong Lan had done much thinking over the past week. Memories constantly flashed before her eyes, memories that she'd forgotten. Sometimes they were about her father and the various beatings she'd received. Other times, she actually remembered the brutal scenes when she blacked out and went berserk, killing people with wild abandon. Every time a memory flashed by, her self-esteem plummeted.

What made things worse was that her brother had yet to visit. She hadn't seen anyone since Feng Ming last came. Such treatment only reaffirmed her initial conviction: that she was a dreadful failure, no matter what cultivation base she had.

She hadn't cultivated all this time. The Blood World Scripture might be powerful, but it had a dreadful side effect: Advancement could only be gained through slaughter and blood. Her next hurdle, establishing her foundation, would either require an unprecedented threat to her life or a special pill concocted from the blood of people and demon beasts alike. The process of consuming the pill would be no less dangerous than breaking through mid-battle. Either way, she would establish a perfect foundation.

A grating sound alerted her as a thin plate of food and a small bowl of water was slipped through an opening at the bottom of her door. The guard shut the opening as quickly as it had opened. This wasn't surprising, now that she remembered how she'd gotten put in solitary confinement in the first place. A few of the male prisoners had been harassing her, so she'd killed all of them with a teacup.

Death by teacup. A terrible way to go. Her solitary confinement was both for her own protection and for the other prisoners. More importantly, it was to protect the jailors. In the process of capturing her, she'd injured three guards and permanently maimed two others. Coincidentally, one of those two happened to be the guard who supervised solitary prisoners. She suspected that one meal a day was an exception rather than the rule, a punishment for her bad behavior.

Hours passed. She hadn't yet fallen asleep when she heard a loud crashing sound from above the ceiling, followed by shouting. Sounds of fighting ensued, and soon the door leading to the basement where she was located blew open. She heard a thump and the sound of a body crumpling, likely the maimed guard.

Who could be breaking into prison at this hour?

To her surprise, she heard the jingle of keys right outside her cell, and the steel door opened. A tall cloaked figure was looking down at her.

"Have you done enough thinking this past week?" a voice asked.

She recognized that voice. Her brother had come to break her out of prison! The very thought brought tears to her eyes. It seemed like her brother hadn't abandoned her after all.

"Let me see your fetters," Gong Wuling said softly. She obediently stretched out her legs, and her brother swiftly unlocked them.

"Come," he said. She followed after him as they traveled through the guardhouse, past twenty crumpled figures. They passed some prisoners on the way, but they didn't dare ask for rescue once they saw Gong Wuling's sharp gaze.

Soon, they were out of the city. Two horses were nicely tied up, their saddles full of provisions for what she could only assume was a long journey. A sudden bout of anxiety struck her as she looked everywhere but didn't see the familiar gleam of her sabers.

"Brother, my sabers are still in the city," she said worriedly.

"I have them with me, but you won't need them where we're going," he said calmly.

"Where *are* we going?" she asked nervously. Did they have to flee the country because of this prison break?

"To get you help," he said softly. "I know a man who works miracles. However, he lives in the mountains. Our journey will take many months, but I refuse to have you continue down this path of slaughter. So, while I'm bringing your sabers, I'm afraid you will never use them again."

Hong Xin hated her life. Months had passed, and she still hadn't managed to save up more than fifty silvers. She knew it was intentional, of course, a prolonged effort by the owner of the establishment to convince her to sell more than just her waitressing services.

It was not that she didn't make money. Rather, the misery of her situation caused her to drink it all away. She was now completely dependent on these few bottles every night, to the point that the friendly bartender now refused to serve her. As a result, she had no choice but to beg the owner, who would smile viciously and sell it to her at twice the price.

The customers today were rowdy and perverted, but she had long gotten used to their touchy behavior and their explicit words. She simply wore a fake smile as she walked around delivering orders. It had been over a month since she had tripped, not that the pay had gotten any better. The owner always found a way to grind her pay down to the bare minimum.

As the night passed by, she kept feeling that there was something missing.

Where is the usual harassment from the owner? she wondered. *Has he finally dropped dead, or did he have a change of heart?*

This was wishful thinking, of course. Later that evening, she finished cleaning up all the tables and sat down and started eating her meal. She waited for the owner to show up, since it was possible that he might confiscate her pay if she didn't wait for him. Soon, she heard the door to the kitchen open and saw the owner stumbling toward her. He was drunk. He pulled up a chair and sat beside her, staring at her in his usual disgusting manner.

"Did you bring my pay for the day?" she said crisply.

The man looked confused, then finally mumbled, "Why do you have to be that way? Aren't we friends? Can't we just chat?"

She looked at him warily. "We aren't friends, and no, I don't want to chat. I just want to get paid," she replied.

"Have you thought about my offer yet? I'll pay you double!" he said hoarsely.

Disgusted, she turned around to walk upstairs to her room. She wouldn't stay around and get treated like this, pay or no pay.

"I'll bring it up to you in a bit," he yelled.

A half hour passed by before she heard a loud knock on her door. As she opened it, the man forced himself inside the room and handed her a small pouch.

She poured out the contents of the pouch, only to discover thirty pieces of silver. She frowned before asking, "What is all this for? Why am I getting so much all of a sudden?"

The owner burped. "It's advance payment for tonight," he said. His face was flushed. His red eyes kept wandering around her beautiful figure, as though taking in a precious work of art.

She frowned. "I've already told you, I'm not having anything to do with your offer. Go to bed, you're being loathsome." She tried pushing him out, only to realize that he wouldn't budge.

Instead, he forced her back against a wall.

"Why do you have to be so mean?" he muttered drunkenly. She wrinkled her nose as the smell of alcohol assaulted her senses. However, before she could push him away, she felt a hand pulling at the edges of her robe.

"What are you doing?" she yelled angrily. She moved to try and stop him, only to have his thick, meaty hand grab her wrist and force it against the wall. She paled as she realized she couldn't free herself of his grip.

He wouldn't dare force me to do anything, would he?

Yet before she knew it, both her wrists were caught up in his one meaty hand. He began grasping at her robe impatiently. It tore under his forceful approach, exposing her fair skin and one of her twin peaks. Her mind blanked. She couldn't think, and to make matters worse, she felt his meaty hand fondle her bare chest, which no one had touched before other than her mother.

Her legs were shaking. *How can this be happening to me?* She tried to scream, only to have a rag shoved into her mouth. He began unbuckling his pants with his free hand.

What do I do? What do I do? she thought frantically. She would rather die than experience this.

It was then that she remembered that she was a cultivator.

She gathered her burning qi and directed it to her raised hands, and a burning dragon shot out from them and hit the ceiling. The owner scrambled back quickly to avoid the falling debris. His previous lusty expression was replaced with fear.

"Spare me, spare me!" he yelled. He was now covered in sweat, but he hadn't had time to pull up his pants, which were down around his ankles.

She summoned a ball of flame into her hand as she looked

down at him with a cold expression. "You deserve death," she said in a deadpan voice. First, she burned his little brother until it was nothing but a black pile of charcoal. His screams rang throughout the bar and into the night sky through the hole in the ceiling.

"You wanted to take me?" she said, her voice full of venom.

The owner's complexion was pale, but he could hardly speak from the shock of his burned extremity.

"Then let's see how you enjoy having someone else having their way with your body." She reduced her flames to the lowest possible intensity, and his skin bubbled as she roasted him alive, one limb at a time.

"I beg you! Please just kill me!" he yelled. She ignored his wailing and continued her grisly task. Soon he resembled a hog roasted on a spit.

"Kill me..." he croaked. Somehow, he hadn't lost consciousness. She ignored his plight and walked out of the room and grabbed the bag of coins on the way out. The corridor was filled with smoke. Her earlier attacks had lit the bar on fire, so time was not on her side.

She crossed the hallway into the owner's bedroom, where she found various pieces of jewelry, some banknotes[9], and a first-level spirit sword. She proceeded to the ground floor, which was completely deserted. Everyone had gone home for the night, and only the wifeless owner remained. She ran down the hall to where his office was and blasted the door inward.

---

9   Paper banknotes on Earth are surprisingly old. They originated from the Tang Dynasty in the 7th century and were fully implemented in the Song Dynasty in the 11th century. This is no surprise, considering that paper originated from China.

She then hastily gathered all the coins and banknotes she saw into a bag and tied it around her belt.

The creaking beams reminded her that the building could collapse at any moment. She ran out of the building, only to see several villagers gathered outside. They were the last people she wanted to face after killing a man. Some people moved to stop her and question her, but they stopped when they saw her torn robe and the tears streaming down her face.

So she ran out from the small town unimpeded, leaving thirty pieces of silver for a horse she stole before going on her way. She galloped out into the night, unsure of where to go.

Should I go back home? she thought. *No, I'm nothing but a bother. I refuse the think the whole world is like this. I'll find a nice town that treats me with respect, where I can settle down and live my life in peace.*

Chapter 8: Regret

Dense crowds parted as a luxurious carriage moved through Songjing City. Many people glanced at the carriage in amazement as it proceeded on the tightly fitted mosaic that led all the way to the palace. After all, even a single piece of the golden carriage would enable a commoner to retire in peace and luxury.

Songjing was the capital of the Song Kingdom, and thus the hustle and bustle of regular cities couldn't hold a candle to it. The streets were clean, and the bricks that made it were unbroken and multicolored. Yet this wasn't the city's most remarkable feature. After the carriage passed a few commercial buildings, lush greenery appeared on every side. Luxurious trees and flowers adorned the picturesque street, on which only a few select businesses could set up shop.

"The heat here is truly unbearable in the summer," said Wang Jun as he sipped tea with Elder Bai. They were both riding in the carriage that was driven by Protector Ren. Such a duty was above his station, of course, but one did not simply deny a core-formation expert's request.

"Young Master," Elder Bai replied, "I've heard that this is in part due to the peculiar formation that encompasses the whole city and allows the greenery to prosper year-round. Think of it as a trade-off for maintaining the city's trademark décor. Besides, I myself prefer excessive heat to intolerable cold. Any slight chill makes these old bones ache."

Wang Jun rolled his eyes. "The weather doesn't annoy me that much. I just hate having to ride around in such an opulent carriage. Isn't being low-key the best policy?"

"Normally you would be correct," Elder Bai said. "However, this carriage has been arranged specifically by the third prince, and we must ride in it to show our continued and official support. This is all because we agreed to play the part as supporters in the light while he garners support from the shadows."

Their conversation was cut short as they entered the palace's front gates. They were soon greeted by a pair of plainly dressed guards, who proceeded to escort them toward the third prince's residence. While their appearance was nondescript, Wang Jun knew that they were experts at half-step foundation establishment. Such soldiers were rare in a national military, so their standing was undoubtedly quite high.

As they proceeded through the palace, Wang Jun took note of the carefully crafted marble pillars that he had seen multiple times to date. They were made entirely with tropical-blue marble, a rare variety that contained both blue and green patches. He figured that they were worth more than their weight in gold, an obvious display of opulence by the Song family, who had ruled the kingdom for the past thousand years.

"Our guests have finally arrived," a high-pitched voice said.

"Please get back to the gate. I'll take them from here."

The guards grunted and headed back, leaving the three guests in the hands of an overly enthusiastic man. He was a chubby man, and clearly very jovial. However, Wang Jun knew that that this eunuch, the right-hand man of the third prince, was not as simple as he appeared to be.

"Both of your guardians may stay in this room here while we visit the prince," the eunuch said. "Our maids will ensure that their every need is taken care of."

"This Wang[10] humbly thanks the third prince for his hospitality," Wang Jun said. "Everyone, please abide by Eunuch Tie's arrangements."

This came as no surprise to his experienced assistants, who immediately darted to the generous refreshments provided. Wang Jun chuckled at the spectacle.

"This way, if you please," said Eunuch Tie, who in the absence of others, became as silent as a mouse. They soon arrived at an ornate door carved from cinnabar oak and gilded with gold. The eunuch led him in directly and seated him on a blue couch near a curious stone fireplace, in which a blue flame flickered.

"Second Young Master Wang, I'm so pleased to see you again," said a man in his early twenties as he strolled into the room.

Wang Jun stood up and gave a curt bow, only seating himself once the third prince gestured for him to go ahead. Eunuch Tie approached them and poured what appeared to

---

[10] A play on words. The character for king, wang (王) is the same character for Wang Jun's last name. In fact, this is also the same character for the most common name in China. Addressing oneself as "this [surname]" is pejorative to oneself, however, it can also be seen as arrogant in the context of "this king," especially when referring to a prince.

be an extremely expensive tea, something that Wang Jun confirmed once he took his first sip.

"Royal Reserve Pu'er tea from the 972nd year of the Song Kingdom's rule. How extravagant, Your Highness," Wang Jun said. "Nearly as extravagant as the Spring Chill Flame in the fireplace."

The third prince, who wore his jet-black hair tied behind his head with a golden clasp, chuckled self-deprecatingly. "There is no need to feign surprise. I'm sure Second Master Wang has seen much more lavish indulgences in his lifetime. Still, I can't deny that my budget can barely tolerate my liberal use of Spring Chill Flame, which emanates the scent and temperature of a cool spring day. However, I can't help but use it during these scorching summer days. As for the tea, I wouldn't dare serve any lesser tea to a connoisseur such as yourself."

Wang Jun chuckled. "Straining the budget. I suppose this is the case, for now. However, the first shipment of weapon exports is set to take place in two days. This kind of expenditure will be nothing more than a drop in a very large bucket."

The prince nodded but couldn't help but frown before looking at Wang Jun with a dour expression. "My father is weakening. I don't know how long he has left, but it can't be more than a few years. He's still fifty this year, however. I refuse to believe that this isn't some scheme by the crown prince and his treacherous oracle, Zhou Li. I know that you advocate caution, but we don't have much time. I fear that he has been poisoned."

Wang Jun nodded. "Relax. Everything is going according to plan. We have chosen the path of superior economy and weapons, while the crown prince has chosen the path of alchemy and the nobility. To our knowledge, he only has a slight military advantage.

"Rest assured that we have chosen the correct path. The nobles are too self-interested to be willing to pay any sort of price, while merchants understand that a proper price must be paid for a proper investment. All you must do is continue drumming up support from the shadows, while we create fanfare and take care of the money aspect of the situation. I guarantee you, no one on the continent is better at generating wealth than our Wang family."

"If you say so," the third prince grumbled. "Has the Zhou family continued to cause trouble?"

Wang Jun shook his head. "They have been very quiet and reserved since their successive defeats. They are currently biding their time, waiting for an opportunity. Which is why I have come today. I have some personal business that I must take care of over the next few days. Please do take care."

Saying this, he took out a carefully wrapped package from his bag of holding. He then carefully unwrapped it under the watchful eye of Eunuch Tie. Soon, a fierce chill spread through the room. A sword was finally revealed from inside the cloth package. The weapon was three feet long and made from a silver-blue metal, while the handle was wrapped in insulating leather. The hilt and the guard were gilded with a sky-blue material, while the blade just above the guard was etched with an exquisite black runic pattern.

"This sword was crafted from cold iron embedded with elemental dust," Wang Jun explained. "The pommel and hilt are adorned with blue gold, and the sword was engraved with a royal frost inscription. Finally, the grip was wrapped with demon-caribou leather to protect the user from the cold. This sword is a mid-grade magic weapon and happens to suit your cultivation method perfectly. Please accept this humble gift."

The third prince looked uncertainly at Eunuch Tie before finally reaching out and grasping the weapon.

"Good sword," he whispered. "Many thanks for this kind gift. Please make sure to take care on your trip and return safely."

"Of course, Your Highness," Wang Jun replied with a smile. "I always take care."

A short while later, a different but much less conspicuous carriage left Songjing and headed to the south. Elder Bai had remained in Songjing. He had been replaced by Hong Ling, who sat in the carriage while performing his work. Protector Ren still vigilantly guarded and guided the carriage as it plowed down the rough road. Fortunately, the road had dried off since their last foray.

"Don't worry, Manager Ling," Wang Jun said. "I'll properly apologize to Xin Er and your parents. It was my fault for naively leading her on."

Hong Ling sighed but did not reply.

It would be a long, grueling trip, but Wang Jun had no choice but to try and ease the knot in his heart. He couldn't sleep as well as he used to, and he had little appetite. The image of that pretty girl with her mauve hairclip haunted his thoughts several times a day. He figured he needed closure, and for that, he needed to give her some sort of explanation. Unfortunately, despite his intelligence and foresight, he was nothing but a child when it came to matters of the heart.

He sighed once more as the carriage continued and finally decided to sit down and cultivate. He didn't bother to set up any precautions, as Hong Ling knew better than to interrupt him, and Protector Ren would keep him safe. As he cultivated, mid-grade spirit stones were consumed one by one as they entered a formation plate, which converted them into a dense fog.

Inside his dantian stood nine short pillars that floated on the surface of his qi sea. The pillars were pitch black at first glance. Only if one looked closely would one see golden runes decorating their exterior. They danced around the black pillars that absorbed the incoming spiritual qi, lengthening little by little, establishing his perfect foundation.

Three wolves looked around nervously as they approached Lord Two Tails's cave dwelling. It appeared like a nondescript cave, but any beast who knew anything in these woods could tell you that entering the cave meant certain death. Two of the wolves dragged over a large spirit deer carcass to the entrance of the cave, where they dropped it and retreated with their heads bowed down. They shuddered as a large paw came out of the darkness and patted down on the corpse and dragged it inside.

After an incense time, the sounds of crunching and chewing stopped, and a whole deer skeleton was ejected out of the cave. It landed neatly on a pile of bleached bones, as though the skeleton was a prized possession on exhibition. The wolves knew, however, that it was a clear message. They would be next if they didn't pull their weight.

"Is that all?" a loud voice boomed from the cave. The third wolf, the leader, approached the cave with his head hung low. He gently placed a blood-red root down on the floor in front of the cave and retreated like the others.

They heard loud sniffing sounds from inside the cave. "A blood ginseng, twenty years old. Not bad, Lang[11] Yi. You have my permission to consume three stalks of crimson dire grass. Keep up the good work."

Despite the mild annoyance with Lord Two Tails forgetting his name, he was suddenly overcome with pure joy. Three stalks of crimson dire grass was more than enough for him to break through and become a dire wolf. As a dire wolf, the future of his pack would be ensured, and the offspring he sired would be much more powerful than a run-of-the-mill spirit wolf.

Tears flowed down the eyes of the wolf as he prostrated himself toward his lord. "Sire, many thanks for your generosity. This subordinate will remember your benevolence for his entire lifetime." Meanwhile, his companions looked at him enviously.

"This is only a matter of course for those who follow me faithfully," the voice said. "Continue your good work, and it won't be out of the question for you to break into the Purification Realm in this lifetime."

The wolf's heart palpitated. The Purification Realm was something a lowly spirit beast like him could only dream of. His bloodline was the lowest of the low, and the only way he could ever hope to break through was by riding the coattails of his betters.

"Yes, my lord. We will continue to work hard!" With these

---

[11] Lang here means wolf. He's literally being called wolf #1.

words, the three wolves left the entrance of the cave. They cleared the area, making way for a group of wild spirit tail chickens.

"Oh, great lord," a spirit tail chicken yelled. "In your mercy, you have declared that these lowly sinners are not beyond absolution and can redeem our entire race by making offerings to your greatness."

The spirit tail chicken motioned with his wing, and a much larger chicken with luxurious feathers walked forward from the crowd. Its face was covered in a transparent white veil.

"As our lord has decreed," he continued, "we have taken the most tender chick of our clutch and fattened her with the finest grains. She has feasted on marbling grass every day after singing hymns to our lord. She has not moved from her perch except to come to offer herself as a trivial sacrifice for the absolution of our infinite sins. She has come to present herself before the first laying, so that her purity may please our lord."

The chickens all bowed simultaneously, waiting in their prostrated position for an incense time before a grave voice announced, "Come hither, my child."

The young chicken, unsure of what to do, walked toward the cave at the urging of her elders.

"Come closer, my child," the voice repeated when the chicken arrived at the entrance of the cave. She carried her overweight body with grace as she walked into the darkness. A loud chomping noise caused the spirit tail chickens to cringe.

It was followed by sounds that resembled the smacking of lips and the licking of fingers.

"Your offering has pleased me," the voice intoned. "Although you are sinners, as my chosen people, you deserve respect."

A wooden token flew out from the cave and landed in front of the clutch of chickens.

"Take this token and claim for your tribe a square half mile of meadow anywhere of your choosing. This shall be your chosen land. On it, you shall build me a temple..." The voice droned on for the better part of an hour with specific instructions, and the spirit tail chicken elders fervently wrote down instructions pertaining to their worship and sacrifice.

Their business accomplished, they walked out proudly toward their chosen land, not making way for the wolves and the foxes, the ferrets and the stoats. From now on, their people could walk with their heads held up high. They would be the true people of their lord.

Where did all of these gullible spirit beasts come from? Huxian grumbled. *I mean, I shouldn't complain, but where did their dignity go? Those wolves were practically begging to serve me, and they do all this legwork just for the permission to eat a few stalks of crimson dire grass.*

The first wolf had practically cried at his generosity. How badly did they get treated for them to pander to such an extent? And finally, those spirit tail chickens. He just didn't know what to say. He'd clearly been playing a prank on them the other day, but they took him seriously and began worshiping him.

The little fox let out a soft burp. He could manipulate his size at will, and whenever no one was around, he shrunk down to the size of a baby fox. In this form, he remembered all the pets and the attention Cha Ming gave him.

I need to get stronger. The annual beast summit is in a few days, and the territory in this forest will be redistributed then.

He looked down at a small blood ginseng, whose wonderful odor filled his cave. With his business completed, he could take his time and savor it.

He nibbled away at it bit by bit, chewing its mushy red flesh and licking up any liquid that dropped to the stone floor of his cave. As he ate, a torrent of demonic energy filled him and remolded his body. It wasn't painful. Rather, it was a very comfortable experience. He felt his joints pop and his bones creak until finally, he felt a soft pop inside his head. As he focused inwardly, he saw that his tiny beast core had finally reached a bottleneck in its growth.

I've finally reached the early Purification Realm.

Beasts that had just formed their cores were quite vulnerable. Upgrading to the early stage had doubled his power. According to his memories, it was similar to the progress that cultivators made. Of course, his personal combat prowess could not be evaluated by this measure alone. As a Godbeast, he had a distinct advantage in combat prowess compared to others at the same level.

Those lesser demon beasts wouldn't stand a chance.

Chapter 9: Dominion

Huxian stretched and yawned before peering outside his cave. He let his eyes rest on his latest skeleton display, the bleached white bones forming a perfect contrast to the forest landscape. He found it hilarious that the beasts outside thought it was for intimidation purposes. After all, it was *clearly* there for people to see and enjoy, a work of art he prided himself on. He lamented that his fellow beasts just didn't have a proper sense of aesthetics.

It didn't take him long to feel bored again. Waiting was a chore, and he needed to get stronger before the summit. Fortunately, night was coming. The night was his home.

His shadow ran through the woods unimpeded. No one noticed when he crossed the newly established spirit tail chicken sanctuary—though to Huxian it was simply a chicken farm—darted through the grass, and finally crossed the border into a neighboring territory. This was but one of many trips, and he had taken special note of the various grasses, herbs, roots, and fruits that would benefit his own purification or his minions.

Regrettably, these natural treasures all had lengthy incubation periods. For example, there were several that wouldn't be ready for another ten years—he left those to the others. By the time they matured, he would no longer have a use for them.

As Huxian slinked through the shadows, he chanced upon a miserable family of stoats. They looked half starved and completely exhausted. The power shift in his territory had affected even neighboring ones. These stoats were the weakest in their group and simply couldn't afford to migrate to another, stronger territory. Not wanting to be cannon fodder, they had no choice but to accept a diminutive existence in this territory.

Everything is as it should be.

He continued sprinting through the shadows until he arrived at a clearing, which contained a single yellow flower. It would mature tonight after a full sixty-year cycle, in precisely a half hour. He didn't dare consume it before then, as its effectiveness would instead be detrimental to his growth. Of course, the plant wasn't technically in his territory, so he would have to rely on subterfuge to steal it, so he remained in the shadows and waited.

Time trickled by, and soon an unreasonably large boar and his entourage gathered near the flower. The smaller boars fanned out in a protective circle while the demon boar waited patiently in front of the flower. Regrettably, even normal demon beasts could sense when natural treasures were about to mature. They knew it instinctively, no hereditary memories required.

"It's been fifty years since I found this glade," the boar said, sighing as he looked at the plant. "Fifty long years of waiting, and I'll finally obtain the last boost I require to propel me into the middle stage of purification.

"Our great lord is the most intelligent, the most patient," a nearby boar declared. This was followed by a wave of compliments as they sought to outdo each other.

"Your enthusiasm and devotion are duly noted," he said gently. "You will not be forgotten. Now I will consume this flower that has just ripened and usher in a new era for boarkind in this forest!" As he spoke, he opened his mouth and lowered it to bite the flower, whose scent was now ten times as alluring.

Unfortunately, he only bit empty air. A swift streak of lightning had brushed past his face and swiped the yellow flower from under his nose!

What the hell is that thing? Huxian wondered. Just as he was about to steal the flower, an unreasonably fast spirit beast plucked it before he had a chance to react. *So, you think you can best me in terms of speed? I'll show you what professional stalking is all about.*

He rushed out to tail the small ball of lightning. Fortunately, his shadow form could avoid any obstacles and traveled much faster than even his original form could. The little ball of lightning flickered and changed directions occasionally to confuse anyone who might be following.

Finally, it arrived at a secluded hovel. Huxian didn't immediately charge in, rather, he followed the shadows and moved in soundlessly. Inside the hovel, he saw a small yellow flower, and beside it, he saw a little gray mouse.

Why does this mouse seem so familiar? he wondered. Its gray color was unremarkable, but it had a small mark on its forehead. Huxian's eyes narrowed when the mouse turned his head, and he finally saw the mark in detail. It resembled a jagged, circular lightning bolt that bit its own tail like an ouroboros.

A Calamity-Swallowing Mouse? This is definitely my lucky mountain. Calamity-Swallowing Mice weren't Godbeasts, but they weren't far off. They were special mutated beasts that fed on lightning storms and calamity lightning. As mutated beasts, they couldn't produce another one of their species. Instead, their descendants would all be lesser kings among mice.

Swift, agile, and an insane complementary ability. This Calamity-Swallowing Mouse would make the best spy, a wonderful addition to my team. He pondered for a few more moments before deciding to act. His figure blurred, and he appeared in front of the mouse, who was just about to consume the yellow flower.

For the first time since he'd arrived at the mountain, he released his aura as a Godbeast. The little mouse, who was only at the seventh level of spiritization, trembled in fear as it prostrated itself. It was a dual suppression of cultivation and bloodline.

"Henceforth, you shall serve me, Bagua Huxian," the fox declared. One of his two tails glowed, and a character appeared and branded itself on the tail. It was one of the eight trigrams

(☲) that represented lightning. "Greet your master, Lightning General."

A glazed look appeared on the little mouse's eyes. It only a few seconds for them to clear, and finally, the mouse looked at him excitedly and bowed down. "Master, it is this lowly general's pleasure to serve," it squeaked and danced around.

Huxian grunted and then looked at the yellow flower. It was a yellow lightning chrysanthemum, and while it would be beneficial to him, feeding it to the small fellow would garner him a demon-beast servant.

"Hide in my fur. We're returning to my cave," Huxian said. "Consume this flower once we return and break through to the Purification Realm."

The mouse shook with excitement and immediately complied. He dived into the same tail where the mark had appeared and slipped into the mark without a trace. Then, Huxian grabbed the yellow flower and scampered off toward his cave. It was a very productive night, and he was very pleased with himself.

One general down, seven to go.

A few days later, Huxian was lying down in his cave, watching the evolution of his newest minion. The Calamity-Swallowing Mouse, Lei Jiang, had devoured the yellow lightning chrysanthemum only two days prior. Due to the compatibility between the flower and the mouse, Lei Jiang had advanced by leaps and bounds.

Huxian watched the little speed demon, who was breaking

through to the Purification Realm. The process left the small mouse contorting in pain as purple lightning enveloped it periodically, remolding its physique to prepare it for the purification process. The little fox wasn't too concerned about success or failure, as a beast of this level would undoubtedly break through without a hitch.

Just then, he heard a rustle outside his cave. Sighing, he grew back to his larger size and peered outside to see two wolves prostrating themselves outside.

"Speak," Huxian growled.

"Mighty lord," one of the wolves stuttered. "The summit is about to begin. The appointed time was a half hour ago. Are you not attending?" He then cowered with his paws over his head.

"This lord's attendance is not any of your concern. Dismissed," Huxian said coldly. The wolves scampered off like their lives depended on it.

Drat, I forgot about the summit, Huxian thought self-deprecatingly. *Oh well, it's best for kings to show up a little late, but I don't want to overdo it in this situation. I'd better take off now.*

He let out a soft roar as he transformed once more, expanding his size to twelve feet in length. This was approximately the proportion of a two-tailed demon fox that didn't possess a special lineage. He then trotted out of his cave, proudly walking toward the peak of the mountain. The location was obvious, for where else would beasts hold a summit save for the peak of a mountain?

During his journey, he passed through many other demon-beast territories. However, none of the lords remained. Their helpless minions could only make way for the ferocious demon beast. As he passed through one territory in specific, he noticed an abundance of weasels.

This must be where the demon ferret migrated to after his expulsion. He thinks he can escape my wrath by traveling toward the peak of the mountain? In his dreams.

Soon, he was greeted by the sight of over a hundred beasts. Some were small, a tiny lightning cat being a prime example. Its tiny white frame resembled that of a normal infant housecat, but its demonic heritage was betrayed by its purple eyes. The largest animal he saw on the peak was a geomantic boa, whose large body was three feet thick and several hundred feet long. He took note of this cunning adversary, who was innately gifted with earth-manipulation abilities. These beasts loved nothing more than setting up traps and labyrinths in their territory.

Huxian was not the least bit uncomfortable as he made his way to the middle of the crowd, where the early-purification beasts were waiting attentively.

"You sure took your sweet time," a panther growled derisively as he approached. "You're lucky the full-moon demon bear always arrives an hour late, or he'd be chewing you up for breakfast. Not that you would make a very big breakfast." The panther was three times Huxian's size.

Huxian snorted. "Order of arrival is based on status. A lowly beast like you is already at the peak of its growth, while I am a king among spirit beasts. Therefore, I showed up later. You would do well to respect your betters, lest they fail to give you face in the future."

The panther's face contorted in anger, but he did not reply. Hierarchy among beasts was extremely strict, dependent on both absolute strength and bloodline. The larger feline had clearly lost out on both counts. Another beast in their grouping chuckled. It was a wolf, whose fur was a mix between blue and silver. His golden eyes shone like full moons on a dark night.

"You would do well to listen to your betters, you stupid cat," the wolf said. "If this younger friend here grows to the next step and becomes a king of the forest, I volunteer to be one of his first subordinates."

Huxian gave him a toothy grin. "In the future, it will be my honor to welcome a moonlight frost wolf as a vassal. You will not be treated poorly."

The bickering continued for some time, until a large pressure emanated from the peak of the mountain. None of the beasts, including Huxian, dared to utter a single sound. As they waited, a large shadow appeared in the mists as loud steps made nearby puddles of water ripple. The figure revealed itself gradually until its hundred-foot-long body was completely uncovered.

It was a large black bear, its fur covered in various silver runes that oozed an aura of strength and suppression. It roared with an intensity that made all the beasts cower in submission. Huxian, who wasn't scared, was forced to feign surrender. He kept the day's memory in his heart, vowing to force the bear to prostrate itself in apology for the humiliation.

"Today's beast summit has officially commenced," the bear growled. "The first item to address is the distribution of territory. Three new lords of the forest have appeared, each with varying levels of power. This means that three older lords have been displaced. Lord Earth Ferret has already offered himself as a vassal to Lord Sky Stoat, so only the three-eyed demon bullfrog and the yin-yang python are without a territory. According to the rules, each lord of the forest must have a territory.

"Do any of the kings of the forest volunteer to take either

one as vassals and reallocate their territory?"

The question sparked an outbreak of murmurs and discussions.

"I will take the yin-yang python under my command and reallocate accordingly," a voice slithered. The geomantic boa had volunteered, which came as no surprise to Huxian. Like species tended to flock together, gathering up strength to assimilate territory from other species. He watched on as the yin-yang python slithered over to his new faction. Huxian could tell there were many dissatisfied faces in the group, but as the weakest ones, they didn't dare protest.

"No one will take this three-eyed bullfrog?" the bear asked. Silence ensued. "Very well, then we will go according to the old rules. Old One-Eyed, do you have any objections?" He looked toward an ancient-looking badger. This badger's black fur had faded to gray, and a large scar ran down one side of its face. Huxian estimated that this beast was 500 years old.

"No problems, Your Grace," the badger said. "Your rules have protected this old one for so long. I will give the three-eyed frog a third of my territory. Anything higher than that, he will have to earn."

The bear nodded. "Now that this is settled, is there anyone who wishes to officially challenge another to increase their territory? If so, state who you are challenging and your request for territory."

Many beasts spoke up and issued challenges. A demon hedgehog challenged a small adder for a third of his territory. He was victorious but suffered serious injuries in the process. Fortunately for him, an official challenge had benefits. Each beast was allowed one challenge, and issuing a challenge granted them six months' immunity from other challengers to heal their wounds.

"Anyone else?" the bear asked.

"I will challenge the midnight panther," Huxian shouted. "I want two thirds of his territory."

This was the highest possible stake in these official challenges. Likewise, if he lost the challenge, two thirds of his territory would go to his opponent.

The bear looked at him and casually glanced at the midnight panther. "Do you wish to fight, or do you concede?"

There was a hidden message in this statement—that according to the bear's judgement, the panther was not the fox's match.

"I…" the panther stuttered. "I concede. As this is a peaceful surrender, please grant my pack two hours after this summit to relocate."

Huxian nodded nonchalantly and granted him his request.

"All right," the bear said, cutting the tension. "Territory has been allocated. Does anyone wish to challenge a king for dominion?"

The ten beasts near the front all shook their heads.

"Good," the bear continued. "Let's discuss the upcoming human tide. These vicious creatures come every year, killing our kin for our beast cores and stealing various lesser herbs in the forest. Sometimes they even manage to pilfer some natural treasures.

"As most of you know, there is a barrier surrounding this mountain. We are at their mercy, as we cannot relocate. Fortunately, the power of our forces is not insignificant. As per our treaty with the cultivators, they will not send out cultivators with cultivation bases greater than early foundation establishment, while we will not send any combatants above lord level to do battle.

"Similarly, lords may only fight foundation-establishment cultivators, while their foundation-establishment cultivators may not fight against our spirit beasts. Anything else is allowed. Be sure to plan accordingly, as the human tide will arrive in six months."

Many of the beasts grumbled in annoyance, while Huxian was perplexed. He had spent much time on the mountain but had not bothered to look at the outskirts. The news that he was trapped here came as a big surprise. He had also never heard of such a "human tide" before. Shouldn't the opposite situation be happening?

Typically, humans settled while spirit beasts procreated rapidly. At some point, there would be too many spirit beasts, so the lords of the forest would send a significant portion of them out to their deaths to fight against the humans who constantly aggravated them. A victory would lead to an increase in beast territory.

Still, he didn't mull over the details. As per their agreement, he accompanied the panther to his territory, who quickly relocated all the felines to the shrunken territory. Of course, Huxian only got the least-productive portion of the territory. After reviewing the territory, he gathered the existing beasts and issued orders benefiting canines and repressing other subservient and opposing species. The felines had mostly disappeared, so there was no need to single them out.

After completing the allocation of resources and laying out his laws, Huxian visited a nearby lord. Unfortunately, the panther's territory was separated from his by a neighboring territory. Therefore, he gritted his teeth and approached the territory lord, Old One-Eyed. The shrewd old fellow knew of the fox's dilemma, so he offered him a strip of land in exchange for one twice as big. Huxian haggled with all his might but only managed to whittle it down to fifty percent more.

Within an hour of the allocation, the badger's minions had migrated, and Huxian's territory was fully joined. He called out a team of his best markers, who subsequently traveled around the territory and urinated with great gusto. Huxian left them to their business and continued to babysit the Calamity-Swallowing Mouse.

The little critter would make substantial contributions to his future plans.

Chapter 10: Path to Life

Five months passed by in a flash.

Cha Ming concentrated as he swiftly covered a blank page with over a thousand brush strokes, filling it with condensed medical knowledge that he'd gleaned over the past six months. Once the page was completely filled, he set it aside to dry and quickly scanned the next portion he needed to copy.

This book was on contagion and the spread of disease. He couldn't help but nod his head in amazement as he reviewed the contents. The doctor had speculated that disease was not a mystical phenomenon but a physical one, and that many steps could be taken to prevent its spread. The same applied to infection. Various procedures for disinfection of tools had been identified, such as washing with distilled alcohol, burning, and immersing in boiling water. The latest one was only a new addition; the doctor had somehow taken the time to evaluate the effects of disinfecting metal via boiling by collecting infection statistics after minor surgeries.

Cha Ming's condition improved with each passing day.

Every week, he destroyed and rebuilt a qi pathway. Soon enough, qi flow had been fully restored to the organs that had been most severely damaged. He felt gratified that he hadn't given up hope.

His brush paused momentarily as Li Yin walked up behind him to inspect his work. Then, he dipped the brush in ink and continued to write. His writing hand was a blur as intricate strokes covered three quarters of the page. He breathed out with relief, then put away the brush and set the page out to dry.

"Not bad," the kind doctor said. "It only took you six months to take in, comprehend, and write out my life's work. I confess myself impressed."

Cha Ming chuckled. "My body was ravaged and my meridians ruined. Fortunately, my soul force remained intact. My comprehension and memorization abilities are far greater than the average person. In addition, my dexterity allows me to write three times faster than a normal person. You say you are impressed with my work, but I'm impressed that you were able to accumulate so much knowledge over the past three decades. The breadth and depth of this work is simply staggering."

"If only they hadn't burned my book," the doctor said mournfully. "It took me a long time to dredge up most of this content from memory. I even had to repeat several key experiments to confirm certain claims. Still, I am proud of what I've achieved over my lifetime." He walked over to the desk and picked up the last two pages, placing them on the stack that would soon be bound together as a single book.

"How is your condition coming along?" Li Yin asked.

"I'm much healthier than before," he replied. "I've restored qi flow to my most damaged organs, so my life is no longer at risk. In addition, I can now exert four tenths of my original strength. I believe things will improve, in time. However, it will still take around a half year to completely connect the remaining organs. Healing the qi pathways in my limbs will come next."

At Li Yin's insistence, Cha Ming followed him into the kitchen. Fortunately, the doctor prioritized Cha Ming's transcription and had taken over cooking for the past half year. They began eating their supper quietly. Li Yin nibbled away at a piece of fish while Cha Ming ate tofu and vegetables.

"So, it seems that you have nothing to keep yourself occupied with for the next half year," the doctor said, smiling. "I have another job for you, if you're interested."

Cha Ming smiled. "I'm eternally in your debt. How can I refuse?"

"This isn't something I can force on you," the man said with a chuckle. "If you don't want to, feel free to do your own thing. I'm looking for an assistant in my clinic. I want to spend time conducting personal health sessions with the town's residents, but I find myself short-handed. I can hardly find a better candidate, given that you've already internalized my life's work."

Cha Ming hesitated. "You know I'll leave after another year and a half or so," he said softly.

"That doesn't matter," Li Yin said, smiling. "You can practice medicine anywhere in the world, not just here. Everything you learn here will be useful to you after your recovery. All you need to do is remember to help those in need whenever you see them. Besides, none of those in the village are keen enough to learn from me yet. There are a few youngsters I have my eyes on, but it will still be five years before I can recruit them."

All I need to remember is to help those in need whenever I see them. Cha Ming had been thrown into the cultivation world so swiftly that he'd forgotten that cultivators could do more than just fight. They could help people.

"Thank you reminding me," he said quietly. "I accept. I'll be your assistant from now on. Though bear in mind that I'll need to commit three days every week to my recovery."

"Good, good," Li Yin said. "You start tomorrow."

"What's your name, little one?" Cha Ming asked a girl who couldn't be more than eight years old. She was much taller than boys her age and had broken her arm while falling down the stairs. As usual, horseplay was involved.

"My name is Luo Xin," she replied. "Are you a doctor?" Her eyes were laced with suspicion. This didn't surprise Cha Ming, as he was considerably younger than Dr. Li.

Cha Ming chuckled. "No, I'm not a doctor. I'm Dr. Li's assistant, which is why he's keeping an eye on me as I treat you. He's always busy, so he's asked me to help him for a while."

The little girl nodded.

"Fortunately, your bone isn't broken very badly," Cha Ming said as he ran his fingers around the blue spot on her arm. "There are no pieces of bone floating around, and your arm hasn't broken in many places. Your circulation is fine as well. All we need to do is put your arm in a splint for two months, and it will be good as new."

To make such an accurate judgement, he relied on his spiritual force. He used a technique that Dr. Li had taught him for scanning injuries, and while his technique was not as sophisticated as the old doctor's, his stronger spiritual force more than made up for it.

"Two months?" she said with wide eyes. "That's way too long. I don't want to." Fortunately, her mother was there with her. A sharp, rebuking stare from the woman quieted her down instantly.

"Don't worry. It won't hurt at all. It will just itch occasionally," he explained. He turned to the mother. "I'll have to trouble Miss Luo to wash her wrappings every few days.

"Of course," the middle-aged woman replied.

He then took a piece of wood from a corner of the room and whipped out a carving knife. He whittled away at it proficiently, shaping it in a way that would accommodate her little arm perfectly. He then carved an opposite piece and placed it around her arm with padding and bandages and wrapped it with cloth and hung it off her neck as a sling.

"You'll need to come back in two weeks for me to check how the bone is healing," he instructed. "Now, let's take a look at that cut on your forehead." He spent a short while applying a salve to various cuts on her body. Fortunately, the gash on her forehead didn't warrant stitches. After the treatment, he placed a glob of salve in a container and instructed her mother on its use.

"You'll need to apply this twice per day for the next three days," he said. "The cuts should heal well on their own. If the area around them gets very red or white, bring her back, as the wound may have gotten infected."

The mother and child soon left, leaving a basket full of freshly baked bread and another basket full of bandages. Her husband was a baker, while she herself weaved cloth. Cha Ming collected the cloth, and after inspecting it, put it in a pile which would be laundered with chemicals for disinfection.

"Good job, young lad," Li Yin said from behind his desk. He was currently writing a program for his upcoming educational sessions. "In a few more weeks, the villagers will begin to trust you, and I'll be able to leave you to treat them on your own while I'm out of the office."

Cha Ming nodded and began cleaning up the area. Shortly after he finished, the door burst open, and a young boy ran in, gasping for breath.

"Doctor!" the boy said. "You need to hurry. Mother is having her baby, and it's not going well!"

Li Yin frowned. "Isn't the midwife there? She's much more experienced than I am in these matters."

"She is," the boy replied. "But she told me to come get you as soon as possible."

The doctor nodded and got up quickly, grabbing a portable medical kit before heading toward the door.

"Come along, Cha Ming," he said. "Things aren't so simple if Madame Su can't handle it."

They followed the boy for a half mile before arriving at a newly built house. The boy's father was a carpenter, and he'd just built the house to accommodate their growing family.

Two little girls greeted them when they arrived, along with a man who was extremely worried and panicking.

"Where is Madame Liao?" Li Yin asked. His authoritative voice snapped the man back to reality. He quickly led them to a small room on the ground floor.

They heard weak panting as they walked in. An older woman frowned when she saw Cha Ming. "Should he be here?"

The doctor nodded. "He is my assistant, and I may require

him during the process. You know I won't always be around to take care of everything." The woman relented and allowed Cha Ming near the bed.

"What seems to be the problem?" he asked while touching the woman's belly.

"She's been in labor for eight hours, and she hasn't progressed much," she replied softly, clearly to avoid alarming the mother. "She's almost out of energy, and I don't know what to do anymore. When I feel where the baby is, I can only feel his shoulder. If that was all, I wouldn't have called you. However, this labor is unreasonably difficult. If it lasts any longer, neither she nor the baby will make it."

The doctor frowned when he directed his spiritual force toward the woman's stomach. He continued examining for just over sixty breaths before stopping. His complexion was pale, and his forehead was covered in beads of sweat.

"Cha Ming, get over here and take a look," he said to Cha Ming, who walked past the older woman. "I need to you to examine the position of the baby, his size, and the position of the umbilical cord. I can't make out these details exactly with my weak spiritual force, so I need your help."

Cha Ming didn't waste time and immediately projected his spiritual force into the woman's body. He felt a small resistance, a person's natural spiritual defenses, but pushed through regardless. Inside the woman's womb, he saw a small, curled-up baby. His shoulder was impinging at an awkward angle, making it difficult for the baby to come through. It seemed like forcing it through would break its neck in the process.

"The baby is at an awkward angle; his shoulder is coming out first," he reported to the doctor. "He won't be able to come out unless this is readjusted. Furthermore, his size is approximately twelve and a half jin, much larger than average. To make matters worse, his umbilical cord is bundled up in such a position that makes readjusting the baby's position extremely difficult. I can sense that her energy stores are only sufficient for fifteen more minutes of active labor."

The doctor shook his head. "Too tricky. I'm not sure what to do, Cha Ming. This is beyond my current knowledge."

Seeing the doctor's mournful expression, Cha Ming recalled a procedure from back on Earth.

"Can we talk in another room?" Cha Ming asked the doctor, who could only shake his head and follow.

Once they were outside the room, Cha Ming asked, "Have you ever removed a baby from a mother by cutting her open[12]?"

The doctor looked thoughtful for a moment. "I've heard of this procedure being utilized before. However, it is almost always performed as a last-ditch effort. I've gathered some oral case histories that show that in nine tenths of cases, the mother dies. Even then, the baby's life is not guaranteed. It's unfortunate that we don't have a healer, because with a healer, the odds would be reversed to a nine-tenths success rate. I have also never performed such a surgery personally."

"Don't you think that we've gained sufficient ground in sterilization and disinfection to make it possible?" Cha Ming pressed. "If we don't do something, the mother will die very soon. Furthermore, if we're performing the procedure on purpose, she won't be completely exhausted and will have a

---

[12] Caesarian sections are older than people might think. Although it is named after Julius Caesar, there is considerable evidence that this procedure was used in both Western and Eastern cultures as a last-ditch effort to save the baby. Of course, the mother's life was no longer a priority, as this procedure was usually used only when the mother had already died or was clearly dying.

better chance of surviving the procedure."

The doctor looked in the direction of the other room and sighed. "We can try. Have them prepare a constant supply of boiling water for disinfection, wash your hands, and prepare to assist me."

Soon enough, with the help of the midwife, they cleaned the woman's belly. She was delirious as they had fed her general anesthetic herbs and numbed the area where they planned to operate with a local anesthetic paste.

Cha Ming carefully poured boiling water over the freshly polished steel instruments. He then stood to the side and awaited Dr. Li's instructions.

"Scalpel," Dr. Li said. Cha Ming handed him the sharp instrument. Li Yin, using a combination of his knowledge of anatomy and his weak spiritual force, carefully cut a curved flap.

"Pincers," he commanded. Cha Ming immediately used these pincers to pull the flap back, exposing a bloodied placenta within her womb. A baby was struggling inside and trying to squirm his way out with no success.

Cha Ming watched as Li Yin carefully cut a thin incision on the placenta, then using his carefully shaved bare hands, pulled out a baby, who immediately started crying. The midwife rapidly wrapped the crying baby in a warm blanket, but Li Yin paid no attention to this. Instead, he quickly scooped up the remaining placenta and laid it out on an empty pan. Then, Cha Ming closed the flap at his instruction.

While one hand kept the flap closed, he used another to grab a second set of pliers, which he used to pinch one end of the cut closed. Li Yin moved quickly as he sewed the wound shut with a freshly sterilized needle and clean silk thread.

Finally, after fifteen minutes, their gruesome task was complete. They carefully washed the wound with cloths dipped in boiling water, and Cha Ming fetched an ointment that prevented bleeding and disinfected wounds. He then took out a clean dressing, which he used to cover her wound.

"What now?" Cha Ming asked.

"Now?" the doctor mused. "Now we pray." He then handed a bottle of pills to the midwife to feed to the mother at four-hour intervals to help with the pain.

Six weeks flew by.

Cha Ming walked into a bedroom, where he was greeted by the cries of an angry baby. He was hungry, which was understandable, given the mother's unfortunate condition.

For some reason, her milk had given out a few days prior. Aside from that, she was perfectly healthy. The wound on her stomach had healed over properly, and she was now the proud mother of four children.

Cha Ming had followed up on the procedure all that time, inspecting the wound and changing the dressings. Naturally, the whole town knew that performing the surgery was his idea. The old doctor held nothing but praise for him, and he rapidly gained the trust of the people in the village. They no longer looked at him as an outsider; rather, he was now an integral part of their small town.

As usual, the mother handed him the child as she went to warm some goat's milk for the baby. Warmth filled him as he played with the infant, who smiled whenever he saw him. Soon enough, the mother returned with a small cup that facilitated dropping milk into the baby's mouth. Cha Ming inspected her wound as she laid down and fed the baby.

"The wound has completely healed," Cha Ming said, smiling. "I won't need to come check up on it any longer, but you should take it easy for the next few weeks as you adapt to moving around. Bed rest is no longer required."

Madame Liao smiled as she continued feeding her baby. "You'll come visit Lin Ming every once in a while, won't you?"

"Of course," he replied with a grin on his face. "Besides, you should bring him in every two months or so for a checkup. We'll be seeing each other often."

Chapter 11: A Kinder Way

A fresh breeze swept through the air, blowing leaves across the rocky ground in the middle of a mountain valley. It was fall, and while not much vegetation grew on the desolate mountain trail, there was still enough grass to feed Gong Lan's and Gong Wuling's horses as they advanced.

Gong Lan's hair had grown several inches since they'd left. Their moderate pace was only interrupted for meals and rest. It was difficult to sleep, however. The wind raged frequently in this mountain valley, and the changing seasons did little to alleviate this.

Her brother seemed unfazed by the wind. He always led the way and often used his qi to dispel intense blasts that swept against them. The mountain pass was narrow, and any slight misstep would spell certain doom.

They continued for several hours that day, only stopping once night fell. Fortunately, they found a cave in the side of the mountain where they could take shelter. A group of adventurers had left a pile of wood there. This was a common act of goodwill. Those who arrived with extra firewood would leave some, and those who were short would thankfully burn what others had left. Life as an adventurer was difficult enough without people being at odds with one another.

Soon enough, a fire was crackling. Gong Wuling always carried a special spirit weapon: a small piece of wood that absorbed fire and released it when required. This piece of wood would never burn; rather, it could be used to modify the intensity of a fire. It could even extinguish it on command.

Gong Lan sat in silence as she munched on a strip of dried meat and drank some water they had collected from a stream a few days back. She looked at her brother, who meditated in silence while recuperating his energy. He didn't eat; advancing from Qi Condensation to Foundation Establishment was a qualitative change. Those who advanced would notice their need to eat plummet, as the energy of heaven and earth they absorbed left them satiated with little need for external sustenance.

After a few hours, Gong Wuling opened his eyes and glanced at Gong Lan, who had yet to fall asleep.

"We'll arrive at our destination tomorrow morning," he whispered. "I'm confident that you'll find the help you need there."

While Gong Lan was skeptical, she noticed that he began fiddling around with a locket hanging from his neck. The locket was golden and shaped like a buddha. She had never noticed it until now.

"Where did you get that locket?" Gong Lan asked.

Her brother chuckled. "I got it here, many years ago. It's what keeps my heart calm and allows me to make good decisions. Without it, I would likely have lost myself to bloodlust. Perhaps you will get one at the peak of the mountain. Or perhaps Teacher will have something else in mind."

Gong Lan was surprised. This was the first time her brother had ever mentioned a teacher to her. In addition, she had never expected that her brother relied on external means in the form of a locket. She had always assumed that he endured through sheer willpower.

"Not everyone is strong enough to handle things by themselves," he said quietly. "Most people can't, in fact. Humans are social creatures. They rely on friends, family, teachers, and even adversaries to maintain their mental state. There is no need to feel ashamed in seeking help. I did it before, and now you will do the same."

Gong Lan thought deeply as she observed the flickering flames of their dying fire. Every person in existence relied on someone else to get to where they are. Even the most primitive savage relied on his parents and his tribe for food before becoming independent. No matter how self-sufficient he was later on, the initial help he received was what determined his life, his fate.

In a sense, those who accomplished great things received more help than anyone else. They were the children of destiny, and the gifts they received were simply advance payment for everything they would accomplish in their lifetime.

How great it would be to be one of those helpers, to enable others to accomplish great things. Not everyone desired to be a hero. Some people, like Gong Lan, just want to help.

The last leg of their journey proved to be the most difficult. Not only was the trail steep and unforgiving, but a thin layer of snow had fallen the night before. It might have been the first snow of the season, yet it continued to fall as they followed the trail, like a final trial set for them before they reached their destination.

Gong Lan shivered as she rode her horse, following her brother's lead. They stopped every few hundred feet in order to let their horses recover to peak condition before continuing. This continued for a few hours of travel until they reached a flat plot of land, where two buildings stood. Gong Lan hopped off her horse at her brother's insistence, and they both approached the smaller shack.

Before they had a chance to knock on the door, it opened and revealed a young boy that couldn't be older than ten years old. He smiled before holding his hands together in prayer, bowing. "This lowly one greets you, benefactors. Are you here to worship at the temple?"

Temple? Gong Lan thought.

"Yes, we're here to see the master," Gong Wuling said after bowing in return. "Is it all right if we leave these horses under your care?"

The monk walked out with a smile on his face and ignored the reins being passed to him. "There is no need for these things," the boy said gently. "These horses will follow me because they enjoy my company and know that I only want to help them and feed them. Any restraining devices are unnecessary."

As though to confirm his words, the horses trotted along and followed him into a barn, where hay and grain was laid out for them. They drank deeply from a small well in the barn, and to Gong Lan's amazement, the water in the well never seemed to diminish.

"Many thanks," Wuling said and bowed in appreciation.

"No thanks necessary," the young monk said. He then sat down beside the horses and began chanting soothing mantras.

They left the monk and the horses behind them and began climbing the largest flight of stars Gong Lan had ever seen. The steps were twenty feet wide, and they seemed to continue without end.

Just how tall is this mountain? she thought.

"The mountain isn't as tall as you think," her brother said cheerfully. "These steps are called the Stairway to Heaven. For those with little hope and faith in their hearts, they appear to stretch out to infinity. For those who believe, they seem rather short. Regardless of what you see, the number of steps has already been determined. Why don't you count them and see for yourself?"

Gong Lan was startled, but fortunately, she had already begun counting them to relieve her boredom. *Thirty-three steps. How could these steps possibly work like he says? Is it all just an illusion?*

She gritted her teeth as she counted and climbed. If she was on her own, she would already have turned back. Was it a defense mechanism or merely a reflection of her heart? Was it to protect this temple from her, or was it simply for her own sake that she experienced this long climb?

586, 587, 588…

She counted as she climbed, and soon she forgot where she was. It was simply a counting game, and she moved her feet to help her count. Darkness surrounded her, and still she counted, a light in the distance growing closer and closer.

877, 888, 889...

Soon, the light became blinding. However, she couldn't help but continue counting. And as she counted, the light began to envelop her. It warmed her and comforted her.

1079, 1080, 1081[13].

As soon as she took the 1081st step, the light and the darkness disappeared. They were replaced by her brother, who was looking at her curiously. He was seated on a bench at the peak of the mountain.

Instead of the bleak plateau that she expected, she was greeted by a lush tropical monastery. The main temple was small and unadorned, built purely out of white stone. Several smaller buildings accompanied it, and many jungle trees grew everywhere around the plateau. Birds flew around as though unaffected by the impending winter. Gong Lan wondered if winter would even touch such a paradise.

What truly stood out, however, was a large tree that stood tall at the back of the plateau. Its gnarled branches spread out in every direction, granting shade to many creatures that gathered beneath it. Despite being far way, she noticed several monks in orange robes meditating beneath the tree. They were accompanied by lions, tigers, deer, and pigeons. All sorts of animals that could not coexist in nature lay down peacefully, as though soaking in the subtle energy that the tree emanated.

Beside the tree, there was a small lake. Just like on land, fish crowded near the edge of the lake to get closer to the tree. Many predatory creatures, like herons and crocodiles, stood by the edge of the water, but they didn't bother troubling the

---

[13] The number 81 is symbolically used in Chinese literature to indicate something impossible. For example, it was used in *Journey to the West* in the form of 81 trials that the Monkey King had to help the Buddhist priest face, an impossible task for most.

ample fish. What amazed Gong Lan more was when a deer got up from under the tree and wandered to the edge of the lake where the crocodiles were gathered. Instead of attacking it viciously, they simply lounged in the sun, allowing the deer to drink its fill before it left and resumed its peaceful session beneath the tree.

"The tree prohibits violence," her brother said softly. "This is an inviolable rule, one that transcends nature. All those who bask in the shadow of the bodhi tree will find their sorrows soothed and peace with themselves. Many who frequent the tree cannot bear to part with it and spend the rest of their lives here."

They continued their journey through the lush greenery. Wherever they traveled, young and old monks alike smiled and bowed to them. They all wore an orange kasaya, a simple garment consisting of a single long piece of saffron cloth. Everyone's head was shaved. To Gong Lan's surprise, she noticed a half dozen women walking by as they carried water. They too had shorn their heads, and several of them had nine burn marks adorning their hairless scalps.

Soon, they arrived at the main temple. Its white walls reflected off a still moat surrounding it. It was all ornamental, of course. The bridge leading to the temple was a permanent fixture. Several orange fish jumped across the bridge as they traveled; they knew that they were not in danger, for no one would dare to harm a living creature in this harmonious paradise.

A young acolyte greeted them at the entrance of the temple. "Teacher will meet you soon," he said knowingly.

Gong Lan was shocked at the man's foresight, but Gong Wuling was unperturbed. They followed the acolyte as he led them deeper into the temple. Soon, they arrived in a well-lit hall. There, a thin figure was seated on a cushion, chanting mantras toward a large golden statue. The golden buddha sat cross-legged with his right hand facing outward, his thumb and index finger pressed together in a circle and forming a teaching mudra[14].

The acolyte seated them on cushions behind the meditating man. Gong Lan felt her mind wandering as she sat down. Much of the tension that had accumulated in her body began to dissipate. Her eyelids began to droop, and before she knew it, she had fallen asleep.

She awakened to the sight of a kindly old man, who was facing them. Like all the other monks, his expression was benevolent and full of compassion.

"I know why you've come, Wuling," the monk said gently. "Is this your little sister?"

"Yes, she's my little sister," Wuling replied. "She's... been through some hard times. Although I promised not to spread the Blood World Scripture, she needed help. But things have gotten out of hand..."

"I see that your solution to everything hasn't changed," the monk said sternly. His smile had faded. "I told you before that the path of slaughter will only hurt the user and those around them. But you didn't listen, and you've even involved your

---

[14] Mudras are hand gestures depicted in Buddhist artwork. These include hand positions for meditation, teaching, generosity, protection, and greeting.

sister. Judging by the aura of sin surrounding her, I can see that she's slaughtered the equivalent of hundreds of men and thousands of beasts. Why on earth would you think this was a good idea?"

"Those were bad men!" Wuling exclaimed. "She's been slaying evildoers. Wasn't it you who told me that slaying those who deserved it was not sin, but merit?"

"That really depends on a few things," the monk replied. "It depends on the state of mind of the person accomplishing things. What is their intent? Is their intent to save, or is it their intent to punish? Are they doing it to protect others, or are they doing it for revenge? All these things factor in. The sin of killing an evil man could be greater than the merit of killing him, if done for the wrong reasons.

"You helped her increase her cultivation and combat prowess, but it did not make her stronger. The Blood World Scripture helped her confront her fears, but she has not resolved them."

"Look, she just needs a calming locket, the same kind you made for me way back then," Wuling implored.

Gong Lan had never seen her older brother ask for something so nicely in her whole life.

"What worked for you will not work for her, I'm afraid," the monk said gravely. "When you quit fighting in the arena, you did it because you were sick of bloodshed. I helped you find a way to be at peace with yourself. I understand that you've started a mercenary company. However, aren't you quite strict on the work you accept? You only protect people. You defend. This is an admirable cause.

"Your little sister, however, had a very pure soul to begin with. You took her grief, and with that, you've turned her into a vicious killer! A single step closer, and she'd become a true devil!" the monk sternly berated Wuling, who was now rather pale.

"A true devil? What do you mean by that?" Gong Lan shot back. Unknowingly, she had released a suffocating murderous intent.

Before she could react further, however, the monk had already appeared right in front of her. He smiled as he took a single finger and tapped her on the forehead. "Calm down," he said pleasantly.

Her murderous intent instantly dissipated. Now she only felt shame. Why had she reacted so violently to the man? Was there really something wrong with her?

"Let me explain, my child," the monk said softly. "Everyone is born with a pure soul, and over time, it gets corrupted by outside influences. Some souls are strong, while others are weak. Those who retain their purity as they age are very kind souls, like you once were. Here, I'll show you." The monk held out his hand, and a soft ball of light slowly materialized.

"Souls are corrupted by sin, which they build up a tolerance to over time. The sins can directly attack the unresisting soul, and a truly kind soul, who is hardly contaminated by anger, greed, envy, sloth, gluttony, pride, or lust, has no resistance to these things whatsoever. Such souls are the bane of these sins, and very effective in overcoming them.

"However, pure souls have a chance to devilize or fall into depravity if exposed to these things too suddenly. Someone who devilizes is not truly human anymore. They lose their empathy and get lost in their sins. For example, had you continued your current path, your anger at yourself and the world would have consumed you, transforming you into a killing machine with no remorse. If that happened, would you be in any position to help or protect anyone?"

The white ball of light was now tainted with red specks. They accumulated little by little, until finally, the ball of light mutated and became a heinous mass of black and red.

Gong Lan shook her head, crying. "No. I guess I couldn't." Now that she thought about it, she was a complete and utter joke.

"That's right, my child," the monk said. "You are very well suited to the path of slaughter, but that is because you're also inherently suited for the path of peace. Would you allow me to show you a kinder way? A way in which you can help your friends without losing yourself?" The monk smiled and held out his hand.

Gong Lan took it without any hesitation.

Chapter 12: Lost in Obscurity

Wang Jun chewed on bitter tea leaves as he waited for news in a tavern. He wasn't used to such rough accommodations, but it couldn't be helped. Stonefell was truly a godforsaken place, one where only seasoned adventurers stayed. According to his previous inquiries, it used to be a thriving village. No more.

Several decades ago, a rare species of spirit beasts had mobilized the entire cultivation world into action. They had banded together and hunted it to extinction, and in the process, the spirit woods and the other creatures it contained had been damaged beyond recovery. Such a story reminded Wang Jun of overfished oceans and lakes and overcultivated fields. Mankind was truly incorrigible in its ways.

"Another pot of tea?" a young man asked.

Wang Jun nodded, and the man returned shortly with a freshly brewed pot. The tavern was the only bar in town, the last one having burned down six months ago. His auguries had at last yielded him limited information on her possible position, so he'd sent out his men to investigate. Meanwhile, he continued his own futile attempts to find her.

For what seemed like the thousandth time, he picked up a fistful of black coins etched with silver runes. He then imbued them with his full soul force and his fate qi. They spun in the air as they collected information that was beyond the grasp of mere mortals, before finally collapsing on the table in a meaningless jumble.

Despite the lack of content, the message was clear: Wang Jun was not privy to the information he sought. Fate was funny that way. Every man had a story to his name, but seers and diviners were helpless when divining their own fate. To make matters worse, Wang Jun was an anomaly. Information on his fate was very difficult to obtain; he was like a shadow that evaded the scrutiny of the most skilled pair of eyes.

This didn't trouble him much. What bothered him was Hong Xin's fate. A year ago, she was simple and predictable. He could have divined her location with his eyes closed. However, none of these thousand auguries had found any hints of her these past six months. Either she had obtained some fortuitous encounter that shrouded her destiny or fate was playing a cruel joke on him, preventing him from seeing her story out of spite or malice.

Or has our short involvement completely merged our stories to the point that hers has become indecipherable like mine?

Such a possibility caused him even greater worry, and it was all the more reason to continue his search. Until he found her, the knot in his heart would to eat away at him little by little. His patience would become increasingly thin.

He recalled a moment that caused him to shudder, the heart-stopping moment when he'd visited her parents with

Hong Ling. Madame Xu had burst into tears, and Xin Er's father had given him the earful he deserved. Afterward, he'd sought any piece of information that might lead to her discovery. Yet for some unknown reason, information that should be easily accessible just didn't reach him. It was as though she were a ghost. Fortunately, he knew she was alive. His auguries let him know that much.

"Xin Er, where have you gone?" he wondered aloud. As soon as he uttered those words, he heard a crashing noise from behind the bar. Something nagged at his mind, and Wang Jun sized the young man up before asking, "Did you work at the original bar?"

The man nodded. "Yes, I was a bartender there. That is, until it burned down with the owner still in it."

Wang Jun directed his piercing gaze at the man, who gulped and continued. "I heard you mention the name Xin Er. Are you perhaps acquainted with Gong Xin?"

Wang Jun frowned. "I know a Hong Xin. Was this lady you speak of this tall, with long black hair?" He held up his hand. "While she wasn't so pretty as to cause the downfall of a nation, she was quite charming with a warm demeanor."

The man at the bar hesitated. "Some of what you describe matches up, but many women fall under that category. Can you show me anything more precise?"

Wang Jun nodded and withdrew a jade slip from his bag of holding. He poured some qi into it until a transparent image of Hong Xin floated out from it and began spinning in circles. She was wearing her mauve dress with green vines, as well as the mauve hairclip that she'd taken with her when she ran away from home.

"Right, that's her," the young man said, his face lighting

up with recognition. "She worked with us for a while. Unfortunately, the owner seemed to have ulterior motives for her. I kept telling her to quit and leave town, but she stubbornly refused. All she would do was drink away what she saved as though she'd never known a happy day in her life.

"After I left work that night, the bar caught on fire. One of my friends told me that Gong Xin had escaped the flaming building. However, her eyes were red, and her face was covered in tears. Her robe had been torn in many places. I really can't help but think that the owner had assaulted her and gotten what he deserved."

Wang Jun's teacup shattered in his hands as he heard the man's story. He looked at his palm and saw that his fingers were coated in blood, jagged pieces of porcelain protruding from them. Yet he felt more alive now than he had these past six months. He ignored the young bartender's panicked expression and began pulling out shards of glass bit by bit, as though reveling in the pain they caused him. Finally, once the last piece had been removed, he withdrew a pill from his bag of holding and ate it. The wound on his hand disappeared without a trace.

"Do you know which direction she left in?" Wang Jun asked in a hoarse voice.

The young man shivered before answering. "She left through the north of town. She stole a horse from a farmer on the way out, though she left him a hefty payment in silver." The young bartender was now sweating profusely.

This didn't surprise Wang Jun, whose aura was now completely unrestrained. He stood up and flicked a pouch over to the young man. The boy didn't know it yet, but he wouldn't have to work for the rest of his life.

As Wang Jun walked out of the bar, he saw Protector Ren and another Wang family guard approaching him.

"I've found out all we need to know. Let's move," Wang Jun said.

His protectors said nothing, and the trio flew out of the village on flying swords, leaving behind many villagers gasping in awe at the spectacle.

The villagers greeted Cha Ming as he walked through the merchant district. He entered a familiar store, the grocer's, where he picked up the provisions he required for their meals. When he arrived at the clerk to pay for the goods he'd gathered, he was waved through with a cheerful smile. He tried to protest and pay anyway—after all, many villagers had left them shards as payment—but then the owner stepped out personally and told him they wouldn't accept his money.

This was a testament to the impact he and Li Yin had on the people's lives. He had treated many diseases, fractures, and vicious cuts. He had also personally performed surgeries, including those used to deliver babies. He had named the surgery a Caesarian section, and although the name had puzzled Li Yin, he couldn't back out on his offer to allow Cha Ming to name it.

With Cha Ming's help, the old doctor had managed to perform many more experiments, as well as hold educational seminars and meetings for the residents. He had spoken on things like hygiene, nutrition, and first-response activities such as bandaging basic wounds and splinting fractures before patients were brought to him.

Cha Ming's only regret was that he couldn't stay for longer. His cultivation was slowly recuperating. As of today, all his organs' qi pathways had been completely reconnected. In fact, they functioned better than before he had been injured. Currently, he could circulate qi through these pathways to achieve one third of his original cultivation rate. In addition, his useable physical strength had skyrocketed, and he could now utilize nine tenths of his original strength.

Still, he planned to stay until he made a full recovery. The cultivation world was dangerous, and he saw no reason not to enjoy the pleasant atmosphere while he could. As he returned to the doctor's house, he noticed a crowd of people surrounding it. Frowning, he walked through the crowd, and after putting away the groceries, he proceeded to the doctor's office.

Li Yin was busy staring at a badly wounded man who lay on the examination table. Seeing the doctor pondering, Cha Ming went ahead and pressed his hand on the man to observe his condition.

Three arm fractures, head trauma, arrow wound to the shoulder... That last one made him raise his eyebrows. Fortunately, the man was not beyond saving.

"What are you thinking?" Cha Ming asked.

It seemed like a clear-cut case. The doctor shook his head and walked up to the injured man. He pulled back the man's shirt, revealing his forearm. There, Cha Ming saw a black mark. It was a tattoo that resembled a serpent woven around a sword. The sword was stained in blood.

"This mark is worn by all members of the Serpentine Sword bandit group," Li Yin explained. "They are a bunch of vicious killers who kidnap, rape, and pillage. I have nothing but utter contempt for them." The doctor then looked at Cha Ming. "I refuse to save this man."

Cha Ming was conflicted. "Why did you save me when I washed up on the river?" After all, it was difficult to judge a book by its cover.

"You want the truth?" the doctor asked. "Very well. I saved you because you didn't have any such markings, and you seemed young and impressionable. Furthermore, it didn't look like you had very long to live anyway. You wouldn't be a threat to this peaceful community. This man, however, is an entirely different case."

The truth hit Cha Ming like a sack of bricks. He had always been taught that doctors should be benevolent and help everyone. He had often heard tales of pure-hearted doctors who treated allies and enemies alike. Yet this old doctor he admired most refused to do the same.

"I believe everyone deserves a chance," Cha Ming said softly. "I will save him."

The doctor shrugged. "I think that's foolish, but I won't stop you. It's your right to choose to save a life. However, you must be willing to shoulder the consequences of your actions." Then the doctor stepped out of the clinic and began to disperse the crowd.

Cha Ming first cut out the barbed arrow that was protruding from the man's shoulder. Then he adjusted the man's bones and set them in place with splints. Afterward, he stitched up several larger gashes, cleaned him, and set him up in the room next to his.

With any luck, he would recover.

A few days passed by before Cha Ming woke up to a crash in the room next door. He yawned and put on his robes. The man's reaction was expected. After all, he'd restrained him, confiscated his weapons and bag of holding, and drugged him so he couldn't harness his qi.

Cha Ming knocked on the door before opening it. He was greeted by an attempted back kick to the mid-section. Snorting, he dove past the kick, grabbing the man by the neck in an instant. Then he squeezed slightly, showing the man that if he wished to, he could kill him in an instant.

"Where am I? Why did you lock me up? What happened to my cultivation?" the man asked ferociously.

"We found you washed up on shore, and I saved you and treated your wounds," Cha Ming replied. "If you don't want me to create new ones, I suggest you get back in your bed and cooperate."

The man hesitated but ultimately agreed to sit on his bed. After waiting for a minute, Cha Ming came back with a flask containing a putrid-smelling potion.

"Drink this," Cha Ming instructed. "You're extremely dehydrated. This will help alleviate the symptoms. Besides, even if your qi was unsealed, a measly sixth level of qi condensation wouldn't pose the slightest threat to me."

The man sighed and drank the potion in a single gulp. He grimaced, but his countenance instantly improved. "I don't suppose I need to drink something like this every day?" he asked.

Cha Ming chuckled. "Only if you misbehave. I've confiscated your weapons and your bag of holding. I'll give them back to you when you leave. In the meantime, recovering your qi isn't out of the question if you behave." He approached the man and directed his spiritual force to the man's arms. The bones had already begun mending.

"What realm of body refinement have you achieved?" Cha Ming asked.

The man shrugged. "I cultivated to the fifth level many decades ago, but I wasn't able to improve any more. It's a hard life out there, and a man needs all the advantages he can get."

"Fair enough," Cha Ming said. "It seems to me like you'll recover within three weeks' time. I'm afraid to say that due to your questionable background, you're under house arrest. I hope that won't pose a problem for you."

The man nodded. "That's very reasonable. I would do the same thing. Very well, I'll stay in this room and won't complain. Besides, if I cause any trouble, it seems like you're more than capable of chasing me down and handling me."

Cha Ming's heart softened slightly at the man's understanding attitude. "It won't be necessary for you to stay in this room. I'll call you out when breakfast is ready."

Weeks passed by uneventfully. Cha Ming continued to care for his lone patient while Li Yin treated the residents in their homes. This was all to maintain secrecy. The less the man knew, the less reason he would have to return to this village after he left.

Cha Ming had even delayed his recovery to ensure that the man, Lei Dong, didn't cause trouble. Fortunately, he had been quite cooperative. Cha Ming eventually allowed him to regain control over his qi so that he could at least cultivate to pass the time.

Finally, the time came to send the patient on his way. While Lei Dong seemed full of gratitude, Cha Ming still didn't dare expose the rest of the village to him. He had Li Yin alert the villagers, who were instructed that everyone should stay in their houses for two hours around lunchtime.

"Is it really necessary to keep me blindfolded?" Lei Dong asked Cha Ming. They were both treading on a barely used path, the only way out of the village. The smell of roses invaded their nostrils as they proceeded. "The degree of secrecy you've treated me with is unusual."

"We just like our privacy," Cha Ming responded. "Outsiders aren't welcome, and while I'm not so black hearted as to leave you to die, I don't want to put our isolation at risk. Outsiders mean trouble, and I don't want you finding your way back."

Lei Dong shrugged. "Quite frankly, I would only need to follow the scent of roses to find this place if I really wanted to. Still, I'm very thankful you've treated me, and letting you keep your secret is the least I can do." Cha Ming wasn't sure how to react to his sarcastic tone of voice, so he kept silent as they walked.

They continued walking for an hour before Cha Ming heard some branches breaking. Sighing, he cast out his spiritual force and located two small silhouettes.

"You can come out now," he yelled.

Two shy children, Yi Qiao and Ling Shen, emerged from the bushes beside them.

"Didn't your parents tell you not to come out?" Cha Ming asked.

"They told us, but we really wanted to see the outsider," Yi Qiao said. "It's been over a year since we last saw one. Ever since you came—"

"That's enough," Cha Ming said, cutting her off. "You've seen him, now hurry back to the village."

Both children looked aggrieved but scampered off nonetheless. Cha Ming's authority in the village was quite high now that he had taken over as the doctor's assistant.

He continued guarding the man as he led him farther and farther away from the village, winding in circular paths to confuse him. Eventually, he took the man to a boat and brought him down the river. After another few hours of travel, they arrived at a small village, where he released him and returned his possessions.

Cha Ming didn't stick around. Instead, he took the long way around and returned to his boat, which he led down the river through an alternate path. He kept a careful eye out for the brigand he had saved, ensuring that there was no chance he was being followed. He had done his best to preserve the village's secret.

If it were to be exposed, disaster could befall them.

Lei Dong was seated at the bar of a tavern. He ordered an ale; it had been far too long since he'd had a proper drink. A pleasant-looking tavern wench brought the drink over and insinuated that she had other services she offered. For a price.

He shooed her off. He normally wouldn't have refused, but his mind kept racing whenever he remembered one of the few scenes he had seen from the village. He had caught a glimpse of those two children while his caretaker, Cha Ming, shooed them away. In the short instance when he shifted his blindfold, he saw a little boy and a little girl.

The two were both unremarkable. They had a different accent than Cha Ming, so it was just like they said—he was a foreigner as well. That meant that there was something in the village that Cha Ming knew would tempt him, thus the isolation. He wouldn't have bothered to speculate what it was, and he had been prepared to never return to the village again.

Until he saw those two children.

The boy and the girl wore ragged clothes, clearly of crude construction. However, they had one thing in common. They each wore a bracelet, and the little girl wore a necklace. They were made of simple rope and clear crystals. But as a cultivator, how could he not recognize those crystals?

It's my lucky day today. If those children could afford to wear spirit stones like jewelry, there had to be plenty more where that came from. *Sorry, kid. You might have saved me, but I'd sell my own mother if enough profit was involved.*

The young healer had thought he was being very clever, leading him in circles like he did. However, there were still a few hints that the experienced bandit could follow. For one, the village was within two hours of a river. Most villages would be built very close to one, so he might have led him the long way for the sake of deception. The second clue was the steep drop in humidity after he left the village. It was as though the village was covered in a perpetual fog. Very few places would have such high humidity in the area. Therefore, he speculated the village was near a waterfall.

The only tricky detail was that the healer was a powerful body cultivator. Fortunately, Lei Dong could feel that as powerful as he was, he wasn't a foundation-establishment cultivator. Therefore, his strength wasn't insurmountable.

He mused at how his failed mission had instead changed into his greatest fortune. "The world of cultivation isn't for the kind-hearted," he muttered. "I'll plead for them to spare you when the time comes."

After finishing his drink, he set off immediately. It would still take a few weeks to track down his leader and gather the bandits for an outing.

Chapter 13: Human Tide

A fifteen-foot two-tailed fox leaped off a cliff, narrowly avoiding a flaming arrow. This arrow was naturally not shot by a beast, but rather a foundation-establishment cultivator. It was a very vexing experience to be chased by such lowlifes. Unfortunately, out of the eighty foundation-establishment cultivators who had come to the mountain, twenty were chasing him. How was such a coincidence possible in this world?

The mountain leader had instructed all the beasts to defend their hovels and abandon those who fell to these early foundation-establishment cultivators—the exact opposite of what they *should* be doing. Huxian felt a conspiracy was afoot, but unfortunately, he had no proof.

Three flying swords zoomed past his head, which he barely avoided. They shaved off three strands of his precious hair. As he dodged, he carefully avoided the various beasts that lived in his territory. Surprisingly, the qi-condensation cultivators had not assaulted these lesser beasts in his territory. It was as though they were avoiding the area on purpose, knowing that there would be much collateral damage from a major fight.

Fine, then. If you want to play, let's play rough. Huxian increased his speed by one tenth, forcing the cultivators behind him to use various exhausting techniques to keep up with him. At the same time, two saber-wielding cultivators flew out in front of him in an attempt to slow him down.

Pitiful fools.

His two tails glowed, summoning the image of a thirty-foot bagua, which imprinted itself on the leafy ground. The ones following him had no time to swerve away. As they passed over the bagua with their flying swords, all eight trigrams and the yin-yang rotated in a hazy swirl. The six cultivators slowed to a crawl as a result, and it seemed like time itself was affected.

Huxian howled and increased his speed by a third yet again, surprising the two saber-wielding cultivators. He didn't dodge them, however. Instead, he rushed at them, biting both their necks in quick succession. Their sabers bounced off his lustrous fur coat, leaving it completely undamaged.

Meanwhile, the six pursuing cultivators regained their initial momentum and resumed their chase. The trap had only delayed them by two seconds, but in such a high-level fight, two seconds was a vital difference.

"Water team. Go!" one of them hollered. Up ahead, he saw another five cultivators coming in from both sides. They formed numerous hand seals, which summoned five icy dragons. The dragons were linked together by a thin thread, and the circular formation condensed into a viscous liquid in the space around Huxian. He grunted and glowed white, his purifying aura forming a film around him and preventing him from being affected.

Instead of trying to flee, he dashed over to one of the ice-dragon controllers. With a determined look, the man took out a complex-looking talisman, which he slapped on his chest before drawing two flying swords from his bag of holding. They quickly slashed at Huxian, who was unable to react in time. The cultivator let out a roar of triumph, as it appeared his swords made contact. He died with a grin on his face as Huxian's mirror image disappeared. The crafty fox had used a decoy to slip behind him, after which he bit off half his body. The protective talisman served as little more than a condiment to the ravenous fox.

"Get together! Don't let him attack us individually," one of the cultivators yelled. The confused cultivators quickly assembled into groups of five. They had clearly rehearsed these actions, and judging by their uniform robes, Huxian figured they were part of a sect and not just lone cultivators.

Fortunately for Huxian, their assembly into groups lost them a few precious seconds, which he used to dart farther up the mountain toward his old friend, Lord Earth Ferret. His fifteen-foot form shrank as he ducked into the lord's burrow.

"What are you doing here?" the ferret yelled. "Get out of my hole, or I'll tear you to pieces!"

However, before he had a chance to act upon his threat, the burrow was torn apart by a large blast. Both Huxian and Lord Earth Ferret burst out of the burrow, their coats singed and full of dirt. Four cultivators floated above them on flying swords. Given their pale complexions, it was clear they had just exhausted themselves to destroy the burrow.

"Fight with me or die," Huxian growled at the ferret. His aura surged as he flew toward the four cultivators. They attempted to block him with great difficulty, but the little fox moved so fast he seemed to have an illusory double. They didn't know he was constantly splitting and recombining himself in order to confuse them and hide his cloning abilities.

"Activate the trap!" the leader of the four shouted. Four more figures appeared, forming rapid hand seals. Multiple earth spikes jutted out from the ground, piercing toward Huxian at a speed much faster than he should have been capable of dodging, but he rapidly shifted back and forth, avoiding forty-eight spikes in total.

As his figure ducked and weaved between the spikes, he saw light at the end of the tunnel. Unfortunately, that light was yellow lightning. An impressive-looking cultivator looked down at him, smirking. He held a totem in his hand, and given its treasure aura, Huxian estimated that it was a high-grade treasure.

I was baited! Lei Jiang, come out! Huxian ordered his general mentally. The small mouse burst out from the rune on Huxian's tail, opening his mouth and forming a vortex. He swallowed the lightning like a light snack. Like Huxian, the Calamity-Swallowing Mouse was now an early-purification demon beast, more than capable of becoming a lord on this small mountain. He sped toward the lightning cultivator as though it were the most delicious prey in existence.

Meanwhile, the ferret had not escaped. Although his rage toward Huxian had not diminished, he was utterly enraged that his entire brood had been annihilated by these damned cultivators. Like badgers, ferrets were not the calmest of creatures. His earth armor manifested, and he flew toward the water cultivators like a natural predator. They only managed to defend a few claws before being torn to shreds. After all, demons were much stronger than cultivators of the same level.

While the ferret engaged in his bloody rampage, Huxian darted past the Calamity-Devouring Mouse and landed in the middle of the four cultivators who had destroyed the ferret's burrow. Seeing that he only had half a second to dispatch them, he unleashed another black-and-white bagua beneath the four cultivators.

This time, however, it spun in reverse. From his perspective, everything outside slowed down to a crawl. In reality, time inside had increased by a factor of four, and he used these seconds to devour the cultivators one bite after another. Those outside could only stare in abject horror at the gruesome spectacle.

What kind of hellish two-tailed fox is this? the leader wondered. He only had around ten cultivators left with him, though another twenty were rapidly approaching.

Our forces should have been sufficient for a simple two-tailed fox. Either they had been lied to or this was new information their informant wasn't privy to. Either way, they could only win by pooling their powers into their sect's battle formation. The situation was quite depressing for Zhong Fa. After all, he was risking his poor life to complete this operation, and he would only receive a few paltry merit points as compensation.

This is all because of the sect leader's stupid agreement and his immediate need for a two-tailed fox's beast core.

Regrettably, any higher-level cultivators were strictly forbidden in this exercise. He could only wait for their forces to assemble before attacking once more.

"Follow me, Lord Earth Ferret!" Huxian shouted. He instilled his words with the bloodline pressure of a Godbeast. Hearing his words, the enraged ferret regained a modicum of sanity and obeyed his command without question. A small mouse wreathed in lightning joined them a few breaths later.

Master, what would you have me do? the Calamity-Swallowing Mouse asked.

Break off from our group and head to the peak of the mountain, Huxian replied. *Stay undetected. I want to know if the sovereign of the mountain is up to anything. If things are as I suspect, he's colluding with the cultivators.*

The mouse's expression contorted in rage at the news. *Colluding with the humans? That's despicable!*

Huxian nodded. *Yes, it's fine for the humans to vie for more territory, but that old bear is too despicable. He is far too worried about controlling the other beasts on the mountain, so much that he's forgotten about his heritage and the nobility of us beasts. I suspect he has been supressing any ambitious spirit beasts with potential. In fact, he will do the same to you, should he discover your identity. This is how the humans have been able to slaughter us year after year with impunity.*

Master is wise, the mouse replied. *If you don't require anything further, I'll be leaving now.*

The mouse vanished, and flickering lightning was the only hint that he had ever been present. Even though they were both early-purification demons, and Huxian was one tier higher, the mouse's maximum speed was still twice that of Huxian's. He was glad to have enslaved the little mouse early, because it would have been impossible to capture it if their cultivation levels were equal.

Now to bait the fish. Huxian and the ferret hurried off at a leisurely pace. The cultivators behind them didn't dare speed up, as both beasts were more than enough to eradicate them. Instead, they lingered behind while reinforcements gathered. Huxian chuckled before leading the ferret into another territory. This time, he didn't instigate by jumping into the wolf's cave like he had with Lord Earth Ferret.

"Lord Frost Wolf, get out here and help me!" Huxian's roar caused the nearby spirit wolves to cower in fear. The birds in the forest all flew away for fear of being drawn into combat by this terrifying lord.

Less than two seconds later, a silver blur caught up to them and ran to his side. "What's going on, little one?" the old wolf asked. "Surely a lord with your vast power wouldn't have any problems handling two or three humans?"

Huxian clicked his tongue. "Try twenty. We've already killed ten, but ten more are chasing. I'm sure reinforcements are coming as well."

The old wolf's eyes narrowed. "So many? What did you do to attract them?"

"Nothing," Huxian replied. "That's what's strange. They attacked my territory as though they knew I was there. There's definitely a traitor in our midst."

"How dare they," the wolf replied while baring his fangs. "I assume my lord wishes to rout them. How can I help?"

"First, we'll gather a few friends," Huxian said. "Then, we'll pick a battleground that's to our advantage."

They continued to flee, picking up a boar, a heron, and three snakes in the process. Meanwhile, the cultivators amassed another twenty Daoists.

We have enough now. Time to turn the tables.

The leader of the cultivators sighed in relief when the reinforcements arrived. They bowed as they reported in, making it evident that his status in the sect was secure. Seeing that they all submitted to his authority, he wasted no time before announcing his plan.

"We now have enough members to use the sect's battle formation. Myself and twenty-three others will join in the formation as the vanguard. The remaining six will stand by to replace any fallen cultivators should the worst happen.

"Before we head out, I want to remind you all that this fox is not only cunning, but his power far exceeds our imaginations. Regardless, while they have nine demon beasts, we have our sect formation. We also have three high-level magic treasures. Moreover, their kings and their sovereign are unable to join the battle. We should have no problem trampling them with impunity."

The team of thirty cultivators advanced through beast territory in a domineering fashion. They didn't bother keeping their auras in check. The various spirit beasts who saw them dodged, ducked, and weaved out of the way. Although these cultivators weren't allowed to attack them directly, it was a different story if the beasts stood in the way and courted death.

After chasing for an incense time, the leader noticed the beasts slowing down. "This terrain must be to their advantage," the lead cultivator announced. "Be careful, everyone. Let's link up to be safe."

The other twenty-three cultivators nodded, and each focused their qi on a silver flying sword. Each sword glowed blue before sending out glowing tethers to neighboring swords. They could now redirect and consolidate their power at will.

With their formation activated, they confidently flew into the canyon the spirit beasts had entered. The sandy pathways were thick and one hundred feet in diameter. Here and there, they saw large scales that seemed to have shed off a large snake.

Is this the geomantic boa's territory? This might get tricky. What a sly fox, finding a loophole in the agreement. A previously established maze that can tell friend from foe did not count as direct engagement by the geomantic boa.

Huxian heard a loud hissing sound as he led the group through the canyon.

What are you doing, young one? the geomantic boa asked. *How dare you bring this fight into my territory.*

Huxian snorted. *Relax, old snake. I won't make things difficult for you. In fact, I'd like to offer you a trade.*

What could you possibly have that would interest me? the snake whispered in doubt.

I have a greater-demon-tier purification technique that I can pass on to you if you cooperate, Huxian sent back mentally. A few moments of silence ensued. *You can pass this on to your direct descendants as well. Take this as a token of good will on my part.*

How can you possibly know such a technique? the snake replied, his voice laced in suspicion. *I demand to have it first. Aside from that, I will only activate the Thousand Illusions Trap and grant immunity to your group. Beyond that, you're on your own.*

Deal, Huxian replied. With but a thought, he transmitted the promised technique to the geomantic boa. This was also a clever ploy by Huxian. By divulging the technique, he was revealing his identity as a Godbeast. Only Godbeasts had inherited memories. By making this deal, his standing in geomantic boa's eyes would increase drastically.

Very well. The maze will activate now. This time, the snake's voice was directed to all the demon beasts in their group, who looked at Huxian in surprise.

The small fox ordered them to turn around, and they were greeted by an enraged group of cultivators attacking the air like madmen. They would be trapped in the illusion until they were attacked.

"Very impressive," Huxian said. "All right, everyone, activate beast mode. We'll attack them all at once before the illusion wears off. We only have three seconds."

The ferret growled as his earth aura intensified and his armor and claws grew. Lord Frost Wolf's fur shimmered as the projection of a full moon appeared behind him, shining down on him and imbuing him with great strength. He grew three times larger under the freezing moon's influence. Then the full moon appeared in the center of his forehead, like a third eye that was constantly open.

The boar also doubled in size. His tusks elongated, and he was filled with a massive amount of vitality that funneled into him from the forest. Brambles grew on his fur, threatening to eviscerate anyone who touched him. Meanwhile, his friend the heron harnessed the power of wind. The projection of a great roc appeared behind him. Evidently, this humble heron held a trace of the great roc's bloodline. The projection's power poured into its wings, strengthening them and elongating them until its wingspan was the width of the canyon.

The three snakes, not wanting to be outdone, coiled together to form a much larger snake. It was a projection of a geomantic boa, like their mother. However, instead of disappearing, it condensed into a physical apparition. The eldest of the three sibling snakes gained control over the large avatar.

Finally, Huxian split into two foxes, one black and one white. The time had come to show his true power. Both foxes were thirty feet long, twice as big as the original size he'd displayed. The other beasts gasped in amazement when they saw this transformation. Their bloodlines thrummed as they sensed the aura of a king among demons. They felt invigorated to be with him, honored to fight with him.

"Now!" Huxian roared. The spirit beasts attacked in tandem. The large snake attacked their feet, launching a corrosive pool of venom at the group of cultivators and breaking the illusion. The cultivators were all alarmed, but the training the sect offered was cold and brutal. They quickly adapted and used their power to fly up in the air to resist the venom. However, as soon as they flew up, they were quickly attacked from three sides by a boar, a wolf, and a ferret. Six of the cultivators in their formation coughed blood from the shock of their charge but still held strong.

They paled when they saw a rapidly approaching figure. The heron flew toward them with its long, sharp wings, threatening to decapitate every one of them.

"Everyone, burn your blood essence, or we'll all die!" cried the leader.

The twenty-four cultivators coughed up blood simultaneously. This wasn't from injury, rather, it was their heart-blood, which was infused with their vital qi. It would take them each a few years to recover from such a large sacrifice.

Their qi gathered together, and their twenty-four blades glowed, forming a giant frosty sword that struck out toward the heron, who wailed in agony. They reveled in their victory, only to realize that they'd celebrated too soon. In the middle of their formation, a large white fox had appeared. A white aura oozed out from it, and the surroundings lost their color. Their blue robes, their frosty swords, and their black hair quickly faded to white and gray. They panicked when they realized that their strength had been supressed, and they could only fight at fifty-percent efficiency.

Their horror only intensified when Huxian acted once more. The white light forced them to project long shadows. However, they saw that the shadow cast by the fox wasn't stationary, like theirs. It was alive. It leapt from one shadow to another, devouring one shadow after another. Each shadow it ate caused the corresponding cultivator to drop to the ground, dead.

The formation crumbled in an instant, and the weakened cultivators quickly fell to the various demon beasts who assaulted them. As they died, Huxian's purifying power turned their corpses into condensed vitality, which he fed into the grievously injured heron. Its wounds healed at a visible pace.

Finally, the white aura faded. Only the brave spirit beasts remained. They feasted together on the corpses of the cultivators, not wasting a single bite from this nutritious meal. After all, while cultivators hunted them for their beast cores, the flesh of cultivators was also full of heaven and earth qi. This was doubly so for body cultivators. This was why spirit beasts and humans hunted each other with great fervor.

The beasts stopped after eating the cultivators they killed, reserving the other half for their battle leader, Huxian. Both his clones recombined into his original thirty-foot-long appearance. He had no need to hide his appearance any longer. Under the beasts' reverent gazes, he consumed the remaining half of the cultivators' bodies in a single gulp.

Afterward, he gathered their treasures and swallowed them as well. Such things weren't useful to normal spirit beasts, but to him, they were of substantial assistance to refining and strengthening his body. His fur grew more rigid, and his skin toughened immediately after consuming them.

Soon he would be immune to even the attacks of a mid-stage foundation-establishment cultivator.

An old cultivator with white hair and a blue robe gritted his teeth when he saw the fight below concluding.

"You told me that he was a two-tailed fox!" he yelled. "That beast's abilities are clearly much greater than you reported. Now

I've lost a good tenth of my sect's foundation-establishment disciples."

The large bear grunted in response. "You can't blame me. Your sect members underestimated the enemy. If all fifty of the cultivators you sent had attacked him in tandem, this never would have happened. Of course, this would have exposed me. Still, with twice as many cultivators, you could have made up for quality with quantity."

The older cultivator looked at the bear coldly. "You need to compensate me for this. I want that fox dead and his core in my possession. During the next 'human tide,' you *will* deliver him to me on a silver platter. Otherwise, our relationship can't continue. I'll find another demon beast to replace you, and we will continue harvesting you like the farm animals you truly are."

With these words, the cultivator flicked his sleeve and vanished. The old bear sighed and closed his eyes. They both didn't notice the small mouse hiding in small hole twenty feet away.

The little rodent had heard every single word of their conversation.

Chapter 14:
A Debt Reneged

Cha Ming woke to the smell of smoke. The suffocating cloud permeated the entire room. Fortunately, his constitution was strong enough for him to handle this little bit of inconvenience. He quickly donned his robe and warily felt the door handle. It was cold.

Opening the door, he kept low and rushed over to the doctor's room, where he saw the old man asleep at his desk. This was a common occurrence—the man was committed to his work and sacrificed his sleep far too often. Looking around, he grabbed the doctor, who was unconscious due to the smoke, and threw him over his shoulder, then proceeded to the doctor's office. Using a burst of his strength, he broke open the locked shelf and willed all the books into his Clear Sky World. Then he opened the door to the clinic and exited.

As soon as he stepped out, a carpet of ten nets flew out, forming an inescapable enclosure. In his prime, it would not have been a problem. Without his qi, however, he had no movement techniques that could help him escape. In addition, he was burdened with the old doctor, who he would never abandon.

The nets struck Cha Ming, and his knees weakened. He crumpled under his own weight, taking Li Yin down with him.

"How do you like our body-restraining nets?" a voice asked. "We prepared these just for you, the only threat in this village."

Cha Ming's eyes narrowed when he heard the voice. It was the member of the Serpentine Sword bandits he had released the other day, Lei Dong.

"Why did you come back?" Cha Ming asked bitterly, already knowing the answer. "What could you possibly have seen to make you want to come back?"

"Normally, I wouldn't tell you," the man responded. "However, you *are* my savior. It was the two kids that gave it away. They wore those spirit stones casually, like they were as plentiful as cabbages. If it weren't for them and your overly protective attitude, I wouldn't have given it a second thought."

Cha Ming's glared at the man. This was the first time he'd encountered such a hateful person in this world. Someone who would betray their savior for material gain.

"You have no one to blame but yourself and your naivete," Lei Dong continued. "If you were smart, you would have cut my throat without another thought." He looked at his companions. "Wrap them up and send them to the cage."

Cha Ming looked around as he was transported by four men. Their house wasn't on fire, and neither was any other house in the village. There were only burned packages that had been set out around the house to lure him out. In the distance, he saw hundreds of people being herded toward the center of town like cattle. There, the bandits were assembling an intricate cage with practiced grace. They had evidently done this many times before.

Cha Ming didn't dare look at his fellow villagers as they were transported away from their homes. He felt immense guilt about what was transpiring. The doctor had been right— he shouldn't have saved the man. Soon, he found himself shackled in a separate cell from the others, who he could still see through wooden bars. Beside him was a group of five men whose wrists were bound with qi-restraining manacles. They were the only cultivators in the village, the ones who kept them safe from spirit beasts.

They looked at him with complicated expressions. It wasn't scorn or loathing. Rather, it was a mixture of disappointment and understanding. After all, he was a healer. It was difficult for him to resist healing a stray cultivator who washed up on their shore, just like he had.

"Everyone listen to what I have to say," one of the bandits said. He exuded a familiar but powerful presence, the aura of foundation establishment. Even in his peak shape, Cha Ming would not be his match. "I, Wei Chen, have captured this village in order to obtain these crystal stones." The man held out a fistful of shards for the thousands of villagers to see.

"You are all worthless as slaves, and we are only interested in harvesting these stones," he continued. "If you provide us information on where to obtain them, we will simply take them and leave. All your houses and storefronts have already been pillaged. However, these stones are far from enough. We are searching for the *source*. What is useless to you is extremely useful to us. Don't force us to act recklessly for something of so little value to you."

He motioned to one of the guards, who brought a little girl

out. It was the one who had unknowingly revealed the village's wealth, Yi Qiao. She no longer wore her bracelet and necklace. Her arms were covered with bruises. Seeing the villagers break out in hushed whispers, he brought a dagger out and nicked her throat slightly. A small stream of blood trickled down her tender skin.

"We will tell you everything," a calm voice said. "After all, these stones are worthless, and our children's lives are priceless. Mr. Zhou, Mr. Xing, Mr. Chen, please step out and help me hold a conversation with these gentlemen." These people were the elders in charge of the village, while the voice that called out was that of the mayor.

"Excellent!" Wei Chen exclaimed. "I knew you would be reasonable people. Men, please gather these four and bring them to my tent."

A tall, slender cultivator in a black robe sat on a large chair inside his makeshift tent. He held a bronze sword covered in intricate blue runes at his waist. Known in his group as "Archaic Sword," Wei Chen was a legend among bandits, and the amount of loot he'd pilfered over the years could allow him to retire several times over.

Still, he didn't stop. People speculated that he robbed and murdered for pleasure. Regardless of their conclusions, they all they knew it was foolish to oppose the Archaic Sword, the vice leader of the Serpentine Swords.

Soon, four older figures were ushered in. They were all

mere mortals with not hint of cultivation in their weak bodies. They sat down meekly, fully aware that their lives were in his merciless hands. Still, to rub the impression in, he let them wait for a quarter hour without saying anything. They sat in silence while Wei Chen stared at them, and they did not dare look up. After enough time had passed, he took out a large chest and set it on the ground. After opening it, he picked up a handful of shards and let them drop back down into the chest.

"So many mid-grade spirit stones," Wei Chen said softly. "It's truly a waste of nature's wonders to leave them rotting in this village. With these stones, a cultivator's power can increase tremendously. I would truly be a sinner if I left them in the hands of you mere mortals."

The elders said nothing in response.

"Tell me where I can find the source of these stones," Wei Chen continued. "And don't tell me they just washed up on shore. It's impossible for such a large quantity of spirit stones to appear out of nowhere. There must be a geological feature where they were extracted."

The mayor, who had been silent this whole time, finally spoke up. "We know where the source is. We can even tell you, as these stones are useless to us and merely used as currency and decoration. However, before we tell you, we want you to make an oath on the heavenly Dao. An oath that your bandits won't kill or harm our villagers, and that you will release us once you are done extracting the stones."

The bandit leader frowned. "You're hardly in a good position to negotiate. I'll have you know that I can simply torture you all to extract the answers. It would be better if you just told me, or this Buddha-like demeanor of mine will vanish and be replaced by a bloodthirsty devil that will destroy the villagers you hold dear."

"The people in the village are all we have," the old man said with a sigh. "Further, I've only brought these three men to confirm the truth of my words. Only the current and past mayors know where the source of the crystals is located, and the past mayor has already passed on. Generations ago, a mayor discovered the value of these stones and made these arrangements. It would be better if the crystals were lost than to make their location known to all."

Wei Chen chuckled. "Such foresight. Very well. I can't confirm the veracity of your words, so we'll continue our search for now. I'll let you know if you're truly in a position to bargain."

Every day that passed by was agonizing. Even though a small stream passed through the village, each prisoner was only allowed a cup of water per day to parch their thirst. Food was completely out of the question.

Cha Ming looked on at the destruction he'd sown. The bandits systematically destroyed their village, dismantling everything bit by bit in their search for the source. All this had started as soon as the leaders returned. They refused to discuss the contents of their meeting, but fortunately, the villagers trusted their elders unconditionally.

All Cha Ming could do during this time was continually destroy and replace old qi pathways. While it was difficult to concentrate with the body-restraining shackles, he was in a far better position than the qi cultivators who had their cultivation sealed. It seemed that the bandits had evaluated his condition and deemed it unnecessary to deal with a cultivator having crippled qi pathways.

Fair enough.

At some point, the old doctor had wandered over near his cell. The cell where he had been placed was a communal one that took up over 95% of the allocated space. He sat beside Cha Ming's cell until the young man opened his eyes. Cha Ming looked away when he saw Li Yin. The old man had been right.

"Let me tell you another story, young man," Li Yin said, sighing. He then looked to the side so Cha Ming could look up as he expounded his wisdom. "After the Spirit Doctor Association banned me from practicing medicine, I didn't listen to them. I gathered a group of young men like you who were eager to learn my craft, and I taught them without reservation. I did this for five years, and we continued treating patients throughout the city.

"Despite their previous judgement, the association didn't really want to bother with us. No one raised a stink, and we were able to continue practicing. One day, however, an up-and-coming spirit doctor came around looking for trouble. He was a noble, and he was keen on proving the superiority of his craft. He came swaggering into my establishment carrying two very badly beaten men. They were clearly on the verge of death, and I strongly suspected that this man had inflicted their wounds himself.

"Then he said, 'One of these men is wealthy and worthy of my care. He's a cultivator, and he's useful to society. The other, however, is a mortal. He is also a thief, so he deserves to die. I will save the wealthy man; save the poor thief if you can with your meager abilities.' After saying these words, he left. It was clearly a provocation, but I couldn't help myself. Even though the man was a thief, he didn't deserve to die.

"I spent the next three months nursing him back to health. I exhausted all my skills, and in the end, the thief's health was restored to seven tenths of his original capacity. He still had some crippling disabilities that I couldn't cure. Once he was healed, I released him. Little did I know that he was a plant by that young master, a pawn for him to squash my budding practice.

"I was arrested two days later on the charge of illegally practicing medicine. My apprentices were incarcerated as well. The thief who I saved, instead of being grateful, complained to the Spirit Doctor Association and said that my care had crippled him. Meanwhile, the young master that had brought him over that day said that while he had offered to treat the man, I had refused to let him treat him and had arrogantly insisted that my medicine was more than adequate.

"Of course, they believed his words over mine. My five apprentices were heavily fined, to the extent that they would need to submit themselves into indentured slavery just to live. Meanwhile, due to my previous offense, I was banished from every major city in the country.

"My actions ruined the lives of five promising young men and affected the many poor residents I normally treated. I was forced away from civilization. I traveled for many years until I finally encountered the current Crystal Falls mayor, who was out to do business. He noticed that I was a doctor but not a cultivator. After all, given the abundance of spirit stones in the village, he dared not invite spirit doctors for fear that greed might corrupt their hearts. He invited me to Crystal Falls, and I have been here ever since, tending to the village in peace.

"In case you didn't pick up on the moral of my story, I'll spell it out for you. I felt guilty for involving those around me, but I don't regret my actions. It's in a doctor's blood to save people, even the guilty. A doctor cannot betray his own consciousness. He can only do what he thinks is right and bear the consequences, just like I did. Just like I hope you will do now."

The doctor left shortly after, leaving Cha Ming in deep contemplation.

Another week passed, and the residents of the village were weakening, and the frequent outbursts of rage from Wei Chen's tent indicated that things weren't going as the bandits had hoped.

Finally, Wei Chen couldn't take it anymore and ordered the three elders and the mayor be brought to his tent. After six hours, a peal of thunder traveled across the clear sky, and indication that an oath to the heavenly Dao had been made. The mayor was dragged back to his cage, bloodied and with broken fingers but with a smile on his face. The three village elders didn't make it back, and Cha Ming soon saw their corpses being dragged out of Wei Chen's tent.

Over the next week, life improved for the villagers. The bandits began bringing them water and food, and they finally regained some strength. They were still weak, but they were no longer on the verge of death.

But the following week, things took a turn for the worse. One by one, the villagers were filed out and separated into three groups: women, children, and men. It didn't matter how old each man or woman was or what their occupations were, they were separated this way regardless. The village got busy as people were organized into construction groups and ordered to build joint accommodations to replace the ruins that were once their homes.

Then increasingly large numbers of young men were led away from the village toward the large waterfall nearby. These men were taken for a full ten days before they came back, filthy and utterly exhausted.

Cha Ming and the cultivators were not part of this group. They remained shackled as things progressed. The once peaceful village had been transformed into a work camp. With every day that passed, Cha Ming's heart ached at the sight of the villagers and their suffering. Fortunately, he saw no deaths. After the first three elders died, not a single villager was killed.

Still, Cha Ming was left with the realization that some fates were worse than death.

Cha Ming woke to the rare sound of his cage door being opened. He looked up to see three burly bandits, who picked him up unceremoniously and dragged him with them. He saw the pitying looks of many villagers as he passed by. Their eyes didn't linger. The bloody lash marks on their arms and backs made it clear that the fear of their captors was being etched into their very bones.

He sighed when he saw a cage full of children; only a handful of mothers were supervising and comforting them, while a handful of men were looking at them from the outside. Off to the side, he saw a group of women performing mundane tasks like preparing food and stitching and washing clothes.

As he walked, he saw a bandit groping one of the women. The others were too fearful to respond, but fortunately, a bandit captain walked up to the offending man and slapped him in the back of the head.

"Use your brain, you idiot," he said. "How do you expect the men to work properly if they see us violating their women? I don't know about you, but I don't want to spend any longer in this shit hole than I have to."

Cha Ming was relieved that things weren't as bad as they could be. At the very least, it seemed like these bandits weren't just another group of devilish cultivators. They were just bad men trying to make a living. Perhaps that was something he could exploit.

Before long, he was led to a small tent. Inside, he was shoved down next to the other five cultivators in the village. He saw Wei Chen, the leader of the bandits, and two of his personal guards. The vicious man looked over at them, smiling.

"Welcome, everyone," he said. "As many of you have speculated, we're looking forward to utilizing your skills to mine spirit stones like the other villagers. However, as cultivators, you are all uniquely useful to us. However, before we do that, we'll need to make you more docile than you currently are."

At these words, another man walked into the room. He was

pale and sickly looking, but his vast spiritual force made Cha Ming feel oppressed. There was a clear difference between a soul at half-step foundation establishment and actual foundation establishment, and this man was clearly in the latter realm.

He felt the man's soul force oozing over him, probing him. He resisted it with all his might, but he was unable to stop the man from inspecting every nook and cranny of his soul. The man grinned when he felt his resistance.

"Interesting. You have someone here with a strong soul, and it will take more than just a small effort on my part to tame him." He looked over to the other five. "Let's get these appetizers over with before we start the main course."

Chapter 15: Slave

A look of excitement flashed across Wei Chen's eyes when the heard the pale man's words. "As you wish, Sigil Master Guo."

Cha Ming had never heard of the sigil master occupation, but judging by Wei Chen's humble tone, they were not to be trifled with. He looked on with both frustration and curiosity as the man approached the five other prisoners. When pale man placed his hand on the first captive's head, Cha Ming felt the man's spiritual force inundating the man's entire being.

"Sixth-stage qi condensation, second-stage body transformation," the man intoned. "I can control him with a Servant Sigil, and he will be amenable to most instructions and perform them without question. I can also forcefully uplift his body cultivation to the fifth stage within three days. This will cost you fifteen mid-grade spirit stones. Do you accept?"

The commander's lips twitched at the cost but nodded nonetheless. Sigil Master Guo smiled and took out a black pen.

He then began painting an intricate rune in midair with black ink.

He's a talisman artist? Cha Ming thought, frowning. He continued to observe as the rune in front of the man became increasingly complicated and three dimensional. The main character was for "servant," but it contained profound mysteries that Cha Ming couldn't understand.

As it continued to expand in scope, the character was complemented by several sub-characters that were joined to it with geometric symbols. Once the complex character was complete, the man painted three other characters beside the existing ones, along with their own three-dimensional supports. These three symbols were the two characters for "master" and "great master."

Finally, after a full one-hour drawing process, the rune was completed. The black symbol gleamed before rapidly condensing and landing in the man's palm. He grabbed the rune and pressed it onto the cultivator's forehead. Cha Ming's eyes narrowed as the man screamed intensely. It was like a dying man's wail, a roar of defiance. Sigil Master Guo ignored these screams and pressed harder, and soon the screams subsided. The cultivator's face was no longer flushed red from exertion, but his eyes were now glazed over. The pale man ignored him and broke off one of the master characters and placed it on his forearm, where Cha Ming noticed hundreds of similar characters were already imprinted.

Then he pressed the other master sigil onto a silver medallion and handed it and the great-master sigil over to Wei Chen. The bandit leader quickly imprinted the great-master character on his forearm, where it joined three others. After this, Sigil Master Guo tossed a bottle of pills to the newly converted servant.

"Take one of these pills every day for the next three days," the pale man said. "No matter how great the pain, you are not allowed to die."

"Yes, master," the cultivator said in a dull voice. All traces of joy or anger had disappeared from the man's eyes, and the complete lack of emotion made it extremely obvious that he could no longer exercise his free will.

The entire proceeding left Cha Ming feeling like he had been plunged into icy water.

Is the same thing going to happen to me? Have I worked so hard to find meaning in my life and restore my vital functions only to be turned into a slave with no choice whatsoever?

Cha Ming had been excited about his new life because of the ample choices it brought him, but now it seemed like these choices would be taken away.

He stirred from his despondent state as the screams of the next cultivator pierced the air. Before long, he too was reduced to a shell of what he once was.

Should I bite my tongue and commit suicide? He quickly banished that thought. Where there was life, there was hope. Things could potentially improve. He need only look within to know that.

The process continued, and soon the five cultivators had each been given medicinal pills and ordered back to their cells. The guards no longer supervised them, telling Cha Ming that they were used to this form of control. The cultivators were easily identified by the black "servant" character on their foreheads. As long as this character remained, the guards knew they were being controlled.

After finishing with the five men, the sigil master walked up to Cha Ming, who was still restrained by the body-restraining shackles. He shuddered when the man ran his finger along his chin, then placed a hand on his forehead. He gritted his teeth and stared at the man in defiance, his eyes bloodshot.

"I have good news, and I have bad news," the man said, looking back toward Wei Chen.

"Start with the good news," the man replied drily.

"The good news is that this man is already very strong," the pale man replied merrily. "I, Guo Jia, do not see such an excellent specimen very often. His base physical strength is 784 jin, as he's a body cultivator of the seventh rank. In addition, his body-cultivation technique is strange. His body has been strengthened by wood, fire, and earth qi and is also imbued with additional regenerative, defensive, and dextrous capabilities.

"In these areas, he can be considered one grade higher. That means that his physical endurance is monstrous, and his working speed will be extremely fast. What's more, it seems that this has been achieved through pure addition of attributes, meaning that his body has not yet been refined. If I refine his body using metal-qi, water-qi, and wood-qi pills, I can bring him up to the ninth stage of body cultivation with the defensive capabilities of a bone-forging cultivator!"

Wei Chen frowned. "What's the catch?"

"Well, there are two issues, one minor and one major," Guo Jia continued. "The first issue is that his tissues are badly damaged from an injury. His cultivation is stalled, and his qi-directing meridians and qi pathways are badly damaged. Qi pathways aside, I will need to use medicinal pills to bring back his base strength and heal the injuries to his muscles and bones.

"The more difficult issue is that his soul is at half-step

foundation establishment. This means that I will need to use a more advanced sigil, a Lesser Slave Sigil. This sigil is sufficient for controlling someone up to Foundation Establishment. It is, however, quite expensive, and it comes with a minor degree of personal risk to me. All in all, the process will cost you 500 mid-grade spirit stones."

"*Five hundred?*" Wei Chen bellowed. "You may as well rob me! Forget it. I'll just kill the boy and be done with it. It's not worth it."

"Come now," Guo Jia said. "A foundation-establishment slave is normally worth 5,000 mid-grade stones. You'd be getting him at quite a bargain. Also, he isn't just good for mining. You can bring him with you afterwards and have a strong bodyguard who doesn't fear death. On account of our long-term friendship, I can knock the price down to 450 spirit stones."

Wei Chen hesitated. "Three hundred fifty, and not a single stone more."

"Let's split the difference at 400 and both leave happy," Guo Jia said, smiling. Wei Chen grunted and tossed him a jingling purse.

"Great! I can't wait to get started. I'm going to *enjoy* him thoroughly."

Wei Chen grimaced in disgust when he heard this, but he didn't leave, lest his merchandise be sullied.

All this time, Cha Ming had remained silent. He knew that his words would change nothing, and he didn't want to give them the satisfaction. He only glared at the both of them, burning their images into his memory. One day, he would have his vengeance.

He looked on as the man took out his pen once more,

tracing out a sigil that seemed ten times more complicated. It wasn't any larger, but the fine details it contained were much more extensive. The single character contained twenty to fifty sub-characters that he couldn't comprehend. He also noticed that, unlike the previous effortless exercise in penmanship, the man was panting and sweating profusely.

The process continued for eight hours, until finally the Lesser Slave Sigil and its master components were fully completed. Cha Ming braced himself for the inevitable fight against the sigil, but to his surprise, the man held it in his hand and sat cross-legged in front of him. He stabilized his condition for four hours before opening his eyes once more.

Wei Chen had not left the tent. He merely sat down and cultivated in peace, occasionally sending out his spiritual force to probe. Time flowed differently for those in the Foundation Establishment realm. They could go for weeks without eating or sleeping, using the energy of heaven and earth to sustain them.

Guo Jia, who had just awoken, stood up and looked down at Cha Ming, who was still firmly restrained. He should have been exhausted, but the strength of his body and soul enabled him to be fully lucid throughout the whole experience.

"You don't like to talk a lot, do you?" the pale man said. "Well, that won't change much by the time I'm through with you." He then took out the complicated Lesser Slave Sigil and pressed it onto Cha Ming's forehead. He immediately began screaming.

It felt like a burning hot iron had been pressed on his forehead, branding into his flesh, his bones, and his very soul. He tried to fight back, but the barrier surrounding his mind was quickly torn open by the sigil.

Suddenly, he found himself standing in a white space that expanded in all directions. Looking down at his hand, he saw that it was slightly transparent. He walked, and his footsteps echoed through the space as though he were wearing dance shoes on a wooden dance floor. The space reminded him of the Clear Sky World, where anything could be shaped according to his imagination.

"Nice mental space you have here," a voice said from behind him. He turned around to see the pale man with shoulder-length black hair. His black robes rustled as though a wind was blowing, despite its clear absence. He held his hands behind his back, and he walked slowly with an aloof expression.

"White is such a pure color, a blank slate," the man continued. "With such a powerful soul, no doubt you would have achieved very much in this life. Unfortunately, you met me. And I very much enjoy destroying such budding geniuses.

"Now, I don't have to do this, but I'm going to explain what's going to happen. I do this solely for my own enjoyment. I will use this piece of my soul to invade yours and force you to submit. The sigil is my weapon. To make things interesting, I'll let you make the first move."

Guo Jia then took out his hands from behind him. In his right hand, he held a writhing black sigil, the one he had drawn earlier. In the outside world, it had seemed tame and docile. Here, in his mental space, nothing could be further from the truth. To make matters worse, Cha Ming could sense that his own soul was very ethereal, while the other man's soul seemed almost palpable.

Cha Ming didn't need to be told twice. It was clearly a hopeless battle, but even if it gave the other man pleasure, he would fight to his last breath. He looked around at the white space and reached out with his spiritual force to see if it behaved in the same way as the Clear Sky World. He imagined four metal walls, and they instantly appeared and enclosed the pale man. Then he imagined a spiked stone, sending it down toward the man to crush him.

However, he didn't relax after this. Sensing an impending threat, he dodged out of the way just in time, and he saw several chains shatter the white "floor" of his mental space. The black chains dragged out Guo Jia, who was still holding the black sigil.

"Interesting," Guo Jia said, smiling and cracking his neck. "It seems you're already a little experienced in the world of mental spaces. Unfortunately, you're far too weak. You don't truly know what a mental battle entails."

The sigil in Guo Jia's hand glowed, and several chains sprouted out of it, forming itself into what resembled a chain devil. It creaked as it moved. Cha Ming, knowing that fire was the enemy of metal, summoned a sea of flames, bathing the intruder and the devil inside it. To his surprise, the chain devil was unaffected, and it walked out with two more companions. The surface of each chain devil was covered in frost.

What sort of metal is this that it can resist such hot flames?

He didn't think for long and willed his Clear Sky Staff to appear. It felt much more solid than his previous manifestations, and the familiar feeling it emanated proved that it was the Clear Sky Staff itself that had been summoned, and not just a representation.

I can win this, he thought. *It looks like Guo Jia has no ability to manipulate my mental space and can only draw power from the sigil he's holding. If I can outlast its power, I'll stand half a chance. Maybe I can even take him down with me.* He held no illusions of living past the battle.

He wielded the Clear Sky Staff as he would normally, drawing imaginary qi through his spiritual body. Fortunately, in his mental space, his cultivation was intact. In fact, it was much more powerful than usual. He remembered the feeling of half-step foundation establishment that Huxian had granted him before, and that was all he needed. Here, his memories mattered more than his actual power.

Not wanting to remain passive, he rushed toward the chain devils with his Swift Staff Art, striking them many times successively. They wailed as the staff struck them, as though they had met their mortal enemy. Guo Jia frowned when he saw this, and his disposition swiftly changed from that of a cat chasing a mouse to that of a tiger using all its power to catch a rabbit.

The sigil erupted with fierce power, and soon Cha Ming found himself surrounded in thick black chains. Seeing this, he willed a set of soul pearls into existence, which instantly surrounded him, glowing red.

Cataclysm Manifestation!

This was the highest manifestation possible, using 108 different pearls. Although they were brought together into a basic flame formation, several pearls flew around violently, incinerating everything they touched.

This time, the flames were hot enough to restrain the chains, and they began to melt. Guo Jia roared angrily as he poured even more power into the chains, manifesting hundreds more from above and below. His soul dimmed noticeably as he activated this function, and so did the sigil.

"You can't run from me!" he yelled. "Even if this is your

mental space, there's no way you can resist the overwhelming difference in power."

Cha Ming continued dodging chain after chain, but he soon began weakening. His soul was also thinning, just like Guo Jia's. Unfortunately, his power was also finite in this mental space, even though he had more tools at his disposal.

Still, he didn't give up. He smashed chain after chain thrown at him. They kept breaking apart and reforming in a split second, continuing their dogged pursuit. Soon he was no longer able to dodge them all, and black wounds appeared on his soul. He gritted his teeth and detonated another Cataclysm Manifestation, destroying one tenth of the chains in the process.

Unfortunately, this was the last of his energy. The chains finally caught up and wrapped themselves around his arms and legs until he was no longer able to move, just like in the outside world.

"I told you resistance was futile," Guo Jia said. "But you didn't listen. No one ever listens. Then again, that's what makes it fun." He then pressed the writhing black sigil onto Cha Ming's forehead, and several chains dug into his soul's "brain."

The world went black, and when he recovered, he was sitting in front of Guo Jia. This was the real world, and they were still in the tent. Guo Jia was even paler than he was before, and sweat covered his forehead. However, he wore a euphoric expression as he reveled in his latest conquest.

Cha Ming noticed that the chains that had held him back had been removed, so he instinctively attempted to lash out and smash Guo Jia's face in. Guo Jia did nothing to stop him, and he soon realized that he hadn't moved, despite his intent to do so. It was as though thick invisible chains restrained his motions as he tried to fight against them. The thought that this person was his "master" surfaced, and that attempting to harm the master was forbidden.

Confused, he walked several steps. Before he could get very far, Guo Jia's voice sounded out.

"Stop!" The chains appeared once more, this time preventing him from walking and moving in general. "Breathe," the man said.

Cha Ming was forced to breathe once more.

Chapter 16: The Mines

You'll have to be careful when controlling him," Guo Jia said to Wei Chen. "He is enslaved, but his soul is still quite powerful. He still has the power to interpret every order given within reason."

Wei Chen nodded understandingly when he heard this.

"Do you mind if I give him some basic instructions to prevent any mishaps?" Guo Jia asked the vice leader, who waved his hand to grant permission. Guo Jia turned to Cha Ming.

"Cha Ming, you are prohibited from harming any Serpentine Sword bandits. You are prohibited from harming the people of this village. You are prohibited from harming yourself. You are forbidden from cultivating. You must sustain your life…" The list continued until Guo Jia was satisfied with the set of instructions.

"Why the prohibition on cultivation?" Wei Chen asked. "He's a cripple, so it's not like he can do anything with the qi."

"Normally, this wouldn't be an issue," Guo Jia replied.

"However, you need to realize that cultivating the soul is different from cultivating the body or qi. This sigil is sufficient to control someone at foundation establishment. But the development of a soul varies between cultivators and is based on their innate soul force. For this man to have such a high soul force with his current cultivation base, he must have had many fortuitous encounters, in addition to full innate soul force.

"His soul is currently at half-step foundation establishment. Everyone who reaches foundation establishment finds themselves able to use soul force, but you might be wondering, if that's the case, then what is the benefit of full innate soul force, or any talent in soul force?

"The truth of the matter is that once a soul breaks through to the next realm, it will immediately grow by leaps and bounds. Depending on talent, fortuitous encounters, and practice in manipulating soul force, the soul will quickly grow to an appropriate level. My dear Wei Chen, you didn't practice soul force, so as soon as you broke through, your soul only broke through to the foundation-establishment equivalent. Therefore, you only had the barest incandescent soul.

"However, when I broke through with an innate soul force of eight, I had a mid-grade incandescent soul. This doesn't mean a lot to you, since you don't practice a profession. However, the ability of every professional is dependent on their soul force. Furthermore, one's future development will forever be determined by their soul force, or so my teacher says."

Guo Jia sighed. "Now back to the initial topic. If he breaks through, his soul will likely jump straight to the late incandescent phase and tear through the control of the Lesser Slave Sigil. Then he might be a substantial risk to your operations."

Wei Chen nodded. "That makes sense. Thank you very

much for your consideration and instruction, Sigil Master Guo Jia. We'll be sure to do business with you in the future."

"It's always a pleasure," Guo Jia said, smiling. "By the way Cha Ming—catch." Guo Jia tossed Cha Ming a bottle of pills. "You must first take the healing pill, then after you have recovered, take one of these pills once per day for the next three days. Grow stronger so that you can be useful to your master. Don't forget to be a good dog while I'm gone."

"Yes, Master," Cha Ming replied through gritted teeth.

Guo Jia then left with a smirk on his face. Wei Chen did not treat Cha Ming like the other cultivators and had him escorted back to his cell. He no longer bore any physical chains, but his mental chains were far harsher.

Once they reached the cell, the guard held one of the command medallions and issued his first order: He was not allowed to speak to others unless it was specifically required for performing his duties. After obtaining Cha Ming's nod, the guard pulled up a chair and lazily guarded his "prisoner."

Just as Cha Ming was about to take the healing pill, he heard a voice from behind him.

"Cha Ming, my boy. Are you all right?" It was the doctor's voice. Although he yearned to reply, he felt as though his mouth were sewn shut. He was forced to ignore the doctor and pull the stopper on the bottle of medicinal pills.

"Cha Ming, what's wrong?" Li Yin said a little louder, prompting the ire of Cha Ming's guard. He smirked before walking up to the large cage.

"He's not the one you know anymore," the guard said. "He's not your friend, either. Cha Ming, tell the man he's not your friend. Look him in the eyes when you say it."

Cha Ming struggled for the fraction of a moment before

slowly standing up as though he were a puppet dancing at someone else's whim. He turned around, exposing his cold face with dead eyes to the doctor. A large black character for "slave" burned on his forehead.

"I'm not your friend," his body said to the doctor. Inside, his heart was breaking. Using the last vestiges of his willpower, he wrested a slight amount of control from the sigil and shed a single tear. When the doctor saw it, he sighed in relief. Cha Ming could still see the sorrow that filled his eyes.

"Get back to recovering and strengthening yourself," the guard said harshly. "And you are no longer allowed to speak to this man unless authorized in the future."

"Yes, Master," Cha Ming's body said obediently. Then he sat down and consumed the first pill that would heal the injuries his body had sustained from the tribulation lightning. As the pill entered his lips, he felt a stream of warmth enter his body that rapidly healed his arms and legs while pushing out the debris that had accumulated. It took him a day to recover.

Immediately after his recovery, he took the first body-refining pill. A violent, metallic force flowed through his body and sliced away at the wood energy that had accumulated. Little by little, he felt the wood energy growing purer and purer, like a forest whose old wood was being removed to make way for new life. A half day later, the force of the pill was completely expended. However, Cha Ming felt the strength of his body increase as the purified wood essence recovered to its original volume.

Ka-cha!

His bones crackled as the strength of his body increased to the eighth level of body refinement. After completing his recovery, he looked at his skin and noticed it was full of impurities. He then looked at the guard, who wrinkled his nose but did not say anything.

Well, if he doesn't instruct me to wash, I won't.

It was the first bit of freedom he had exercised since his enslavement, and he found that even wallowing in his own filth would be a wonderful experience as a free man.

Seeing that the guard would not interfere, he ingested the next pill in the sequence. An icy cold sensation raced through his body as destructive water energy rampaged through his veins. The natural heat that was generated from the fire energy accumulated in his body rapidly decreased, to the point where he felt like a block of ice. Not all heat was lost, however. A much more concentrated fire still remained, and he felt his strength increase greatly as the fire qi in his body recovered. Soon enough, he was able to move once more.

Finally, he popped the last pill, which was full of destructive wood energy. It bored through his body, attacking the frail defenses set up by the original earth qi that strengthened his skin and bones. His skin and bones cracked, but in the process, their structures changed. They were no longer smooth like before. These localized fractures caused the earth qi in his bones to change on a fundamental level. It became more crystalline, and as a result it became far firmer than before.

As he recovered from this last treatment, he felt power welling up in him as his physical strength broke through to the next level, the ninth level of body cultivation. His work complete, he stood up and stretched his joints, which had stiffened over the past three days of cultivation.

"All done?" the new guard on duty asked.

"Yes, my body refinement is complete, and I am currently at the ninth level of body cultivation," Cha Ming replied mechanically. He was then escorted to Wei Chen's tent. Wei Chen was a powerful foundation-establishment cultivator and could see the changes in Cha Ming's body almost instantly.

"Good," Wei Chen said. "Guo Jia didn't lie to us. This man will be a solid addition to our workforce. He'll be able to do the work of five men, but he will be able to continue around the clock. And he won't take up as much space as five men, freeing up four additional slots in the mine. Take him up to the mine and put him to work right way."

The guard saluted, but just as they were leaving, he heard Wei Chen's rebuking voice. "And get him to take a bath, for heaven's sake. Just because you're a pig doesn't mean everyone else can tolerate that stench."

The journey to the mines was far less dreadful than Cha Ming imagined. On the way there, they encountered several worn-out and dirty villagers, but no one on the verge of death. It seemed that the bandits cared about their productivity, so everyone was moderately well fed. As they walked, Cha Ming saw parts of the forest he never knew existed. After all, when he was weak and recovering, he didn't dare to venture out into the woods. Later, he had been far too busy to bother.

Occasionally, a small spirit beast crossed their path. They were harmless ones, like spirit rabbits and spirit cats. All of them shared a common feature—they were far too small to be worth the effort of catching. Cha Ming speculated that the bandits had grossly overhunted the spirit deer and other larger animals during their stay.

Soon, they arrived at a wide river. The readjusted their path and traveled toward the large misty waterfall that gave the town its name. Droplets of water formed as the waterfall crashed down into the water below, resembling small crystals that shone in the sun and refracted daylight. The entire area near the base of the waterfall was covered in a thick, rainbow-colored mist.

Just outside the misty area, Cha Ming saw several silhouettes carrying pails of water up a hill, where the work camp was located.

Must be some of the village women, he thought. *The bandits get them to carry the water to preserve the men's energy, but more importantly, to show them that their wives are safe.*

They plowed on ahead until they arrived at a large shack at the top of the hill. It was surrounded by forty guards, making it obvious that everything valuable in the work camp was located in this building. The guards at the entrance of the shack hesitated when they saw Cha Ming. That is, until they saw the slave mark on his forehead. Then they started jeering.

"I see you have a fresh fish there," one guard said.

"He looks big and strong, just the way I like them," another commented.

The guard escorting Cha Ming snorted derisively. "Cha Ming is the personal property of Vice Leader Wei. You're not allowed to damage him." Then, looking at Cha Ming, he added, "If these men try to defile you or beat you, and it's unwarranted, you have my permission to break a bone in a non-lethal manner."

"Yes, Master," Cha Ming replied dully. However, he grinned inwardly. Perhaps he could use these words to his advantage.

Before long, they entered the secure shack and arrived at a desk. Behind the desk, Cha Ming noticed several pieces of equipment—buckets, large containers, pickaxes, and shovels. He whistled inwardly when he noticed that several of them were spirit weapons, specially crafted for extra durability to withstand the mining process.

Behind these was a door leading to a small room. Judging by the density of spiritual energy in the area, it was undoubtedly full of spirit stones.

That is the least-safe storage method I've ever seen, Cha Ming mused. *Why wouldn't they just use bags of holding?*

Still, he said nothing. He wanted nothing more than their plans to crumble due to their lack of foresight.

"Quartermaster!" the guard beside him shouted. A short, stocky fellow quickly ran from one of the back rooms and bowed to the guard. They were clearly not of equal standing. "I need four of your best pickaxes and a tool belt for this man. The most durable you can find."

"Of course," the quartermaster said, then he broke into a run to retrieve them.

"We found this runt in a small village," the guard smugly said. "Not a shred of cultivation in him, but we heard he was a good accountant. We *convinced* him to come along with us. See how he's moved up in the world?"

Cha Ming didn't bother to reply. At least for now, he had the freedom not to talk and entertain this annoying fellow.

The quartermaster came back quickly, holding four pickaxes that were much larger than most Cha Ming had seen on the wall. "I-I-I hope that this is what you're looking for," the short man said, quivering.

"Yes," the guard replied, admiring the large durable spirit

pickaxes. "For once, you're actually using your brain and following instructions. Good job." He then instructed Cha Ming to don the belt and tools.

After gearing up, they continued climbing until they reached the base of the cliff, where the waterfall originated. Cha Ming noted a newly built stone pathway that led to the back of the waterfall.

No wonder they couldn't find the source, he mused. *The mine was hidden behind the waterfall. How could the bandits possibly imagine that a mortal villager would have the courage to wander behind such a powerful force of nature?*

Cha Ming walked carefully, making sure not to slip on the wet stones and gravel that littered the path. He used various handholds that had been pierced into the side of the cliff, easing his way along the slippery path just behind the soldier. Several others were climbing behind him, impatient with his slow pace. However, he couldn't be bothered to accommodate them. After all, his orders were to ensure his own safety.

As they climbed, the line behind them became increasingly long, but Cha Ming didn't heed their insults or demands to speed up, and the bandit that led him didn't ask him to speed up either. At one point, he even stopped abruptly, causing the people behind him to lose their balance. One of them plunged down to the rocky waters below with a loud scream.

The guard looked back and glared at Cha Ming. He wasn't sure if he'd done it on purpose, but just to be safe, he issued a new order. "You may not stop if it endangers the lives of any bandits or villagers," the guard said sternly.

Cha Ming smiled, which looked awfully eerie given the gray shade of his eyes. "To clarify, Master, if I find myself in danger, I must stop to reduce the risk to my personal health. Those traveling behind me are impatient and putting themselves at risk. Should I slow down in consideration for their reckless behavior and endanger myself? If so, what degree of risk is acceptable for myself as opposed to others? Could you please supply me with an exact formula?"

The guard was stumped. It was a very ambiguous case, and Cha Ming was well aware that the guard knew he could not intentionally murder one of their members. However, such an ambiguous situation, combined with the death-seeking behavior from the other bandits, had given rise to a perfect storm.

"You must behave yourself with utmost loyalty to your great master, Wei Chen," the guard said sternly.

"Of course, Master," Cha Ming replied eloquently. "But as far as I know, I am a precious asset that has been purchased for 400 mid-grade spirit stones. Furthermore, I am a perfectly obedient ninth-level slave. I am inclined to believe that I am worth far more to Commander Wei Chen than these trashy fifth-level cultivators behind me. So forgive me if I cannot endanger my own precious life for their worthless ones."

This reply caused the guard's face to blacken like a kettle.

"Of course," Cha Ming continued, "if it was Master who was in danger, I would sacrifice my life in a heartbeat."

The guard's complexion recovered slightly after regaining this small amount of face. He then looked at the ones behind Cha Ming angrily.

"Stop seeking death, and stay far behind!" he bellowed.

The bandits indignantly backed away slowly, allowing Cha Ming and the guard to continue their ascent in peace. After a quarter hour of travel, they finally arrived at the entrance of a cave. It was one and a half times Cha Ming's height, and as they entered, Cha Ming saw a security checkpoint.

He and the guard proceeded directly through the checkpoint, as their loyalty was assured. The miners were not so lucky. He spotted several of them being strip-searched, with the bandits going so far as to search their rectal cavities for smuggled spirit stones. Cha Ming knew that the villagers wouldn't bother with such a futile act, but the bandits were suspicious by nature.

Cha Ming and the guard continued walking for another half hour, passing light after light in a large tunnel, which eventually widened into six different directions. The walls were bare and dirty and littered with exploratory holes that sought to discover errant parts of the mineral vein. Before long, they arrived at a group of villagers under careful scrutiny of six nearby guards.

"Cha Ming!" one of the villagers yelled, looking at him with a bright face. But Cha Ming was under strict orders, and he could not talk to the villagers unless it was necessary for his work. Under the direction of the supervising bandits, he took one pickaxe in each hand and began tearing away at the wall in front of him. He had been instructed to work at optimal speed, balancing recovery and digging speed to maximize his efficiency.

For once in his life, Cha Ming cursed himself for being good at math. Or being a good engineer, for that matter.

Chapter 17: Improvement

Sweat dripped down Gong Lan's brow as she swept the stairs to the temple for the hundredth time. She remembered every crack and every plant that grew beside the massive Stairway to Heaven. She even remembered each rodent that passed through and shot them a menacing glare every time they crawled onto the stairway with their dirty paws.

Her gaze held no killing intent. Rather, it threatened to punt them all the way back down, causing them to restart their climb from scratch. Not long after, the rodents chose to stay off the stairway. For now.

Satisfied, she swung her broom over her shoulder and ran a hand over her now-bald head. Regrettably, it was a rule in the monastery. All those residing here, whether male or female, monk or not, needed to shave their heads. Her teacher said hair encouraged vanity, and shaving it built character. However, so far her rehabilitation had her questioning whether this was a legitimate reason or if the old monk was just a neat freak, cloaking his personal, albeit overly neat agenda in a mantle of righteousness.

Regardless, the months of toiling, cleaning, and manual labor had reduced her anxiety significantly. She felt her worries surfacing from time to time, but instead of beating them back like she usually did, she let her mind wander. Her teacher had told her that much of her mental suffering was from unprocessed trauma[15]. She had kept it bottled up all this time.

Unlike much of what she had been told in the past, the answer to her problems was not to unleash her bottled-up anger. This didn't solve the problem. There were many triggers that interrupted her way of thinking and prevented her from behaving rationally. This had served to protect her mentally in her most vulnerable moments.

The only way to deal with these triggers was to process the very thoughts that caused them in the first place. When she had asked how to process them, her teacher had handed her a broom and instructed her to sweep every tile in the monastery and every step on the large flight of stairs. This was to be her task every day. He also said that whenever the thoughts that bothered her surfaced, she shouldn't fight against them. Instead, she should let her mind wander as she continued sweeping, carefully moving her broom left and right, moving her eyes left and right as she swept.

She had been very skeptical at first; the more she swept, the

---

[15] Much of this is drawn from the author's personal experience undergoing EMDR psychological treatment. It is a rapidly paced PTSD treatment and used extensively in the armed forces and with emergency response personnel worldwide. It has also proven to be effective in treating depression and anxiety, something the author can personally attest to. Please note that this should not taken as any sort of medical recommendation. Readers should consult with their medical doctor for actual advice on psychological treatment.

more thoughts resurfaced, and only scenes of bloody carnage came up. But as she swept and focused on her broom, the scenes bothered her less and less. They were still horrifying, but they didn't make her tense up like they used to. Her blood no longer boiled when she thought of battle.

The afternoon sun beat down on her as she traveled back to the Bridge of Redemption, a large stone pathway that traveled from the monastery to the bodhi tree. Crossing this bridge was the only way to travel to the other side without swimming or flying. Legend had it that the founding monk of the temple had achieved Buddhahood beneath its branches.

She observed these branches as she swept, and her mind wandered once more. She thought of a scene of bloody carnage, which caused her to instinctively focus on the broom and her sweeping motions. A few moments later, she thought of her brother smiling at her. Then she thought of a scene in her childhood where her father had told her he was disappointed. She thought of the smiling face of a woman who she did not remember. She thought of Cha Ming and his little fox. There was no rhyme or reason to her train of thought that she was aware of. She followed the monk's advice and let her mind do what it had to.

After a half hour of sweeping and dreaming, she suddenly felt a strong urge to cry. She dropped her broom and knelt in her orange kasaya, shivering, allowing tears to flow down onto the Bridge of Redemption. She wasn't sure why the bridge was called that, but she often felt these sorts of emotions whenever she swept it. And no matter how hard she tried, she couldn't sweep to the end of it.

After crying for an incense time, she felt much more clearheaded than before. Her taut muscles crackled as she stretched out her limbs in satisfaction. Regardless of whether or not the monk's method was correct, one thing was certain: She had never felt so relaxed in her life.

A cart struggled along a worn-out clay road, bringing root vegetables to town for sale at the market. A man was driving it, his long gray hair tied behind his head in a messy topknot. His shirt was cut from coarse cloth, and it had obviously not been washed in many weeks. There was a simply dressed but beautiful lady beside him. Her black hair ran all the way down to her shoulder blades, and it was fastened in place with a beautiful mauve hairclip. The piece of purple jewelry had seen better days. Despite this, she wore it proudly. It was her only hairclip, and she treasured it.

Hong Xin was feeling considerably better than she had months ago after her time at the inn. Fearing she'd get caught by the authorities for murder, she ran until she couldn't anymore and found refuge with an old farmer and his lovely wife. Seeing her pitiable and frightened appearance, they had taken her in. It wasn't purely for charity, however.

She soon became aware that the couple was aging and having trouble making ends meet. It wasn't due to the quality of their land, but rather that their poor, aging bodies were falling apart. Before they could even ask her, she immediately volunteered to help with the fields. She tilled, planted, and hoed the cracked ground. She weeded an extensive garden as an eruption of foreign plants threatened to choke out their crops. Finally, she harvested said crop, the same one they were now bringing to the market. The experience was life changing.

Being raised in a city, her life thus far had been completely devoid of hard labor. Now she had the calluses to prove she was more than just a pretty face. Her beautiful skin, which she had carefully kept out of the sun for so many years, was now weather-worn and tanned. And unlike many months ago, she now wore a gentle smile on her face.

Nevertheless, it was time for her to leave. She had stayed long enough, and she aimed to improve her lot in life. She missed the city life and its conveniences, as well as its magical appliances and accessories. The couple she had dwelt with offered to recommend her to a local inn, an offer which she gratefully accepted. Birds of a feather flocked together, and she was sure that anyone the old man recommended would be a nice person.

I hope they manage to find someone to help them out with the fields, she thought. Old Gui could barely kneel, and his wife didn't have the endurance she used to. They needed a strong pair of arms to help them. *When I find a job, I'll be sure to write to them often, and if they don't find anyone, I'll see who I can convince in town.*

Soon, they arrived at the gates of Castle Town, a medium-sized village completely enclosed within stone walls. It was a refuge for the local residents, who would otherwise live in fear due to their proximity to the spirit woods. After arriving at the gates, the old farmer paid their communal toll of three coppers, and they entered the village with no issues.

Hong Xin accompanied the old farmer all day, using her natural charm to coax buyers from the busy streets. For the first time in a long time, the man sold his entire load at a reasonable price. Normally he would have sold at least half his crop to a bulk buyer, who would take on the trouble of redistributing it over a longer period. The profits greatly reassured the old man, who wasn't healthy by any means.

After having sold the lot, Old Gui led Hong Xin to the inn he had mentioned. It only took a half hour before her employment was finalized, and she soon had a full belly, a warm bed, and a new set of clothes to wear for her first day at work the next day. Unlike last time, this new boss was an older gentleman, and his smile radiated kindness. She could not sense any wicked or covetous intent in his expression.

Life is taking a turn for the better, she thought. Then, for the first night in a long time, she cultivated.

"Go!" Feng Ming said to his squadmates, who immediately pounced toward a nearby group of dark-robed cultivators. They screamed as the soldiers' spears found their marks and ended their pitiful lives. Feng Ming looked up when he heard a chiming bell, an alarm of sorts to warn the remaining cult members of an attack.

He snorted and pulled out a bow from his bag of holding. An arrow quickly left his bow and was followed by an agonizing scream. He didn't aim as he shot, simply letting loose one arrow after another, and they somehow found their marks. The ringing stopped.

His team assembled and began charging toward a group of fifty cultivators. Twenty of them had bows, and the remaining members held swords in hand, ready to fight. Behind them, a significantly larger cultivator stared at them with red eyes. He emanated a baleful aura, and Feng Ming could practically taste the sin oozing out of him.

"Loose!" the large man, who was clearly the leader, yelled. A flurry of arrows rained down on Feng Ming's squad, but they remained expressionless and didn't even bother raising their shields. To the surprise of their opponents, the arrows either bounced harmlessly off their armor or fell to the ground, barely missing the soldiers as they advanced.

"Charge!" Feng Ming yelled. He released his foundation-establishment aura, causing the opposing troops to cower. Half of them recovered after a small amount of effort, their bodies transforming. Some grew larger, and others sprouted weapons on their limbs, but all of them shared a similar feature—they were all inhuman and pure evil.

"I thought so," Feng Ming said. "Tonight, drinks are on me, boys!"

The troops cheered.

"Captain is definitely the luckiest son of a goat I've ever met," one soldier said. "Every mission he picks ends up successful with no casualties, and the high-priority targets are always there when we need them to be. He's like our guardian angel, always looking out for us."

"Shut your trap and deal with these buggers first," a sergeant snapped. "If I didn't know any better, I'd think you'd taken a fancy to our dear captain."

The remainder of the troops snickered before focusing on their enemies, who were less than fifty paces away.

"You guys take care of the small fries," Feng Ming yelled. "I'll take care of the big one." As they approached, the opposing forces held out long spears in an effort to impale them mid-charge. A veritable wall of shields came up behind them, and they were all covered in vicious spikes.

Feng Ming snorted and stomped his foot, which caused a large pillar of earth to come out from beneath him, propelling him upward and over the shield line. Archers tried to stop him mid-flight, but all arrows missed him due to a strong breeze that happened to blow at the right moment. A few threw spears, but those that hit him broke due to faulty construction. As Feng Ming landed, he grabbed his spear and began attacking the leader wantonly. The large creature could only grit his teeth and unleash one saber art after another.

On the battlefield, several other freakish strokes of luck occurred. The soldiers accompanying Feng Ming noticed their armor shifting unusually, avoiding lethal strikes one after another. Their enemies' blades shattered on first contact, clearly a manufacturing defect that had not been corrected through proper tempering of their blades. Sometimes the soldiers even slipped in pools of blood, only to find out that they had avoided a lethal blow, which was then absorbed by another enemy fighter.

"It's better to be lucky than good," Feng Ming always told his soldiers. And he was right. Unlike the rest of the army, the special forces operated on a contract basis. Often, there were optional objectives to be completed that were more lucrative than the original mission posting. Their team *always* completed these. As such, their cultivation bases advanced by leaps and bounds.

This was the biggest reason for Feng Ming's current early foundation-establishment cultivation base. As the group leader, he obtained half the spoils. The sheer amount of resources he consumed, combined with a good dose of luck, enabled him to easily break through to foundation establishment with a nine-pillared foundation. A foundation with nine pillars was flawless, something that only one in a thousand cultivators could hope to obtain.

He used this power to his advantage, oppressing his opponent, who was at middle foundation establishment but had unfortunately established a low-grade foundation with four pillars. This was his lot in life, and he could only be trampled underfoot by Feng Ming's better foundation, equipment, and luck.

The battle was over after sixty breaths. Feng Ming let out a sigh of relief as the golden glow that surrounded him condensed into a golden rune. It floated around him like a guardian spirit, a reward for all his virtuous behavior. Two other runes floated around his head.

Three down, six to go, he thought. The first volume of the Good Fortune Scripture had nine treasures that could be obtained. Only then would he be able to proceed to the next step.

A loud yawn broke the silence in Wang Jun's office. His eyes were rimmed with black due to severe sleep deprivation. Unfortunately, he had no choice in the matter. Business deals that should have gone through didn't, and the market wasn't responding as he'd planned. He was sure that, in addition to Zhou Li's interference, another figure was manipulating the scenes from the shadows.

There was nothing he could do about that. All he could do was work as hard as he could with every waking hour to compensate for it. On the bright side, his increase in cultivation base had made it far easier to concentrate and sustain himself without eating or sleeping. Exhausted, he wrote another letter to the third prince, informing him of his successes and failures.

Elder Bai entered the room with a pot of tea and quietly poured a cup for his young master, who sipped it with closed eyes. "It's nice to see that you still have the sense to treat yourself to a cup of tea. You know, there was a study a few years back that proved that those who drank one to three cups of tea lived up to five years longer than those who didn't."

Wang Jun smiled. He'd read that report and knew that it was utter hogwash. Still, he appreciated the older man's humor in such trying times. He needed all the help he could get.

"Remind me again where we are with our targets," Wang Jun asked while massaging his temples.

"Well," Elder Bai said after clearing his throat, "we've fallen behind schedule, and our total revenue thus far is less than 500,000 high-grade spirit stones. We still have a long way to go to achieve the family's goal of three million. Aside from this, our operating margin targets are slightly lower than required, mostly due to the loans we've had to take to prioritize growth. In addition, our market share in key sectors is way off track. We'd need a miracle to get things in order by the deadline."

"Or a war," Wang Jun retorted.

The older man raised an eyebrow. "Duly noted, Young Master." He then continued listing off various key items. Wang Jun found himself uncharacteristically nodding off in the process. He asked the ever-patient Elder Bai to repeat said information whenever he caught himself in the act.

"Where are we at in the search?" Wang Jun asked.

Elder Bai sighed before setting down a stack of papers and seating himself in front of the young man.

"Young Master," he said gently, "you need to let her go. You're spending an unhealthy amount of time on this matter, and you're letting it eat you up from the inside out."

Wang Jun simply continued staring blankly.

Elder Bai sighed. "How will you get your revenge if you don't complete the family's task?" he asked.

Wang Jun's eyes narrowed when he heard this, and the exhaustion he felt instantly dissipated.

"Quite right, Elder Bai. Please keep up the good work, and let me know if you catch a whiff of something big."

"As you wish, Young Master," Elder Bai said. He then picked up the teapot and retreated from the room, leaving Wang Jun to his brooding.

Chapter 18:
Rebellion

Huxian hopped over a small and fearful family of spirit mice as he wandered through the mountain woods. Using his natural control over darkness, he slinked through the shadows, cleverly bypassing a demon bear's territory. The bear was weak, but he was one of the mountain sovereign's staunchest followers. Alerting him wouldn't be wise at this juncture.

He had less than half a year remaining before the next summit. As the mountain's official method to distribute power, it was the only place he could publicly accuse the bear of colluding with the humans. Before that, he needed supporters. More importantly, he needed strength.

Strength was everything on this mountain, and without it, the mountain sovereign would simply laugh away his accusation. If the strength of his follows didn't make the cut, they would simply be slaughtered under the sovereign's orders. With strength, he could talk on an even footing with the despicable bear.

Huxian checked over his back before entering a small tunnel hidden under a rock near the river. It was barely large enough for his reduced form to navigate, but he didn't care. Discretion was key in this operation. Soon the tunnel expanded by connecting into a larger one. There, he met the demon ferret he had tamed a short while ago. Technically, the beast was a follower of Lord Sky Stoat, but Huxian's strength made it impossible for the lesser demon to refuse his orders.

They continued traveling together for some time before the tunnels enlarged yet again. This time, the walls were made of stone, and the tunnels were a hundred feet in diameter. This allowed them both to assume their original forms. Naturally, Huxian no longer hid his original black-and-white form. Instead, he used it to cow and intimidate his growing circle of influence.

They were soon joined by three herons, one badger, four wolves, and a mastiff. One of the wolves was the moonlight frost wolf who had pledged his support during the last summit. By the looks of it, he'd found a few friends who were also ready to throw their lot in with him.

Eventually they arrived in a large underground cavern. Three other large tunnels led into the massive chamber. A mid-sized group emerged from the one to Huxian's left. There were two deer, one moose, a boar, and three owls. The owls were predatory and nocturnal animals, so there were no conflicts of interest between them and most of the other beasts present. They competed fiercely with the cats, who were followers of the bear sovereign.

The deer, moose, and boar, on the other hand, were preyed upon by many of the animals. Their lot in life wasn't so great, given the great power held by the bears and the cats, and so they were willing to entrust their fates with Huxian for amnesty and better living conditions. The ancient moose was a king-level beast, and very few who had accumulated in this tunnel would dare tangle with him.

From another tunnel, Huxian saw many insects. Two twenty-foot-long Hercules termites spearheaded the group, which also contained a massive praying mantis and a swarm of bees, though the swarm could be considered a singular entity rather than a group. The worker bees couldn't think for themselves, and only the queen bee counted as a person. It was no wonder that such a prideful demon beast had shown up— the bears had stolen her honey for far too long. Despite her small size, she was a king-level demon beast and commanded enormous respect.

Finally, a symphony of slithering sounds echoed through the fourth tunnel. A dozen snakes emerged first, all lord-level existences. Then three small boas entered the large cavern. They were followed by their mother, the geomantic boa, who had created this network of tunnels. In addition to being very powerful, this king-level beast was the most cunning demon beast on the mountain. Her faction was the most powerful king-level influence on the mountain, and her territory was a natural fortress.

The beasts gathered at the center of the cavern in front of an elevated platform. Then, at the geomantic boa's insistence, Huxian moved to stand at the top of the platform. As was customary, he first released his bloodline pressure, causing many of the beasts present to cower. The only ones who didn't were the moose, the boa, the queen bee, and strangely enough, one of the owls. This caused Huxian to reevaluate this cryptic figure, and it also simplified his plan.

"Everyone, I have an important announcement to make," Huxian said. "My follower, Lei Jiang the Calamity-Swallowing Mouse, overheard an important conversation a few weeks ago. It was a conversation between the mountain sovereign and a human cultivator."

Murmuring, bleating, and chirping ensued. Many voiced outrage while others voiced skepticism.

"May we see this Calamity-Swallowing Mouse?" the geomantic boa slithered.

Huxian obliged and sent a mental command to the small mouse, who erupted from a rune on one of his two tails. The many beasts gasped when they saw this early-purification demon beast. Most of them felt a bloodline suppression. Just like Huxian, this mouse was many levels above them.

"It's true," the mouse said. "I overheard them talking after we noticed the strange behavior of the cultivators during the last human tide. They seemed to have information that only insiders would have, and they sent twenty cultivators in a direct attempt to overwhelm my master. It was only with the help of many of the noble beasts here that we managed to stop them."

"You overpraise us," Lord Frost Wolf said. "It is our responsibility to fight against the humans, for the benefit of all beasts."

"Nonsense," a badger yelled. "The law of the jungle is sacrosanct. We should all fight for ourselves. When has there been a need for beasts to stay united?"

"And that," Huxian said, "is the problem." The whole crowd hushed in response. "The orders of the sovereign make no sense. Instead of fighting the humans as a team, we've become a farm to be harvested every year. Furthermore, I suspect that he has been using this to exterminate budding threats. I trust that the current kings in attendance have noticed something."

The geomantic boa hesitated before speaking. "It's true that many promising beasts have died mysteriously. And often, they have been killed by cultivators during a human tide. Still, that's not enough reason to prove the charge you've brought forth."

"I, for one, have always been suppressed," the queen bee replied. "My species is a higher tier than most here—I am a Celestial Rainbow Queen Bee, and my advancement is heavily based on my stored honey. Unfortunately, the sovereign always comes to bully me by taking my honey, making it impossible for me to advance."

"It is true that there is something suspicious going on," the great owl hooted. "As a True Seer Great Owl, I have also suppressed my advancement. My prophetic abilities have sensed that I will be eliminated should I proceed one step further."

His words made Huxian grin from ear to ear. "As a True Seer beast, you should be able to validate the truth of what happened that day, should you not?"

The owl hesitated. "I can. However, to validate the truth, the recipient of my inquiry must be willing to open up his mind and soul to me. Any resistance will cause the recipient to sustain damage to his true soul. In my opinion, it is hardly appropriate to subject a beast of Lei Jiang's caliber to this technique. It is a great loss of face to bare one's soul."

"Loss of face isn't an issue," Huxian said with a snort. "Lei Jiang, prepare yourself to be examined."

"Yes, Master," the Calamity-Swallowing Mouse said obediently.

Under the stares of the many spirit beasts, the owl fluttered up to the top of the platform. Then, after bowing to Huxian, he hopped over to the small mouse, who sat docilely on the ground despite facing its natural predator.

With a sudden motion, the owl grabbed the mouse with a claw, and the claw began glowing like a full moon. A beam of light shot out from the mouse's head and traveled to the top of the cave, expanding into a two-hundred-foot-wide viewing screen.

There they saw things not from Lei Jiang's perspective but from an omniscient one. Everything within two hundred feet of Lei Jiang was revealed. In the projection, Lei Jiang was cowering in a small crevice on a cliff. Above him, they saw a large bear speaking quietly with a white-haired cultivator wearing a Daoist robe. They could see their lips moving but couldn't hear any sound.

Huxian cleared his throat. "Your ability is indeed amazing, and I wasn't wrong to have you come up here. However, would it be possible to hear what they're saying?"

The owl's feathers shook nervously as the True Seer Great Owl realized the problem.

"My apologies, Great King," the owl said, stammering. He then made a gesture with his claw, and five small gray demon energy cables appeared. They were accompanied by three smaller cables: one white, one red, and one yellow. The owl began fiddling around with the cables, and the screen above sometimes blacked out and sometimes became a blue screen. At some point, they heard the rustle of the wind clearly, as the conversation in the memory was already over.

Huxian massaged his brow with his paw. Unfortunately, setting up audio and video at the same time was a huge problem for spirit beasts, and despite the many instruction manuals that had been released over many aeons, the problem never seemed to go away.

After a quarter hour, the issue was finally resolved. Just as the owl was about to resume the movie, Huxian cleared his throat once more. "Can we get subtitles, please? Many of us are hard of hearing."

The owl shivered and resumed his work. A half hour later, the issue with the subtitles was finally resolved. The owl then brought the film back to its original starting point, and the recording started again.

"You told me that he was a two-tailed fox!" the white robed Daoist yelled. "That beast's abilities are clearly much greater than you reported. Now I've lost a good tenth of my sect's foundation-establishment disciples."

The large bear grunted in response. "You can't blame me. Your sect members underestimated the enemy. If all fifty of the cultivators you sent had attacked him in tandem, this never would have happened. Of course, this would have exposed me. Still, with twice as many cultivators, you could have made up for quality with quantity."

The older cultivator looked at the bear coldly. "You need to compensate me for this. I want that fox dead and his core in my possession. During the next 'human tide,' you *will* deliver him to me on a silver platter. Otherwise, our relationship can't continue. I'll find another demon beast to replace you, and we will continue harvesting you like the farm animals you truly are."

With these words, the cultivator flicked his sleeve and vanished. The old bear sighed and closed his eyes. Lei Jiang kept deathly silent before finally finding an opportunity to slip out.

On the way down, the mouse encountered some seeds, which he ate. Then he proceeded to the True Seer Great Owl's territory and urinated on his tree, snickering. Then he went to Lord Sky Stoat's territory and impregnated one of his concubines. Then—

"I think that's enough, Lord Great Owl," Huxian said, coughing. He shot a reprimanding look at the mouse, whose consciousness had finally returned.

"Lei Jiang's antics aside," Huxian said in an authoritative voice, "it's clear that the old bear is colluding with the humans. The situation is downright deplorable. *We* should be the ones unleashing a *beast tide* every few years, not the other way around. While personal territory and food-chain order is important, it's equally important to band together against the humans that want to invade our territory. There shall be no more cowering, no more giving in. I won't have it!"

He nodded toward the screen. "This is why we need to rebel. Only once we overthrow the old bear and start a cooperative relationship can we shake these despicable humans off. This isn't a human city, this is the *forest*. The forest belongs to us beasts, just like it always has. But let me clarify: I don't hate the humans. They are just fighting for more territory like the rest of us. What I won't stand for is treachery. That old bear has been lining his pockets and preserving his power long enough. Who's with me?"

The beasts all looked at each other hesitantly. Only the wolves gave their immediate approval.

"Regrettably," the geomantic boa slithered, "this force is not sufficient. Our kings are fewer, but we are more powerful. Our lords are sorely lacking. The only way that we can make up for this is by having a strong enough leader. And I regret to say that you are not strong enough yet."

The fox smirked. "I can be strong enough. I need a drop of each of your purified essence blood. With that, I'll break through to middle Purification Realm, and I'll be a cut stronger than that old bear."

The beasts murmured in dissent.

"The price is high," the geomantic boa said. "What do we get in return?"

"Of course, I wouldn't ask you to do this for free," Huxian said. "This loss of essence blood will weaken you slightly and delay your purification by five years. In exchange, I'll gift each of you with a beastly purification technique suited to your species. This will allow you to easily recover the lost essence. Some of you may even break through to king level."

Immediately, every beast but the snakes were enthusiastic about the idea.

"And for us?" the geomantic boa asked. After all, she had previously been gifted with such a scripture before, and it had been more than adequate for her and her children.

"Seeing as you are a long-term business partner," Huxian replied, "I will pass on to you the Triple Lotus Venom Strengthening technique."

"Trip-Triple Lotus Venom?" the geomantic boa exclaimed. "Very well, My Sovereign. This humble one subjects herself to your authority."

After their meeting, the beasts all returned to their homes and began training intensely. The upcoming summit would be the deadliest in the history of their small mountain. They would either overpower their opponents or perish.

Inside Huxian's cave, Lei Jiang served as a scout while Huxian purified the blood essence he'd collected and began devouring it through his laws of darkness. They were converted to pure demonic energy, which he used to purify his bloodline, which in turn strengthened his muscles and bones.

After a few days, he heard a snap, and the energy surrounding his cave traveled toward him in vast amounts. He'd broken through to middle Purification Realm, and now there was only one being on the whole mountain who stood a chance against him.

At the peak of the mountain, a large bear was eating honey from a pot. It was the honey that he'd been extorting from the queen bee for years. He was sure she resented it, but he couldn't resist. The honey was great sustenance for him, and he was sure that in a year, he would be able to break through to the upper Purification Realm. By then, he wouldn't even need to rely on those humans to reign unhindered.

But as he ate, he noticed a vacuum in the mountain's ample demonic energy.

A breakthrough? He narrowed his eyes when he noticed that the commotion was coming from Lord Two Tails's cave. *He's getting far too strong. I need to take him down soon, otherwise I won't stand a chance.*

Regrettably, he couldn't do that on his own, so he resigned himself to the fact that Lord Two Tails would become a king of the forest, wrecking the precious balance that he'd carefully crafted over the years.

Chapter 19: Incandescence

The rhythmic beating of a pair of hammers caused Cha Ming's bones to shake with every blow. Every strike caused large chunks of ore to crumble from the wall into large carts that were parked near him.

He had been hammering away for the past five days, a new personal record. His endurance grew with every passing day, but he also felt an external strength seeping into him. It was an ever-present energy that continuously refreshed his aching muscles and gave him sufficient energy to keep mining. It wasn't that he *wanted* to work; a very specific set of orders kept him working as long as he possibly could.

Thus far, Cha Ming had caused twenty-seven non-lethal fracture injuries to the bandits and had indirectly caused the death of seven others. He was able to accomplish this due to loopholes in the rules, contradictions between his well-being, production capacity, and the safety of the bandits. This had prompted Wei Chen to fetch a lawyer and contract specialist, who investigated the case data and patched any loopholes.

After three repetitions of this grueling process, Cha Ming found himself unable to act directly or indirectly against the guards.

Now all he could do was work until his bones ached. But there was a silver lining to his current predicament. The incessant pounding and hard work had made him completely comfortable with his 1,080 jin of physical strength.

Like that's any use, Cha Ming thought. *I can only continue mining until I encounter a stroke of luck and break free from this mental prison.*

His hammering continued, and he took one slow step at a time, synchronizing his movements with the swinging weapons and splashing debris. Moving forward was difficult because his entire body was covered with pieces of gold-weighted clothing while he wore gold boots on his feet. After all, exerting one's full strength was very difficult without a sufficient counterweight. His suit enabled him to exert his full fist strength with every blow without a hint of recoil. While it increased the vibrations and the pain he felt, he couldn't question the efficiency of this method. In fact, it was very similar to what he did using his Mountain Stance or his Hard Staff Art.

Months passed this way, until he had spent a total of six months in the mine. His endurance grew with time, and eventually he was able to continue mining for ten days without rest. His good behavior and insane productivity made it so that his jailers no longer supervised him. They would only come to check up on him every hour and deliver meals, which he wolfed down in as short a time as humanly possible.

One day, he was pounding away and mining like he had been for the past week. No guards were around, only workers who rapidly removed the debris and spirit stones that he'd smashed away with his vicious hammer strikes.

Suddenly he heard a loud crack throughout his entire body. His mind shuddered, and he almost lost consciousness. The nearby miners were completely stunned when he paused his mining for a few breaths. It was the first "break" that they had seen this monstrously strong man take in months.

Cha Ming resumed mining shortly after, careful to conceal any signs of what had occurred. Fortunately, the miners beside him were all normal mortals, and they didn't recognize the sharp sound that come from Cha Ming.

The sound of him breaking through to the next level of qi condensation.

Wei Chen sighed with boredom as he reviewed the notes on the progress of the mining operation. They had only mined a third of the mine's total reserves. At least, that was the current estimate based on their exploration and calculations.

This worried the normally calm and calculating man. The movements of his bandit group had not gone unnoticed, and their absence even more so. It wouldn't be long until the leader came looking for them. If they were found with such a large amount of unreported wealth, the fate of Wei Chen and his group of loyal bandits would be sealed. As the weakest of the three vice leaders, it was difficult for him to compete for benefits.

Will I need to abandon part of the mine and flee with the profits?

In his greed, he quickly shoved this thought out of his head.

Nothing could make him abandon a sliver of these generous profits. They were his ticket to absolute domination, and he wished for nothing more than to move unhindered in these lands. He wanted freedom from oppression and the ability to protect those he loved. Or what was left of them. He also wanted the ability to avenge those who had moved on.

This was why, despite his vast wealth, he kept pushing himself to perform increasingly atrocious acts. His bar was lowered further and further, and it wouldn't be long before he felt that killing for intimidation and devil sacrifices were completely acceptable practices. His present morals were willing to excuse the wanton murder of innocents with sufficient reason. What that sufficient reason was, only he knew.

Suddenly he felt a jolt on his forearm where his slave sealing marks were located. He quickly bared his arm and discovered that all the symbols were intact and functioning properly. Frowning, he looked suspiciously at Cha Ming's slave mark.

That man has been nothing but trouble. In fact, he's completely unusable as anything but a miner. Should I send someone to observe him again? Cha Ming had been obedient for months, but he sorely remembered the effort it had taken to completely tame him.

Eventually he gave way to his worries and sent out a message. He would no longer take chances with that unpredictable slave, and once the mining project was over, he would silence him. After all, he wasn't one of the villagers, he was just an outsider who had taken refuge there for some time.

The heavenly oath did not prevent the shrewd bandit leader from killing him once his usefulness had run out.

Cha Ming continued mining as he observed the changes occurring inside his dantian. The membrane surrounding his qi lakes had been breached, like a dam after a reservoir had exceeded its capacity. He looked on as the five qi lakes in his dantian, joined by five white and five black rivers, began growing into qi seas. A massive amount of qi suddenly rushed in from his surroundings, reducing many spirit stones he had mined to rubble.

How the hell am I going to hide this? Cha Ming thought worriedly.

Under the assistance of the surrounding spirit stones, it only took an incense time for his dantian to fill to the brim. His new qi seas were many times vaster than the original qi lakes, and it was obvious that this was an important watershed in the cultivation process. Regrettably, he still couldn't cultivate normally, but he was sure that the process of restoring his meridians would be much smoother from now on. That was, if he survived that long.

Still mining, he looked inward into his spiritual sea. It was white, just like when he had fought Guo Jia. But now, instead of seeing his chained, nearly transparent body, he saw that his body was glowing ever so slightly. He also discovered that a new piece of information had appeared in his mind: He had cultivated his soul into the Incandescence Realm. He also noticed that his soul was growing increasingly bright. He felt his soul pulling from a mysterious force in his surroundings to strengthen itself.

The glowing eventually reached a bottleneck, where it stopped briefly before pushing through to the next level. His soul continued its accelerated growth, until it glowed like a dim lightbulb. There it stopped once more before a popping sound signaled yet another breakthrough. His soul continued to grow stronger until the glowing resembled a bright lightbulb.

Crack.

A shattering sound ensued, and the glow from his soul became so bright he couldn't bear looking at it. His soul now glowed as bright as the sun. After a short while more, the growth of his soul halted.

The upper level of the Incandescence Realm. It was not the peak, but controlling his qi and spiritual force was much easier than it was before.

Upon closer examination, the glow gave his soul great strength. The slave sigil chaining his soul was now offering nothing more than a light resistance. It was like a garment that he could tear off at his leisure. He knew that as long as he willed it, the slave sigil would shatter, severing his connection with the other master sigils. He was now halfway to freedom.

Suddenly the sound of footsteps and weapons being drawn caused his perception to be drawn back to the outside world. He had received no orders to stop, so he resumed mining as quickly as possible. The guards tentatively approached him with spears, but he ignored them.

Soon a guard holding a master sigil approached him. "Halt!" the man said.

Cha Ming, who was mid-swing, instantly halted his motion in midair.

"Attention," the guard instructed.

Cha Ming instantly turned around, standing straight as a

rod with his hammers crossed in front of him subserviently. After a subsequent command, he dropped the hammers and kept his hands firmly by his side.

"What happened here?" the guard asked.

Cha Ming kept a straight face that didn't betray his newfound freedom.

"Reporting to Master," Cha Ming replied docilely. "This slave has broken through to the seventh level of qi condensation due to the ambient spiritual force in the air. It was a natural breakthrough, but it caused this slave to pause for three breaths before this slave was able to continue mining." He said no more or less than was expected.

The guard turned pale when he heard this but quickly regained his composure and instructed Cha Ming. "We will be taking you to see the leader now. Submit yourself to the application of body-restraining and qi-restraining manacles."

Cha Ming did not put up any shred of resistance. As they put on the manacles, he became weak as a kitten while simultaneously controlling his soul force and suppressed his apparent soul cultivation base until it resembled half-step incandescent realm. Only those with a higher soul force than he had would be able to tell the difference. He was sure Wei Chen wasn't one of those people.

The journey out of the falls was uneventful, and soon Cha Ming found himself standing face to face with Wei Chen. They were alone in his private quarters. He waited patiently as Wei Chen walked around him and observed him. He didn't react when the man reached out with the great-master sigil's powers, checking the link between them. He also didn't react when Wei Chen uncomfortably walked up to him and gently touched the mark on his forehead.

Walking behind him, Wei Chen asked, "What happened?"

"Please clarify, Great Master," Cha Ming replied dutifully.

"Did you break through to the seventh level of qi condensation?" Wei Chen asked.

"This slave broke through to the seventh level of qi condensation."

"Did your body break through?" Wei Chen pressed.

"It did not," Cha Ming replied.

"Then why did you pause for three breaths after breaking through?" Wei Chen asked.

"The immediate breakthrough caused this slave's body to lose all energy before it was finally stabilized by external heaven and earth qi," Cha Ming answered.

"Why would your body enter a state of energy deprivation?" Wei Chen asked. "Usually, there is sufficient qi throughout the whole body to stop an interim interruption. Breakthroughs mid-combat are not unheard of."

This was a tricky question. Truthfully, it had occurred because of his shock at his newfound freedom. Thankfully, Cha Ming had anticipated this question and come up with a conceivable answer. "This slave's body is crippled. This slave's non-core meridians and qi pathways are broken and barren, causing there to be a qi deficiency in this slave's body as a whole. Therefore, this slave's body's qi was overdrawn. Had it been mid-combat, this slave would have died."

Wei Chen looked pensive as he walked out from behind Cha Ming. Pensive, but doubtful. As Wei Chen walked behind him once more, he sensed a fist approaching his vitals. He avoided the fist ever so slightly but didn't retaliate.

"Why did you dodge?" Wei Chen growled.

"Master has ordered that this slave preserve his body's

functions unless directly ordered by a master or great master to do so," Cha Ming replied calmly.

"Was my fist approaching you not a direct order?" Wei Chen asked.

"No, it was not," Cha Ming replied.

This was obviously a trick question and a trick action. Should Cha Ming have taken the fist on purpose, he would have been obeying an implicit order but not his explicit orders. Wei Chen was simply a cunning old fox, and it was no wonder that he had become a vice leader of this bandit group.

"Allow me to attack you," Wei Chen said.

Before Cha Ming could reply, a rapid boot strike approached the side of his head. It was a near-lethal blow, one that he could just barely react to in time if he so chose. Of course, he did nothing of the sort. He was knocked down to the ground with a severe concussion, and his strong constitution barely stopped him from passing out or throwing up. He stayed there, not getting up until ordered.

"Get up!" the leader yelled.

Cha Ming attempted to stand up but was prevented by a boot. While his cultivation was no longer restricted, the leader had reinforced himself with qi, making it impossible to resist. Still, Cha Ming didn't give up and attempted to squirm out of the way of the foot. He struggled for an incense time and was beaten bloody in the process.

Finally, Wei Chen allowed him to stand up. As he did so, Wei Chen handed him a short sword. It was a third-grade spirit sword.

"Cut your arm off with this sword," Wei Chen growled.

What a vicious man.

Cha Ming quickly grabbed the sword and hacked into his

arm. A splash of blood sprayed onto himself and the leader, but he didn't stop after just hitting bone. He struck it over and over again, and cracks started to form on his bone. The strength of his body caused cracks to appear on the spirit sword as well. Fortunately, Cha Ming's soul was extremely strong, and he could withstand the pain. In fact, it had been strong enough at half-step incandescence, so regardless, he did not have to fake any screams. Cha Ming figured this was yet another ploy to get him to commit a mistake.

"Stop!" Wei Chen yelled just as Cha Ming's arm bone was about to be severed in two.

Cha Ming halted the blade an inch from his arm, which was now a bloody mess. Without any kind of medicine, it would be two weeks before he could use this arm properly again. As he stood there in pain, Wei Chen walked out of the tent and came back with another two men, who immediately began to clean the floor and his arm.

"Take this pill and eat it," the leader said.

Cha Ming complied, and he felt a surge of vital energy transferring to his arm. It began knitting together the ravaged flesh and chipped bone. "Rest for six hours before continuing your work at maximum efficiency."

A half day passed by before Cha Ming was finally back into the full swing of things. This was, of course, the final test by the shrewd man. The medicinal efficiency could not fully heal his arm in six hours, so he could only start mining with a damaged arm. After some quick calculations, he adjusted the rate of mining between his arms, ensuring that he could heal adequately while mining at the maximum average rate. After twelve hours, his arm was fully healed, so he resumed his mining at peak efficiency.

Over the next two weeks, the guards became increasingly complacent and began leaving him alone again. In their absence, Cha Ming began doing two things. First, he began embezzling spirit stones, keeping them inside his Clear Sky World. Second, he began using his superior spiritual force to guide qi down his ruined pathways, destroying them and rebuilding them as time passed. It was much easier than before, and the pain was much easier to bear. It was a risky process, but he had to do it. Besides, he was sure that Wei Chen was untrained in spiritual detection abilities and would have trouble inspecting his meridians and qi pathways without outside help.

And so, Cha Ming bided his time and waited for an opportunity to escape. He could not train his body-transformation technique, and making another breakthrough in qi condensation was not an option.

However, he was sure his chance would come. It always did.

Chapter 20: Escape

A cloud of dust burst out of one of the mining tunnels, forcing out the majority of the miners. Amidst the sounds of coughing and wheezing, a muscular figure waited for the cloud to settle before deciding how to proceed. This was a reasonable course of action, and well within the confines of his instructions. At this stage of the mining process, proceeding without care was tantamount to suicide.

This was the fourth tunnel that Cha Ming had almost mined to completion. They liked to use him for these final excavations because his resiliency didn't lose out to a demon beast's. He was a veritable human cockroach, and ideal for surviving potentially fatal cave-ins.

As the dust started to clear, Cha Ming walked forward and stealthily stole several large spirit stones, placing them in his Clear Sky World. Inside this spatial dimension lay a small mountain of spirit stones. Failing anything else, it was a piece of fortune that would never land in the bandits' hands. They were also the resources he would rely on to break through after making his escape.

Over the past several months, Cha Ming had completely remade his qi pathways and meridians. His new set could accommodate eight types of qi, seven of which he had at his disposal. He had undergone several additional inspections by Wei Chen. Fortunately, Wei Chen's plots were no match for Cha Ming's cunning. The vice leader had no way of confirming the truth of Cha Ming's statements with inquisitors, as they abhorred injustice and would never stoop so low as to aid a bandit group. As such, Cha Ming continued to mine while Wei Chen's suspicions eased up little by little.

One of the bandits assigned to guard him approached. "What do you see, Cha Ming?"

Cha Ming could tell where the guard was both by sound and through his superior soul. He noted that the guard did not have his weapons drawn as he once used to, as it had been nine months since Cha Ming's last outburst. They now assumed that he was tamer than a farm animal. The guards walked past him leisurely and began inspecting the surrounding passageway.

In this latest collapse, it appeared that a large cavern had been cleared out in the tunnel. It was roughly a hundred feet wide and tall, and it led to eight other passageways. These were existing pathways that they had not excavated.

Could this be my chance? Cha Ming's heart jumped. He was under no illusions that he would be kept alive. The bandits had hinted as much in the many conversations they held near him. They assumed that he was only a workhorse, one that they could slaughter at their leisure. In order to gain an opportunity to escape, he had played the part of the grunt to perfection.

It's time, Cha Ming thought.

In Cha Ming's mental space, his incandescent soul opened its eyes. It looked down at the slave sigil and grinned as its hand grasped it, shattering it like a porcelain vase. In the outside world, the black slave sigil on his forehead also disappeared. He willed the Clear Sky Staff into his hands, and before any of his guards realized what was happening, he used his Swift Staff Art and immediately appeared beside one of them.

Crash.

Bones broke as he unleashed months of pent-up fury, smashing the man's neck with 1080 jin of brute force. Then, using the recoil from his blow, he struck another guard in the face. A sickening crunch rang out as he crushed the man's skull. Then he channeled the power of wind to rapidly strike the remaining four bandits in succession. It only took two breaths' time. All the bandits guarding him were crumpled on the ground, dead.

Wei Chen was cultivating in his tent when a dull throbbing on his arm caused him to focus on it in annoyance. He lifted his sleeve to check what was happening, and he only just caught the disappearing traces of Cha Ming's slave brand.

"I was right all along," he whispered, feeling vindicated. He had always suspected the shrewd boy despite his numerous examinations. He sighed and exited his tent, preparing to head into the mines to execute Cha Ming, the misbehaving animal. He only hoped the damage Cha Ming had caused wasn't too extreme.

"Vice leader, the life slips for six of our group have crumbled!" a bandit yelled from a few tents down. The man was in charge of supervising a room filled with jade slips that contained a trace of each bandit's soul. These slips would shatter upon the death of their owners.

"Stop panicking already," said Wei Chen authoritatively. "It's just that vicious slave again. It's time to put that suffering dog out of his misery."

With these words, he summoned his archaic sword from his bag of holding and quickly flew up to the mines behind the waterfall.

Cha Ming wasted no time after his brief fight, not even bothering to loot the guards' bodies. He knew that Wei Chen would be arriving soon, and his only chance was to make a run for it. He looked at the eight different passageways, approached one of them, and using earth qi, caused a thick wall of earth to rise from the ground and block it off. It wasn't perfect or flush, but breaking it down would cause debris to cover his tracks.

Such a technique was completely unsuitable for battle, as each wall took five breaths to erect. After setting the first, Cha Ming sealed off six other passageways before heading down the eighth remaining one. He turned around to seal this entrance as well, using ten breaths this time in an effort to mimic those formed from the outside. Thankfully, his incandescent soul was strong enough to penetrate the earthen barrier he erected, and the task was completed without a problem.

After finishing his hasty work, Cha Ming gripped his staff and ran down the passageway at full speed. He didn't know what he would encounter, but it was far better than staying behind and awaiting his death. His tunnel branched multiple times, all while leading him in a downward direction before finally leveling off.

That was when he heard a blast from behind him.

Shit, they've found the right tunnel this time. He used his Seven Cloud Steps to move at maximum speed.

"You think a pitiful worm like you can escape me?" Wei Chen yelled, not far behind him.

Unfortunately, Cha Ming could only continue advancing along the straight pathway. Soon, a flying sword came hurtling at him, forcing Cha Ming to defend blow after blow while retreating.

It looks like this might be the end of the road. Dodging another sword blow, Cha Ming continued down the pathway, which finally opened up into a large black cave. Even while using light crystals, he could barely see the end of it. The small ledge leading into the cave ended in a sharp precipice, revealing a world of darkness below.

Gritting his teeth, Cha Ming threw down three of the light crystals he'd salvaged from the mine. They fell rapidly, shrinking as they went, before finally vanishing. The pit was clearly too deep for light to escape.

"So you've finally met a dead end, my little dog," Wei Chen said, his voice echoing in the tunnel. He appeared fifty feet away from Cha Ming, floating on an ancient-looking flying sword. As Wei Chen stepped off it and onto the ground, the sword danced around the man's body before aggressively pointing itself at Cha Ming.

"I admire your tenacity," the vice leader said. "If you surrender now, I can make this quick and painless. I'm a man of principles, after all."

"What principles?" Cha Ming replied coldly. "You're just as bad as that turncoat subordinate of yours, enslaving an entire village just because you can. How could this possibly be the actions of a principled person?"

"Well, I obviously can't let them go until I'm ready to leave," Wei Chen replied. "Otherwise they would expose this place's secret. It's already extremely benevolent that I didn't slaughter the lot. I had sufficient reason to do it, but I didn't."

"Didn't, or couldn't?" Cha Ming retorted. "I saw the lightning in the sky. You swore a heavenly oath, and since then, not a single villager has died. I'd wager you made an oath to spare the villagers. Do you dare kill me?"

Wei Chen chuckled. "Yes, I did swear a heavenly oath not to kill the villagers, and to leave them here once I'm done retrieving the minerals. In fact, it was the mayor's negligence that enabled me to enslave them in the first place. I would have agreed to not enslave them and to bring in external labor. Everything was on the table, if only I could obtain the location of the mineral vein.

"However, you seem to be mistaken about something. You and I both know that you aren't one of these villagers. You're just a man who washed up here and is staying temporarily. So I *can* kill you without violating the oath."

Cha Ming chuckled dryly. "I figured you'd say that."

"Any last words before I kill you?" Wei Chen asked.

Cha Ming pondered for a moment, thinking of the black abyss below. Suddenly, the fall into the unknown didn't seem so bad.

"You better hope the fall kills me," Cha Ming said coldly before flinging himself backward.

But Wei Chen had noticed Cha Ming's intent, and he sent his ancient sword out at lightning speed. Cha Ming had barely left the ground when the sword came piercing toward his heart. Unfortunately, he had no time to block, and evasion was impossible mid-jump. Or was it? Cha Ming's mind quickly determined the best course of action before he poured his incandescent force into the Clear Sky Staff. It elongated rapidly and struck a wall in the cave, causing him to swerve and barely avoid the flying sword in the process.

The rapid acceleration caused Cha Ming to plummet into the darkness. The flying sword, seemingly unsatisfied with his retreat, adjusted its trajectory. It entered his shoulder, barely avoiding key organs as Cha Ming plunged into the darkness. Wei Chen had no choice but to retrieve his sword and could only glare at Cha Ming's falling figure.

Darkness enveloped Cha Ming as he fell into the unknown. Before long, he saw a pale blue light approaching him rapidly from below. It was a relief to see that the chasm had an end to it, but he wasn't very optimistic about his chances of surviving the fall.

He waited for the impact for a hundred breaths, the blue speck growing as he fell. Unfortunately, the glow was too far away, and he could no longer adjust his trajectory. Seconds trickled by, and just when he thought he would impact the ground, his body swiftly decelerated. To his surprise, his fall was cushioned by what appeared like a soft cloud of intangible energy. Then, due to the blood flowing out of the vicious wound on his shoulder, he fainted.

Cha Ming woke up some time later. His wound had partially healed over, and the blood no longer flowed like a small river. In the center of the massive black pit, he saw a tall building made with light blue stones that emanated soft light. They were the same ones he'd seen while falling. There was flat ground beneath him, so he stepped off the soft material that had cushioned his fall. It dissipated as soon as he set foot on the cold, hard ground.

Having nowhere else to go, Cha Ming approached the blue building. The massive structure was a strange sight compared to the traditional Chinese architecture of this world. It looked futuristic, even by Earth's standards. Despite its advanced appearance, Cha Ming could instinctively tell it was positively ancient. It emanated an archaic aura that spoke of a time far removed from the current age.

The details of construction slowly grew clearer as he approached. Before long, he was able to see the individual blue stones in detail. Each one was engraved with a complex runic pattern. To his surprise, he didn't recognize more than one in a thousand. Those few he did were written in the same runic script that he had learned while crafting talismans.

Seeing no exits in the cave, and bedazzled by the building before him, Cha Ming continued advancing. He walked forward carefully, his staff in hand, admiring the building as he circled it. It took three hours to fully travel its perimeter, and to his surprise, there was no entrance to be found. He returned from the place he'd started, which he assumed was the front of the building. Where a door should have been, there was only a large blue wall that, unlike the rest of the building, was empty of runes.

Perplexed by the peculiar construction of the building, Cha Ming approached the stone wall until he was only two feet away and could make out the characters more clearly. They were pure white, much like the creation qi in his dantian and the characters that Sun Wukong had painted to craft the circle of protection. Each rune emanated a profound sense of meaning. One character in particular caught his attention. When he saw it, he immediately felt refreshed, as though he had just finished cultivating beside a mountain stream.

He reached out to touch this character, and when he did, it felt like cool spring water. Images flashed through his mind, as though the rune yearned to convey its name to him. It seemed to contain some sort of spirit or truth.

"Amazing," Cha Ming whispered.

Only a single character on a single stone in this massive building gave him this feeling. He felt that by comprehending this character, his water techniques would improve by leaps and bounds, and so would the water-related talismans he drew. He sat down in meditation before the building and pictured the character in his mind. To his surprise, he couldn't imagine the shape he'd clearly seen on the wall. Instead, he only saw a blurry image in his mind's eye.

What if I try picturing a small part? he thought. The character seemed to be separated into four distinct pieces, so he focused on the first piece, which gave him a massive solid feeling. An image came to mind as he imagined one piece of the character, that of a small forested mountain in the wilderness.

The more he focused on this image in his mind, the clearer the piece became.

He continued to study it until he could no longer bring further clarity to the individual piece, which was still slightly blurred. Then, moving to the next one, he was overcome with a strong sense of tranquility and focus. In his mind's eye, he pictured himself in meditation. His soul couldn't help but sit cross-legged in his mental space and imitate what he saw.

This piece must symbolize meditation.

This realization brought instant clarity to the second piece of the character. Further, his understanding of the first piece increased as well, clearing it up even more. He realized that it wasn't just the pieces that held meaning but their combinations. Following this epiphany, he quickly moved to the next part of the character, where the picture of a stream appeared in his mind. Specifically, it was a mid-sized mountain stream, filled with fish struggling against the current in an effort to reach the pool of water that bred them. As his understanding deepened, the first, second, and third pieces of the character materialized even further.

Finally, he looked at the last piece. Instead of a picture, a feeling came to mind. He felt thoroughly refreshed, as though new life had been breathed into him. It was the refreshing feeling one felt in the spring, just after winter, when a draft of wind rapidly cooled the new warm weather.

It's a cool spring breeze. The combined character represents that feeling you get when a cool spring breeze brushes past you as you meditate near a mid-sized mountain stream. What a profound character!

As soon as he finished this thought, he noticed that his mental image of the character was now clear and substantial.

Then, looking into his mental space, he also noticed a character hovering around. It was simply there, waiting for him to use it. He felt completely comfortable with the character, to the extent that even painting it with only his qi would have some sort of effect.

He yearned to try out this hypothesis, but before he had a chance, the wall before him began glowing brightly. He stepped back cautiously, only to see that many runes had lit up on the blue stone wall. They traveled upward and downward, forming a straight line.

Twenty feet away from him, another character began glowing, and another line parallel to the first began appearing. Finally, a much thicker line of characters began glowing up above. It lit up brightly, forming the outline of a doorway. And then, the blue stones in the middle of the doorway vanished as though they had never been there in the first place.

At the top, he saw characters that he could instinctively read in his native tongue.

"Fuxi's Library," he whispered in awe.

Chapter 21: Fuxi's Library

A soft blue glow accompanied Cha Ming as he walked through a hallway in Fuxi's Library. The illumination wasn't all encompassing. Rather, it seemed that the walls "knew" where he was and lit up just enough to accommodate him. Such a design reminded Cha Ming of modern technology that had begun appearing before he left Earth.

The temperature was no longer cool like before. It was now just the right temperature. The humidity dipped as well, mimicking the dry sensation that made him most comfortable. He was an inhabitant of the plains, after all, and he had found the high-moisture environment in Crystal Falls somewhat suffocating.

Before long, he arrived in a dimly lit room furnished with a couch, a small table, and a lamp. On the table, there was a small bowl filled with white pellets that smelled wonderful and another one filled with water. His stomach grumbled when he realized he was indeed quite famished.

"The food is suitable for human consumption," a pleasant voice said behind him.

He turned around rapidly and saw the semi-transparent figure of a middle-aged man. His hair wasn't dark like those outside, rather, it was brown and cropped short. He also wore a full beard on his face, and his clothes were very unusual. The man reminded Cha Ming of his own unusual appearance. However, he was a foreigner in this world. Was this man one as well?

"Greetings, Elder," Cha Ming said, clasping his hands together and bowing. "My name is Du Cha Ming. How might I address you?"

The middle-aged man looked at him quizzically, a bemused expression on his face. "Is this the current form of greeting?" the man asked, mimicking Cha Ming's movements awkwardly. "It has been far too long since I have received visitors. Regrettably, I hate to inform you that I don't have a name. You may call me Custodian, as I am the perpetual keeper of this library."

"Why wouldn't you have a name?" Cha Ming asked curiously.

The man smiled before gesturing to the chair, urging Cha Ming to sit down. He materialized another one and sat down as well. "I don't have a name because only those with souls may have names. I am a soulless entity, so I have no name, no story."

"A soulless entity?" Cha Ming breathed in sharply. "Then you are not a ghost? Are you just a projection, then?"

"A projection..." the man mused. "Yes, I am a projection of a program, entrusted with a mission. It would be more accurate to call me a construct, a servant of my master, Fuxi. I am curious, are there such constructs in your world? Aeons have past since I last saw a living person."

Cha Ming hesitated before replying. "This world does not have such things, but in my memories, I am aware of another world. There, no one cultivated. Rather, they aimed to develop technology to the pinnacle, and were on the cusp of designing something called artificial intelligence."

"Oh, so you're a reincarnator?" the man replied in surprise. "That makes things much easier. Yes, it is as you said. I am an artificial intelligence, and I have been programmed with a mission: to preserve knowledge in case this material plane falls to the devils. The hope was to grant a small advantage to the local righteous cultivators.

"I was never found since the library was established. Aeons passed, and the world switched quietly to the control of the devils. Then, many aeons ago, the control switched back to the angels. A switch in control leads to a change in the laws of this material plane, so it is quite easy for me to determine this despite the library's seclusion."

Seeing Cha Ming's confused expression, the Custodian looked at him apologetically. "Relax and eat while I tell you a very condensed history of my purpose, and the lucky chances that are available for you here today."

Cha Ming glanced at the bowl of white pellets. His guards had never fed him adequately, so he wasn't sure how long he would last against politeness. As a compromise, he picked up the bowl and drank, then popped a white pellet in his mouth. His body was instantly filled with vitality, and he felt as though he'd just eaten a full, nutritious meal.

"Amazing!" he exclaimed.

The Custodian simply smiled and continued his story. "Each material plane was created inherently good. The laws of the world rewarded acts of kindness and mercy while punishing those who performed evil. However, the universe was created fair. It left a path of survival open to evil and its devilish souls, enabling them to convert worlds to suit their own kind. Since the beginning of the universe, the custody of many worlds has changed multiple times.

"The war in which my master participated was particularly intense. Therefore, he created libraries throughout the many material planes, where he stored the knowledge he prized the most: the power of words and names.

"Here you may take a single opportunity to learn various words, many of which may have been lost to the passage of time. Words contain power, as I'm sure you realize, since you were able to enter the library in the first place. Only those who practice runic arts may enter. In addition, only those with positive karma on their bodies may enter as well. This is to prevent the devils from learning these runic arts for themselves.

"In this library, there are three smelting trials in which you will gain the opportunity to gain knowledge. Your performance during these trials will earn you rewards, which will scale based on your cultivation level. Each level in cultivation comes with certain expectations, so as a qi-condensation cultivator, you cannot be blamed for performing poorly. After attempting these tests, you may stay here to digest your learnings, but you may never enter the library again.

"Do you understand?" he asked.

"I think so?" Cha Ming said hesitantly.

"Relax and recover," the Custodian said, smiling. "There is no rush. Once you are ready to challenge the library, simply shout out for me and let me know." With these words, the Custodian left Cha Ming in the comfortable room.

Cha Ming noticed that the room not only contained a couch,

but also a bed. Since he was dirty from his work in the mines, he was pleased to find a small room that contained washing facilities, where he cleaned himself up before collapsing in exhaustion. It was his first time sleeping in months.

Cha Ming calmly cultivated and adjusted his state of mind for the next few days. After almost a year in slavery, he took pleasure in exploring his newfound freedom. His mindset had transformed greatly. Before, he took cultivating for granted. Now he saw it as something that he did willingly and proactively. It was a privilege to improve himself.

After finishing his cultivation session, he drank water from a bowl that always refilled itself and ate a single white pellet. It melted in his mouth like mana from the heavens, and the energy that traveled to his limbs when he ate reassured him that it wasn't just empty calories.

It took a week for Cha Ming to finally relax and relieve the tension in his sore body. After recovering to his peak condition, he didn't dare delay for too long. After all, the villagers were still mining up above, and who knew what kind of tricks Wei Chen would pull once the harvesting was completed. Moreover, he was concerned about the latter's status as vice leader. Who was the leader? Could the activities of the bandit leader be restrained by the oaths of his subordinate?

So Cha Ming had to use every shred of available time to increase his strength. The reason the village was in such a situation was due to his carelessness and compassion. But as the doctor had said, it was his responsibility to make up for his actions and save the villagers.

"Custodian, I'm ready," Cha Ming said to the empty room.

The middle-aged man instantly appeared. Surprisingly, he now wore cultivator robes. Seeing Cha Ming's surprised expression, the Custodian chuckled.

"No need to worry," he said. "I simply surveyed the outside world and studied the culture while you rested. It's interesting to see a world so primitive yet so advanced in the Dao. Often, cultures first discover technology before cultivation."

Then, as though realizing something, the man motioned to the sofa in the common room, and a set of light blue robes appeared. "After looking around, I realized that you were dressed much like a beggar, so I used up a little energy from this facility to craft these new robes for you. They should be a lot more durable than the rags you are wearing, and they will always stay clean. Further, they will provide you some level of defense against the elements and various weapons.

"Everyone out there is so violent nowadays. You could hardly tell this is an angel-controlled material plane. I mean, isn't the whole point of cultivating to seek peace and live forever?"

Cha Ming wasn't sure how to respond, so he took the opportunity to change robes. The fabric felt soft and pleasantly cool. The robes were weaved with a sky-blue material he had never seen before. Even using his full strength, he wasn't able to tear the fabric. The robes were covered in various white and dark blue runes, which made it clear to Cha Ming that the garment was at least a magic treasure.

"There," the Custodian said when Cha Ming walked out of the room. "Now you look like a proper cultivator. These robes should last you during your stay in this material plane. You can change their appearance at will."

"During my stay here?" Cha Ming questioned.

"Oops, I said too much," the Custodian said. "Still, you have karmic threads linking you to individuals outside this material plane. Given your current foundation, I see no reason why you wouldn't surpass the limitations of this realm. In any case, you're as weak as an ant, and there are tens of thousands of existences in this realm that can trample you with impunity. Work hard."

Cha Ming followed the Custodian down a wide hallway that eventually led into a large room containing three large obsidian steles. They were covered in white characters, which he figured were instructions. Beside each stele, he saw a bowl filled with blue liquid and a brush. The stele on the left had the smallest bowl, and the stele on the right had the largest bowl.

"Each stele contains a trial," the man explained. "As part of each trial, you will receive the opportunity to absorb knowledge related to words. Each stele has its own rules. You must past the first stele to proceed to the second, and so on."

Cha Ming nodded and chose the stele on the left. He sat on the meditation cushion provided. As soon as he sat down, he saw the world around him fade, and soon he was surrounded by darkness. The only things he could see were the obsidian stele, the bowl, and the brush.

"First trial, the trial of words," a voice said inside his head. "Words are the basic building block of civilization. Each word provides insight into the Dao and contains a trace of the true nature of heaven and earth. Without words, no one can speak, write, read, or listen. Conversations cannot be held, poetry cannot be created, and stories cannot be read or written. As such, it is necessary to have a sufficient understanding of words for civilization to flourish.

"As part of this trial, you will be shown increasingly complicated runic characters. You may study them as long as required, but you will only have five chances to write out the character. Use the liquified elemental essence in the bowl. You may use the brush provided or your own brush. The pass rate is determined based on the percentage of characters completed. Only basic material plane characters will be tested."

Suddenly, a character appeared in front of him. It was a character he recognized, one that he had used to craft multiple frost talismans with in the past. He summoned the Clear Sky Brush and withdrew all the elemental essence from the bowl, pulling it into the white brush. With the infusion of liquified elemental essence, the two remaining characters of his body-cultivation technique lit up. He was sorely tempted to give up on the test right then and attempt to break through to the Bone Forging Realm.

However, he pushed the thought out of his mind and focused on the task at hand. This was a once-in-a-lifetime opportunity. Liquified elemental essence could be found, but such a chance would disappear forever. He used his brush and quickly painted the familiar character on the obsidian stele.

"First attempt, failure," the voice said coldly. "Four attempts remaining."

Cha Ming frowned, confused. Wasn't this the character that he had painted so many times in the past? This caused him to be very doubtful about the legitimacy of the exam.

No, there must be a reason. Maybe I need to sense the character like I did before.

Cha Ming sent his incandescent force into the lightly

glowing character in front of him. His mind focused on the different pieces of the character. As he gleaned insights from it, the character became increasingly clear in his mind's eye.

After half an incense time, when he felt that he sufficiently understood the character, he tried to paint it once more. His strokes were exactly the same, but this time he attempted to use his soul to imbue the various insights he had gleaned from studying it. The character on the stele glowed brightly, then peeled off the stele and plunged into his mental space, where it hovered joyfully and awaited his whims and wishes.

"Character is satisfactory," the voice intoned. "Proceeding to the next character in sequence." A new character now appeared on the stele, this one relating to fire.

It seems I never truly understood frost after all. Cha Ming sighed inwardly. *But why do I feel like I've only scratched the surface? Why is it that, despite obtaining a satisfactory grade, I feel like there's so much that I didn't understand about it?*

It was clear as day what the library was trying to convey: You can only properly use words you understand. Simply copying them will only produce a weak shadow.

The trial continued, and days passed. Every morning, Cha Ming saw a bowl of water and three white pellets appear in front of him to meet his basic nutritional needs. In the beginning, he could understand and copy 500 characters per day. After the first 5,000, however, the characters became much more obscure, and the time he used increased. The failures increased as well.

Soon enough, three weeks had passed. He sat down calmly, observing the 10,000th character in succession. The past nine characters had required five attempts before he obtained one success. He sweated profusely as he attempted to draw the next character, aware that he was reaching his limits. This would be his last attempt.

He painted the last character as though in a trance, reflecting on the meaning hidden within. The character was one related to a gentle wind. He held his paintbrush and traced the character with gentleness and care. It took fifteen strokes, but these were filled with the various insights he had gleaned over the last three weeks.

With the last stroke, the character glowed brightly like the others before it. Success! It peeled off from the stele and dove into his mental space, joining the 9,999 others before it. The instant it joined the others, each of the ten thousand danced with joy, as though the presence of this last character brought them additional meaning.

Soon, the blackness faded, and he found himself in the room with the three steles. Ten pieces of jade appeared before him. A quick scan of the pieces of jade confirmed their contents: all 10,000 characters he had just learned.

Cha Ming suddenly felt an overwhelming urge to cough. He did so, and ten drops of blood flew out of his mouth and imprinted themselves on the pieces of jade, like a forcefully acquired signature. He now intuitively felt a golden thread of karma connecting him to the building. An *obligation* of sorts.

"Congratulations on perfectly completing the first trial," the Custodian said. "As a reward for a perfect pass, you may choose one of the following items."

Suddenly, a multitude of items were floating in the trial room. Each item had a description floating beneath them. Cha Ming, who had now memorized 10,000 characters, could easily decipher the descriptions. There were various peak-magic weapons, talismans, and formation plates. He even saw several crafting-related items, such as talisman brushes, carving knives, pill cauldrons, and spiritual hammer cores.

Yet Cha Ming was hesitant to pick.

"Is that all?" he asked the Custodian.

The Custodian frowned. "Yes, that is all. Are none of these treasures pleasing to your eyes? They are all peak-magic treasures, and more than a few are well suited to you."

"Would it be possible to obtain liquified elemental essence?" Cha Ming asked shyly. "My cultivation method requires it, and I am currently impoverished. I am a talisman artist with no crafting materials. I have a brush, but no ink or paper. Furthermore, I've noticed that there seems to be an adequate amount in this building."

"Ah!" the Custodian exclaimed. "This is actually very easy to resolve. This library has an elemental-essence-gathering formation. As for paper, I can find a way to make you some. In fact, this is much more convenient for me. I only have a set amount of treasures to give out, and I have no way to replace them. Meanwhile, elemental essence is a renewable resource.

"Just wait until the three trials are over, and I will make sure you are well stocked. I'll reward you based on your performance in all three trials."

Cha Ming was overjoyed. He could now relax and complete the trials without worry.

"Oh, one more thing," the Custodian said. "Since you have perfectly passed the trial, you have been given jade slips containing a record of all you have learned. Since the trial has been of special benefit to you, your obligation is greater than others. Before breaking through to transcendence, you have a karmic obligation to teach ten others the content of these slips. Further, they must all be morally upright individuals. The slips are there to aid you in your teaching endeavors. Once this is accomplished, you will owe Master Fuxi nothing.

"You may now rest before attempting the second trial," the Custodian said before disappearing. The entrance to the hallway appeared once more, allowing Cha Ming to catch up on the sleep he had missed for three weeks.

Chapter 22:
Yu Wen

The next day, Cha Ming returned, fully refreshed. He calmly sat in front of the second obsidian stele, fully prepared to tackle the next challenge. As before, his surroundings faded. However, he was not greeted by pitch blackness. Instead, he found himself at a desk.

Cha Ming was now in a small room. A dozen young men and women were also seated at strange desks. Their hairstyles were very different from what he was used to—some even had blue or green hair. In addition, they wore clothes similar to what the Custodian had initially worn.

A sliding sound instantly brought perfect silence to the room of chattering young adults. A middle-aged woman had just entered the classroom. She wore a pair of spectacles, which he found strange considering none of the children wore them. Her clothes were simple but well maintained, and her tidy, militaristic hair hinted at a rigid personality.

"Welcome to the first lecture on compositions," the woman said. "You have all achieved outstanding grades on the vocabulary unit. As you now know, words hold deep meaning that allows us to harness the secrets of the universe."

It seemed he'd been sent to a classroom for this trial. Would he only have this one chance to learn everything? Also, why would the Custodian send him to learn with a bunch of other constructs? Wouldn't it be easier to teach him the same way as before?

"I would like to take this chance to introduce a temporary transfer student," the instructor said, giving Cha Ming a meaningful look. "He will only be here for one month. Please do your best to help him learn while he's here."

"Yes, teacher!" the students intoned.

"Very well," she continued. "First, I will teach you about addition. Different words bear different meanings in combination with one another. Some words combine easily, while others do not. Can anyone tell me why that is?"

A pretty girl with lightly curled black hair held her hand up to answer.

"Yes, Yu Wen?"

"Word compatibility depends on many factors," the young lady said cheerfully. "First, fueling relationships between elements tend to add better than destructive relationships. In addition, some words are simply well related in an abstract sense. For example, the 'mountain' and 'stream' characters seem incompatible based on elements, but their underlying concepts are not.

"Second, it depends on the user. A user must be compatible with the words used, and different words are compatible with each other because they are compatible within the user. What is possible for one might not be possible for another.

"Third, it depends on intent. Deep emotions can make

certain words compatible with one another. Although this seems closely related to the second principle, it is separate. The second principle involves physical compatibility, while the third principle depends on the individual's will."

"Very good," the teacher said. "Continuing…"

The girl who had just finished speaking, Yu Wen, was seated right beside Cha Ming. Her black curls were in sharp contrast with her pale, jade-like skin[16].

Such a pretty student, he thought. *If she wasn't a construct, I might try befriending her.*

As though sensing his gaze, she looked at him, winked, and motioned her head toward the three-dimensional equivalent of a whiteboard. There, the teacher was writing out the lesson in midair with a brush containing gray ink. It was a similar gray to what he'd seen before on his qi pathways once all the elements were joined.

And so, he spent the next twelve hours participating in an extremely long lesson. Fortunately, it wasn't just a lecture. Sometimes, he participated in group activities. At other times, there was self study. When divided in pairs, he took the initiative to ask Yu Wen, who smiled shyly and accepted his invitation.

Soon enough, class was over. Everyone was free to depart to their homes. The students filed out of the classroom, leaving only Cha Ming and Yu Wen. She was no longer studying. Instead, she was reading a book. He wondered at

---

[16] Jade is not only restricted to the color green. In this context, the jade is white. In China (as well as several other countries in Asia), snow-white skin is a sign of beauty, and dark skin is considered ugly. In fact, many people carry umbrellas on hot summer days to avoid the sun. Instead of using sunscreen, they use whitening sunscreen that will take away any bronzing your skin may have "suffered" in the past.

how sophisticated an artificial intelligence would need to be to enjoy simple pleasures like this.

Unfortunately, time was not Cha Ming's ally. He only had a month to learn as much as he could, and the first day's lesson had already been extremely overwhelming. He could only grumble inwardly and dip his Clear Sky Brush in the pot of elemental essence on his desk and participate in the optional assignments that he could access by toggling through several of the desk's menus.

The current exercise was a sort of fill-in-the-blanks exercise. He would fill in the words he felt were appropriate in context. A few easier questions passed in succession before he was finally confronted with a difficult problem. He thought for a while before painting in a guess on the screen, which crumbled and counted as a single strike.

"You should have used the character for 'acting' instead of 'behaving,'" a soft voice said behind him. It was the pretty girl that he had worked with all day, Yu Wen. He couldn't help but smile when she came over.

"May I?" she asked. Cha Ming nodded, and to his surprise, she grabbed his Clear Sky Brush before leaning over the top of him and painting the character she'd mentioned. "Acting implies deception, while behaving implies knowledge of what's proper. Both indicate a method of action, but the context of the sentence mandates the other."

His face flushed as he looked up at her charming face. She leaned over him, her face turning beet red as she realized the awkward position she was in.

"*Aiya!*" she yipped, scrambling away in embarrassment. "I'm sorry I acted inappropriately. I just love to solve puzzles, and everyone else in the class is so boring and caught up in their own lives. Only you would bother to stay at school and do these kinds of exercises."

Cha Ming found her embarrassed rant amusing. He chuckled. "It's no problem, no problem at all. May I have my brush back?"

Yu Wen suddenly noticed the impropriety and handed it back to him hurriedly.

"I'm so sorry," she said. "I shouldn't just grab people's soul-bound treasures like that. It's the highest form of rudeness."

"Soul-bound treasure?" Cha Ming asked, perplexed.

"*Aiya*, you don't know?" she asked with a shocked look on her face. An impish smile appeared. "If you forgive me, then I'll explain it to you." Her coquettish attitude made Cha Ming blush slightly, and he could only nod while massaging his brow.

Yu Wen ran back to her desk joyfully and pushed it toward Cha Ming. A loud screeching sound like nails on a chalkboard caused him to shiver as it moved. Soon their desks were only a foot apart. She sat down beside him before sighing in satisfaction.

"That's much better," she said. "It's so boring in class with all the desks separated. Now, where was I? Ah, soul-bound treasures. Soul-bound treasures are the rarest of treasures in the universe. They choose their owner, granting him or her many benefits. They tend to grow with their owner as well, provided that they are supplied enough materials.

"Unfortunately, it's not easy obtaining one. There are only a handful of them in the universe, and only those with a strong destiny can inherit them. They are called soul-bound because they will shatter when their owner's soul is destroyed, and their owner's soul will perish if the item is destroyed. Of course, destroying such an item is an extremely difficult feat. Even the ruler of Heaven might not have such formidable power.

"In any case, only the soul-bound partner of the treasure can use it. Having one will surely spark jealousy among many people, but fortunately, most people will just assume that yours is an artificial soul-bound treasure, just like this hairclip."

She pointed to the back of her curly hair, where a green jade hairclip fastened all but her bangs into a loose ponytail.

"Wait a minute, I'm puzzled," Cha Ming said. "Didn't you say that only the soul-bound partner could use it? If you're so certain this is a soul-bound treasure, how could you use mine?"

"It's. A. Secret," she said coyly and buried her face back into her book.

Cha Ming could only sigh.

What an unusual construct. Since his time was limited, Cha Ming continued to study hard and completed a variety of exercises on his desk. He studied all night, and strangely enough, Yu Wen stayed all night as well. She simply sat beside him, reading her book, occasionally correcting his mistakes.

Class resumed the next morning. After receiving several glares from male students in the class and receiving a quizzical look from the teacher due to the proximity of his and Yu Wen's desk, the teacher launched straight into the concept of subtraction.

Unlike addition, subtraction was used to eliminate undesired properties from words. This could either weaken the word or refine the word. Cha Ming realized that this was much like the concept of purposefully weakening a talisman beyond one's reach. It was important to draw the weakening character first so that the intent was known.

Similarly, refining was much like the body refining he had suffered under Guo Jia's pills. After consuming metal, water, and wood pills, the wood, fire, and earth energy in his body had been greatly concentrated and strengthened. The principle took advantage of destructive relationships. Like before, the physical capabilities of the individual and their intent influenced the result.

A week flew by in a flash. Cha Ming spent all his time learning in the classroom during the day and studying at his desk at night. Yu Wen accompanied him and helped him the entire time. No other students in the classroom came to interact with him. He wondered why they were there in the first place. Did it depend on his disposition and preferences? Would they take the initiative to befriend him if it suited his learning style? He had many doubts in his heart, especially after those glares he had received on the second day.

At the end of a class during the second week, Cha Ming felt exhausted. He held his hands on his head as he tried to digest the latest content—geometry. The principle was that shapes, lines, and circles could be used to establish relationships and channel the power of words. There was no limit to the size of these lines and shapes—they could either be the size of insects or span entire cities.

Yet despite their high potential for application in formation arts, talismans, or weaponsmithing, none of these subjects were ever breached. It was as though they were simply teaching concepts and letting the students' imaginations run wild. It was much like engineering school teaching calculus or chemistry.

"You look positively exhausted," a soft voice said. Yu Wen's familiar voice snapped him back to reality, and he looked down at his desk, which was filled with doodles and notes. "What seems to be causing you problems?"

Cha Ming sighed self-deprecatingly. "I'm having a lot of issues learning all these concepts. While they feel simple on the surface, every time I apply them, I feel overwhelmed."

Yu Wen looked at him with pity. "Of course it's very difficult for you to learn. Your soul is barely in the Incandescence Realm, while everyone else in the classroom is leagues ahead of you. Quite frankly, I don't know what they were thinking, arranging for you to transfer to this classroom for one month."

"Still," Cha Ming replied, "I am here and can only learn as much as I can. Even if I can't learn everything to perfection, I can tell that everything here is useful." An awkward silence followed.

"How about I be your personal tutor?" Yu Wen suddenly asked.

"You understand all this?" Cha Ming asked in a surprised manner.

"Of course," she said proudly. "I learned all these things decades ago. I'm only here for fun and to pass the time."

Cha Ming hesitated. "What do you want in return?"

"I just want you to call me Wen Laoshi[17] from now on," she said with an impish grin on her face. "That's fair, isn't it?"

Cha Ming coughed lightly. "Isn't that a bit much?"

Yu Wen said nothing and held her hand in front of her mouth.

"How about I only call you Wen Laoshi *after* school

---

[17] Laoshi means teacher in Mandarin Chinese. Adding laoshi behind someone's name is a formal way of addressing your teacher. Effectively, you admit the other's superiority to you.

hours," said Cha Ming. "This way, I won't make the teacher feel awkward."

"It's a deal!" Yu Wen said. "Now let's see where you were having problems."

And that was how Cha Ming managed to power through two more weeks of school.

It was the last day of class. Cha Ming wasn't sure what would happen once class was over, but he had already been told that there would be no final exam. He took advantage of every moment and continued studying what he was taught. Fortunately, he had managed to stay for the whole lesson segment on grammar. The next lesson segment would be sigils, which he unfortunately would not be able to attend.

Cha Ming regretted not being able to stay to learn more, but he understood that the owner of the library must have had a purpose in limiting class time to only a single month. He guessed that it had to do with testing aptitude or something along those lines.

At the end of class, Yu Wen accompanied him to study. Unlike before, her expression wasn't as excited as usual. Rather, she seemed sad. Although she was only a construct, Cha Ming had come to see her as more than that. He felt that she was an actual person. As such, he guessed that her sulky demeanor had a lot to do with this being his last day.

After studying for a few hours, she let out a deep sigh. "You will be leaving at midnight. That only leaves us a few minutes together. It was very nice studying with you, Cha Ming." A single tear ran down her cheek.

He smiled and used his finger to catch her tear. "It'll be all right," he said reassuringly. "I'm sure you'll find some other good friends after I'm gone." She nodded in response, but it was obvious that she wanted to continue crying.

"Before you leave," she said in a quavering voice, "I want to play a song for you."

"Sure," Cha Ming replied. "What do you play?"

She didn't reply. Instead, she waved her hand and summoned a guqin[18]. It was carved out of pure jade. Resplendent silver strings that shone like the moon were draped across the majestic instrument.

Pluck.

The first note seemed to put him into a trance. He felt as though he was lying by a river in the mountains, beneath a tall oak tree. He quickly realized that he had been dragged into an illusion. He did not struggle. He simply enjoyed this illusion.

As the music continued, Cha Ming slowly drifted into a deep sleep. When the clock in the room struck midnight, the music stopped.

"Congratulations on passing," the excited voice of the Custodian exclaimed. Cha Ming awoke in the usual blue room with a hint of sadness in his eyes.

---

[18] A classical Chinese stringed instrument in the zither family. It is too large to be carried and is played while seated.

"What score did I obtain?" Cha Ming asked blankly.

The Custodian, not noticing his unusual mood, made a hand gesture. Instead of dozens of items, a long, blue candle in a bronze platter appeared.

"You scored eighty-two percent," the Custodian explained. "The prize for obtaining this score at your low cultivation base is ten uses of enlightenment incense. You simply need to burn it, and it will help you meditate on the Dao. It is very useful for creating unique techniques, talismans, weapons. You name it!"

Cha Ming sighed and accepted the candle, drawing it into his Clear Sky World. "Can I ask a question?"

"Of course," the Custodian replied. "What would you like to ask?"

"Why was a simulated classroom used this time?" Cha Ming asked. "Why couldn't I have learned from books? The people there seemed so real, and now that I've left, I feel a little lost."

"It had to be a classroom because some things can't be taught through books," the Custodian replied awkwardly. "Besides, that wasn't a simulated classroom. It was a real classroom, with real people."

Chapter 23: Truth

The truth hit Cha Ming like a sack of bricks. He suddenly felt ashamed at his own stupidity.

All that time that I was in the classroom, all that time I spent with Yu Wen, was real? No wonder she was crying when I left. And all this time, I didn't know. He didn't know where she lived or if he'd ever see her again. Then again, it seemed she knew this. She probably knew they could never meet again.

"The reason you could only stay for one month is because the energy stores in the palace are limited," the Custodian said apologetically. "Your soul was transferred to one of Fuxi School's classrooms in the celestial realm. If this was a transcendent-grade library, I could have extended the duration. Unfortunately, this library is only in a mortal realm, and the energy available is quite pitiful."

Cha Ming closed his eyes to calm down before standing up. "Thank you for telling me, Custodian. I need to go rest before the third trial."

"One moment, young man," the Custodian said. Three jade

slips flew out of his hands, and a drop of blood flew from Cha Ming and imprinted on them. "Your score was exceptional, but not top tier. As a result, you are obligated to teach only three students. You are only required to teach the material which you've mastered, which is imprinted on these jade slips."

Cha Ming nodded in acceptance and went to rest.

Cha Ming's mood improved considerably by the next day. Unfortunately, there was nothing that could be done—he could not return to the classroom, so he would only meet Yu Wen if fate willed it. All he could do was continue and take care of the task at hand. Passing the trial and obtaining the knowledge in Fuxi's Library was of paramount importance in saving the villagers. After all, the better he performed on the third trial, the more liquified elemental essence he could obtain. If he could obtain the capital to complete the first cycle of his Seventy-Two Transformations Technique, the task would no longer be so insurmountable.

"I'll give you a fair warning," the voice of the Custodian said from behind him. "This trial is extremely difficult, especially given your cultivation base and the prowess of your soul. Don't feel too discouraged if you don't do well."

"How long will this trial take?" Cha Ming asked. He was getting increasingly worried about the amount of time he was spending away from the villagers.

"Two months if you are fast, three months if you are slow," the Custodian replied.

"Very well, please activate the third trial," Cha Ming said, seeing the time was still within reasonable limits.

Like before, the world around him faded. This time, there was no darkness, there was no classroom. There was only a pure white space.

Huxian and three wolves residing in his territory trotted proudly as they scaled the mountain to attend the summit. These ambitious followers had proven themselves multiple times over the past months. As such, he had gifted them with compatible cultivation techniques. They had broken through mere days before the summit, a welcome addition to the meager forces at his disposal.

Instead of avoiding the other beasts' territories, he walked through them proudly. In fact, he went out of his way to walk through cat territory and bear territory, wasting no opportunities to upset the bear's staunch supporters. While they yearned to bite back, what could they do? Even king-level beasts wouldn't have half the guts required to challenge Lord Two Tails.

As they climbed, they were joined by multiple other beasts: Demon deer, boars, birds of prey, and insects all gathered under his banner. It was an impressive display, only eclipsed by other king-level figures. In the distance, he saw King Aquatic Moose accompanied by the vast majority of prey-type animals. He also saw Queen Bee leading a veritable army of insects. She had seemingly hidden her strength for a long time. All for this day and her chance for vengeance.

Huxian saw another familiar figure as he neared the peak. It was the geomantic boa and her brood. Their numbers looked to be three times higher than he remembered previously. He wasn't surprised, however. Deception came naturally to those belly draggers. An increase in numbers wasn't the only trump card they had. He noticed a three-colored sheen on the geomantic boa and her three children's fangs, a clear indication that they had successfully cultivated the Triple Lotus Venom Strengthening technique. With this, their attack prowess had surely doubled, increasing Huxian's margin of safety considerably.

Instead of proceeding to the middle of the lord-level beasts, he cut straight to the front. Even the cats, the bears, and the stoats didn't dare say anything in protest. They could all tell instinctively that he was their superior in every way. In fact, he was only a formality away from becoming a king-level existence.

Huxian didn't wait long before a large hundred-foot bear came prowling down from the peak of the mountain where he resided. The bear's gaze swept across kings and lords like a monarch examining his troops. When the bear looked at Huxian, their eyes locked. The demon bear snorted and projected his killing intent toward Huxian, who didn't bat an eyelash. Instead, he yawned. The bear sovereign could only contain his fury and ignore him, continuing to inspect the remaining beasts.

"Welcome, everyone, to this year's summit," the bear announced. As usual, we'll start with the division of territory. Are there any new lords that wish to challenge existing ones to capture their territory?"

The targets of this question were obvious: He was referring to Huxian's three followers and the latest swarm of insects and snakes.

"This humble follower of Lord Two Tails challenges Lord Nightmare Forest Leopard for two thirds of his territory!" the eldest of the wolves beside Huxian yelled.

"This humble follower of Lord Two Tails challenges Lord Swiftwind Jaguar for two thirds of his territory!" the second wolf yelled.

"This humble follower of Lord Two Tails challenges Lord Midnight Panther for two thirds of his territory!" the youngest wolf yelled. Despite being the youngest, he was the most powerful of the trio. His bloodline was slightly stronger than the other two.

The Sovereign's and the savanna lion king's eyes narrowed at when they heard this. This was an open provocation, a deliberate attempt to shift the balance of power. The savanna lion king shot Huxian a murderous look. "It's best not to bite off more than you can chew, little runt. You might become a king-level figure today, but you'll be the lowest of the low."

"Enough with the posturing," Huxian said aggressively. "Will you scaredy-cats fight or surrender? This king doesn't have much time to waste today on petty matters."

"You!" The savanna lion king could barely contain his anger. After all, these three challenges would deprive him of a third of his total territory.

"Fine, if you want a fight, we'll give you one."

The bear looked at the three wolves beside Huxian worriedly. They didn't seem exceptional, but the one beside them was an unfathomable wildcard. He had to curb Lord Two Tails's power, lest the runt overthrow him before they had a chance to kill him during the next human tide.

King Savanna Lion, have your subordinates go for killing blows. If they kill the wolves, I'll take the heat. That fox must not be allowed to gain territory during this summit.

The large feline king had long since thrown his lot in with the Sovereign. Therefore, he complied with great glee. The Sovereign soon received King Savannah Lion's confirmation. Now, he could rest easy.

Unlike the usual tradition, the three battles would take place simultaneously. Huxian did not oppose this; he was sure that the Sovereign would try something dirty this time, so he quietly informed his faithful lapdogs of the circumstances.

"Fight!" the Sovereign bellowed.

The battle began, and the three wolves, a small jaguar, a pitch-black leopard, and an impressive-looking panther went into their fighting stances. The battle was much more vicious than all the past battles between lords of the forest. It was clear that the three wolves were being supressed and could barely defend. Red claw marks quickly appeared on their muzzles and their gray fur coats. Still, they didn't give up and kept fighting back with their all.

"You should call off your little mutts if you don't want them to die," the lion king said, gloating. "After all, claws and teeth don't have eyes in the thick of battle. It's difficult to control one's attacks when faced with life and death."

You said it, Huxian said, chuckling inwardly. Then he looked toward the three wolves. *Keep up the good work, boys!*

Keep showing that same opening, right at your jugular. Act on my mark!

Suddenly, the battle took a turn for the worse. All three cats simultaneously lashed out with vicious claws. Each of them was different—Lord Swiftwind Jaguar's claws were veritable sickles of wind, the sharpest and most vicious of all the elements. Nightmare Forest Lord's claws shone with a blackish-green tint, clearly poisoned. Meanwhile, Midnight Panther Lord's claws were more subdued and deceptive. They were laced with the power of darkness, and it was clear that avoiding them was now a matter of life or death.

"Foul play!" the geomantic boa roared when he saw these three lethal attacks. But the Sovereign pretended he didn't hear or see anything.

Huxian grinned when he saw the lethal attacks. *Use it now!*

Suddenly, a vicious light appeared in each of the three wolves' eyes. Their round blue pupils shifted and became dark narrow slits. Their irises took on a yellow hue and now appeared like the eyes of a basilisk. The audience gasped in shock when they saw this development. Were these truly wolves?

The three cat beasts weren't amazed, however—they were petrified. They paused mid-strike due to their crippling fear, and before they knew it, they were paralyzed in this position. The wolves wasted no time and did what wolves did best: They bit at the cats' necks without any hesitation. Their sharp execution led to a swift reversal of positions. After taking a deep bite, they tossed the three cat corpses on the ground and proceeded to chew on their corpses.

"Impudent wretches!" the savanna lion king roared, jumping in front of the corpses of his followers, the presence of a king radiating down on the three wolves. They had no choice but to cower in fear. However, they didn't have to wait long before Lord Two Tails's radiant aura burst out, and he jumped in front of the savanna lion king.

"Oh?" Huxian barked. "I'd like to see why you think my subordinates are being impudent."

"This was a friendly battle for territory, but your lapdogs went for killing blows!" the lion king roared indignantly. "There is a strict rule on this mountain against killing, and your followers have broken it. I demand their deaths."

Huxian chuckled. "How convenient. You and I both know that your minions simultaneously went for killing blows against these three brave wolves. It was only due to their good luck that I passed them all a skill as a trump card for insurance. They originally didn't plan on activating it, but seeing as your cats were disregarding the rules, they had no choice but to act. And now you have the face to argue against me?

"Since all three acted at the same time, it was clearly a premeditated act. As a punishment, I demand that the full territory of these three cats be handed to my wolf lords as compensation."

"You!" The lion king was boiling over with rage. Fortunately for him, the Sovereign came to his rescue.

"This is a very serious charge, Lord Two Tails," the Sovereign said solemnly, seemingly impartial. "This Sovereign did not see any such treacherous acts from the cats. Furthermore, it's the cats that have died. This truly calls into question whose act was premeditated."

"Shameless!" Huxian roared. "So if this cat's minions want to kill mine, I should have them wash their necks and prepare for death? I see that there is a severe double standard at work here."

The Sovereign's eyes narrowed. "This is a grave accusation, little one. You had better think twice before laying down this kind of challenge."

"I support this challenge!" the geomantic boa yelled.

I support this challenge! the Celestial Rainbow Queen Bee said mentally to everyone present.

The bear sovereign gazed at these beasts coldly, unsurprised by their insubordinate behavior.

"I support this challenge!" another voice yelled out. It was surprisingly the moose king. The moose king was usually the most passive of the kings. However, this time he stepped out to support the challenge against the cats.

The surrounding animals weren't stupid. It was clear that things were not going smoothly for the cats and that a new faction was emerging and challenging the Sovereign's ruling.

"Very well," the Sovereign announced. "The challenge will proceed. Do you have any proof to offer?"

"I saw what happened with my very eyes," the geomantic boa slithered. "In fact, I yelled out about it, but no one took my warning to heart. This queen's heart feels wounded at this neglect." As the most powerful queen, the geomantic boa's words held huge sway.

"This is still all hearsay," the bear said calmly. "Do you have actual proof?"

"How convenient," Huxian interjected. "If they had killed my wolf brothers, you would have denied any wrongdoing and asked for proof. Now that they are dead, I need proof that the cats tried to kill them first. Truly an impartial sovereign."

"Impudence!" the savanna lion king, the brown bear king, the panther king, and the stoat king roared. Meanwhile, the turtle king, the eagle king, and the badger king stood by. These were neutral existences that never took sides.

Suddenly, a soft coughing sound emerged within the minds of all the beasts. Everyone turned to stare at a non-descript owl. "I have a way to shed light on this situation, if these kings wouldn't mind this humble lord's interjection."

"What proof could you possibly offer?" the lion king shouted.

"Seconded!" Huxian yelled.

"Seconded!" the geomantic boa slithered.

"Seconded!" the queen bee buzzed.

"Seconded!" the moose king roared.

Seeing this support, the Sovereign had no choice but to concede. He looked at the owl with disdain.

"This is serious business. If you can't prove the results beyond a shadow of a doubt, I'll still give you a chance to withdraw. Otherwise, you won't be able to escape punishment."

The owl ruffled his feathers when he heard this. "I'm confident in my abilities!" Then, he bravely hopped up beside the bear sovereign, and a three-dimensional projection of the battle was thrown up into the sky.

"This is my inherent ability," the owl said proudly. "I can replay any scene that I've seen. Notice that until now, no one has truly landed any killing blows, and the battle is one-sided."

They continued watching the battle, until finally, the three cats launched attacks all at once.

"Notice how their claw attacks are all swiftly directed at the wolves' jugulars, and all with precise timing," the owl explained. "The wolves are apparently defenseless. Most abilities would be useless to defend against this. Now, moving along, notice how the wolves activated their abilities in retaliation. The end result is evident given the three corpses beside us. This humble

servant will not pass judgement, but the result seems clear."
The owl then fluttered away immediately and floated behind
Huxian. His stance was clear as well.

"Stop being shameless and pass the verdict," the geomantic
boa slithered. Her brood also began slithering as a group,
giving the most powerful queen an ominous backdrop.

The Sovereign's expression was one of cold fury. "Very well,
the result is clear. All of these three rebellious cats' territories
will go to these noble wolf lords as compensation. Are you
satisfied?"

Huxian nodded and looked tauntingly at the savanna lion
king, who could barely contain his temper.

"Are there any *other* lords who wish to make a challenge?"
the bear sovereign asked, not bothering to hide his imposing
presence. Despite his best efforts, several small figures stood up
to challenge. Unsurprisingly, it was twelve snakes, followers of
the geomantic boa.

"I challenge Lord Unrivaled Stoat!" one yelled.

"I challenge Lord Skulking Ferret!" another yelled.

One by one, they challenged all twelve lords of the stoat
family. After the insects and snakes, the stoats were most
numerous. Unlike last time, they did not fight all at once, and
the stakes were much lower. Each snake only challenged the
stoats for one third of their land, the minimum amount.

It took a good hour for all of the challenges to finish, and
by the end of it, half the challengers had won, leading to only a
mild exchange in territory. The stoats and ferrets had all been
poisoned in their battles.

"Since this is a friendly match, I will give you all the antidote
after the summit ends," the geomantic boa said in a nonchalant
voice. Since he had taken the initiative, the stoat king and his

minions could only choke back their tears. The poison wasn't lethal, at least not for the next few hours.

The Sovereign massaged his temple with his paws. "Does anyone else want to challenge?"

Fortunately, the swarm of insect lords didn't issue any challenges. Two bear lords issued challenges to two bee lords, who eventually lost half of their negligible territory.

"Now then, since all these petty disputes are settled, it's time to welcome a new king of the forest, King Two Tails!" the Sovereign announced.

Chapter 24: Sovereign

The sea of demonic beasts spoke in hushed whispers as Huxian stepped up. His black-and-white appearance was regal, befitting of a true king of the forest. Even many of the other kings couldn't help but lower their heads instinctively.

"King Two Tails, as a king of the forest, you will be allocated a portion of the forest's territory depending on your rank and merit," the Sovereign said gravely. "In exchange, it's your responsibility to protect all those beneath you during every human tide. Do you accept?"

"Of course I accept," Huxian said proudly. "It's my duty to protect all the spirit beasts on this mountain, even those I dislike. I will even protect the lion king if he's in a pinch."

"Your enthusiasm is commendable," the Sovereign said. "We will all count on you to make this mountain stronger. Since you are the most junior member, and your current territory and that of your underlings is sufficient, you will not be gaining any extra territory. Would you like to challenge anyone?"

Huxian shook his head. "There is no need. I'm satisfied with what I have. I only seek to protect my brother beasts." Mumbles of approval in the sea of beasts ensued.

"Such a king lacking in ambition is not deserving of his territory," the savanna lion king said, cutting the moment of appreciation short. "I challenge King Two Tails to regain the territory of my subordinates."

The group of demonic felines behind him hissed, reinforcing his menacing atmosphere.

"Are you sure you wish to do this?" the Sovereign asked, frowning. "Sometimes it's best not to let your anger cloud your judgement."

The lion king shook his head. "I refuse to let him do as he pleases. He is unlawful with no regard to his seniors. Someone has to discipline him, and that someone may as well be me!"

The bear sighed. "Very well. Do you accept his challenge, King Two Tails?"

"How can I not accept the challenge of this pompous buffoon?" Huxian said. "Leaving his territory in his incapable hands is a wasteful use of nature's riches. This territory will be much safer under this king's supervision."

"Very well," the Sovereign said. "Proceed to the battle platform to fight."

Lord-level battles could be performed on the spot, but the potential for collateral damage in king-level battles mounted significantly, so they proceeded to the peak of the mountain. Huxian widened his eyes when he saw that the "battle platform" was an immense slab of jade. It was covered in all sorts of runic lines that he could barely understand. At a glance, he could tell that no matter how hard they fought, the jade slab would remain intact.

"Are you ready?" the Sovereign asked. Huxian and the lion

instantly assumed their combat stances. "Fight!"

As soon as the words left his mouth, the two king-level figures became a veritable blur. Only the other kings of the forest could see them, and even then it was difficult. After all, cats and foxes were known for their speed. Despite having just broken through to the middle of the Purification Realm, Huxian could still match him blow for blow.

"How boring!" Huxian said, taunting the savanna lion king.

Not wanting to be outdone, the lion king drew on the heaven and earth energy of the mountain, causing every strand of fur, his teeth, his claws, and his glorious mane to become coated in a film of gold energy. He then clashed with Huxian with renewed vigor.

To Huxian's surprise, his opponent's speed didn't drop despite the substantial increase in weight and power. Instead, it increased. The lion king used his increased muscular strength to unleash his power to the max. If he had been a lesser-spirit beast, Huxian would have had a difficult time.

"Nice one!" Huxian said mid-combat. "Now I'll need to use a full fifth of my strength to defeat you!"

The crowd gasped when they heard this arrogant claim.

"Is he courting death?" a bear asked. "How could he be so bold?"

"A young cub doesn't know the immensity of heaven and earth," the stoat king snorted.

However, the neutral spirit beasts' well-honed senses noted a sharp increase in Huxian's speed. In addition, the small fox's bloodline power erupted with full force, causing most of the kings on the mountain to tremble. Even the Sovereign couldn't help but shiver.

Huxian used the impact of his bloodline to dart between the

savanna lion king's paws and appear behind him. He then bit deeply into the back of the cat's neck and threw him down on the platform like a pathetic kitten being scolded by his mother. The lion collapsed into a mangled heap, barely breathing. The battle was over.

"You were lucky I showed mercy and only want this mountain to be stronger," Huxian said disdainfully. "However, I'll gladly accept your tribute of territory. Perhaps the life of a pauper will teach you a well-deserved lesson."

The entire crowd, including the Sovereign, were greatly shocked by the tremendous display of power. The mountain became so quiet one could hear a leaf drop. Many of the neutral kings, who had been ambivalent about the addition of a new king, started looking favorably on the young pup King Two Tails.

"Anyone else?" the Sovereign asked. Seeing no response, he continued with the meeting. "The next item on the agenda is the human tide. I have received a message from the humans, where they state that they will be sending out mid-level foundation establishment experts. Therefore, all the kings in the forest will need to be on guard this time around."

"Why the sudden change?" a timid porcupine lord asked amongst the whispering demon beasts.

"I do not know the reason," the Sovereign said gravely. "However, this has happened two times in the past. Unfortunately, I am unable to participate. All I can do is warn all the beasts on the mountain to protect themselves and hide to minimize losses. We will move on, and they will leave when they are satisfied with their gains."

All the kings in the forest grumbled with discontent. However, one voice dared to speak up.

"What a load of hogwash," Huxian said loudly.

"Excuse me?" the Sovereign asked menacingly. "Would you care to repeat what you said?"

"I said it's a load of hogwash," Huxian said proudly. "Your strategy of dividing us up is deplorable, and tantamount to treachery. We lose countless beasts every year because you instruct us to spinelessly hide and not support each other. Not just that, you are conveniently excused from this scuffle. Have you no shame?"

The Sovereign's eyes narrowed. "I have nothing but the best interests at heart for every beast in this mountain. How dare you accuse me of treachery."

"If only it was just an accusation," Huxian continued, sighing. One of his tails glowed, and a small mouse darted out and landed on his back. "Everyone, I have an announcement to make. My subordinate Lei Jiang overheard a conversation between the bear sovereign and a human cultivator during the last human tide. He colluded with the humans and leaked my existence and location. As a result, they ambushed me immediately after with twenty cultivators. Later, they were joined by twenty more. It was only with the assistance and cooperation of many of the beasts here that I managed to survive!"

"How dare you!" the bear roared, growling menacingly. "I've treated you so well, yet you have the guts to accuse me of treachery? Kings, seize him! We don't need a beast like him on the mountain."

The brown bear king and the panther king immediately walked up, and some of the fence-sitters also reacted. The eagle king circled overhead while the badger king stood up on his hind paws, revealing vicious claws.

"You think you can do anything you want because you are the mountain sovereign?" a voice slithered. The geomantic boa pulled up beside Huxian, glaring at the other four menacingly. "I've seen his proof, and it's beyond a doubt. You are a traitor to this mountain, and we've had enough of your ways."

"Right," the queen bee said, bringing her horde of drones. "You've suppressed me by stealing my honey all this time, stopping a sovereign-level beast from maturing. If I had been able to evolve, our mountain's strength would have increased greatly. You're just a cowardly bear that relies on the humans to clean up any threats to your rule."

"I have also seen this proof," the moose king said, walking up beside Huxian. "The Sovereign's acts are deplorable, and he must be deposed."

"I will support my master," Lei Jiang yelled while releasing his aura. Surprisingly, despite being a low purification beast, the aura he emanated matched that of a middle purification beast. Their forces were evenly matched.

The bear king looked around, but unfortunately, the turtle king didn't move. Meanwhile, the savanna lion king could do nothing to help; he lay prone on the side, licking his wounds. The stoat king looked like he wanted to speak up, but he was immediately shut down by a menacing glare from the geomantic boa. The threat was obvious: If you speak up, I won't give you the antidote to your minions, and they will all perish. The geomantic boa's devious ploy had come to fruition.

"It seems we're at an impasse," the Sovereign said calmly. "However, who will you nominate as sovereign? There are no upper purification realm beasts aside from myself. It will be difficult for you to protect this mountain without me."

"You need not concern yourself with this, traitor," Huxian

growled. "I challenge you for sovereignty of this mountain in a battle to the death. Our other forces are evenly matched. Whoever wins, the others will follow. This is the ancient law that has been passed down by our ancestors."

The Sovereign looked at Huxian's supporters. "Are you agreeable to this condition?"

One by one, the other beasts nodded.

"Very well, I shall kill this pup and teach you all humility!"

It didn't take long for all the beasts on the mountain to congregate around the giant jade slab. Every beast, whether they were insects, birds, mammals, or reptiles paid close attention. After all, their destiny would be determined by the winner of this single battle.

"Are you ready?" the Sovereign asked. "When you die, I want to make sure no one thinks I relied on trickery."

Huxian snorted and split his body into his two black and white clones. "I was born ready. I'll even give you the chance to attack first."

The bear sovereign's eyes narrowed. "You've truly hidden yourself deeply. However, I refuse to believe that this sovereign, who has achieved the late purification realm, can be thwarted by a mid-level runt like yourself."

The black rune-covered bear stood up on its hind paws, its hundred-foot frame looking down on all the beasts present. Like Huxian, it chose not to hide its strength any longer. One by one, the silver runes on its body lit up and glowed in a soft green color, not unlike the jade platform beneath them.

Huxian gulped. *Is he drawing from the jade platform to cause his bloodline to evolve? Does that mean that I'm no longer fighting a normal late-purification beast, but a variant beast instead?*

The demons in the world were known for their adaptability. As such, it wasn't unusual for variant beasts to rear their ugly heads. However, this meant that the challenge for sovereignty had just become a deadly crisis for Huxian.

The bear, who had grown to a height of 150 feet, stomped his paw down as soon as the last jade rune on his body lit up. Huxian was suddenly overwhelmed with a gravitational field ten times greater than normal. According to his senses, this field encompassed the entire jade platform, making it impossible for Huxian to ignore this suppression. Huxian's white clone activated its purification aura, but the gravitational pull was too difficult to ignore. He could only halve its suppression, and only for his white half.

You say you're upright, but you play dirty. He gritted his teeth, and both his clones began attacking the bear in tandem, carefully avoiding the vicious swipes of the bear's paws. Even Huxian's unreasonably tough body would have trouble defending against such overwhelming strength.

His two clones expertly dodged the two paws. His white clone, the least affected by the extra gravity, leaped up and tried to bite the bear's knees. As he bit down, however, his mouth ached as one of his teeth cracked. He swiftly retreated after barely drawing blood.

I feel like I've bitten into a block of immortal jade. This is too unreasonable, too unfair! His white clone could only begin looking for weaknesses on this seemingly invincible bear.

"Do you now see the gap in power between us?" the bear yelled with glee. "No matter how hard you bite, you'll never be able to do more than draw a little blood. In fact, I heal faster than you can damage me!"

Huxian witnessed the truth of his words when the small

bite mark he had inflicted swiftly regenerated.

It's all up to my shadow form now.

Unfortunately, his shadow form wasn't faring much better. Despite being able to directly attack the bear's shadow, it seemed like the bear had somehow reinforced it. It wasn't pitch black like most shadows but contained a greenish hue. Meanwhile, it could still be affected by the bear's attacks. The ten-times increase in gravity affecting his clone was no laughing matter.

Let's try my newest abilities, Huxian thought. *I sure hope this works.* His shadow form instantly dissolved, covering the jade platform in an inky substance. From this substance, shadowy awls suddenly darted out, threatening to pierce the bear.

The bear sovereign swung his paws fiercely to try and deflect them, to no avail. Unfortunately, they bounced off his skin harmlessly. Then, they snaked around his arms and legs and restrained his movements. The bear sovereign roared as he used his entire strength to attempt to free himself.

Meanwhile, Huxian was feeling the impact from every jerk of the bear's massive body. He couldn't hold on for very long under the strain. After all, both his clones were part of his true self, and injuring one was the same as injuring the other.

Seeing that the bear was trapped for the time being, Huxian's white clone began shining like the sun. Around him, eight glowing sigils sprang to life and began absorbing all light in the surrounding area. He was clearly charging up for a fierce attack.

The bear's eyes narrowed when he saw the bright glow, and he redoubled his efforts. His every attempt to move resulted in cracks forming on the black chains.

I can't let this attack hit me or I'm done for!

Seeing that the situation wasn't looking good, he initiated a technique that was taboo for all demon beasts: burning his blood essence.

Blood essence was far more precious for a demon beast than a human. Every amount lost not only decreased one's power, but also lowered the strength of one's bloodline. He had struggled for many centuries to upgrade his previously pitiful bloodline of a silver-runed black bear. It was all thanks to the insights he'd gleaned from the jade platform that his bloodline was able to undergo a quantitative leap.

Burning his blood essence would mean that after this fight, he would require many natural treasures and dozens of years to recover his power. Yet, if he didn't do it, death awaited him.

With his newfound strength, his muscles bulged, and one of the chains holding him down shattered into motes of shadow. Three more chains followed, and finally, he roared and unleashed his power to the maximum. The chains shattered and agglomerated into a pitiful black fox coughing blood.

However, he didn't have time to deal with the shadow clone. Instead, he began building up energy to resist the incoming blow. Light was too difficult to dodge for him. He was a slow but powerful demon beast, and he knew to play to his strengths. With but a thought, his front paws glowed jade green in preparation for executing his trump card—Jade Executioner!

Huxian coughed out a mouthful of blood as his shadow clone was forced to revert to its original form.

Not good. I'm not sure if I can take this guy if he can defend himself. He had thought about unleashing his beam prematurely, but before he knew it, a jade glow appeared on the bear's front paws. Huxian scoured his genetic memories but could find nothing like this ability.

It must be a self-created ability. That bear is a lot shrewder than I gave him credit for. Two more tense breaths passed as both beasts built up power to unleash a devastating strike. The surrounding beasts held their breath. They knew that this attack would surely decide the victor.

Suddenly, the eight sigils surrounding Huxian congregated near his mouth and fused together into a tiny point. The bear's eyes narrowed. He brought his claws out to defend with all his might.

Eight-Sigil Light Beam!

Jade Executioner!

The explosion of white and green pushed back all the nearby beasts. They had wished to see the final outcome, but their vision was obscured by clouds of dust. Then, little by little, the clouds faded. Both the white and the black Huxian had blood leaking from their five orifices[19].

The bear sovereign was breathing raggedly, and various cuts could be found covering his entire body. Three of his claws had broken in the process of blocking Huxian's monstrous

---

[19] Two ears, two nostrils, and one mouth.

attack. In addition, it seemed like his regenerative abilities were having difficulty healing him. Yet, upon closer observation, the bear's vital areas were all intact.

"You lose, little fox," the bear sovereign exclaimed. "Now be a nice pup and go to sleep."

As the bear approached, many of the beasts allied with Huxian offered to help bail him out. Lei Jiang was poised to evacuate his master at a moment's notice. However, Huxian swiftly sent a mental message to all of them. As injured as he was, he still had one last resort he would use. He was just hesitant to use it, since it would delay his progress for over a year.

Oh well, no sense in moaning about it. On the bright side, it'll give Cha Ming a chance to catch up. That guy's talent is so terrible it's not even funny.

This thought removed the last bit of hesitation from Huxian's mind. He gazed upward, looking at the bear's menacing jade paws, which were about to crash down on him.

Unfortunately, this ability of his couldn't be used for very long. If his timing was slightly off, he would perish instead. So he waited until an ominous glint appeared in the bear's eyes and his paws came crashing down. In only a tenth of a breath, he would be smashed into a meat patty.

Now!

Both of Huxian's clones suddenly disappeared, and the jade platform was cloaked in pitch-black darkness. No one could see anything, and it was like a tank of water had suddenly been filled with a giant glob of ink.

After a breath of time had passed, however, everyone became aware of a faint glow where Huxian's body had once been. It didn't look anything like a fox, but rather like a small bead of concentrated sunlight.

A loud shout alerted everyone to the name of this technique: *Light in the Darkness.* The ball of light flashed toward the bear sovereign, who didn't have a chance to defend. It dove into one of his eye sockets and came out the back of his head.

As suddenly as the darkness had appeared, it disappeared entirely, leaving behind a single black-and-white fox. Huxian, exhausted from the fierce battle, collapsed on the stage. The winner was clear. The large black bear, who now had a hole passing through his head where his beast crystal would normally reside, fell to the ground in a dead heap of demon-beast meat.

Lei Jiang darted to the side of his master protectively. "Step out of the way," a slithering voice said coldly.

"I refuse," Lei Jiang shouted. You can get my master over my dead body!"

A puzzled look suddenly appeared on the geomantic boa's face. "Oh, you misunderstand, little one. We were going to bow to our new sovereign, but there's no way we can stand by bowing to a little shrimp like you."

The small mouse looked around and saw earnest expressions on all the nearby beasts. All beasts, no matter if they were demon beasts, spirit beasts, or god beasts, obeyed the strong. Lei Jiang let out a sheepish laugh and scampered off to the side. Then he joined all the nearby beasts in bowing to their new sovereign.

A new sovereign who would lead them against the human cultivators and would help these beasts defend what was rightfully theirs: their home on the mountain.

Chapter 25: Sigil

Gong Lan wiped the sweat off her brow as she admired the freshly swept bridge behind her. It was white like alabaster, a clear contrast to the lush greenery and the clear blue sky up above. She was proud at having managed to sweep the bridge in its entirety.

Turning around, she took her first step onto the emerald-green grass. When her bare feet touched the grassy carpet, a cooling sensation ran up her legs and released all the tension that had accumulated during her full day of sweeping.

She took another step, plunging her entire body into the calming shadow beneath the bodhi tree. The few worries that remained in her mind after sweeping the bridge vanished instantly. They were replaced by clarity, and her self-criticism transformed to thoughts of self-reflection.

She continued walking for a short time before arriving near the front of the crowd, where several monks and animals peacefully sat in meditation. There, even lions and antelopes could sit together in peace, so she followed suit and sat cross-legged as well. As soon as she shut her eyes, the soft sound of mantras that emanated from the wind whispered to her through the leaves of the bodhi tree.

You've finally resolved the memories that cause you the most problems, a small voice said inside her head. *What will you do now?*

Oddly enough, the voice didn't trouble her. It simply triggered peaceful self-reflection.

I'm not sure what I should do, she thought. *It seems that whenever I do things, I cause people to suffer. I also cause myself to suffer as well.*

That's right, the voice replied. *Whatever you do, you will cause suffering for someone or something. More importantly, you will cause suffering for yourself. You have accumulated far too much negative karma in this life. Your actions cannot help but reap it. As you are now, you would cause more harm than good regardless of your intentions.*

Gong Lan paused as she contemplated this notion. At the same time, it made her feel rather helpless. Was there no way for her to interact with the world without causing one death after another? Would she simply have to hide herself away from the world and do nothing?

There is a way, if you are willing, the voice said. *The problem is due to the karma you've accumulated. Since that's the case, if you are willing, you can suffer your karma here, little by little, under my protective shadow. It will be painful, but it will soothe your soul.*

Gong Lan hesitated. *Are you the bodhi tree?*

I have been called this by some, the voice replied.

How long will this process take? she asked.

It could take a day, or it could take a lifetime, the voice replied. *Your progress will only depend on yourself. First, it will depend on your willingness to face your past misdeeds, whether intentional or unintentional. Then it will depend on your willingness to admit your wrongs and beg forgiveness. Finally, it will depend on your willingness to change.*

She thought about her current counterproductive state before making a swift decision. "I accept," she said softly, breaking the silence surrounding her. The ones around her didn't hear it, however, as they were all entranced and in deep contemplation. Only one being heard her, and that was the spirit of the tree.

Bear with it, my child, the tree whispered to Gong Lan. Then, the inside of Gong Lan's mental space was covered in a soft yellow light. Her soul let out an agonizing wail that no one could hear. She could only sit under the shadow of the bodhi tree and suffer in silence.

The familiar atmosphere in the world of white was very comforting to Cha Ming. It gave him a feeling of control, a certain confidence in his abilities. He waited patiently in the world of white for what seemed like hours.

Finally, he heard footsteps in the distance. He looked over and was surprised to see an old man with gray hair wearing a green Daoist robe. The man carried himself with grace, giving the impression that he was a natural-born sovereign. Yet despite this innate mightiness, Cha Ming felt no pressure from the man. Instead he found only gentleness and care.

The man walked over to where Cha Ming was seated, leaving him no choice but to stand up and bow in greeting. The old man smiled at the polite gesture.

"Have a seat, my young friend," the man said while waving his hand. A surge of white mist traveled from his fingers, and a short table with two cushions appeared. This greatly surprised Cha Ming, who thought that he alone could manipulate his mental space. "I don't often get to meet people from the younger generation. Welcome to my library, young man. I am Fuxi."

The revelation left Cha Ming in a daze. After all, Fuxi was a legendary figure, an emperor credited with creating humanity along with Nuwa. He seated himself but couldn't help but doubt the man's identity.

"No doubt you are confused about why someone so prominent as myself would come meet you in person," the old man said understandingly. Then, seeing Cha Ming nod, the old man chuckled. "Your honesty is appreciated. I am, in fact, only a fragment of Fuxi's soul. Each of these libraries that I established throughout the universe carry a small fragment. A conservative estimate is that I have millions of such avatars. Fragments like myself exist solely to educate and test those who come into the library and will continue to do so as long as my main body lives."

"My apologies for doubting you, Senior," Cha Ming said. "Please allow me to pour you tea to repent." With but a thought, a steaming pot of water appeared in front of Cha Ming. He then imagined the best tea he had ever tasted—coincidentally one that Wang Jun had poured for him—and prepared two small cups using a gaiwan[20]. He did this over a wet tea table that he

---

[20] A small lidded bowl without a handle used to brew tea leaves in small quantities.

summoned in conjunction with the tea set.

Fuxi waited patiently for him to serve the tea before knocking his index and middle finger twice[21] on the table and receiving his cup. He inhaled deeply, savoring the smell, and then drank a small sip.

"It's been so long since I've drank tea from a material plane," Fuxi said appreciatively. "These leaves are definitely some of the better ones among those I've tasted across the aeons. Tell me, do you like music, young man?"

"All kinds," Cha Ming replied.

"Good, then I'll summon some ambiance music for us," Fuxi said. He then snapped his fingers, and a single blue guqin appeared beside them and began playing itself. It was as though a phantom master musician had appeared and began playing for them. Cha Ming soon found himself lost in the process of brewing and drinking tea and enjoying the music. He had no idea know how much time passed.

"Cha Ming, it's good to take time to calm down every once in a while," Fuxi said softly. "Otherwise, you will burn yourself out."

Cha Ming didn't find it odd in the slightest that the man knew his name.

"It's not like I've been left with much of a choice," Cha Ming said helplessly. "There are people relying on me, and I must learn all I can before going to help them." The villagers up above needed his help, and if he didn't hurry, he could only imagine their fate.

"You misunderstand me, Cha Ming," Fuxi said. "Right now, you rested while drinking tea and listening to music. Much of

---

[21] This is a traditional way to thank the one preparing tea. It's not overly formal.

the tension you've accumulated over these past months has dissipated. You're sure to be of much better help to them now that you've rested.

"Sometimes it only takes an incense time or an hour to show sufficient care for yourself. But many people still don't bother. So no matter what anyone says, that is a choice that you can make, regardless of what's happening around you. It's a matter of attitude."

Cha Ming took in a deep breath and pondered these words as he continued brewing and drinking.

"Now then, for the last trial," Fuxi said suddenly.

Cha Ming put his cup down, and the table and tea disappeared. The calming guqin music stayed, however.

"As I'm sure you've guessed by now, the first step to language is the use of words. Words describe many things, and we abbreviate them with runes. We then use our knowledge of their relationships and relate them through grammar and geometry. However, it is still an abbreviation. It is far from the truth.

"The meaning of words is best expressed through sigils. These are three-dimensional constructs, much like the three engraved in your chest. However, the requirements for crafting them is very strict. Like runes, a cultivator can only write what he knows. It is very taxing on the soul and qi to trace out sigils, which is why this exercise is taking place in your mental space. It will allow you to partially exceed the limits of your qi.

"Unfortunately, nothing I do can make you surpass the limits of your soul. As such, this trial will be immensely difficult, but the benefits to your future cultivation will be staggering." Fuxi then materialized a gray brush in his hands. It was plain and unadorned, but Cha Ming could sense that it was a frighteningly powerful artifact.

"Try to follow my motions," Fuxi said.

A small stream of liquified elemental essence poured out from the brush as Fuxi slowly painted a sigil. As Cha Ming observed, he noticed that it was a very familiar character. It gave the impression of a solid tree and fluttering leaves and exuded an aura of rich vitality despite being incomplete. It only took the man an incense time to complete the full sigil. Its base form seemed to be the character for wood, however, it was a hundred times more complex than the simplified sigil he'd drawn before. Once the sigil was complete, it began glowing with a vivid green color.

"Now it's your turn," he said, motioning to Cha Ming. "We will repeat this process three times for each of the characters being tested. At your level, I suggest not pushing yourself to complete it. Instead, focus on gaining insights from the sigils you draw."

Cha Ming gulped but soon took out his Clear Sky Brush. Noticing that it was missing liquified elemental essence, he dipped the brush in the bowl that appeared beside him. Real or false, he would use this essence to complete the trial.

Instead of striving for perfection, Cha Ming decided to start off improving on what he had imagined previously as a suitable base for the wood sigil. He began drawing leaves, but now he combined them with vines and bark. Even so, there were many pieces of the sigil that he couldn't fathom and thus couldn't draw. For example, on one part of Fuxi's sigil, he sensed an aura of death and decay. How could these abstract concepts be painted so easily? Before long, he finished a simplified but slightly improved version of the wood sigil he had drawn as part of the Seventy-Two Transformations Technique.

"Not bad!" Fuxi said. "Let's try again."

They repeated the process twice, and Cha Ming's wood sigil grew increasingly complex. They then moved on through the other four material elements—wind and lightning and through a multitude of other sigils.

Weeks passed, and soon the number of tiny, incomplete sigils he'd painted numbered almost a thousand. He began realizing that many of them could be joined together if he so chose, like pieces of a great puzzle. When he explained this epiphany to Fuxi, the older man simply laughed and told him he wasn't wrong.

Finally, after many months, Cha Ming began his last feeble attempt at the 10,000th sigil. It didn't even materialize. Instead it crumbled, as Cha Ming's understanding could not support even the most rudimentary form of the character.

"Don't be discouraged," Fuxi said, seeing Cha Ming's sad expression. "It's only natural that you can't complete it. Truth be told, it would take someone at the peak of core formation to even stand a chance. Their soul would need to be a single step away from breaking through transcendence."

Fuxi then stood up, and Cha Ming anxiously rose with him. It was about time for Cha Ming to leave, and who knew if he would be able to meet the legendary man again. He clasped his hands together and bowed deeply in thanks.

But when he rose up, Fuxi was gone. His white mental space was completely blank, like it had originally been. The message the man was trying to convey was clear: There was no need for thanks. The man was simply doing what he felt was right—spreading his knowledge throughout humanity. He was just like the legends described, selflessly teaching mankind the tools it needed to survive.

Cha Ming awoke shortly after Fuxi left. After traveling back to his body from his mental space, he realized he was famished. His body was also stiff, as though he hadn't moved in months. *Had* it been months? The only way to be certain would be to ask the Custodian.

"Congratulations on completing the trial," a pleasant voice said from behind him. The Custodian soon walked around him at a leisurely pace and set down a bowl full of white pellets. Cha Ming swiftly picked up a few and ate them, instantly relieving the extreme hunger he felt.

"It's normal to be hungry like this," the Custodian explained in a friendly manner, placing a bowl of water in front of him. "You were in the trial for three months. During that time, you lost about twenty pounds. I suggest resting and stretching for the next few days while you eat these nutritional supplements. They are very good, and you'll gain the weight back in no time."

The duration didn't surprise Cha Ming, as this was well within his expectations. He was more impressed to find out that he could now meditate for so long.

"You wouldn't mind giving me a bag of those before I leave, would you?" Cha Ming asked jokingly.

"I certainly can," the Custodian said. "However, they have a shelf life of one hour. I can teach you how to make them if you like. You can use creation qi, right?"

It hadn't occurred to Cha Ming that they were being made on demand. However, given that he had been gifted a set of custom-made cultivation robes, this wasn't too surprising.

"Deal," Cha Ming replied.

"Now, where was I," the Custodian said, pondering. "Ah yes, it's time to finalize your prize for completing the trial. Your completion rate was frankly abysmal—only sixteen percent. As a result, you aren't required to teach anything. In fact, you're strongly advised against it."

"I'm flattered," Cha Ming said dryly.

"In any case," the Custodian continued, "you accomplished sixteen percent despite being at a harsh disadvantage in terms of soul and cultivation level. Due to this, you will be rewarded with a prize one tier higher than your first prize."

With a wave of the man's hand, ten items floated around Cha Ming. They appeared much more powerful than the last set he had witnessed.

"Are those... peak-magic treasures?" Cha Ming asked.

"Of course they are," the construct said. "Besides, you should be able to advance your realm rather quickly, so these items will be immensely useful to you. Strictly speaking, I wouldn't have offered these specific ones, but *someone* put in a good word for you. So here we are."

Knowing that his time was limited, Cha Ming began sifting through the items. He instantly disqualified three of the prizes, as they were weapons that he was not proficient with: a sword, a saber, and a spear. The staff was also redundant, as his Clear Sky Staff was a superior weapon. Another four magic treasures were tempting but didn't suit his current needs. They were a magic pill cauldron, a magic hammer focus, a set of formation flags, and a magic carving knife.

The final four items would all be extremely beneficial to him. The first was a cloak that could hide his appearance and obscure his presence. It would be incredibly useful if he wanted to ambush the bandits one by one. Another item was a pair of bracers. According to their description, anyone wearing the bracers would gain resistance to the five elements. He wasn't sure what element Wei Chen practiced, but it would likely be incredibly useful to be prepared for so many.

The third item was a mysterious-looking silver plate. It had an intricate runic design carved into it and exuded an otherworldly charm. After reading the description, Cha Ming realized that it was a peak-magic treasure, a cultivation formation plate. With this plate, he could greatly increase his cultivation rate. Unfortunately, he didn't have the luxury of time. Otherwise he would have picked this item in a heartbeat.

The fourth and final item was a wispy piece of cloud. To Cha Ming's surprise, the item's description didn't match the item at all.

Stormchaser Boots? Looking at it again, he saw lightning crackling within the cloud.

"Sir Custodian," Cha Ming asked, "are these really boots?"

"Yes, these are fine boots," the Custodian replied. "You just can't see them in their current form." He then proceeded to slap the cloud a few times. "Get back into your original form this instant!"

The cloud shuddered for a bit, looking aggrieved, before condensing into a pair of white boots.

"They are very stylish, albeit temperamental boots. You can even wear them to upscale events, as their color will shift to match anything you wear."

"What do they do exactly?" Cha Ming asked hesitantly. He didn't want to waste his pick on a fashion item.

"Ah, these boots allow you to run with the wind," the Custodian replied. "They are imbued with the powers of wind and lightning, the fastest of the natural elements aside from maybe light. While they won't increase your movement speed by a full sub-realm, they are equivalent to having a top-tier movement technique. With a complimentary technique, they could very well increase your speed to the next sub-realm.

"In addition, they allow you to run in the air. It's very similar to a flying sword, but it's decidedly slower. However, you can run at a higher altitude than a flying sword, which is very convenient in many situations."

"I'll take the boots, then," Cha Ming said. The increase in movement speed was already enough to sell him on the item, but this last function cinched the deal.

The Custodian nodded understandingly. "He thought you would like them. Now then, here is the other prize that I promised you. Due to your excellent overall score, I'll reward you with ten jin of liquified elemental essence. Also, I took the liberty of making you 1,000 slips of talisman paper. Do let me know if you need more paper before you leave."

Two items floated out from his sleeves: one small bundle and a large crystal bottle.

Hearing he would be receiving a whole ten jin of liquified elemental essence, Cha Ming's eyes sparkled. If he wasn't wrong, he had enough to write out the next two sigils of the Seventy-Two Transformations Technique!

"Many thanks for fulfilling this request," Cha Ming said. "You've saved many lives."

Over the next few days, Cha Ming ate, slept, and stretched his limbs as he recovered from his extended meditation session. He also performed some simple calisthenics and bodyweight exercises to circulate the blood in his body.

Finally, after sufficiently resting, he secluded himself in a small room to execute what he had been planning over the past few days: a breakthrough unlike any other he had ever attempted.

Chapter 26: First Cycle

Taking in a deep breath, Cha Ming summoned the Clear Sky Brush and began painting the next sigil in succession for the Seventy-Two Transformations Technique: the gold sigil. He started at the end of the character as always, this time starting with the elementary shape of a blade. He painted these blades together in a crystalline fashion and with practiced ease. After all, his soul was much stronger than it had been when he painted the first three. In addition, he'd practiced 10,000 sigils during the third trial. Although he was hardly proficient in painting complete sigils, he was experienced in painting parts of them.

The crystals formed with blades were clustered around a sharp main spike, just like he had done for the wood sigil and the groupings like trees. He carefully painted eleven other identical spikes before finishing by painting the gold (金) character as per his usual convention. It wasn't much different from the first three. While he could have painted a much more powerful gold character filled with myriad profound truths, he knew instinctively that balancing the five elements was paramount. Therefore, he could only draw up the simplest version possible.

The silver-gold character suddenly shimmered upon completion and shot itself into Cha Ming's chest, just like the last three. The energy from his surroundings surged into him, augmenting the element of metal in his body and strengthening it little by little. The sigil completed, he patiently waited for the strengthening process to take effect. Unlike before, he was barely phased by the pain that wracked his body. After all, he had been through too much over these past months, and his soul was far stronger than it used to be.

Days passed before the process was completed. A resounding crack ran through his body as he got up, wielding the power of half-step bone-forging realm. His physical strength had increased by a large amount. It was now on par with his defensive abilities at initial bone-forging realm. The metal had reinforced his tendons and muscles, transforming them into wires that could handle far more weight than they initially could.

Cha Ming didn't waste any time getting used to his new abilities, however. He immediately used another dose of liquified elemental essence to draw the water sigil. This time, he joined up several tiny droplets into groups, which were breaking off from the main droplet, which served as a stem of sorts. Then he painted eleven more of these and joined them with the final water (水) character.

His body was once more encapsulated in heaven and earth energy, which transformed him. Little by little, all the water in his body was being strengthened. His blood became more concentrated but somehow less viscous. It was an extremely mysterious process. Once the transformation finished progressing, he knew all his senses had increased by a step. His hearing, sense of smell, taste, sight, and sense of touch had sharpened. His control over these senses also increased. For example, he could now choose to reduce them significantly—but not eliminate them—at his leisure.

The strength of his body increased until it arrived at a bottleneck. The strength stored within his body surged, but it had nowhere to go. Unfortunately, he knew the method but not the theory behind pushing through to the next realm. And try as he might, he couldn't push the strength into his bones as was suggested by the description of the bone-forging realm. He could only passively wait and observe as the technique executed itself.

Days passed, and he still struggled at the bottleneck. His strength didn't budge an inch despite the flood of power summoned by the water sigil. Finally, the sigil dimmed and faded, blending with his skin just like the other four. The process was completed.

Just as he was about to get up, however, all five symbols began to glow at once. They were surrounded by a white circle that had not been there before. A large suction force emanated from the white circle, demanding sustenance from Heaven and Earth. It trickled in slowly, and to Cha Ming's surprise, the creation qi accumulated in his dantian migrated to the surface of his chest via an obscure route through his body. It didn't use his existing meridians; rather, it permeated through his cells without triggering creation or growth.

The wisp of qi traveled from his dantian to his chest, and after it made contact with the circle, the five elements and the white circle began to grow increasingly bright. The process continued until all the creation qi in his dantian was depleted, and the growth of the white circle slowed to a crawl.

Cha Ming was surprised at the development, but fortunately he could still move his body and react to the situation. He quickly retrieved the mortal-grade formation plate from the Clear Sky World and placed it in front of him, tossing a pile of mid-grade spirit-stone ores he had accumulated while mining. He then circulated his cultivation base, replenishing his creation qi little by little. Meanwhile, he used the excess five-element qi in his dantian to repeatedly attack the barriers in his qi seas. He held no illusions of breaking through during this process, but even mosquito meat was still meat—it would save him much trouble later.

He continued to cultivate this way for a week. A small pile of dust accumulated before him from the residues and impurities in the raw ore from which he absorbed qi. In truth, he could only absorb thirty percent at best from these unrefined ores and the remaining energy that had dissipated into his surroundings. Fortunately, the lost energy was quickly absorbed from his surroundings through the Seventy-Two Transformations Technique, strengthening the white circle in the process.

By the end of the week, the forces of the five elements in his body had changed substantially. They had all increased to their maximum volume. Even his organs were completely full of energy that patched up various injuries that had accumulated over more than a year of mining. However, he noticed a sharp imbalance between the first three elements and the last two. He knew the reason for this—the body-refining pills that Guo Jia had forced him to consume had increased the purity of these three elements. There was nothing he could do about this.

Soon enough, yet another change occurred to the white

circle with five colors. The thin outline of a black star suddenly appeared. Like before, the suction force increased, drawing the energies of Heaven and Earth. In addition, all the destruction qi in his dantian began mystically migrating to the formation on his chest. To his relief, it also passed through his dantian and cells unhindered, feeding the black star on his chest.

Unlike the previous time, the appearance of the black star brought Cha Ming great pain. While it was still bearable, he dumped all of the spirit stones he had accumulated onto the formation plate and focused his efforts purely on absorbing and refining qi.

The process was akin to what he'd suffered with Guo Jia's body-refining pills, only this was ten times worse. Pain ravaged his bones, his marrow, his organs, and his muscles. Even his skin and nerves weren't spared, which made the process all the more unbearable.

Hours turned into days and days turned into weeks as his body was simultaneously destroyed by the black star and recreated with the white circle. With each cycle, the impurities that had accumulated in his body since his birth were eliminated. Even the large portions of his organs that were damaged beyond repair swiftly regained their original functionality. The only things that were not created and destroyed in this process were the new qi pathways and the meridians he'd created. These were already perfect, having been baptized through creation, destruction, and the five elements.

Time passed by slowly. Every time he thought the pain had reached a peak and his body's impurities had been completely eliminated, the pain increased by a single step. The formation was testing the limits of his soul and his ability to tolerate the pain. It would seemingly continue until he could bear it no longer.

Finally, when he'd reached his limit and felt his mind would break from the endless pain and solitude, the technique stopped. The absence of pain left him at a loss, and his enhanced senses wandered around his pure body in search of... *something.* His senses wandered through his meridians, which were now perfectly elastic and much larger than when he'd started cultivating. They then wandered through his organs, whose functionalities had all greatly increased during the process.

Cha Ming was no longer sure what his current talent level was, but he knew one thing for certain: It definitely wasn't at the fourth grade like he'd originally speculated. This had to have something to do with remaking his qi pathways, qi seals, and meridians. The calamity that had crippled him was now a blessing in disguise.

After marveling over his increased talent, his soul force wandered over to his bones—the source of his increased curiosity. To his surprise, small crystalline seedlings had appeared, covering the entirety of his bones. He instinctively thought that they had always been there. That the conditions hadn't been right for them to make an appearance before. Only by achieving a basic level of body refining and purification would they appear.

He counted them one by one and concluded that there were seven sets of seventy-two crystal seedlings, for a total of 504. Their distribution didn't seem random; rather, they resembled the outlines of some sort of formation.

With the appearance of these seeds, the Clear Sky Brush trembled, and a piece of information rushed into his mental space. It took the form of an ancient scroll. A look of shock and surprise appeared on his face as he read through the contents.

Seventy-Two Transformations 12/72: First Cycle Complete

First Reward: Physical capabilities increased one sub-realm.

Second Reward: Talent increased according to body's circumstances.

Third Reward: Limited Transformation

As he focused on the third reward, his eyes widened. He quickly became aware that he could change his appearance and aura to that of another being within his species—someone that he'd seen in the past. Unfortunately, it wouldn't allow him to vary his height by more than one foot taller or one foot shorter.

Despite this limitation, the value of this skill was evident. It would be very useful in his upcoming battle against the bandits. In addition, he would even be able to avoid the detection by experts that were specifically trying to chase him using his aura as a guide. This was not an illusion technique but rather a physical change resulting from readjusting his skin, hair, and bones.

After reviewing this technique, he moved on to a second scroll that appeared in his mental space. Unlike last time, this was a complete set of instructions on the next cycle of the Seventy-Two Transformations Technique. He frowned when he saw that there were many ways of completing the technique, many paths to choose from. However, the instructions stated that choosing one would set the path for future advancements in the technique:

Seventy-Two Transformations: Second Cycle Instructions—Bone Forging

Nature Path: A morally neutral method of forging the bones. Using this technique, the bones will be forged and refined like green jade. It is neither the weakest nor the strongest path, relying purely on natural treasures to strengthen the body. The materials required are:

Immortal Wood Jade: 1 jin
Immortal Fire Jade: 1 jin
Immortal Earth Jade: 1 jin
Immortal Gold Jade: 1 jin
Immortal Water Jade: 1 jin
Immortal Jade Core: 1 jin

The list was followed by instructions on the applications of the materials. The five-element jades could be used in any order, but the Immortal Jade Core could only be used as the finishing touch. After noting the materials, he proceeded to the next path.

Malevolent Path: Use the power of sin to forge the bones. Using this technique, the bones will be forged and refined like black obsidian. It is the strongest path, relying on the bone essence of the masses to forge the bones. No sin is incurred in using the technique, but gathering the materials will automatically incur sin. Materials can only be gathered by the user. The materials required are:

Bones of 4 bone-forging experts with a merit halo, alchemically imbued with wood
Bones of 4 bone-forging experts with a merit halo, alchemically imbued with fire
Bones of 4 bone-forging experts with a merit halo, alchemically imbued with earth
Bones of 4 bone-forging experts with a merit halo, alchemically imbued with gold

Bones of 4 bone-forging experts with a merit halo, alchemically imbued with water

Bone essence of 4,444 qi-condensation cultivators with a merit halo

This morally repugnant method forced Cha Ming to reevaluate the Clear Sky Brush. It was no righteous tool that could only be used by the pure. Rather, it allowed complete freedom in one's actions. If the user wanted to use it peacefully, it would allow it. If the user wanted to take an easy path, that was also fine. It would simply obey the whims of its master.

After overcoming the revulsion in his heart, he read the third entry:

Exalted Path: Use the power of Heaven to forge the bones. Using this technique, the bones will be forged and refined like purple dragon bones. It is not as strong as the Malevolent Path but incurs no sin in the process, relying on the approval of dragons to forge the bones. No merit is gained by executing the technique, but only those with sufficient merit will obtain the approval of dragons. Materials can only be gathered by the user, and they must be willingly given. The materials required are:

Arm Bone of 1 Transcendent Silver Dragon
Leg Bone of 1 Transcendent Copper Dragon
Leg Bone of 1 Transcendent Iron Dragon
Arm Bone of 1 Transcendent Gold Dragon
Skull of 1 Transcendent Cobalt Dragon
Bone fragment of a Five-Clawed Gold Dragon: 1 tael

Cha Ming couldn't help but swallow when he saw the list. This path seemed insurmountable to him. For starters, he didn't even know if dragons existed on the continent. Then, he would somehow need to gain their approval. According to the description, they were a lofty and noble species.

Among the three methods, there was only one that he could reasonably practice if he could find the materials: The Nature Path. He refused to take the Malevolent Path, and the Exalted Path would depend on his luck in the following years. Unfortunately, he was on a strict timeline, as he was worried about the issues in the Song Kingdom.

After completing his review of the next cycle, he ended his seclusion, washed himself, and sought out the Custodian. The middle-aged man had a surprised look on his face.

"Oh, a breakthrough so fast?" the Custodian said. "And in body cultivation no less? It's too bad that you won't be able to use magic treasures until you advance your qi cultivation."

Cha Ming chuckled. "This is merely the first step. I will soon establish my foundation. However, I want to acclimatize myself to this new strength. Is there an exercise facility in this library?"

"Of course," the middle-aged man said. "Please come this way."

He followed the Custodian to a significantly larger room. It was completely empty, save for a single pillar in the center of the room. "My apologies, but our limited resources can't accommodate anything fancy. We only have this empty space and a strength-testing pillar. Don't worry about breaking it, though. You'd need to transcend to have even the slightest chance."

Cha Ming's eyes brightened, and soon he found himself holding the Clear Sky Staff and executing the various techniques that he'd learned over a year ago: Soft Staff Art, Swift Staff Art, and Hard Staff Art. All the subsidiary movement techniques and staff techniques were included in his practice.

As he moved, he noticed that his increased speed and power caused significant drain on his qi resources, and that he would need to upgrade his capacity as a qi cultivator in order to fully apply his combat techniques. Still, familiarizing himself with these limitations was very useful, so he continued for a full day. At the end of the day, he walked up to the strength pillar and punched it with a single fist.

Peng!

A number written in runic characters appeared above the pillar. He rubbed his eyes and re-checked the number before confirming that his physical strength had increased to 4,320 jin and increase of four times compared to a few months ago. This was because he had not only broken through to the Bone Forging Realm, but his strength had increased by a sub-realm thanks to the metal transformation. The normal fist strength of someone who had just broken through to the Bone Forging Realm was 2,160 jin.

Cha Ming returned to the seclusion chamber immediately after completing his tests. While he was satisfied with the increase, he knew that he had a long way to go if he wanted to stand a chance against Wei Chen.

It was time to proceed to the next step of his plan: breaking through to Foundation Establishment.

Chapter 27: Foundation Establishment

A pile of spirit-stone ore crumbled to dust as Cha Ming filled his dantian to the brim. The process was effortless compared to the past, thanks to his increased talent. His qi pathways were thick and flexible while his tempered organs made circulating his qi so much easier than in the past.

It took less than a day to fill up his nearly full dantian, and his qi seas were at their maximum capacity. A boundary, much thinner than before, prevented the qi from expanding past its natural borders. Without much thought, Cha Ming swallowed a Barrier Breaker pill and urged his qi to burst through the thin and weakened membrane. The membrane shattered effortlessly, allowing the limits of his qi sea to double.

Having achieved his first objective, he urged his cultivation forward, reducing spirit-stone ores to dust with the formation plate to fill his dantian. A week later, another effortless breakthrough brought him to the peak of qi condensation. Since his soul was already in the Incandescence Realm, it no longer received nourishment from these two breakthroughs.

Two weeks later, his qi seas were once again filled to the brim. The small room he'd secluded himself in was filthy, but he didn't care. All he cared about was increasing his cultivation rapidly. It was reckless to do so on his part—after all, rapidly increasing one's cultivation could lead to instability and lack of control over one's qi. But what others worried about, he used the force of his soul to overcome. The control offered by his late-incandescent soul was far greater than most qi-condensation experts could manage.

Having reached the peak of qi condensation, he now focused on the next task at hand—establishing his foundation. From what he'd gleaned from his cultivation method, one established a foundation by condensing their qi into one to nine pillars, which started at the base of where the qi seas were located. Establishing a one-pillar foundation was a difficult process for most people but could easily be achieved using pills. Even a pig could be forced into foundation establishment with sufficient spirit medicine.

The second, third, fifth, and sixth pillars were much easier to condense than the first, but the fourth and seventh pillars were watersheds that were difficult to overcome, save through sufficient talent. The eighth and ninth pillars were more difficult to establish compared to the previous seven combined. Nine pillars signified a perfect foundation.

Regrettably, Cha Ming wasn't completely sure how to proceed. His cultivation method highlighted several possibilities, but the specifics had yet to be determined. For example, he could attempt to make nine mixed pillars, but where would he place them? In theory, he could attempt to produce ten pillars, whether mixed or single element. However, ten pillars were much more difficult to produce than nine, and they would be less potent than a perfect nine pillars.

After exploring these points, his Perfect Five-Element cultivation technique suggested establishing five pillars, then using the creation and destruction qi to establish a supportive matrix that could grow with these five pillars. This way, the five pillars would as effective as a nine-pillar foundation plus a little bit more. The genius of this method was that establishing five pillars was relatively simple, and the process would enable one's pillars to be much larger than normal foundation-establishment pillars due to the sheer amount of qi available compared to other cultivators.

As such, Cha Ming directed his consciousness into his dantian, first drawing his wood qi together to form the outline of a pillar. It felt sturdy compared to the liquid qi in his dantian, and it radiated an aura far superior to what normal qi could emanate—the aura of foundation establishment. Once this outline was completed, he used his incandescent force to direct his qi into the pillar, where it began filling out its empty shape and solidifying little by little.

A day passed by as he condensed his first pillar, and finally, the entire wood-qi sea was dry. He then moved on to the fire sea, the earth sea, the gold sea, and the water sea in succession, each easily forming a pillar. Then, with slightly more strain, he laid out a white circular foundation that connected the pillars, then did the same with the black star formation. On the whole, the process took a full week.

Most of the process was finished, and if he wanted to, a single push was all he needed to step into foundation establishment. However, he didn't do so. With but a thought, these five pillars and their foundations collapsed, melting back into the qi seas they were originally formed with. While he wanted to achieve foundation establishment as soon as possible, he felt that with his powerful soul, he should be able to improve upon the technique.

He used the next two days to recover before proceeding with the next step. If he failed and his idea couldn't come to fruition, he could always revert back to establishing a traditional foundation. This time, he withdrew three spirit pills and placed them just within arm's reach. The spirit-stone ore that he hadn't used yet for refining his body was still in a dirty pile next to the formation plate, ready to be used at his leisure.

After breathing in deeply, he began the process once more. This time, however, he did something most people would find unthinkable. First, he used his wood qi and shaped it into a tiny leaf. The process was akin to painting a sigil with his brush. Once the first leaf was formed, he drew five more and joined them with a stem. This process took much longer than when he first made a qi pillar, and the process caused great strain to even his incandescent soul.

Gritting his teeth, he continued and drew another eleven stems each containing five leaves. Finally, he used another wisp of wood qi to form the character for wood, completing what he saw as the most elementary wood sigil. Once the outline was completed, he rapidly drew in the remaining qi from the wood sea, fully materializing a solid sigil pillar.

The completed pillar gave off a far different sensation than the original one he'd condensed. It resonated with an aura of truth and subtle mysteries of the universe. In addition, he felt that the power emanating from it was at least fifty percent stronger than the original pillar he'd condensed.

Elated with his success, he proceeded to the fire pillar, forming it in much the same way as he had when drawing sigils for the Seventy-Two Transformations Technique. This second pillar was formed even more easily than the first, but it still took a considerable amount of mental energy on Cha Ming's part. To make things worse, there was no stopping the process to rest once he started. He could either establish his foundation or fail.

The third sigil he crafted was the earth sigil. This time, however, the pillar was formed with much greater difficulty than before. He felt an intense vibration as he built it, and it threatened to crush the foundation he was trying to build. Gritting his teeth, he continued forming the earth sigil brick by brick until he finally managed to solidify his entire earth sea into a pillar. Only once it was complete did the shaking and instability stop.

Next, he focused on forming the gold pillar. The process was even more difficult than the last. With every blade he formed, it attacked the wood pillar. Meanwhile, it was being strengthened by the earth pillar but melted by the fire pillar. It was a nightmare of unbalanced forces, and this pillar almost collapsed in the process.

Finally, he started the water pillar. Worse than any of the others, he felt four different forces threatening its stability. The power of the water pillar began leaching into the fully formed wood pillar. Meanwhile, additional energy from the water pillar was diverted to attack the fire pillar, and while it received some support from the gold pillar, the earth pillar constantly sapped away at its strength. After building only half of the water pillar, he was forced to swallow one of his precious foundation-establishment pills.

The pill provided a much-needed boost to both his mental strength and to the stability of his pillars. Using this window of stability, he finally managed to complete the fifth and final pillar. Unfortunately, only a third of the pill's medicinal efficacy remained.

I hope it's enough, he thought, mobilizing the white creation qi and forming a lattice similar to what he'd done in establishing the original formation. After successfully establishing the circle, he began forming the star line by line. While the first two lines were successfully drawn, he finally noticed some instabilities in the formation as a whole.

Frowning, he could only continue the process. He didn't want to waste a foundation-establishment pill simply because he didn't yet understand the root of the problem. He slowly proceeded in drawing the black star, paying attention to every minor detail. Before long, he'd finished the third stroke.

Kacha! A cracking sound alerted him that a small piece of one pillar had crumbled. Such a flaw would make it very difficult to complete the process. In fact, his intuition told him it was impossible. He continued to the fourth black stroke, well aware that the process would ultimately end in failure. In the process of failing, he would note where the sigils cracked and how he could improve the process next time.

Kacha! Kacha! Kacha!

Several other fragments fell once he completed the fourth stroke, and he finally noticed a pattern in all the defects. He gulped at the implications but still continued. After the fifth and final stroke, the remaining destruction qi was used, and his qi seas were dry. Yet dozens of fragments fell from the sigils, and finally from the black-and-white framework supporting them.

Still, he decided to proceed with the final step: condensing his foundation. As he concentrated his spiritual force onto the formation, another few dozen cracks formed, and eventually the formation became incapable of supporting itself. It crashed into five mixed pools, and the failure caused Cha Ming to cough up blood as his qi flowed in reverse. He nearly passed out but managed to stabilize his cultivation and ultimately separate the qi into their five distinct qi seas.

So dangerous. However, it was all worth it. Next time, I'll be able to do it. If I fail, I'll just have to fall back to the standard formation.

During the reconstruction of subsequent destructions of his foundation, he discovered multiple flaws in the process. The first flaw was very similar to when he'd originally condensed qi. That is, he needed to keep his five qi pools in balance at all times. Building a pillar upset the balance. Therefore, he would need to build the pillars simultaneously. Forming the creation qi and destruction qi matrices had similar issues.

In addition, he realized that while he could use flawed sigils to complete the Seventy-Two Transformations Technique, his foundation would not allow such unbecoming structures. At the very least, he would need the core pieces of each elemental sigil. A full sigil wasn't necessary, but his most primitive sigils contained far too many imperfections and instabilities. It was precisely these flaws that broke off whenever his foundation crumbled to pieces. He needed to correct them to stand a chance at success.

As a result, his pillars would need to be much more complex than he'd originally expected. He needed to draw extra support from foundation-establishment pills. In other words, to attempt the process, he would need to use the last two remaining pills. He would only have a single chance to succeed.

Sighing, he swept the dust off himself and cleaned the mess

in his room. Afterward, he spent a week recovering from his injuries and stabilizing his cultivation base. Finally, he sent his spiritual force into his dantian once more and began the process anew.

This time, he painted the leaves in a livelier fashion and intertwined them with vines. He added more flickering to the fire, and more cracks to the earth. He added crystalline grains to the gold blades and added ripples to the water. All of these might seem unstable, but they were what added life and energy to these sigils. These instabilities in the drawing process would benefit the overall stability of the sigils upon completion.

And so he painted them despite the great mental strain. After completing fifty percent of the characters, he saw them shaking and was forced to swallow one of the foundation-establishment pills. The characters began to strain once again at ninety percent completion, so he ate the final foundation-establishment pill. If he failed this time, he would need to double back and tread on the path of mediocrity.

The last ten percent involved drawing the final strokes of these characters. He painted them with great precision and completed all five characters simultaneously. To his delight, they showed no signs of the instabilities from last time. Instead, they let out joyful and lively hums of approval. They had been built in accordance to Heaven's laws, and he felt that should he choose to do so, he could immediately condense them and achieve a five-pillar foundation. This foundation would be akin to an eight- or nine-pillar foundation due to their special construction.

Still, he chose to strive for perfection. He took a deep breath and simultaneously began drawing the intricate creation framework and the complex destruction framework, moving from ten separate points at the same time. He had effectively divided his mind into ten parts, each accomplishing a task just as strenuous as building an individual elemental sigil. He knew that he could not continue for long—only a fifth of the time he'd originally used to build the five pillars in the first place.

Working quickly, he encountered the first major hurdle in the process: the intersection of the destruction lines. Each line intersected with another once to complete the star, and the interacting energies made it difficult to complete the destruction structure that stabilized the entire formation.

Cha Ming coughed up blood in the process but managed to overcome this hurdle. Pale faced, he continued and brought the black and white lines to mere millimeters away from their connection points. Then he clenched his teeth and let out a roar as he used the last of his mental strength to force them together.

The ten connections sent shockwaves through his body. He bled through his five orifices as a power much greater than he should be allowed to wield at his realm surfaced. He didn't have the mental capacity to continue the process, but to his delight, it didn't matter. He smiled as he passed out, realizing that his foundation was so perfect that it instantly condensed itself and lay down gently where his qi seas used to be.

In these last few moments of lucidity, he felt euphoria as heaven and earth qi rapidly rushed into the gaping void, filling his qi seas all the way up to the top of his foundation pillars with a much thicker qi than had previously been present.

It was foundation qi.

Cha Ming woke up a few days later. During his long slumber, the Custodian had thoughtfully tidied up the dirty room and prepared a basin of water. Smelling a fishy scent in the air, Cha Ming disrobed and began washing off a grimy residue from the surface of his skin. These were impurities that were not truly such a thing when he had entered bone forging. They were residues formed by qi from his previous realm, which were completely incompatible with the foundation qi that now resided in his body.

After washing himself, he directed his consciousness to his dantian, where he saw five stable runic pillars surrounded by vibrant oceans of thick qi. They were joined by thick white rivers of creation qi and separated by raging rivers of black qi. Strangely, these ten rivers didn't seem complete. Rather, he felt that there were only three much larger rivers of each color, alternating so rapidly between each state that they superimposed, giving the illusion that there were five rivers. It was similar to a situation he had studied on Earth, where a benzene molecule alternated between several resonant structures.

He inferred from his previous experiences that he could, in theory, ignore two destructive interactions and two creative interactions. Effectively, this meant that he was no longer restricted to using only "allied" elements collectively, such as water, wood, and fire. Instead, he could also mix opposing elements, such as metal, wood, and earth, which contained two destructive interactions. Exact applications would need to be determined, and he would need to evaluate the potential of ignoring creative interactions in depth in the future.

With but a thought, he summoned the five different types of qi as a barrier. This was an ability that was automatically granted to those having achieved foundation establishment. Unfortunately, he knew no advanced skills that could take advantage of his newly upgraded qi. The only thing he could do was make rudimentary improvements to his staff arts and then use his remaining qi to shield himself against incoming attacks. With any luck, he would be able to contend with Wei Chen.

After examining his qi for a moment, he moved to the last item that might provide him an additional boost to his power: the black-and-white orb left behind by Elder Ling. Withdrawing it from the Clear Sky World, he filled it with his newly minted foundation-establishment qi. The ball shattered, slowly revealing three items that carried his teacher's familiar aura.

Chapter 28: Life is a Dance

The golden light embracing Gong Lan's soul was no longer burning as intensely as before. Instead of a searing light repeatedly piercing her, it now felt like a warm blanket that brought heat to even her coldest extremities.

The first few weeks had been hellish, and there was no way she could isolate her senses or even pass out. She could only endure. Her soul had been safe the entire time, being nourished under the bodhi tree's gentle embrace. It was completely voluntary, of course. She could have ended the process at any time. But by doing so, she wouldn't be able to help her brother, her friends, and herself.

Throughout the painful process, she was forced to relive the many atrocities and sins she'd committed throughout her lifetime. Fortunately, her soul had been wiped clean during the Yellow River's cleansing process, meaning that she didn't need to pay anything for any of her past incarnations.

Despite the golden light's warming glow, she still felt a little cold. Her soul curled like an infant to conserve the warmth that permeated it, certain that one day she too could feel a world full of warmth and be free from suffering.

Weeks passed, and her soul, which was clothed in a cocoon of light, finally showed signs of emerging. A crack appeared on the cocoon, and a flood of information surged into her mind.

Peak resplendent soul. Only a resplendent soul's light can banish the darkness in other people's hearts.

Using her soul's strong arms, she ripped open her silky cocoon and emerged into her mental space. To her surprise, the cocoon didn't disappear. Rather, it shrank and transformed itself into a golden raiment made from the finest soul silk. A wondrous sight greeted her, a world filled with golden light. Animals wandered peacefully as they traveled to and from a golden bodhi tree that had established itself in the middle of her mental space.

Why did this place change so much? she wondered.

It changed because of your willingness to change, the voice said in her mind. *It is radiant because you allowed the light to burn away your impurities. Is this not what you wanted? Now that your karma has burned away, you no longer need to fear the influence of karma in your everyday life. You can sever your attachments with ease, transcending to the Buddha realm to live a life in peace.*

Gong Lan's soul frowned. *Isn't that a little too easy? How can I just sever my attachments?*

It is quite easy, the voice assured. *I have ensured that you no longer owe karma. You may leave when you wish. Besides, attachments are the source of suffering. Acquaintances lead to conflict and complex feelings; possessions lead to greed; even the simple act of eating leads to gluttony. By ignoring these things, you can maintain your newfound purity and improve yourself in the heavens above. Isn't this the goal of all martial artists?*

But what about all the people who rely on me? she asked.

What of them? the tree replied. *They care for you, but they can never help you. Wouldn't it be a great relief to them that you are well off and going to a better place? Those who care about you will be happy for you. Only selfish people would think otherwise. In fact, I challenge you to think of those you care about and their reactions.*

At the bodhi tree's prompting, she had a vivid dream. In this dream, she visited her brother and told him she was leaving to be happy for all eternity. A great smile appeared on his face, and he told her not to worry about petty things and to move on.

In another room, she met Cha Ming, who smiled and said he was glad that she had found what she was looking for. They would be fine without her. In one final room, she saw Feng Ming. After hearing her wondrous tale, his eyes widened, and he said, "It's better to be lucky than good! Good luck on your travels."

She didn't think of anyone else. All the other people she really cared about had long since passed away.

You see? the tree said. *Those who truly care about you just want you to be happy and free from suffering. Why don't you follow my guidance and transcend? Leave this mortal plane and contribute to spreading peace in a transcendent realm.*

Why can't I do the same in this realm? Gong Lan retorted.

You can. There's nothing wrong with it. However, it would be akin to a master physician applying ointment to a stubbed toe. Or an exorcist listening to a confession while devils and ghosts ravage the countryside. The greatest good can be done in the higher realms. As a benefit, you will be able to live much longer and help so many more people. Here, you will only grow old and wither away.

The tree's urgings made sense on an intellectual level. However, how could things be so simple? When she'd imagined the conversation with her brother, she didn't miss the fatigue he tried to hide so carefully. When she imagined Cha Ming, she didn't miss his disappointment at not being able to fight alongside her. When she thought of Feng Ming, she could see the silent taunting hidden behind his eyes. He was thinking, *I thought you were out to get me. Have you given up already?*

More to the point, she still remembered the ghastly memories and the remnants of the massacre she encountered on the way to Jade Spring. The thousands of lives that had been lost in Fairweather. By leaving, she could help those in a realm up above. She would only need to give up on those she had seen and that she *knew* needed help *right now.*

No... I won't leave, she said. *There are far too many things to do, too many people to help, and too many villains preying on the weak. How can I just abandon them?*

Very well, the bodhi tree replied. *But how will you stay? Your soul is on the cusp of transcending. If you do not stop it, you will transcend regardless. And then you will not be able to help anyone without karma interfering in your endeavors. You will have no choice but to leave.*

Hearing these words, Gon Lan examined her soul once more, realizing that many invisible shackles that bound it were beginning to break. She didn't panic, however. Instead, she looked back at the golden tree in her mental space and smiled. *Since you asked me all these questions, you must have a way to prevent this.*

I do indeed, the tree replied. *However, the price is a very serious obligation. As long as you are within this realm, you must protect me when I am in danger.*

Gong Lan was confused. *This is a serious amount of trickery for such a righteous tree. And who would dare to cause you harm while you still cast your shadow? Who could ascend the Stairway to Heaven and pass the monks that guard you?*

The tree was silent for a moment before replying. *Desperate times call for desperate measures. And that day will come, my child,* it whispered. *It will come sooner than you think.*

Hong Xin danced to the joyful sounds of music and laughter as she served drinks to her cheerful patrons. She skillfully balanced her tray as she twirled through the crowd with a flourish. Unlike her previous job, they didn't attempt to trip her. Rather, they quickly cleared the way to give sufficient room for her performance.

Quick as lightning, she placed six drinks in front of her thirsty patrons before holding her hands to her chest. They watched in anticipation as she raised her hands, sending a colorful flicker of flames into their drinks and lighting them on fire.

Life in Castle Town was much different than life in Stonefell. Here, she could be herself and not be persecuted. The pay was good, and her manager didn't withhold her tips. Over time, she had managed to save enough resources and push her way to the seventh level of qi condensation. There were few people in town that could contend with her—not that she had to.

Hong Xin hated fighting. While there were much more lucrative occupations, such as guards and adventurers, Hong Xin preferred to stay away from these things. Thankfully, the patrons in Castle Town were all decent human beings. Whenever one of the younger men or adventurers acted up and tried to lay their hands on her, a few of the older men would give them a long lecture on human decency. Most people didn't require a second lecture, which involved a good dose of corporal punishment.

After delivering the latest batch, she spoke to their guests and ran up to the bar, where the innkeeper spent his day. "Three more flaming reds, three baiju, and a cinnamon ale," Hong Xin said cheerfully.

The innkeeper chuckled. "Hiring you was the best thing I ever did. Business is booming, and it's all thanks to you."

"Nonsense," Hong Xin said bashfully. "It's because you have such a great atmosphere. Even the most miserable worker or traveler would find a smile by visiting this inn."

The afternoon passed by joyfully, and soon the people who shouldn't have been drinking had passed out and returned home. The rest of the patrons were there for the atmosphere and intended to stay well past midnight.

Suddenly the door to the inn burst open, revealing a figure cloaked in red. The person's aura was stifling, forcing everyone to stop what they were doing. But the supressing aura left as soon as it arrived, and people went back to drinking as though nothing had happened. Hong Xin looked to the entrance and saw the most beautiful woman she had ever laid eyes on lowering the cowl of her cloak.

Fortunately, none of the younger folks were present, and the older men had the decency to limit their catcalling and speak about her in whispers. The woman ignored this light conversation and walked up to the bar, where she sat down and placed a large case on the ground beside her.

"Innkeeper," she said pleasantly, "I'm looking for a place to stay for the night. Do you have a room?"

The innkeeper gulped. "Yes, ma'am, I have just the room for you. We're pretty fully right now, so I'll bump you up to our luxury suite free of charge."

A young waiter who overhead this began whispering to him, "Sir, one of the other rooms just cleared out. It's not necessary to—" The man clenched his teeth as he was rudely interrupted by a stomp of the owner's foot.

"It will be three silver for the night," the innkeeper said. "Is that all right?"

The woman, whose lustrous black hair was draped halfway down her back, smiled and replied sheepishly, "Unfortunately, I am a little short on silver right now."

The innkeeper frowned, which Hong Xin found understandable, given that he'd already given her preferential treatment.

"However," the woman continued, "I make my living playing music. If you let me play for a few hours tonight, I guarantee your patrons will be happy, and you won't regret it."

"Oh, a musician?" he said, his face breaking into a grin. "It's been a while since we've received a traveling musician in this establishment. Don't worry about the room, or a meal, for that matter. As long as you play some interesting music, the men will surely appreciate it. Hong Xin, please clear some space for our guest."

"Sure thing, boss," Hong Xin said enthusiastically. She had only ever heard two performances since starting at the inn, and both performances were memorable experiences.

The woman bowed slightly after seeing Hong Xin. "Thank you very much for your hospitality."

It only took an incense time to clear a few tables at the back and set up a small platform where she could play. The woman carefully climbed onto the hastily constructed platform, placing the large case on the ground in front of a cushion. Then she opened the case and removed a light seven-stringed instrument from it. The delicate guqin was a fragile instrument, and it complemented the pretty lady perfectly. It was constructed with a blood-red wood, and its strings were made from a deep-red fiber.

"What's your name?" Hong Xin asked her while watching her set up.

"It's a happy coincidence, but my surname is also Hong," she said. "My name is Hong Yinyue[22]."

"Red Music?" Hong Xin said. "How fitting, given that you play a red instrument."

"More than you know," the woman replied as she finished unpacking her guqin. She seemed calm, but Hong Xin spotted a hint of sorrow that briefly flashed across her eyes, so she remained quiet and asked no more questions. After checking that Yinyue had everything she required, Hong Xin continued serving drinks. Her movements became a blur as she quickly filled one order after another, since the patrons all wanted to drink as they enjoyed the music.

A half hour passed, and Hong Xin had finally filled every order. Exhausted, she sat down on a stool and made eye contact with the mysterious musician, who had remained silent while

[22] Hong means "red" and "Yinyue" means music. Note that both instances of Hong are the same.

she worked. The gentle murmurs in the bar were suddenly silenced with the single pluck of a string.

Hong Xin felt as though she'd slipped in a trance when the slow, gentle music began. She began to reminisce about her childhood. It was a pleasant, lighthearted tune that spoke of naivety and innocence. As the song progressed, she realized how much she missed her parents and how much suffering she'd likely caused them by running away.

Soon, the tune changed ever so slightly. The lightly plucked strings spoke of first love and the initial fluttering of a human heart. Hong Xin's heart began to pound as these memories invaded her consciousness, enabling her to remember those blissful moments. Unconsciously, she touched the used mauve hairclip that she had worn ever since she and Wang Jun had first met.

The warmth in her heart didn't last for long, however. The pace became hurried, and she imagined herself fleeing out in the wilderness, running away from home. When she finally found refuge, it was more hellish than she could ever imagine. The rhythmic thrumming of Yinyue's fingers caused her heart to palpitate when she remembered that awful night when she was forced to burn the bar owner to a crisp.

Then… silence. From this quiet atmosphere, a gentle melody slowly reached a crescendo, building up momentum. Everything before this had felt like Hong Xin's life was crashing down on her, but now, she felt only hope and calm. She remembered the kind farmers and helping them plant their fields. She remembered coming to Castle Town and finally enjoying her life like she should. She remembered the invigorating feeling when she had finally started cultivating again.

Then the music stopped. The song felt unfinished, yet for some reason, no one felt that it was inappropriate. One by one, the patrons began clapping and cheering for the beautiful musician playing her bewitching tune. She no longer wore her red hooded cloak, but rather wore a traditional red qipao. She didn't seem to pay attention to her audience. Instead, she smiled and looked at Hong Xin, hinting that this song was for her and her alone. Then she turned back to her audience and began strumming some joyful tunes.

"Are you all right?" the owner asked Hong Xin in a concerned voice. Hong Xin immediately realized that she had been crying this whole time.

"It was just so beautiful. I just need to go wash my face and I'll be fine," she replied, running off to her room.

The music ended early that night, but everyone was so pleased with the performance that they didn't complain. Instead, they sat around and drank while talking about Yinyue, the lady in red who was so talented in music.

Midnight eventually came, and the boss was forced to chase the last of the men out. Finally, Hong Xin was able to eat her meal in peace. She didn't go straight to bed, however. Instead, she went to the backyard of the inn where she could get a bit of exercise. She wore a set of cultivator robes that she had bought at one of the shops in town.

Breathing in deeply, she closed her eyes and practiced a fluid punching and kicking routine, using the few techniques that she knew in quick succession. For some reason, the motions came much more naturally than before, and she finished her routine in record time. Still, she felt unsatisfied about her performance. Something was missing.

She continued practicing, but instead of firing off a predetermined set of punches and kicks, she began to improvise. As she practiced without thinking, she heard a soft piece of music. It was the song she'd heard previously, beginning at the part that represented her arriving at the farm on the road to recovery. Her motions slowed as she recalled the torrent of emotions passing through her after killing the bar owner, yet they gradually improved as the tempo of the music in her head increased.

Before long, she was moving much faster than before. The tempo of the music increased, reaching a feverish rhythm. Hong Xin felt like a fire was burning in her heart, banishing the cold that had invaded her soul on that fateful day. Sweat dripped down from her brow and soaked her training shirt as she danced, but she didn't care. She felt like all she wanted to do in her life was dance.

Finally, the music stopped. She stopped as well. She looked around but found no one. The music had been in her head all along, but it was music she could never forget. It was music that kindled her heart and soothed her soul, and she wished that she could hear it every day.

After calming her ragged breath, Hong Xin returned to her room and immediately went to bed. It was best sleep she'd had in over a decade.

It was past midnight in Castle Town. Yinyue wasn't sleeping. Rather, she just stood at her window and stared at the moon. It had been a long time since she'd taken up her old profession as a traveling musician. After all, someone of her renowned talent could invite herself at a king's banquet to give a performance, forget a small town like this.

Yet a few years back, she'd felt the urge to wander. She didn't know why, but she followed her heart.

Life is a dance, and sometimes you need to follow the music life gives you. It was a saying that she'd followed countless times in the past, and it had never led her astray.

Tonight, like many other nights, she pondered the reason why she traveled.

Why did I have to come here of all places? Why not a big city or somewhere scenic like the Fire Mountains? She knew the answer would come to her eventually. Every time she asked herself this question, she came a little bit closer to the truth.

Suddenly she noticed a flickering figure downstairs in the courtyard. It was that little girl that seemed so enamored by her presence. The reason she'd played the first song earlier was because she felt a lingering darkness in her heart, an ache that was difficult to remove. Yinyue's music art could heal the wounds in a person's heart and light a blazing fire from a heart's dying embers. It was a song that she had played for that little girl alone, and the many bystanders could never understand its profundity.

Yinyue smiled as she looked down at the figure, stiffly

executing one stance after another in a rehearsed manner. *If only she would learn to let go, I'm sure she'd be a great dancer.*

To her surprise, the forms changed after about an incense time. It was as though the girl had subconsciously taken her advice and began dancing to a tune only she could hear. A surprised expression flickered over Yinyue's face when she realized that her rhythm and movements were according to the song that she'd performed for the poor girl earlier that day.

She learns surprisingly fast for having such terrible talent, Yinyue thought. She then continued watching her appreciatively from the window up above, not making a sound. *Very few people have what it takes to dig themselves out of a pit of darkness. Only those who have lost all their light can learn to kindle the fire within their hearts.*

Then, it struck her. Perhaps her reason for wandering was related to this girl? The more she thought of it, the more amazed she became. Fate worked in mysterious ways, but she couldn't fathom what it was thinking by sending her to pick up someone with such trashy talent.

Oh well, she thought. *Life is a dance, and I don't lead, I only follow. If fate wants me to teach her, teach her I shall.*

Chapter 29: Beast Tide

A group of six young qi-condensation cultivators traveled swiftly as they kept their eyes peeled for natural treasures that grew in abundance on the mountains. There were many precious materials that would do wonders for their cultivation; even a six-month-old blood ginseng or a one-year-old qi-gathering berry would go a long way for these youngsters who had barely stepped on the path of cultivation. The probability of finding such things was quite high, however, and spirit beasts would find eating these severely unripe natural treasures an unpardonable crime. To them, it was only appropriate to eat them at the peak of their maturity cycle.

Or so they thought before they set foot on this dreadful mountain. They were greeted with clear-cut, barren woods. The natural treasures, which should have been abundant, had been picked clean, forcing them even deeper into the beasts' dangerous territories.

"I don't think we should be going in so deep," a young lady that couldn't be older than eighteen complained to a boy that looked several years older than the rest of the group. She didn't want to speak to the man initially, but the other four were simply yes men, followers of their elder brother.

The older man chuckled. "Relax, Fei Er, your elder brother Xiao Jintao is already at the eighth level of qi condensation. And with my superior combat prowess and this peak-spirit weapon, only a lord of the forest would stand a chance against me. And besides, because of that stupid treaty, they wouldn't dare lay a finger on me."

"Who allowed you to be so familiar with me?" Li Fei said with a sniff. "You may call me Miss Li or Li Fei at most, but don't think that your status is sufficient enough to be so intimate with me. If you really want to prove your worth, find me a six-year-old iceflame lingzi[23] and break through to mid-foundation establishment. Then my father will likely offer me to you on a silver platter."

She watched in amusement as the older man seethed with rage and trudged forward. A six-year-old iceflame lingzi was a precious item coveted by the entire sect. Even if he found it, it wouldn't belong to him. By the time he found one, Li Fei would have been married for many years.

Suddenly, Xiao Jintao held up his fist and signaled for their group to halt. Li Fei was about to speak up and ask what was happening when the older man shot her down with a rebuking glare. While she was upset and felt mistreated, she decided to bide her time and reprimand him later.

At Xiao Jintao's signal, they proceeded at a fifth of their original speed. The short-haired man had drawn the peak spirit-tier saber that he had been awarded by the sect just prior to this mission. Its faint blue glow reassured her that, as he'd

---

[23] A small round fruit. A lychee.

boasted, not many creatures could pose a real threat to them in these woods.

Before long, they heard a rustling noise behind a group of bushes. At Xiao Jintao's signal, the four men approached from the right while he and Li Fei approached from the left. He held Li Fei back for a few breaths just before they emerged from behind the bushes in order to allow his followers to scout. Soon, they heard some loud chuckles coming from the fattest cultivator in their group, Yuan Tao.

"I nearly died of a heart attack," Yuan Tao said. "But after all this caution, we only found a cute little spirit rabbit. Look, he's even carrying a small twig in his mouth."

Xiao Jintao shot him an angry glare. "Quiet! Even a lion must use their full strength to catch a rabbit." His overreaction over such a small threat was truly a huge loss of face, especially in front of Li Fei.

"He's so cute!" Li Fei said, approaching the small white rabbit. The rabbit was now trembling uncontrollably, so much so that it dropped the twig it had been carrying.

"What's this?" Li Fei said, picking up the twig. A small round fruit was growing on it. Half of the fruit was a frosty blue color while the other half was crimson red. She clearly felt the concentrated energy it contained. It was marked with six distinct lines that would only grow on such fruits, one for each year it aged.

"A six-year-old iceflame lingzi?" she said, gasping in surprise. "With this, I'll be able to break through to foundation establishment in one fell swoop! Such a lucky rabbit. I'll be keeping you as a pet." She reached down to grab the rabbit, but as she did, she noticed a small black spot on her otherwise flawless white hand.

Frowning, she used her robe to try to wipe it off, but to no avail. "Senior Brother Jintao, could you please pass me the gourd of spirit water?" she asked, embarrassed. She loathed asking for anything from him. But to her surprise, she heard no reply.

She turned around with a cold expression, preparing to scold the entire group. To her horror, all five men had collapsed on the ground, their faces full of black spots. Trembling, she looked at the single black spot on her hand and pulled up the sleeve of her robe. Her entire arm was peppered with spots.

"Poison?" she said hoarsely before she crumbled to the ground.

How?

This was the last thought that passed through her mind. Had she been more observant, she would have noticed that strands of a rare herb, pockmark death grass, were growing in the grass where they passed to circle the bush. The herb was quite lethal to low-level human cultivators, but harmless to spirit beasts. They had fallen into a meticulously planned trap.

The bait was the little white rabbit and the six-year-old iceflame lingzi.

"Be careful, men," a cultivator in blue robes said to a group of twenty-nine other cultivators. They were an elite group at middle foundation establishment. "This time, our target is the king-level beast, a variant two-tailed fox. It's vicious and cunning, and it will require our entire strength to trap him.

"Fortunately, we know exactly where he is. Our patriarch spared no expense to divine his location just prior to our departure. This fengxue compass will lead us straight to him."

"Don't worry Vice Leader Li," a short, stocky cultivator said. "We all know that it's vitally important to capture him. Our patriarch's life and the future of our sect is at stake."

"The sect is grateful to have committed elites like you, Elder Han," Vice Leader Li said emotionally. After all, he was more than just the vice leader—he was the patriarch's beloved grandson.

"In any case," Vice Leader Li said, "we brought the sect's protective treasure, a peak-level magic spear with us. With this spear, there's no way that wretched fox will be able to overwhelm us." He said this while holding said spear in his hand. The mighty power emanating from the spear renewed the elite group's confidence.

"Thankfully we won't be going anywhere near the geomantic boa's territory," one of the younger cultivators in the group said. "That place is a death trap, and I daresay that even the patriarch wouldn't want to fight that beast in its own territory." The other cultivators all nodded in agreement. In fact, the reason they had been routed so badly the previous year was due to the illusions in the geomantic boa's terrain.

And so, the cultivators continued traveling toward the two-tailed fox's location. They had been going for three hours before their leader frowned and glanced at the fengxue compass that still pointed due east.

"Strange," Vice Leader Li said. "We should have arrived at his position long ago. Somehow I feel that we've been traveling in circles. For example, look at that tree. Brother Meng, didn't you urinate on it only an hour ago?"

The older cultivator's face flushed in embarrassment, but he approached the tree and sniffed. He paled when he realized this was indeed the case. "How is it possible for superior cultivators like us to be trapped so easily?"

"There's only one possibility," the vice leader whispered. "The geomantic boa's territory has changed."

Suddenly their surroundings shimmered, and the lush forest they had seen previously was now a desolate wasteland. Here and there, they saw geomantic runes that were created using the boa's natural ability.

"How perceptive of you," a voice said. Soon after, a forty-foot black-and-white fox walked out from behind a large rock that was situated near them. "Are you confused as to why I'm revealing myself? You see, we had a betting pool going on. We each wagered a drop of blood essence on how long it would take you to realize your predicament. Unfortunately for you, I'm angry now. I bet on six hours, and that tricky geomantic boa bet on three hours. I should have known that she'd rig the game in her favor."

"Aren't you looking down on us a little too much by facing us alone?" Vice Leader Li said angrily, hefting his spear. A confused expression appeared on the fox's face before it realized what had happened.

"Oh, I get it. You guys are still trapped in a secondary illusion. Bowie, don't slow-roll them. Dismiss the illusion."

The illusion faded, and the thirty cultivators were shocked to discover that they were now surrounded by eleven lords of the forest. Furthermore, they seemed to have fully charged their most powerful attacks, which could be unleashed at a moment's notice.

"Any last words?" the fox asked calmly.

"Damn you!" Vice Leader Li said. He didn't have the chance to say any more. The fox quickly unleashed its purifying and devouring power, while the various beasts unleashed their attacks and decimated the group of cultivators with their most powerful strikes.

All around the mountain, similar scenes were occurring. Lords teamed up with lords, using the terrain and their overwhelming physical strength to their advantage. Smaller beasts played tricks. In a funny turn of events, even the spirit-tail chickens were useful. In their devotion to Sovereign Two Tails, they had developed priests that studied Huxian's natural abilities like scripture. Their faith had somehow allowed them to harness the power of the bagua, enabling them to trap groups of cultivators very efficiently.

After one long night of cold and merciless slaughter, the humans on the mountain were eliminated. The beasts rejoiced in the knowledge that, at last, they had repelled the human tide.

Huxian didn't rest on his laurels, however. He and the geomantic boa were both creatures with inherent knowledge of formations. One by one, they cracked and devoured the various seals that shut them off from the outside world. After two days and three nights, the air above the mountain shimmered and shattered.

For the first time in decades, the various spirit beasts and demon beasts on the mountains walked out of their caves and admired the beautiful setting sun. It wasn't optically different than before; rather, they could now feel the warmth more intimately on their furs and feathers.

"This, my friends, is the feeling of freedom," Huxian said in a loud, booming voice. "No longer will we wait here passively as the humans invade our territory and rob us. It's time for us to reclaim what's rightfully ours: the valley at the edge of our mountain.

"It used to be covered in pristine forests, but the humans chased us out and took our lands. They took our medicinal herbs, roots, and fruits, limiting our population and growth. No more. Stand with me, brothers and sisters, as we assemble our beast tide and show the humans what we're made of. It's our turn to rule!"

The beasts on the mountain, enlivened by their leader's glorious speech and too frightened to say anything due to bloodline suppression, began their heroic charge toward the human settlement below.

Tears appeared in Cha Ming's eyes when he saw the three items appear before him. They bore his teacher's aura, a man who had dedicated much energy and attention to his fledgling growth. Even now, when he was no longer there, he had left items to help Cha Ming on his future path of cultivation.

The first item was a letter, which he read immediately.

> *Dear Cha Ming,*
> *As beautiful as my writing is, I'm really bad at writing letters. However, I'm fully aware that you bear a great destiny*

on your shoulders, and I'd feel guilty if I didn't leave you at least something to help you on your way.

First off, I've left you two talismans. They are both mid-grade magic talismans with incredible offensive power. However, there's a catch. Both talismans have been created differently. One of them was created using mathematical and geometric rules along with advanced symbols. The other was created using an expression of my extreme emotions.

This is, first and foremost, a demonstration of the field I excel in the most: runic poetry. Each character has its own nature and intent. However, the intent of the writer and their state of mind can greatly affect the power of a talisman. Words from the heart have power, Cha Ming. These two talismans will show you that difference.

The second item I've prepared for you is quite speculative on my part. I performed a few divinations on you and a few items, but due to your inscrutable fate, I couldn't get an answer that was more than fifty percent accurate. What I'm trying to say is that there's a fifty-fifty chance that this nifty gadget that I've left for you will be very useful on your journey. Worst case, it should be moderately useful in fighting against that twerp, Zhou Li.

In any case, I'm sure I won't be able to see you again for quite some time. I've been feeling antsy lately, which means that my wife is definitely coming to retrieve me. And let me tell you, she's not gentle. Be sure to take care while I'm gone, and if you ever get a chance, come visit me at the Inky Sea Sect after you transcend.

Cheers,

Elder Ling

P.S.: I discovered that Zhou Li's henchman, Protector

Song, is the regional Angels and Devils *champion. I'm going to wipe the floor with him before I leave. Do be sure to continue sharpening your skills before we meet again.*

P.P.S.: Deep inside, Mao Mao is sorry for being so territorial with Huxian. The little fox has great potential, and he's a little bit jealous. Tell him not to hold it against him.

Cha Ming chuckled as he read the letter. It perfectly reflected his eccentric teacher's character. After reviewing it one more time, he turned his sights toward the two talismans his teacher had left him.

The first was an elaborate talisman, filled with complex geometric shapes that he could now recognize. It was also written with some fairly impressive characters, like "sovereign king of beasts," "annihilation," and "blood devouring." However, the characters were all centered on two elegantly drawn characters in the center. They were two of a single runic character he had ever seen before, but when he read it, he was overwhelmed with Mr. Mao Mao's overbearing and haughty attitude. Putting two and two together, he assumed these characters meant Mao Mao.

Cha Ming rubbed his eyes in disbelief when he saw this but shook his head and moved on. The next talisman left him sweating in embarrassment.

Instead of being covered with elegant geometric symbols, it was covered in boldly written characters.

Ode to Mr. Mao Mao
Mr. Mao Mao, my love for you knows no bounds.
It is like a tyrannical beast,
Destroying everything in its path.

How I envy those who perish under your gentle claws.

Cha Ming wasn't sure whether to laugh or cry after reading the talisman. Originally, he'd doubted the authenticity of the first. Now, however, he found the original talisman to be a bastion of knowledge, an elegant and unparalleled creation. In his heart, Cha Ming swore never to use the talisman unless it was a life-or-death situation. Only then could he bear the humiliation it entailed.

Cha Ming took some time to lower his expectations before moving on to the third item. It was a thin jade slip containing characters he could barely decipher. It read:

Devil Sealing Scripture
A single scripture to seal all evils in the realms.
Can you see what I see with these eyes of pure jade?
Only those who share my will can understand my resolve.

As he read it, he felt a sharp pain in his eyes. Aside from this, he was only left with a cryptic lack of understanding concerning what he had just read. He felt there was now knowledge inside his mind that he was not yet privy to. Shaking his head, he stored the two talismans and the Devil Sealing Scripture and began to recover his strength for when he would leave Fuxi's Library.

Chapter 30: Theft

Cha Ming exhaled a breath of turbid air as he opened his eyes, expelling the last bit of impure qi that had remained in his system after his advancement. The stone walls, sensing his awakening, illuminated the pitch-black room in a soft blue light. Based on his experience, the light would intensify gradually, acclimatizing his eyes to normal illumination.

He stretched his limbs and back, relieving the tension from sitting in meditation for so long. Then, looking at his palm, a miniature white formation appeared, which absorbed the creation qi in his body and concentrated it into a single white pellet. It was the same as those that the Custodian had made during his time at the library, complete with its dense, easily absorbable calories and perfect nutritional value.

The pellet melted in his mouth, rejuvenating his slightly weakened body. While a foundation-establishment and bone-forging dual cultivator like himself did not need to eat more than once every two weeks, his advancement had required a great deal of energy. Most of it had come from his surrounding environment and spirit stones, but they could only do so much to supplement his bodily functions.

He wasn't creating something from nothing. Every object in the universe was created with the qi of heaven and earth. His cultivation method gathered the qi and converted it into foundation qi in his dantian. A portion of this qi happened to be creation qi, which was ideal for producing such an item. It was also suitable for creating something like physical water, which he did with a simple thought.

Soon, a clear ball of liquid appeared in his hand, and he took several sips of it before using the remaining amount to wash his hair. Water created from ordinary water qi couldn't do what he'd just done. It could wash him, certainly. It couldn't sustain him, however. It was an illusory imitation of the real thing. The same applied to flames, earth, and other such manifestations created with qi. However, those things created with the white qi were all *real*. He wondered if one day all his qi could behave this way.

Sighing, he stood up and called out for the Custodian, who appeared immediately.

"Must you leave so soon?" the Custodian said with a sad expression on his face. "I may be a construct, but I still have feelings. I've been lonely for aeons, and your company has been marvelous."

Cha Ming smiled. "I would stay longer if I could, but I have doubts about the safety of the people up above. I must leave to free them and help them start a new life. Besides, my brother fox Huxian is still out there. I need to find him and make sure he's safe."

"Where would you like me to send you?" the Custodian asked. "I can manipulate space to send you anywhere within

100 miles from your point of entry."

"Oh?" Cha Ming considered that pensively. After thinking for a moment, he decided not to return through the mines. "Can you send me into the forest up above, away from any humans?"

"Not a problem, young man," the Custodian said, smiling. Then he bowed. "It was nice meeting you, Cha Ming. Don't forget your promise to teach. In addition, no one will be able to learn from this school for the next twelve years."

Cha Ming returned his bow. "I understand your intent, Custodian. I'll be sure to find someone to keep you company after twelve years have passed."

"Thank you," the Custodian said.

Then Cha Ming felt a jarring sensation before being overwhelmed with a brightly lit sky he hadn't seen in months. The sweet smell of leaves, sap, and flowers mixed in with the decaying underbrush assaulted his nostrils. He appeared next to a fourth-level spirit boar, who roared in rage and instantly charged at the threat to its territory.

Cha Ming exerted a slight amount of spiritual pressure, causing the boar to stop mid-charge and sit down respectfully. He walked over to the trembling boar and petted its head, directing a kind, calming intent to the creature, who became as docile as a pet dog. Then he held his hands out and projected his incandescent force outward.

He sent out a gentle, non-intrusive projection outward one mile, sensing nothing but spirit beasts in the surrounding area. Sensing no one, he expanded his sense to five miles, spotting a dozen odd bandits scouting the woods and hunting in the process. Then he expanded his incandescent force to his limit of eight miles. An incandescent soul granted the user the ability to project his soul out to sense things in a radius of two miles. Every sub-realm thereafter increased this radius by two miles, to a maximum of ten miles for a peak incandescent soul.

Found it, he thought. He saw the fuzzy outline of what used to be the village in his mind's eye. He saw the bandit tents, the cages, and the many prisoners going about their duties. He saw the shack containing tools, spirit stones, and the pitiful accountant going about his duties. He saw groups of exhausted men and crying children, and the downtrodden women who reassured them.

After confirming the position of the village, Cha Ming sat cross-legged in meditation to formulate a plan. His past experiences in trying to rescue prisoners had scarred him greatly, and he refused to be reckless like before. These bandits may not be devils, but he wouldn't put anything past these immoral beasts who had enslaved their fellow men. He had to be cautious, and he certainly couldn't expose his identity to these men, lest they hold the village hostage.

Thinking of this, he remodeled the bones in his face and took on the appearance of his late nemesis, Zhou Xian. The mystical technique transformed both his appearance and aura, and he complemented this new appearance by transforming his cultivation robes to a set of black robes with a deep cowl. He now had the appearance of a vicious assassin who hid his features.

There were three problems he needed to consider in rescuing the villagers. The first problem was that he couldn't kill Wei Chen first. The bandits were currently restrained by Wei Chen's heavenly oath. If he died, he wouldn't put it past them to at least attempt to threaten him with hostages, even if he did not let on his relation to the villagers.

Next, he needed to lure the bandits out of the mine, disrupting their activities and making it difficult to endanger the hostages. He couldn't expose his appearance or true purpose, so he would need a motive for invading their village in the first place.

Should I pose as an assassin? A thief? But what could I steal that would cause such a ruckus? The shack containing spirit weapons and spirit stones came to mind. While he doubted that *all* the spirit stones mined were there, he also didn't think that Wei Chen would be so concerned about picking them up every day, especially given that his men had the area surrounded.

However, stealing such a small amount would unlikely achieve the effect he required. He would likely need to repeat the thievery multiple times. In fact, robbing other things from their group might be necessary.

Lastly, he was likely barely a match for Wei Chen. While his qi cultivation and body cultivation were both equivalent to early-stage foundation establishment, Wei Chen had experience. He also likely had foundation-establishment techniques, and Cha Ming could only use the insights he'd gleaned in Fuxi's Library and his newly improved qi to enhance his techniques. At the very least, he would have a slightly larger qi pool than an early-foundation-establishment cultivator.

Either way, this meant that he could not confront them directly. He would need to divide and conquer. His main advantage was his physical body's endurance, his multiple varieties of qi, and the Stormchaser Boots, whose appearance he had altered to black to match his outfit. He thought briefly of the two mid-grade talismans Elder Ling had gifted him but chose not to account them for now, for fear that they might be ineffective. At the very least, he could use them in a pinch for an unexpected effect.

He then thought of a glaring flaw in his plans. *Why is the Clear Sky Staff so obvious in appearance? Can I change its appearance to something plainer like the rest of the magic items I'm wearing?*

He summoned the staff, which reluctantly altered its appearance. Instead of being crystal clear, it was now a dark brown. For some reason, it refused to turn black, white, or gray. In addition, he was only able to dim the runes to a dull glow. Like before, the staff refused to see them extinguished, as though he were crossing its bottom line.

Quite picky, are you? he thought. To his surprise, the staff shivered indignantly and began reverting to its previous appearance. Cha Ming panicked and apologized profusely before it finally halted its progress and returned to its dark mahogany color with dull runes. However, he could see that the wood was slightly lighter in color than before and the runes slightly brighter, as though in protest. He didn't voice his displeasure, however, for fear that the brush would revolt once more.

His clothes complete, he waited for night to come. To his surprise, a family of a dozen boars arrived just before sunset to offer greetings. The boar he had spared approached and put a root on the ground, as though paying tribute to its king. Cha Ming chuckled when he saw that it was an ocher spirit root, one that had matured at least six years. The family of boars sat obediently, waiting for him to devour it.

And people use the saying "worse than a beast" to insult others, Cha Ming mused. *Truly, these boars have enlightened me. While I cowed them previously, the boar didn't have to come back. However, it acknowledged its defeat and now seeks to give me the honor it thinks I deserve. Many humans aren't so thoughtful.*

Then, chuckling, he held out his hand and sent a surge of qi into his closed palm. He opened it up and dropped twenty nutrition pellets that he had just created. Seeing the boar's confused expression, he moved away rapidly, giving the impression that he had disappeared. In the distance, he used his incandescent force to see their reactions.

After a while, the lead boar walked up to the root Cha Ming left behind and ate it, then after sniffing the white pellets, it ate one as a test. Then, noticing that these were good nutritious things, it invited each of the boars in its family to eat as well.

Cha Ming's figure fluttered in the darkness. His footsteps made no sound as he walked in the air using his Stormchaser Boots and his Seven Cloud Steps technique. Fortunately, using this basic technique was very economical for him now. His foundation-establishment qi allowed it to be used far longer than before. He estimated that it was to the extent that he could use the movement technique for a half day.

He used his incandescent force to avoid the many patrols around the camp. There were many more bandits than in the day, likely due to Wei Chen's vast experience as a bandit. Bandits and thieves came at night, not during the day. Still, avoiding them and remaining in the darkness was easy to accomplish. As one sentry walked passed him, he quickly zipped through the camp, avoiding the notice of the many bandits that were huddled around a fire. He flew through the darkness until he arrived at a second well-lit and heavily guarded area: the storage shack.

He walked around the perimeter carefully, probing for any potential weaknesses. He could only sigh in disappointment and proceed to his backup plan, which involved using brute force. Then, summoning his Clear Sky Staff, he ran toward the bandits like a gale force wind. They barely had the chance to react before Cha Ming's staff hit six of them in quick succession. His footwork was fleeting and the motions of his staff eccentric. Despite the staff's lightness, its quick movements and Cha Ming's great strength were enough to pulverize their bones and internal organs, killing the six bandits instantly. He wasted no time with the others and kicked the door in.

He ignored the quivering accountant, who he had just woken with his brusque entry, and proceeded to the back of the shack, where he felt the densest energy of heaven and earth. Opening the door, he saw various locked chests. He wasted no time and broke them open with fierce blows of his staff. The crystal ore they contained scattered all over the floor, but he instantly whipped them up into his Clear Sky World. Then he proceeded to another four rooms and repeated the process.

As soon as he had finished looting, he felt a powerful spiritual force projecting outward and focusing on the shack.

Time to go, he thought. He used his spiritual force to avoid the probing and rapidly burst out of the back wall of the shack, where various bandits welcomed him with weapons drawn. He snorted and stepped down onto the ground heavily, increasing his weight using Mountain Stance. Then he extended his Clear Sky Staff to fifty feet in length, using his entire strength to smash across a dozen of them with Sword Staff.

Previously, his Sword Staff would only glow with a silver sheen. Now, however, he could see the blurry outlines of various runes in the staff art, complementing the blade-like qi projection that made the technique effective and increasing the density and sharpness of the blade. As a result, the Sword Staff cut through them like butter, bisecting them before he withdrew his staff and ran like the wind.

He didn't pause for even a moment and flew away, well aware that a frightening presence was approaching from behind: Wei Chen and two others he had not noticed previously were approaching on flying swords, tailing him in hot pursuit. Wei Chen led the pack, but before long Cha Ming noticed the man break away from the pack and begin catching up with frightening efficiency.

Cha Ming clicked his tongue and tried using his Seven Cloud Steps to increase his speed, but to no avail. He then remembered what the Custodian had said—that the boots were good for fighting and flying but weren't great for absolute speed compared to a flying sword.

Do I have no choice but to fight?

He wasn't very confident in his odds of winning against the three experts pursuing him, so instead he focused on his previous experience with the Sword Staff Art. Somehow, some blurry runes had appeared that supplemented its functions. Could he do the same for the Seven Cloud Steps technique? While using the technique, he felt the wind qi beneath his feet and the path it traveled, combining awkwardly with the functions of his Stormchaser Boots.

What runes would truly be useful right now? He instantly though of the Seven Cloud Steps talismans he had crafted for the auction in Fairweather. To his surprise, the qi beneath his feet became more tangible, and some blurry runes formed of qi appeared. His speed increased substantially. However, Wei Chen was still closing in on him. He was only a few hundred meters behind, almost in range to lash out with a flying sword.

Cha Ming's mind rapidly sifted through the many characters he had learned in Fuxi's Library. Whenever he found a character related to wind or speed, he willed it to appear, and it materialized beneath his boots. Sometimes, his speed increased. Other times, it decreased due to incompatibility.

"You can't escape!" Wei Chen shouted as he closed the distance. "Surrender and return what you stole, cut off your right arm, and we'll let bygones be bygones."

Cha Ming ignored him and continued focusing on gaining insight with compatible characters. Unfortunately, things became much more difficult once he sensed a sharp sensation from behind. He used his boots to sharply change directions in midair, barely avoiding a flying sword. It turned around to head back toward him, but its efficiency was much lower. Cha Ming thanked his lucky stars and no longer regretted the choice he made in choosing the boots. While they were slower than a flying sword, their ability to change trajectories on demand was invaluable.

"You might be able to avoid a single flying sword, but how about three?" Wei Chen yelled, taunting him. Cha Ming was well aware of the other two cultivators who would soon close in on him. He continued thinking as he evaded, and soon he found three runes that seemed to complement his movement technique perfectly. Unsurprisingly, they were all runes that represented different types of clouds.

Perhaps seven clouds are optimal. He poured through his

memories, and before long, he found four additional ones. The seven runes represented "cirrostratus," "altostratus," "stratus," "nimbostratus," "noctilucent," "polar stratospheric," and "cirrus". These were all clouds that didn't move much, and the logic behind his deductions were that they would enable him to push off with greater force. In addition, he was strapped for time and had already determined the first three.

Sharply evading another sword, he began tracing geometric lines between the fuzzy qi runes between his boots. At this time, the other two foundation-establishment experts had arrived and sent their flying swords out to intercept him. He dodged the various flying-sword techniques, barely avoiding death multiple times before finishing the formation of foundation-establishment qi.

As soon as the final line connected, establishing a firm relationship between the characters, the blurry characters condensed and cleared. His footsteps quickened and his instantaneous acceleration increased dramatically.

"It was nice spending time with you," Cha Ming said with Zhou Xian's voice. "However, I don't have a lot of time to waste. I have things to do, things to steal. See you around."

Then, using his newly created technique, he darted off into the distance. He heard loud cursing as the three fell further and further behind before finally giving up.

Cha Ming continued for an hour before stopping to catch his breath and count his gains. Overall, he'd stolen the equivalent of 30,000 mid-grade spirit stones. Regrettably, he estimated that this was only two weeks' of total output from the mine.

Still, it was a start. He refused to believe that they wouldn't react after he repeated the theft several times. It was a game of patience, and he was sure theirs would give out first.

Chapter 31: Luring the Tiger from the Mountain

Cha Ming looked on grimly from his vantage point in the trees, carefully watching for any openings. He had fully restrained his incandescent force since discovering that, while he had a stronger soul than the other foundation-establishment experts, they could still sense him when their incandescent force intersected.

Keeping it withdrawn and concentrated enabled him to both avoid detection and overpower the senses of others that came nearby. Regrettably, he could now only rely on his normal, albeit greatly improved, eyesight. His eyes were as sharp as an eagle's, enabling him to identify complex details a few hundred meters away.

Over the past week, Wei Chen had visited the small shack every day to collect the stones obtained from the mine. Cha Ming's plan to rob them several times evaporated into thin air, and he had no choice but to reevaluate his options.

Now that Wei Chen and the other two had been alerted to his presence, he didn't have a large window in which to act. In addition, the many patrols in the woods had been withdraw. Everyone ate dry rations, and the mining operations had intensified. Based on the conversations he overheard, the mine would be completely excavated within two months. If he tarried too long, they might just cut their losses and abandon the remaining amount.

However, there was no such thing as a perfect defense. After many days of observation, he finally saw a crack in their patrols. Swift as the wind, he used his Seven Cloud Steps to descend on the bandits like a god of death, instantly killing six men with his Swift Staff Art. Then, noticing the three strong experts moving out toward him, he retreated back into the woods.

Wei Chen cursed as he looked at the six bodies. They had arrived just a moment too late, enabling the thief to escape with no consequences.

"Just what is his game?" one of them said. "What grudge does he have against us?"

"It's likely not a grudge," Wei Chen said after examining the wounds that were the result of blunt trauma. Although he had not fought with the thief directly, he could now assume that the man's weapon was a staff or a cudgel, much different from the sword they had originally assumed given the metal qi and the sharp wounds that had bisected the bandits guarding the shack previously. "The thief is probably trying to lure the tiger from the mountain, hoping that we'll chase him so he can obtain another small fortune. His speed is his advantage, but have you all noticed that his cultivation is no greater than someone who has just broken through to foundation establishment? He's not a match for any of us, so he can't help but resort to these means."

"Even if he was a match, he wouldn't be able to defeat either of us in less than a few minutes," Xue Shen said with a snort. He was a promising youth, one that focused on cultivating water and practiced ice techniques. "Why did you keep us all together? If we were spread out, we could defend the entire camp, and he wouldn't stand a chance against us. You're much too cautious."

"Caution keeps a man alive," Wei Chen said calmly. "However, caution won't catch this one. He'll keep nibbling away at us, and it will wear down the morale of our group. The mining efficiency will drop, and I'm afraid of staying much longer. If we dally too long, the leader will come to inspect. We won't be able to hide the evidence of such a great find. We need to finish mining as soon as possible and run away before it's too late.

"Can't we just abandon the rest of the mine?" another young man asked.

"You want to abandon nearly 200,000 mid-grade spirit stones?" Wei Chen asked incredulously. "I thought you were poor, but I must have been mistaken. If you're so rich, Fang Yao, why don't you give me a hundred thousand as a small gift."

The young man kept silent. As bandits, they were all greedy. Such a fortune would enable them to escape and live their lives in luxury without risking their necks.

"But you have a point, Xue Shen," Wei Chen continued. "We don't have to kill him immediately, just stall him. Let's all separate and stay at key points of the camp. Whoever encounters him will need to restrain him until the others arrive. You two will stay on the outskirts while I will guard the mineral shack itself."

"How nice of you, boss," Xue Shen said in a disgruntled voice. "We'll be risking our necks while you get to relax."

Wei Chen shrugged. "The guy is sneaky. Who knows if he'll circle around to the shack if we're all on the perimeter. Someone has to do it, and I'm stronger than you guys. Besides, I'm the boss. I deserve preferential treatment."

Looks like things are getting increasingly difficult, Cha Ming thought as he observed the movements in the camp. The two experts on the perimeter made it impossible to sneak up on them, even when trying to conceal his presence. They had completely retracted their incandescent force, focusing on covering only the nearest 500 meters they each covered.

This meant that he now had to pick a fight with them directly if he wanted to get anywhere. Over the past few days, he had observed the mannerisms of the two experts on the perimeter. Eventually, he settled on the best target, Fang Yao. The man used a spear as a weapon, which Cha Ming saw as an aggressive but slow weapon. At the very least, this man would not be as difficult to escape from if push came to shove.

The plan this time was risky, and for it to succeed, he needed to kill or severely maim one of them before retreating. If not, he wasn't sure he could survive their combined onslaught.

Cha Ming summoned his darkened Clear Sky Staff,

gathering his power before bursting out with explosive speed. He flew swiftly and silently, striking out with the swiftest staff strike he had ever executed. The staff shimmered with blurry runes that Cha Ming could not decipher, but fortunately, he felt their intent. The incisiveness of the blow was far greater than the original staff art he had modified to form his own Swift Staff Art. He called this new technique Gale Strike.

As he approached, Fang Yao's head turned rapidly and faced him. While Cha Ming had not made a sound, the sixth sense of a cultivator was extremely efficient.

"I knew you'd pick me!" the man said with an excited smile on his face. His muscular body flexed, and he swung his spear out to deflect Cha Ming's blow. The haft of his spear collided with Cha Ming's staff, sending waves of recoil back to both fighters.

He's a dual body and qi cultivator? Cha Ming was surprised, as this was an uncommon path. This meant that he'd accidentally picked the second strongest in the group, assuming Xue Shen was only a qi cultivator.

Cha Ming smirked as Fang Yao's smile disappeared and his expression turned grave. The fierce man coughed up blood as a force of 4,320 jin, combined with Cha Ming's Gale Strike technique, completely overpowered the strong man almost twofold. Still, the man was experienced and didn't lose his calm. A defensive talisman flew out from his bag of holding, covering him in a translucent jade armor. Then he poured his foundation-establishment qi into his spear, holding the point toward Cha Ming, who had been pushed back ten feet due to the recoil.

Fortunately, this was exactly what Cha Ming wanted. He could deal with increased defenses but couldn't hope to contend against a fleeing opponent or an opponent that could restrict his movements. Cha Ming ran toward Fang Yao on the ground this time, his feet leaving deep impressions as his weight increased along with the weight of his staff.

The Clear Sky Staff was now shaking madly with the earthly power of vibrations. Fang Yao could only grit his teeth and hold his ground as Cha Ming's staff bore down on him, strike after strike. Each strike caused his bones to crack and his ligaments to tear. The most frustrating part was that, as a spear wielder, he was outranged by Cha Ming's elongated staff. It was now fifteen feet long, more than enough to contend against the man's ten-foot spear.

I won't be able to hold out if I let him continue, Fang Yao thought. His initial impression that he was unmatched by those in the same realm had completely vanished. This mysterious thief was not only a dual cultivator as well, but his strength was more than double his, despite being of the same cultivation realm.

I have to take the initiative, he thought while carefully evaluating the thief's aggressive blows. Fortunately, the attacks were clumsy and predictable, likely the reason that the man was able to strike with such vicious and numbing blows in the first place. It struck him as odd that a thief would use such techniques, but he didn't have the luxury to figure out why.

After twelve strikes passed, Fang Yao finally saw an opening. He charged forward, his spear like a raging earth dragon as he channeled all his foundation qi into his strongest killing blow,

Earth Dragon's Raging Spear. He took a blow to the shoulder as he struck out, not caring for his personal safety. It was all or nothing, and he could only bet his life to delay the thief while he waited for reinforcements.

Cha Ming's incandescent soul focused on the man as he stabbed with his spear. He felt suffocated by an overwhelming presence, and it felt like his chest was slowly being drawn toward the tip of the spear.

Fortunately, Cha Ming was prepared for this sort of retaliation. He swiftly manipulated his weight and shifted into a stance of his Soft Staff Art, White Willow Shade, and executed Wading Through the Reeds. His body was rapidly pulled toward the spear's head as the transparent figure of an earth dragon appeared behind Fang Yao. Cha Ming softly held out his staff, brushing past the tip of the spear and then using it to roll himself slightly to the side. He coughed up blood as a fifth of the spear's potential was absorbed by his torso, but using his forward momentum, he used his Soft Staff Art to throw Fang Yao forward in the direction of his spear strike while tripping him at the knees.

The man plunged into the earth, but Cha Ming was ready, manipulating his weight and landing firmly on the ground. He poured his incandescent force into the Clear Sky Staff, aiming to land a finishing blow. Using all his strength, he smashed his staff, which was now thirty feet long, straight into the helpless man, whose exhausted qi shield shattered instantaneously.

As he crushed Fang Yao, he felt a jolting sensation that caused him to direct his incandescent force backward. There, he noticed two swords flying toward him. One emanated an aura of frost, while the other emanated an aura of decay. Unfortunately, he had no choice but to get hit by one of them.

Cha Ming clenched his teeth and chose the frost sword, manipulating his body slightly as he dove toward Fang Yao's corpse, grabbing his bag of holding and the man's spear in the process. The instant he grabbed the bag of holding, a sharp pain pierced through his side, followed by a numbing sensation. He had positioned himself to avoid any organ damage, but the pain from the blow forced him to scream.

He saw Wei Chen's archaic sword up ahead, readjusting its trajectory. Knowing that the frost sword was impeding his movements, he gritted his teeth and pulled the sword out the way it came. A stream of blood flowed onto the ground. Fortunately, he was a bone-forging cultivator, and such a small amount of blood loss wouldn't cause him to faint.

The archaic sword was in close proximity, so he immediately activated his Seven Cloud Steps, and seven green runes appeared beneath his feet. He quickly dodged out of the way and disappeared into the woods.

"Don't let him get away," Wei Chen yelled as he hopped onto his sword and flew off after the thief. "He's injured, so there's no way he'll be able to continue for very long after such a fierce struggle."

Xue Shen shot him a skeptical look but followed anyway. "You heard Fang Yao. It seems he's a body cultivator, and somehow his combat prowess is an entire realm higher than he lets on. He'll likely heal within a short period of time."

"You fool," Wei Chen said. "That's exactly why we can't let him escape. If we let him heal and ambush us again, he'll be able to nibble away at the entire camp with impunity. If Fang Yao died so easily, that means he and I are likely evenly matched. What if he ambushes us the next time and finishes *you* off? Wouldn't that mean the rest of us will be ripe peaches ready for him to pluck?"

Seeing Xue Shen's expression turn somber, Wei Chen spoke some reassuring words. "Look, he used to be able to run away at his leisure, but now he can barely keep ahead of us. We can easily follow the trail left behind by his blood. I refuse to believe that he can withstand this sort of blood loss indefinitely."

Two hours later, Cha Ming was exhausted. It wasn't because of his consumption—fortunately, Fang Yao's bag of holding had several qi-recovering pellets. It was because of the repeated blood loss over the course of the chase. Even a bone-forging cultivator could not sustain losing blood for so long.

He looked grimly at the wound on his side that was just healing over. Then he heartlessly grabbed a knife from his Clear Sky World and cut it open once more.

This last time should be enough. Any more, and they'll begin to suspect. Cha Ming continued running in the air for another fifteen minutes before finally darting to the side, using his superior agility to outmaneuver his pursuers and disappear.

Then he flew back the way he came, running like the wind at a pace that was fifty percent faster than the pace he'd used to bait them away in the first place.

Wei Chen stopped where the trail of blood ended, looking around and sending out his incandescent force to sense the thief's location. The man had disappeared, much like the morning mist in the head of the summer sun.

"Where could he have gone to?" Wei Chen pondered out loud. Then he looked up at Xue Shen, who had just returned from investigating the surroundings. "Have you found anything?"

"Yes and no," Xue Shen replied. "I didn't see anything, but his sudden disappearance makes me believe that he wasn't that wounded in the first place."

"What are you saying?" Wei Chen asked, furrowing his brows.

Xue Shen shook his head. "I'm saying that he brought us out here on purpose. The both of us at once. I suspect that stealing spirit stones was not his goal all along. I believe he actually wants to help those villagers."

Wei Chen's eyes narrowed. "If that's the case, we need to rush back immediately. My life depends on it." He didn't doubt the truth of Xue Shen's deduction. However, if the thief wasn't stopped and the bandits got desperate, who knew if they would try to execute villagers to threaten them? By then, Wei Chen's life would be forfeit. As their superior, he was directly responsible for their actions.

Xue Shen snorted. "You can go ahead, but I'm not going to go commit suicide along with you. It's your fault you made that oath in the first place. We could have safely waited for the leader to come and have him interrogated. Instead, you chose to get greedy," the frosty man said.

He turned around to leave, only to find a dreadful sword pointing straight at his forehead, the aura of decay rapidly corroding the barrier of qi protecting him.

"I don't think I asked for your opinion," Wei Chen said icily. "You *will* come with me and fight him. We're in this boat together, dead or alive."

Xue Shen gulped before nodding and hopping on his flying sword, flying back toward the village alongside Wei Chen.

Chapter 32: Freedom

Cha Ming had fully healed by the time he returned to the village. Unsurprisingly, the rest of the bandits were still going about their business. The guards were guarding, the miners were mining, and those with special functions were performing them at peak efficiency, lest they get caught for slacking by the tyrannical Wei Chen.

Here and there, he heard whispers and musings. Some people questioned whether the thief would be caught, while others berated them for lack of faith. Cha Ming used the many things he heard to organize his thoughts and formulate a plan.

The first thing he did was sneak past the many tents, rushing next to Wei Chen's tent and swiftly killing the six guards in the vicinity. He dragged them into the captain's tent as soon as he realized that the Clear Sky Brush refused to take in the corpses. It did not appreciate being a corpse repository, and Cha Ming didn't have time to burn them.

After dumping the corpses, he entered the tent that held the life slips of the various cultivators, just in time to see a bandit with a panicked expression rushing out toward him. The reason for his panic was obvious—six life slips had suddenly shattered, and the leader was nowhere to be found. Cha Ming didn't think twice before clutching the man's throat and snapping his neck, tossing him aside unceremoniously. He didn't bother to pick up his belongings, as his time was limited.

Cha Ming rushed out of the tent soon after, looking like the bandit that he'd just killed. The man's weapon, a large saber, was strapped on his back. Many of the bandits greeted him as he passed by, but unfortunately Cha Ming didn't know the man's voice. He waved curtly and ignored them, heading out toward the caves. He wanted to settle the caves first, lest the bandits hole up there after he defeated the rest. That would make rescuing the villagers extremely difficult. While he wasn't aware of the exact terms of the oath Wei Chen made, he wasn't willing to risk a single life on its efficacy.

Soon, Cha Ming finished mounting the steps to the waterfall, where he was greeted by four guards.

"Xing Bao, what are you doing here?" one of them asked. "Shouldn't you be guarding the life-slip tent? Did something happen?"

Cha Ming didn't reply, instead choosing to summon the Clear Sky Staff and dispatch the four guards in quick succession. He then ran into the nearest tunnel after taking on the appearance of one of the guards.

"What are you doing down here? Did something happen?" one of the mine guards in the tunnel asked, worried.

Cha Ming nodded gravely and replied using the voice of the guard. "The camp has been invaded many times recently, so we need to escort the prisoners back to their cages. Come help me gather them."

The guard looked uncertain, but seeing Cha Ming's authoritative demeanor, he followed his lead. Soon they encountered three more guards who were supervising a dozen hardworking men. Cha Ming recognized every single one of them. He'd treated some of them, treated some of their wives and children, and had helped them with miscellaneous tasks. He was relieved that while they had been mistreated, that glow in their eyes from when they'd lived freely had not yet faded.

"Shackle these prisoners and lead them back to the cages," the guard he accompanied said.

"That won't be necessary," Cha Ming said. Then, quick as lightning, he took out his staff and instantly dispatched the four guards as easily as cutting grass. The miners looked at the corpses in horror, not daring to speak. Cha Ming then swiped his hand over his face, revealing himself to the prisoners.

"Stay here calmly and don't cause trouble," Cha Ming said in his soft, kind voice. "You will all be free soon, mark my words."

Seeing Cha Ming's face, the villagers were overcome with joy. After all, they had heard he was dead, but now their assistant physician was here in the flesh and saving them.

Cha Ming then reverted back to the form of the previous guard and calmly walked into another tunnel, repeating the process. This time, one of the village cultivators was there, mining with peak efficiency. After gathering the guards, Cha Ming dispatched them all quickly. The enslaved cultivator, who had previously been mining mindlessly, suddenly turned around and rushed toward Cha Ming, who he now identified as an invader.

Cha Ming sighed and gripped the man, pinning him against the wall. He ignored the screams of the nearby miners and their pickaxes, shrugging off the slight cuts they gave him, which quickly regenerated. The cultivator's strong physical blows also couldn't do a thing to Cha Ming's sturdy body. After observing the servant character on the man's forehead, Cha Min materialized the Clear Sky Brush and began drawing four intricate characters and geometric shapes, linking them to the sigil imprinted on the man's forehead.

The characters he drew were those of freedom and breaking shackles. He linked them together with the sigil in a subtractive sense, using them to weaken the cultivator's mental restraints. Soon, the cultivator stopped struggling and regained clarity in his eyes.

"Stop!" the man yelled. The villagers looked at him in astonishment, as this was the first word the man had said in over a year. The servant character was still there but seemed slightly faded. "Who are you?" the man whispered.

Cha Ming smiled and revealed his face to the cultivator and the rest of the villagers, prompting shock and happiness. "I need to go save the rest. You are not free yet, but it should be no problem to maintain your consciousness and control over your movements for the time being. Once this is all over, I'll free you once and for all." After seeing the man nod, Cha Ming rushed off and killed all the guards and set the other four cultivators free.

Having saved the most difficult cases, he looked down toward the village and assumed the appearance of the life-slip guard. The man's position was clearly very influential, and Wei Chen trusted him greatly. He descended the slippery stone steps behind the waterfall, and after walking past the guards at the spirit-stone shack, he proceeded to the area where the cages were.

Cha Ming walked over to the few guards surrounding the

cage and yelled in an authoritative voice. "Gather together. On Vice Leader Wei Chen's orders, we are to gather and resist the thief, who is on his way. We must hold out together until the vice leader arrives.

"What about the prisoners?" a guard asked suspiciously.

"You stupid oaf, what's more important?" Cha Ming scolded. "Do you like your life so little? Come now, if you refuse to follow orders, I'll just kill you myself."

In this way, Cha Ming gathered the bandits little by little and led them to the center of the camp, where their tents were erected.

"What is this all about?" one of the men grunted. "Wei Chen doesn't usually use you to give orders."

"Oh, it's quite simple, really," Cha Ming said, suddenly transforming to Zhou Xian's appearance and changing his clothes back to a black cloak. "It's time for you all to die."

Cha Ming suddenly whipped his staff out, striking guard after guard like a tempest.

"Run away!" a remaining bandit yelled, fully aware that they weren't his match. The bandits were the cowardly type to begin with, fearing the strong and bullying the weak. They would have abandoned their fellow bandits countless times to save their own skins. Only a charismatic and powerful figure like Wei Chen could keep them in line, and only barely at that.

Cha Ming slaughtered them as efficiently as possible, using the Swift Staff Art to leap between targets. Despite being his weakest strikes, they were already far too much for the bandits to bear, and before long, one hundred of them were lying on the ground, dead.

After slaying the closest batch, he rushed toward the group that was moving toward the prisoners' cages, slaying them before they had a chance to use them as hostages. He slew them one by one, and finally, none of the bandits below foundation establishment remained. The camp was now deathly silent, and the only noises he could hear were the sounds of wailing children. Even the man who had betrayed him earlier, Lei Dong, lay dead with the others. Gloating wasn't Cha Ming's style, and he had not had the luxury of confronting the man. No matter. In his opinion, all the bandits received a quicker death than they deserved.

Cha Ming chose not to free the villagers just yet, sitting down in meditation to recover his strength instead. He took out the well-used energy-gathering formation plate, using it to quickly convert spirit stones into useable energy. It cracked under the strain of the increased volume of energy he pumped through it. But he didn't care and continued to turn a frightening amount of spirit stones to dust. He continued until the formation plate finally shattered. He had managed to recover nine tenths of his qi. It felt like a huge waste, but he didn't have the luxury of time. He opened his eyes and materialized his staff just in time to see Wei Chen and Xue Shen approaching with murderous looks.

"Who are you?" Wei Chen said, nearly erupting with anger. Seeing the vice leader's livid expression, Cha Ming chose to stoke the flames.

"I'm just a dog," Cha Ming said, regaining his original appearance. "A dog you would eventually put down, but a loyal dog all the same. Yet I'm this village's dog through and through. I will protect them with my life."

Wei Chen became red as a tomato when he saw Cha Ming's appearance. "I knew you were no good. I should have killed you when I had the chance."

Cha Ming smiled calmly. "And now you do. I'm not going anywhere." Both men looked at each other briefly before rushing him, unleashing a multitude of techniques. Clearly they had recovered their energy with pills before arriving.

Cha Ming rushed to meet them and clashed intensely with their flying swords in a frontal confrontation. His qi weakened as the corrosive power of Wei Chen's sword enveloped him, while his movements slowed as his staff clashed with Xue Shen's frost sword.

Xue Shen, who was not a frontal combatant, formed multiple hand seals that summoned nine swords of ice. They began attacking Cha Ming in tandem, restraining his movements. Cha Ming could only evade with great difficulty, using Flaming Wheel Defense to cover the area where his staff traveled with red runic characters that fended off the nine icy swords. Most of his attention was centered on Wei Chen, who grabbed his sword and dove toward Cha Ming, causing its aura to surge. The vice leader rapidly formed hand seals with a single hand, and vines shot up from below and attempted to entangle Cha Ming. He quickly evaded them using his Seven Cloud Steps and Stormchaser Boots.

Cha Ming felt greatly pressured by both cultivators, and realizing he would surely fall by fighting them both at once, he focused his attention on Xue Shen. He ducked and weaved, deflecting various blows with heavy metallic staff strikes as he moved elusively toward Xue Shen. The blue-robed man, realizing Cha Ming's intent, began retreating in a circular fashion, trying to move himself behind Wei Chen. Cha Ming tried to chase after him but realized that frost lotuses had bloomed behind Xue Shen and were invaded the surrounding air with a frosty aura.

Cha Ming, seeing that it would be difficult to eliminate this man, clenched his teeth and withdrew one of the talismans from his Clear Sky World. It was the Mao Mao talisman covered in geometric shapes, the one that looked the least dubious between them.

Here goes nothing, Cha Ming thought while throwing the talisman at Xue Shen. The man snorted and sent out one of the nine flying swords toward the talisman, hoping to cut it down before it activated.

Much to Cha Ming's dismay, the sword reached the talisman before anything happened. To his surprise, however, the sword of ice shattered on contact. Xue Shen paled as the massive apparition of a bobcat appeared and fiercely charged toward him like a vicious beast from the depths of hell. Cha Ming was equally shocked at both the apparition and its presence. He noticed that it shared many features with Elder Ling's territorial cat, Mr. Mao Mao.

Is that his true form?

Still, he was overjoyed to see such a powerful ally. Wei Chen diverted his assault on Cha Ming to attempt to deal with the summoned animal, striking at it with his Archaic Sword. Cha Ming snorted and used Seven Cloud Steps to jump in front of the middle-aged cultivator, deflecting blow after blow with great difficulty. Fortunately, he used his Sword Staff Art, which seemed to have a restraining effect on the wood-based power of corrosion.

Xue Shen let out an agonizing wail as a large chunk of his body disappeared, leaving behind a gaping wound. His lifeblood quickly left him, and soon after, the apparition of Mr. Mao Mao disappeared along with the last vestiges of the man's life.

"I refuse to believe that you have more than one of those," Wei Chem shrieked, increasing his rate of assault. They exchanged multiple blows, but unfortunately, Cha Ming wasn't able to dodge all of the sneaky man's cuts. They were soon both covered in wounds, but Cha Ming's wounds seemed worse than Wei Chen's. This was because the man continuously restored the various bruises and breaks with a powerful wood-qi healing technique.

"You're much too young if you think you can defeat me so easily," the man said, cutting Cha Ming for the seventy-second time. This strike felt different than the others that came before, and he noticed that the vast majority of the qi in his body had disappeared. Even the creation qi he used had eroded to nothing.

"What have you done?" Cha Ming said, shocked.

"You should feel honored to fall victim to this technique," Wei Chen said, chuckling. "Only three people have seen it, and they are all dead now. I am named Archaic Sword because I control the power of corrosion."

Wei Chen swiftly attacked Cha Ming with his sword after saying these words, forcing Cha Ming to block with impaired technique and only his physical body strength. The staff was knocked out of his hands, and he felt a wave of enfeeblement hit him.

Cha Ming's mind raced as he saw the looming specter of death. *What can I do?* he thought. *All of my qi has disappeared, so I can't activate any talismans. I don't have any qi-recovering pellets either.*

He looked into his dantian, noticing that the thick qi surrounding his five qi pillars had completely vanished. The creation-qi matrix was no long brimming with the usual white fluid that he could use interchangeably with all of the other types of qi. He focused on the black star at the center. To his surprise, the destruction qi inside the matrix was still flowing freely, unaffected by what Wei Chen had done to him.

Can I somehow use this destruction qi? he wondered. Unfortunately, none of the runes or sigils he'd learned contained any elements of destruction. It was as though a character formed of destruction qi or energy couldn't exist, not without the support of anything else.

I'll have to take a chance, he thought, directing it toward both his hands. The violent black qi struggled as he urged it down his qi pathways, forcing it through the meridians that had been formed after he cleared the rubble.

Wei Chen's eyes narrowed as a black film formed on Cha Ming's hands and began wearing away at his skin. His heartbeat sped up. An overwhelming and threatening sensation was coming from the black substance on the younger man's hands.

He was a master of the power of corrosion. However, he felt like an ant struggling before a mountain when he saw the corrosive qi that was eating at away at the man's hands. It only took a single breath for Cha Ming's bones to become exposed. Wei Chen wasted no time and rushed in for the kill.

Cha Ming's hands ached like they had never ached before. He knew he didn't have much time, so he rushed toward Wei Chen, who was doing the same. This was the final clash, and the victor would be determined in mere moments. As Wei Chen's sword bore down, Cha Ming chose to dodge only slightly, allowing it to pierce a nonlethal part of his abdomen. He howled as a searing, corrosive pain lanced through his blood vessels near the deadly wound. However, the pain wasn't anything compared to what he felt in his rapidly withering hands.

Cha Ming pulled himself closer to Wei Chen, using the man's forward moment against him. The older man panicked and tried to move away, but it was too late. Cha Ming reached out and grasped the man's head with both his hands, and they penetrated his flesh like a hot knife through butter. After all, Cha Ming's body had been tempered by destruction, but Wei Chen's had not.

Wei Chen crumpled to the ground, and Cha Ming collapsed, unable to remain conscious much longer. He looked at his ruined hands but didn't despair. He had been through an extensive recovery process before, so he was confident in his odds of success.

Epilogue

Hong Xin looked on sadly as the woman in red walked out through the village gates after a long stay. She had truly enjoyed the nights when the woman played her songs, allowing Hong Xin to dance to her tunes. In fact, it was only a few days after Hong Yinyue's arrival that the woman had requested she join her act, dancing to her graceful music.

The act had been a success; working-class men and nobles alike had frequented the tavern to watch the graceful show. Hong Xin had lost count of the marriage proposals that flew her way. She had refused them, of course, following a script that the experienced performer shared with her to minimize hard feelings.

And now, it seemed like all of it would disappear and vanish into thin air. Hong Yinyue had long since told her that she disliked staying in one place for very long. She simply followed where fate pulled her, going with the flow. And now fate was pulling her back toward her home city. *Life is a dance*, she always said.

Hong Xin sighed as she thought of the wonderful weeks that had passed by so swiftly. Not only had her mood fully recovered to her usually cheerful disposition, her cultivation had also advanced by leaps and bounds. "It's natural for a dancer to progress when there is music," Yinyue had told her. "Everyone needs music in their life, and some more than others."

"Why don't you just ask her if you can tag along?" the innkeeper said an hour later while chopping and preparing vegetables for the upcoming night. He didn't make as much as usual, as business was sure to slow down with Hong Yinyue having departed.

"Wouldn't that be rude of me?" Hong Xin said, thought she was seriously considering the matter.

"I don't see why it would be," he said. "You guys get along great. I don't think she'd refuse."

By the time he looked up, Hong Xin was gone, running upstairs to her room and hastily gathering her possessions. She had learned her lesson last time and was always ready to leave at a moment's notice.

"Thank you for everything!" she yelled before darting out the door.

"Don't forget to come back if she says no!" the man yelled back, smiling and shaking his head.

Hong Xin ran through the city streets, running into various patrons that she had met over the past few months. They looked at her with knowing smiles. The guards waved as she passed through, and they pointed her in Yinyue's direction.

It took a few hours for Hong Xin to catch up. As she approached, an overwhelming feeling of nervousness invaded her thoughts.

What if she says no? What if I need to go back? Can I really ask her?

As she was pondering these things, Yinyue stopped. "Is it really so hard to ask?" she said, turning around. Her alluring, bright red cloak was in stark contrast to the flat fields that surrounded them.

"Can I?" Hong Xin said, her eyes tearing up.

"Of course," the woman said dotingly. "But you can't slow me down, and you need to listen to me in all things. Otherwise, things might get dangerous."

"Of course!" Hong Xin said, running over. "Where are we off to?"

"We're going back to my home town," Yinyue said, grim faced. "It's a long way back, especially when walking. However, I think you'll like the city I'm from."

"What's its name?" Hong Xin said curiously.

"Perhaps you've heard of it before," she said. "Gold Leaf City."

"Finally, fresh meat after so long," a skinny, greasy-haired man said to his eleven companions. "It's tough being a bandit when there's no one to rob."

The others chuckled as they looked at the approaching figure. They couldn't make out the figure's features, as the sunlight was shining from their direction.

"Let's play it safe and wait until he gets close," the leader said, his hand quivering in anticipation. It had been so long since he'd drawn blood. Unfortunately, he was different than his companions. They could survive with nothing but gold and food to fill their bellies. He *needed* to kill to survive, to sate his inner rage.

Soon enough, the figure in the distance became clearer. "It's a monk!" one of the bandits whispered. "Awful bad luck to rob a monk. Plus, they're always poor. We should just let this one run along."

"Nonsense," another bandit said. "Don't you know that they take offerings all the time? Their temples are gilded in gold and filled with jade. Of course he'll have something on him." This was also one of the more eager members of the group, one that the leader appreciated greatly.

"I don't think that's a he," another said, shaking his head. "She might be bald, but I can tell a woman from a mile away. It's bad enough luck to attack a monk, much less a helpless woman monk. Let's let her pass, boss."

"Do I pay you all to think?" the leader snapped, holding his saber. He could barely control it, and killing a monk would go a long way to sate his thirst for blood. If he killed her, he might be able to go for a month without killing again. At his signal, the bandits readied themselves to jump out for an ambush. The bald woman wore an orange kasaya, and she walked without a care in the world.

Suddenly, only a few feet from the ambush point, the figure stopped. Her eyes seemed bright like diamonds as she looked toward their hiding place. "Come out," she said, smiling, "there is no need to hide. I'm sure we can talk this through."

The leader cursed as his eleven companions sheepishly stepped out from the bushes. He could only follow suit. One of his companions mumbled apologetically, "I'm sorry, my lady.

It's really bad luck to try robbing a monk. You may pass."

"It's no problem," she said. "Here, take these few gold pieces so that you may fill your bellies. There is no need to kill or rob innocents to make a living."

All of the bandits, including the bandit leader, were all filled with a sense of deep shame. Three of them even collapsed on their knees, unable to restrain their sorrow.

"I'm so sorry," the fattest bandit said, weeping. "I killed a man once. I deserve death."

"I can't continue living," another man said, his eyes red. "How can I stand myself after all the harm I've done?"

The leader shivered when he saw this monk's charisma. He also felt a sense of crisis. As he thought this, the monk simply smiled and walked up to them, placing a gold piece in each of his eleven companion's hands.

"I'm sure you have learned your lesson," she said. "Repent and help others. Protect them. And if you can't do that, lay down your weapons and become farmers or pick up a craft. Use your good deeds to atone for your sins."

The bandits nodded and wept.

Then she looked over in the leader's direction. Her blue eyes felt like vast oceans filled with light. "Show yourself," she said gently.

Shivering at her command, the bandit had no choice but to show his true form. His red eyes glowed like blood, and his veins bulged as he held his saber firmly.

"Don't you feel ashamed at what you've become?" she continued.

The other bandits paled when they saw this. Only now did they realize they had been in the presence of a monster.

"I do," he said, shivering. "However, there is no repentance for me. I can only continue this way. In my next life, I will surely be reborn in Hell."

The monk smiled and walked up to him slowly, ignoring the saber in his hands. She stopped only two feet away from him. "There is repentance for everyone," she said. "Allow me to relieve you of your burden." She laid her hand on his forehead. A red projection appeared behind him, wailing in agony as it was pierced by multiple beams of bright light. Wherever they pierced, whiteness spread. It only took thirty seconds for the red soul projection behind him to turn completely white.

Then it disappeared into the distance, and the man collapsed, dead.

"Was it necessary to save that man?" Gong Lan said as she walked along the dirt road. All of the bandits had chosen to renounce their former identities and spread out in every direction. Some said they would become farmers, others decided to become guards. This she understood. These men were not beyond saving, just like her.

"It is most difficult to show mercy to your enemy, but in this case, it was necessary," a childish voice said to her. Green tendrils spread out from a locket on her neck that was made with an exceptionally large bodhi seed. "You saved a man's soul, and while he is not deserving, this is one soul deprived from the devils, one less soul they can use to turn this plane against us. You have weakened the devils in Hell by depriving them of fresh blood. Saving this man hurt the real enemy."

Gong Lan sighed. "Very well. We will continue doing such things. When must we return?"

"I'm not sure," the seed replied. "It could be years or decades. Less than a century. However, rest assured that the time will come. When this is all over, you can transcend without worries."

Gong Lan nodded, and they continued on.

Huxian lay at the peak of the mountain, licking his wounds as he listened to the spirit-tail chicken choir. They sang hymns of praise for him, and before long, they brought forth their latest sacrifice. Soon the chickens left with solemn appearances. The offering was no more.

Huxian sighed, depressed at the failure of their expedition. The beast tide he had been so confident in had ended up floundering at the last moment. The reason behind it was quite simple: walls.

Walls had been an enemy of spirit beasts since ancient times. Despite understanding their construction, and despite having the strength to tear them down stone by stone, every spirit beast held an instinctual fear of walls. Only kings amongst them could urge the lesser beasts forward, and only barely. This crushing blow to their morale had caused countless spirit beasts to fall like flies, and Huxian had no choice but to call them back to the mountain.

Unfortunately, he was now too weak to do much. His fight with the bear sovereign had cost him precious blood essence, and he would need to recover it before making his next move. He glared at the mountain beside them. It had its own sovereign, comparable in strength to the previous sovereign. If he couldn't invade the humans and their walls successfully, so be it. He would go for the next best thing: annexing the nearby beast territories. He was a king after all, and he deserved his own dominion.

"Are you sure you want to do this?" Cha Ming asked the village mayor.

"Yes, I'm confident," the mayor replied. Cha Ming nodded and activated a line that he'd drawn. It glowed brightly as it traveled up the stone trail, into the waterfall, and through the tunnels. An incense time passed before a sudden explosion shook the land nearby. Rubble flowed from behind the waterfall in great quantities before finally stopping.

Cha Ming probed the collapsed tunnel before turning to the mayor. "It's all done. The cave is collapsed, and it shouldn't be obvious that it's a spirit-stone vein unless they do significant digging. Not that it matters, since over nine tenths of the mine has already been excavated."

The mayor nodded. "Make sure you take all of the stones with you. We want nothing to do with them."

Cha Ming smiled and tossed a medium-sized bag to the man. It jingled loudly. "Here are five thousand low-grade spirit stones. It's not a vast sum of money, but it should be enough to purchase a currency that the village can use."

The man was hesitant but accepted it nonetheless. Then he looked at the buildings that were quickly rising from the ashes. The entire town had come together, and soon it would be fully rebuilt. "Thank you. It will be difficult to survive the winter without purchasing provisions."

"From now on, you won't have to hide anymore," Cha Ming said before leaving.

Before long, he arrived at Li Yin's tent. It was Wei Chen's old tent, and it had been serving as a temporary hospital. The man smiled when Cha Ming came in. "Is it done?"

"Yes, it's done," Cha Ming replied. "Soon the village will be back to normal."

"As normal as it can be," Li Yin said. "Mental scars like this stay with people for a long time. We were fortunate, however. It could have been a lot worse. We were enslaved, but our women and children maintained their dignity. By the way, how are your hands?"

Cha Ming revealed a nimble set of pure white fingers that were covered in freshly grown skin. It had been an easy but excruciating process to regrow the lost flesh.

The doctor sighed. "My greatest regret is that my life's work was lost. How will I be able to teach without those books? It will be very difficult."

Cha Ming chuckled before sweeping out his hand. A dozen large books appeared on the table. Li Yin looked shocked for a moment but instantly recovered. "I saved them just before the bandits came," Cha Ming said. "I didn't think you would want your life's work burnt to the ground."

The doctor, who had lost all hope earlier, was now grinning ear to ear. Cha Ming left him to flip through the pages and returned to his own tent. After closing the flap to ensure he wouldn't be disturbed, he took out a gray candle in a bronze holder. He needed to gain strength as quickly as possible. After all, he had discovered much information relating to the bandit leader from Wei Chen's bag of holding, and one thing was certain: The leader would come soon, and he would come with a vengeance.

This small village had finally found their light in the darkness. And he would protect it with everything he had.

— End Book 3 —

A Note to Readers

If you've enjoyed this book, I would greatly appreciate it if you left a rating on the site where you purchased it. Ratings lead to credibility in this competitive marketplace, and by leaving one, you signal to the world that this book is worth reading.

As some of you might know, I release each book as I write it. It wasn't necessary for you to buy this book, but your support is greatly appreciated. If you are so inclined, you can continue reading as I write at:

https://royalroadl.com/fiction/16320/painting-the-mists

I can't promise fully edited or proofread content, but I will do my best to continue maintaining frequent and high-quality releases.

If you would like to receive bimonthly updates on writing progress, releases, and the life of Patrick Laplante, subscribe to the Painting the Mists newsletter at:

http://eepurl.com/dymvO1

You can also find a link to the newsletter at www.paintingthemists.com. As a bonus for subscribing, you'll receive exclusive biography sketches for each of the key characters, starting with Huxian!

Other ways to contact me or keep in touch:
Facebook: https://www.facebook.com/RedMiragePtM/
Twitter: @RedMirage_PtM

The Cultivation Systems

Qi Cultivation

- Qi Condensation – condense the qi of heaven and earth into a liquid in your dantian
    - Stages 1-3: form a qi pool
    - Stages 4-6: form a qi lake
    - Stages 7-9: form a qi ocean
- Foundation Establishment – form pillars from your qi, setting a firm foundation for your future cultivation.
    - Traditionally, a cultivator forms between one and nine pillars, which are affixed to the bottom of the qi oceans.
    - The liquid qi in this stage is more viscous, its quantity and quality is dependent on the number of pillars.
    - Pillars are grown from the bottom up, gradually forming the foundation with which to form your core
- Core Formation – condense your foundation into a core, the basis of your future growth
- Rune Carving – ???

Body Cultivation
- Body Strengthening – basic body strengthening and purification. Typically, the body is fed with qi and then refined with an opposing qi, removing any impurities
- Bone Forging – bones are the basis of strength and durability. The strongest body is nothing without strong bones supporting it.
- ???

Soul Cultivation
- Innate Soul – cultivators are born with an innate soul, and it grows as the cultivator advances in qi condensation. Eventually, the soul will make a rapid breakthrough into incandescence.
- Incandescent Soul – the soul begins to shine with incandescent light. Advanced soul manipulation of objects and mental communication is now possible.
- Resplendent Soul – wrap the soul in a resplendent vestment

Acknowledgments

As I continue to write, I find that this list of acknowledgments grows. There are far too many people to thank—if I missed you, I'm sorry. It wasn't intentional.

Just like before, I would like to acknowledge my wife and my parents parents, who continue to encourage me on my journey in writing this novel series. Likewise, thanks go to my two brothers and my sister. More specifically, thank you to Denis, who has finally started reading the series after much persuasion. Levi will fall in line eventually.

Thank you to all my friends once again. I recently took some time off work to focus on writing, and after talking to them, I'm convinced that I've made the right decision. Thank you to Dave for once again beta reading Book 2. And once again, thank you to my friend Usama, who is now a recurring character in my prologues.

Many thanks to Crystal Watanabe for her excellent support while editing my novel. My writing continues to improve with her help, so I'm glad to have her on board. Thanks also go to Samuel Alves for the excellent cover remake on this new edition.

Finally, thank you to my readers. I write to tell stories to people, and a story is worth nothing if it isn't shared.

About the Author

Patrick Georges Laplante was born in a small town in the Canadian prairies in 1987. He began publishing *Painting the Mists* online under the pseudonym RedMirage in January 2018.

An engineer by trade, he graduated from the University of Alberta in 2009 and completed his master's degree in 2011. While writing and engineering have little in common, he actively utilizes his experiences and attention to detail in fleshing out a vivid world and answering the "whys," which are often left unanswered in Xianxia fiction.

As an avid vegan, he aims to prompt internal reflection in his readers through various themes like non-violence, choice, and begging the question: Is personhood restricted to humanity? And what is proper conduct, morality, and love?

His work is inspired by a combination of Western fiction, *Dungeons and Dragons*, Chinese web novels, and various Japanese, Korean, and Chinese comics and illustrated novels.

www.ingramcontent.com/pod-product-compliance
Lightning Source LLC
Chambersburg PA
CBHW021426240626
47153CB00001B/49